ABOUT THE AU

Meredith Appleyard lives in the Clare Valley wine-growing region of South Australia. As a registered nurse and midwife she practised in a wide range of country health settings, including the Royal Flying Doctor Service. She has been an agency nurse in London and a volunteer in Vietnam. When a friend challenged Meredith to do what she'd always wanted to do – write a novel – she saved up, took time off work, sat down at the computer and wrote her first novel. Realising after the first rejection letter she needed to learn more about the craft of writing, she attended workshops, joined a writers' group and successfully completed an Advanced Diploma of Arts in Professional Writing with the Adelaide Centre for Arts. Meredith lives with her husband and border collie Lily, and when she's not writing she's reading!

meredithappleyard.com.au

Also by Meredith Appleyard

Home at Last
All about Ella
When Grace went Away
Becoming Beth

DAISY
and
KATE

MEREDITH
APPLEYARD

First Published 2023
First Australian Paperback Edition 2023
ISBN 9781867271185

Daisy and Kate
© 2023 by Meredith Appleyard
Australian Copyright 2023
New Zealand Copyright 2023

This is a work of fiction. Names, characters, places, and incidents are either the product of the author's imagination or are used fictitiously, and any resemblance to actual persons, living or dead, business establishments, events, or locales is entirely coincidental.

Published by
HQ Fiction
An imprint of Harlequin Enterprises (Australia) Pty Limited (ABN 47 001 180 918), a subsidiary of HarperCollins Publishers Australia Pty Limited (ABN 36 009 913 517)
Level 19, 201 Elizabeth St
SYDNEY NSW 2000
AUSTRALIA

Printed and bound in Australia by McPherson's Printing Group

MIX
Paper | Supporting
responsible forestry
FSC® C001695

'The truth is rarely pure and never simple.'
– Oscar Wilde

1

Daisy

It was early. Twelve days into another new year, heralded without resolutions. The weather was unseasonably cool and the sky above clear and blatantly blue. A flock of swallows swooped in and settled on the power line. They preened and a brisk southwesterly ruffled feathers. When Jess and I journeyed below, they lifted, only to resettle in our wake. This road out of town was uphill, a gentle but steady climb. Steeper than I'd remembered. Jess's lead slackened as we huffed and puffed our way to the top. She eyed me and grinned, and I grinned back. Two old girls out together, vaguely overweight and more grey-haired by the day. I did my best to ignore the grey hairs and I'd just about given up on losing the extra two or three kilos. I'd been trying to shift them ever since the boys were born and Gareth, the eldest, would be forty-three this year.

We walked on as far as the first farm gate and then crossed the road to retrace our steps back to town. A car sped by, spitting dust and gravel. Jess and I plodded on. Today we didn't pause to take in the familiar view from the top of the hill. We'd done that on the first morning we'd trekked out this way, a week ago now. With home and breakfast in sight, the tension increased on Jess's lead.

Home. If you could call couch-surfing at my granddaughter Georgia's place home. But when Gareth turfed me out of the family home in order to knock it down and replace it with two townhouses, I had no comeback. After all, Gareth owned the property—I'd sold it to him way back in an effort to ease my burden of debt. Debt that had snowballed ever since Charlie Toogood, errant husband and father of our three boys, had headed north in search of work. Twenty-three years ago. He must have found *something* because he never came back. The old house was past its prime, but the land it was built on was in a much sought-after area and Gareth's plan made sound business sense. One townhouse would be leased out and I'd live in the other. 'Best thing is, Mum, you won't be uprooted for too long,' he'd said in his pitch to me. 'And you'll have a brand-new townhouse to move into.'

No denying that, on paper, the floor plan looked amazing. A new townhouse with a garage and the smallest of gardens was beyond anything I'd ever dreamed of living in. I couldn't pack fast enough. Along the way I'd discovered the limits of my meagre income: it wouldn't stretch to renting a place while I waited for my new townhouse to be built. Not a place with a yard suitable for a dog. Not any place, really. That's when Georgia had agreed to take us in. Realistically, she was the only family member in a position to do so.

But with me bearing down on seventy and Georgia barely into her twenties, there'd been adjustments to be made. As the interloper, the burden of those adjustments had fallen squarely onto my shoulders. After living in blissful solitude in a three-bedroom house for a decade, I discovered I wasn't as amenable to change as I'd thought I would be. Or wanted to be. Already there'd been several tense moments; no doubt there would be more. Unless, of course, she threw us out. I was on my best behaviour because at this point in time there was no Plan B.

After we'd crossed the last street, I let Jess off the lead a few doors from home and she bounded on ahead. This morning the hairs on the back of my neck prickled when I bent down to unclip the lead. That weird sensation you get when you think someone might be watching you. It wasn't the first morning I'd experienced a similar sensation. A furtive glance behind yielded nothing but an empty street, yellow-lidded recycle bins lined up along each kerb. With a shiver, I quickened my pace.

Georgia was on a morning shift and my elderly Mitsubishi station wagon stood all on its lonesome in the narrow driveway of her rental. A tangled potato vine clung precariously to the side of a galvanised iron single-car garage that leaned at an unhealthy angle, rendering the door un-openable and the space unusable. Beside the garage, an old rainwater tank slowly rusted away. It was hard to tell which structure was propping up the other. The single-bedroom weatherboard workers' cottage Georgia paid a ridiculous amount of rent for wasn't in much better condition.

'It is a bit of a dump,' she'd said with a dismissive flick of her wrist when I'd arrived on her doorstep ten days ago. 'But it was this or the nurses' home at the hospital. And guess what? A fortnight living it that smelly, damp hole was enough for me.'

I hadn't commented. It'd been dark and although I'd been filled with gratitude that she'd agreed to take us in, I'd been exhausted. With Gareth's business closed between Christmas and New Year we'd used that time to clear out the house and move my furniture and belongings into his shed. Plus, I'd totally understood the bit about the nurses' home. By Georgia's description, it hadn't changed much since I'd lived there decades before. Except perhaps for the salt damp. That'd sounded much worse.

Jess panted her way around to the water bucket and then scoffed the handful of dry food I threw into her bowl. The back door was unlocked. There wasn't a key, only a deadbolt on the inside. Apparently, the landlord had only supplied one front door key. Georgia hadn't mentioned having another key cut; it was on my list of things to do. I went inside and was swamped by a wave of despondency. So much so, I had to prop myself against the wall for a moment in order to regain my equilibrium.

When I said I was couch-surfing, I'd meant that literally. I slept on a sagging pull-out sofa bed in a corner of the 'cosy' living area, the only privacy afforded by an old hospital screen. My bedroom, when the sofa wasn't being used as the place to sit. That was determined by Georgia's rostered shifts, what she wanted to watch on the television, and if she could drag her attention away from her phone long enough to watch it.

A camping wardrobe with a broken zip and a suitcase held my clothes and the other paltry belongings I'd brought with me. Plus two sets of sheets and towels. There wasn't a washing machine, only the laundrette downtown, alongside the dog wash. I hadn't taken dirty laundry to a laundrette since I was Georgia's age. On the upside, Jess had never been cleaner nor more sweet-smelling. Instead of watching my clothes go around and around in the Maytag, I'd bath the dog.

But beggars couldn't be choosers, or so I'd been told, and it *was* only temporary. The part that bothered me the most was that, to date, my old home remained standing; stripped bare but otherwise untouched. I know it hadn't been long and it was the summer break, but my main fear was that 'temporary' might prove to be longer than any of us had bargained for. Especially me. In this time of shortages, from building supplies to foodstuffs and toilet paper, it wouldn't be wise to get too far ahead of myself. It might be prudent to consider a Plan B.

On top of everything else, I had mixed feeling about coming back to *this* country town. Why couldn't Georgia have chosen someplace else to launch her nursing career? It's where I'd moved as a newly trained registered nurse at about the same age as she was now. And, like Georgia, I'd been brimming with excitement in anticipation of the opportunities and possibilities life had on offer. This town was where I'd met Charlie Toogood and spent a sizeable chunk of my life thereafter. Some happy times and some not. And here I was back again. Like I said, I wasn't sure how I felt about that. The irony of Georgia following in my footsteps hadn't escaped me either. 'But how cool is that,' she'd said when I'd voiced my thoughts aloud to her. All I could wish for was that she had the sense to make better life choices than I had.

Rather than succumb to a jag of self-pity this early in the day, I heated water in the microwave and made a cup of tea. Barely palatable. But Georgia didn't own a kettle, electric or otherwise. Not even a saucepan. Kitchen appliances and utensils were scant. There was an electric stove that had seen better days, a newish microwave oven and a fridge, the freezer compartment stacked full of Lite n' Easy meals.

Fortified by the tea, I tidied my 'bedroom' before I had breakfast: a handful of muesli and a tub of low-fat yoghurt. We'd agreed that I'd fold away the bed and return the living area to its intended purpose as soon after rising in the morning as was practicable. No lying in for me. No leaving the bed unmade. No tea and toast, with me propped on pillows and the newspaper spread out on my lap.

But it was only temporary. And I *was* grateful. If not for Georgia's generosity, I have no idea where Jess and I would have ended up. Probably sleeping in my car.

2

Kate

There she was again with that unattractive bitzer of a dog in tow. Every morning for the past week, they'd trotted by at around the same time as if they didn't have a care in the world. Some things never changed. Like her dress sense. Women over a certain age should *never* wear lycra. But Daisy Miller hadn't ever been bothered about what she should or shouldn't do. Or what people thought about any of it.

When she'd first walked past my house last Wednesday morning, I couldn't quite believe it was her. I'd stepped outside to throw the rinsed-out milk carton into the recycle bin. She hadn't seen me. It had been decades since I'd last clapped eyes on her and age did unkind things to women. But there'd been something familiar about the tilt of her head, her confident step and the way she'd smiled down at the dog.

The following morning at the same time I'd hovered at the loungeroom window, more certain this time after they'd passed by that it was her. Then, Friday morning, I'd been almost one hundred per cent sure. If there'd been any doubt, Valma Parrish confirmed it for me that same afternoon at book club.

'Guess who I ran into at the supermarket this morning?' she said. 'Daisy Miller. Remember her? Apparently, she's staying with her granddaughter. She's a registered nurse at the hospital. Talk about history repeating itself.'

'Gee, Daisy Miller. That is a long while ago. I reckon my James was the first baby she delivered here after she'd done her midwifery training in Adelaide, and he'll be forty next year,' Evelyn Roberts said. She turned to me. 'Kate, surely you remember her from when you were nursing?'

'Oh, yes,' I said with feigned indifference. 'You say she's back in town? Well I never.'

Evelyn's gaze narrowed. She wasn't fooled by my insouciance. 'Weren't you friends?' she said. 'I seem to remember—'

'Back on topic, ladies,' Rose Timms commanded and tapped her pen on the tabletop. 'You can finish gossiping over afternoon tea.' Rose had been a schoolteacher and then a school principal and always assumed she was in charge. No-one ever challenged her.

Rose had moved us on to the next question in the back of this month's read and I'd sighed with relief. I didn't want anyone, including myself, to probe too deeply into that era of my life, or my friendship with Daisy Miller.

Seven days had passed since I'd first spotted her and here I was again standing in what had become my usual spot by the window. I'd watch until Daisy and her dog walked by and were obscured by the neighbour's bottlebrush. It was as if I couldn't help myself. Easing from one foot to the other, I stayed put, knowing I'd catch one final glimpse of them when they crossed the street near the intersection. Impossible to miss her in that hot pink T-shirt. Hot pink and lycra at her age? Really?

A part of me could acknowledge how pathetic I was, watching her through the wooden venetians each morning, she oblivious to my scrutiny. Another part of me experienced a thrill of satisfaction each time: me knowing she was there and she not having a clue I was watching. Or even that I lived in this house.

But the distraction was short-lived; it wasn't long before a familiar emptiness returned and with it the longing for things lost that I refused to acknowledge at all. Instead, I imagined what she might do if I waited in the front yard and called out as she walked past. A sort of ambush. Not that I had any desire to do that. Or the necessary courage. Or the need. Daisy Miller was from the distant past and she could stay there, for all I cared.

Lips pinched, I let the wooden slats of the blind clunk back into place.

With horror, I realised how tightly I'd been pursing my lips. I swear there were more lines and wrinkles every morning when I looked in the mirror. I stretched my mouth wide into a parody of a smile—more of a grimace really—repeating the action several times on my way to the kitchen to turn on the coffee machine.

The house hummed with silence and the faint scent of orange oil cleaner lingered from the cleaning lady's efforts of the previous afternoon. That reminded me, I must talk to her about the second bathroom: there'd been smears on the mirror and a dust bunny in the shower recess. She'd been instructed to clean it regardless of whether or not it had been used. Four bedrooms, three toilets and two bathrooms, a study, family room, dining area, formal lounge and kitchen was a lot of space for one person. Not to forget the yard and garden; the outdoor living area and swimming pool. The pool had been Dennis's idea, not mine. Now Dennis wasn't here any more but his swimming pool was and it always needed maintenance or cleaning.

A while back I'd had to let my cleaner go. It'd been a stressful time, but after I'd found what I strongly suspected was a pubic hair on the kitchen bench, there'd been no other option: individual colour-coded cloths were provided for each area of the house and I had been very clear in my instructions on what colour was to be used where. The thought of finding *another* cleaner if this one didn't work out was depressing.

The usual snarl of emotions too complex to comprehend, never mind unravel, balled up inside of me. With steely resolve, I squared my shoulders and did what I always did: shoved the lid back on that Pandora's box. Instead I focussed on a caffeine fix. The first coffee was undoubtably the best one of the day.

Sun slanted in across the breakfast nook and single Wedgewood place setting. It was my favourite spot in the whole house. Although I hadn't intended to, all I could think about, as I dawdled over a second espresso and sourdough toast spread with strawberry jam, was Daisy Miller and how we'd once been the best of friends. Not ever having had a close girlfriend before Daisy, not even at school, no-one knew how much I'd cherished the friendship.

We'd first met when Daisy came to work at the hospital in the mid seventies, a newly minted registered nurse fresh from her staffing year. Three years her senior and having worked at the hospital as an RN for all of those years, the Matron instructed me to take the new recruit under my wing. Daisy was like a sponge, soaking up knowledge and milking each experience for what it was worth. At first I'd resented her quick intelligence and lack of guile; her enthusiasm for life. The patients loved her. Daisy was one of those what-you-saw-was-what-you-got people. Even back then I'd had enough insight to see she was many things that I was not. Although I tried, it proved impossible not to like her.

On the job, we worked well as a team. Together, we experienced the challenges and uncertainties of country nursing. These shared experiences, the highs and lows and the vulnerabilities, grew into a friendship. Another nurse is often the only person who knows the right thing to say to pick you up or gently lower you down.

When I met Daisy I'd not long been engaged to Dennis Hannaford. He was a farmer, the most comfortable in his own company. But he'd slowly warmed to Daisy's outgoing and optimistic manner. As my friendship with Daisy progressed past the professional, it'd often be the two of us trekking out to the farm to visit Dennis and share a meal, or a picnic and a swim at the waterhole. Sometimes she'd sleep over as well.

Dennis and I were married in June the following year, about eighteen months after Daisy had come on the scene. The wedding reception was held at the bowling club, and that's where Daisy Miller met Charlie Toogood. He wasn't a wedding guest, rather a mate of a member of the bowling club who'd volunteered to help out behind the bar, or so I learned afterwards.

Dennis knew Charlie vaguely because at the time he was working as a farmhand for a neighbour. Dennis had never had a thing to say about Charlie, good or bad. But that was Dennis. I, however, was never as circumspect in venting an opinion and my first impression of Charlie Toogood was not positive.

Not so for Daisy, and so began a subtle shift in our friendship. Daisy began to spend more time with Charlie. Consequently, she didn't visit the farm as often. When she did, it was only to blow in, stay long enough to drink a mug of tea and then be off again.

'You're newlyweds now!' She'd laugh and wink. 'Wouldn't want to overstay my welcome.'

We saw each other just as often at work but there'd been a definite change in our relationship. Admittedly, I'd married and moved out to the farm, but my share of her free time and attention shrank while Charlie's grew.

Then one afternoon, several months after she'd taken up with him, she'd unexpectedly come out to the farm. I'd been on night duty and we'd only seen each other for a few minutes at shift change. When she walked into the kitchen I was standing at the sink. I'd turned to face her, taken aback by her pallor and eyes that were red-rimmed and puffy. You'd think she'd been the one on night shift.

'What's happened?' I said.

'I'm pregnant.' The words landed heavily in the quiet kitchen.

I'd grabbed a kitchen chair and plonked myself down seconds before my legs gave out from under me. Daisy sat on the opposite side of the table. Lost in her own private purgatory, she didn't notice my reaction. Mouth open, I'd stared at her. How dare she have a baby before I did? She wasn't even married to Charlie, the good-for-nothing loser.

She sniffed and blew her nose.

'What are you going to do?' I'd said, not really caring.

'Get married, I suppose. What else is there to do?'

'There are other … options. You know that.'

It was as if she hadn't heard me. She'd rested her elbows on the table and dropped her head into her hands. 'This is not how I'd imagined my life would go,' she wailed, the sound muffled by her hands.

I'd tried to push aside the grim satisfaction I'd felt at that revelation. Not very kind or charitable of me. But I'd desperately wanted to be pregnant, and wasn't.

Our friendship changed even more. Only weeks later, Daisy married Charlie at the registry office in Adelaide. Dennis and I witnessed the union. My emotions had been all over the place on the day. Daisy looked lovely in a colourful polyester wrap dress and gold platform sandals. But I couldn't take my eyes off her baby bump. She would have been five months pregnant by then. I'd resigned myself to tolerating Charlie for Daisy's sake. But the wedge had been driven firmly between us.

All I remembered of Charlie from the day they were married was his keenness to get to the pub afterwards. Except to say, 'It's their business, not ours,' Dennis remained mute on the subject of Daisy and Charlie.

Life happened. Over the years that followed, situations and circumstances stealthily drove the wedge deeper, millimetre by millimetre, until that one fateful day when, for me, the friendship split irretrievably. Even now, decades later, the memory of that day brought a bitter taste to my mouth.

I tipped the dregs of my coffee down the sink and put the breakfast things into the dishwasher. As I wiped the table in the breakfast nook I grudgingly admitted that, in all fairness, the demise of our friendship did not rest solely at Daisy's feet. To blame her for everything and totally freeze her out of my thoughts and my life had been the easiest way for me to deal with the situation at the time. And for a long time afterwards. Even now, after all these years, knowing myself the way I did, it was unlikely I'd ever be able to make that admission to her.

3

Daisy

It was Georgia's weekend off and she'd invited a handful of girl-friends over for drinks and nibbles on Saturday night. She asked me to make myself scarce for a few hours. In the interests of domestic calm, I readily complied. The weather was mild and Jess and I shared a takeaway hamburger and watched the kids at the skate park until dark. They gradually drifted off home or to get up to mischief some place else.

We walked along the main drag, detouring up a side street to gaze in the window of the book shop. Preloved books, it said, meaning they'd been loved once and there was hope they might be loved again. A bit like me. I bought an ice cream from the service station and shared it with Jess. A bit after nine, we were back at Georgia's. We sat in the car on the opposite side of the street and listened to music and laughter emanate from the open doors and windows.

'I wonder how often we'll be banished like this?' I said to Jess, curled up on the passenger seat. Her tail thumped once. 'Not much fun, is it? Given I'm paying a fair share of the rent.'

The dog stood up, wobbled around a bit and awkwardly resettled herself on the seat. I shifted my seat back as far as it would go and wiggled about until I was comfortable. We both yawned.

'Eww!' I shrieked moments later and lurched forward in the seat. 'You farted! You dirty dog.'

Jess had the good sense to keep her head down. She didn't move at all. I opened the windows. 'Do *not* do that again,' I said, and imagined the reproachful glance she'd be throwing my way in the gloom.

I woke with a start. I must have dozed. A cool breeze wafted in through the open windows and Jess snored softly beside me. My feet were cold and I had a crick in my neck. When my gaze crossed the street to Georgia's place, time shifted for a moment and I was parked outside a house not dissimilar to this one, waiting for Charlie's boozy friends to depart so I could go inside and go to bed. Home after a flat-out afternoon shift at the hospital and six months pregnant with Gareth. We'd been married a month. The house we'd lived in then had been two streets away from this one. It wasn't there any more—I'd walked past to check. Some entrepreneur had pushed it over and replaced it with six equally unattractive flats. Besser-block breezeways and Mission Brown woodwork.

My eyes drifted shut and I sighed. What an unremarkable life I'd lived, stumbling from one domestic drama to another, barely surviving from one payday to the next. Doing my best as a parent but more often than not feeling as if I'd missed the mark. Charlie there for the good times but glaringly absent whenever the going got tough. Until he wasn't there at all.

The boys had turned out okay, regardless. Gareth was an electrician and ran his own lucrative business. His wife Tess was a sensible, practical woman who didn't let her husband boss her around. They had three children, Georgia being the eldest. Jay, my middle child, had had problems. Life sometimes got the better of him. He was perpetually single and what a relief that was. Adam, the youngest, was a registered nurse. He and his partner Bec, also a nurse, had recently given birth to their second child, another daughter; Stella and now Nadine. Will, Adam's teenage son from his first marriage, also lived with them.

There was no denying that the past decade had been my most contented. After Mum died, I'd had no-one to please but myself. Gareth had relieved me of the mortgage but there'd been other debts and I'd lived from one payday until the next; and now, although I had no significant debts, I lived from one pension day until the next. While I didn't need much, a bit more would have been nice.

Across the street, Georgia's screen door opened. Light spilled onto the verandah. There was a flurry of laughter and goodbyes followed by the slam of car doors, engines revving and then tail lights blinking into the night. I started the station wagon and puttered across the road into the driveway.

'How long have you been parked over there?' Georgia said when Jess and I climbed out.

'Two hours.' I was chilled to the bone. I felt old and tired and grumpy. I locked the car and closed the front gate. Georgia and I went inside. A disgruntled Jess flopped down onto the mat. 'Sorry, sweetie,' I said through the screen door. We both knew she wasn't allowed indoors. Neither of us was happy about that.

'Why didn't you come inside?' Georgia said. Her cheeks were flushed. There were several empty wine bottles and the remnants of a deli cheese platter on the kitchen bench.

'Didn't want to gate crash.' A scalding cup of tea would have been lovely right then but I made do with a glass of tap water.

'I'm sorry, Gran,' Georgia said. She loosened her hair from its elastic band and let it fall to her shoulders. It was thick and dark and lustrous, a lot like mine had been at her age. And then she yawned wide enough to make her jaw crack.

'Don't be sorry.' I rinsed the glass and upended it on the sink. 'You work hard and you're entitled to a social life.' My turn to yawn.

'Next time we'll go to Lisa's place. She broke up with her boyfriend and he's moved out.' She covered what was left of the cheese platter with cling wrap and put it in the fridge. 'I'll clean up in the morning. And don't you dare do it.'

We both knew that I would. Together we pulled out the sofa bed and re-assembled my bedroom. The task was easier with two.

'I'm on nights next week, remember?'

I nodded and dragged the privacy screen into position.

'What'll you do during the day?'

'Keep very quiet so as not to disturb you,' I said.

She looked sceptical but shrugged and said, 'I'll clean my teeth and then the bathroom's all yours.'

When she came out of the bathroom I was waiting for her. 'Georgia, sweetheart, If you don't think this is working—me staying here with you, sharing expenses—all you need to do is say so and Jess and I will find someplace else.'

'No … no,' she said, the second 'no' sounding way more convincing than the first. 'All good. Besides, Dad said you couldn't afford to rent on your own and Mum said it's his fault you're homeless.'

'Did she,' I said. Had Georgia been coerced by her parents into letting me stay? Or bribed? Neither option was palatable. But homeless? 'Temporarily displaced' was how I'd thought of myself. Not homeless. Homeless sounded desperate. Final. Hopeless. They were almost the same words, only one letter different. The prickle of tears surprised me. I blinked.

'Don't worry, Gran,' Georgia said, and squeezed my shoulder. 'If I think this isn't working any more, I'll tell you.' She pecked me on the cheek, her breath toothpaste-fresh. She wafted off in a cloud of florally fragrance. I think it was the body lotion she used.

After I heard the snick of her bedroom door closing, I went into the bathroom and closed the door. Homeless. At the largesse of my family. I leaned heavily on the hand basin. Not for the first time since Gareth had run his plan past me, I felt exposed. Extremely vulnerable. Even more vulnerable than I'd felt when the boys were little and Charlie would just take off, in the guise of looking for work. More often than not he'd only be gone a week or two, but other times it would stretch into several months. Rarely did I see a wage packet.

I had a hot shower to warm up, cleaned my teeth and slathered on Olay night cream. The bottom of the tub was visible, reminding me to be more frugal with it. After saying goodnight to Jess, I tiptoed around the house and checked the doors were locked.

As tired as I was, sleep hovered just out of reach. Bedclothes pulled to my chin, I stared into the darkness and considered what Gareth might have done if I'd said no, that I wouldn't be moved out of my home, albeit temporarily. Even with the promise of a new townhouse at the end. While I hadn't paid him rent, I had met all the other expenses, from rates to utilities and any minor repairs. The yard was huge and the upkeep and general maintenance had been my responsibility. No small task or expense.

Who was I kidding? If I'd said no, he would have tipped me out anyway. And as well as being homeless, my relationship with him would have been damaged, perhaps beyond repair. He owned the property and I'd continued to live there only because of his generosity. It had bothered him that he wasn't earning anything from it, apart from the appreciation of the land's value. My eldest son worked hard and wasn't one to miss an opportunity or challenge, especially if it would make him more money.

Then, for the first time, I had a horrifying thought. I lurched into a sitting position. What if he succumbed to the lure of the dollar and decided to lease out both townhouses? Changed his mind about me living in one and paying a peppercorn rent? After that, sleep was nigh impossible.

4

Kate

When the time came, it did not go well. However, hubris was the last thing I would have expected from a cleaning lady. After I said I wasn't completely satisfied with her work, she glowered at me and, hands on hips, said, 'Well! None of my other clients have *ever* complained.'

I returned her glare from across the kitchen's granite-topped island bench. 'Perhaps not, but did you ever consider they might have wanted to but weren't game enough?' I said, recklessly adding fuel to the fire.

Her face turned an unhealthy puce, beady eyes disappearing into folds of skin. In that moment I realised how much I disliked her and how I didn't trust her one iota. That I hadn't from the very beginning. But she was there to clean my house, not to be my best friend. On the flip side, if you couldn't trust the person you employed to clean your house, better to let them go.

'You know where you can stick your lousy job!' she said, effectively upstaging me. She snatched her car keys and mobile phone off the bench. 'People said I was crazy to clean for you. That you were a mean old cow. I should have listened to them.'

'What people?' I said after I'd digested her words. But she'd gone, slamming the door in her wake. I rushed after her, howling when I banged my hip on the corner of the island. 'Just a minute—'

I caught her just as she unlocked her car. 'What people?' I repeated, indignant.

'As if I'd tell you. But don't ever think you'll find another cleaner in this town.' She flung open the car door and heaved herself in, started the car, gunned the engine and reversed out of the driveway. She'd obviously forgotten I'd asked her not to park on the driveway because her car had leaked oil onto the cement.

For a minute all I could do was stand there gawping. Then I did a quick scan of the neighbours' houses to see if we'd had any witnesses. Unlikely, because the folk either side of me worked and the elderly lady across the street spent all her time in the kitchen, which was at the rear of her house.

A ginger cat slunk across the street. It glanced back at me over its shoulder. Feeling nauseated, I went inside. My hands were shaking. After a glass of filtered water and several deep breaths, I felt marginally better. But who were these people who thought I was a mean old cow?

Later, after I'd rehashed the clash for the umpteenth time, I decided my biggest regret was that I hadn't waited until after she'd cleaned the house. I'd accosted her before she'd even started and the situation had spiralled out of control. Now I had a grubby house and no cleaner. You'd have thought after years of people management I would have made a better job of dealing with her poor performance. I poured myself a generous glass of wine and took it outside to the patio.

★★★

Between rubbers of bridge the following afternoon, I recounted the episode to the girls at my table. Of course I left out the part where she called me a mean old cow.

'Does anyone know who I could employ to do my cleaning? I'd prefer they came with references. I pay the going rate, which isn't cheap,' I said.

The three women sitting at the table remained straight-backed and tight-lipped, not one of them making eye contact. I'd known these women for years. Two of them had worked for me when I was the director of nursing at the hospital and I counted them as friends. They just sat there.

And then Lorraine, being my bridge partner and the more outspoken of the trio, said, 'You might have to clean your own house, Kate. Like the rest of us do.'

'None of you has a cleaner?'

They all shook their heads.

'Not ever?'

Another head shake.

'But you all had jobs ... families ... busy lives ...'

'And?' Lorraine said, raising a pencilled-in eyebrow.

'I'd just assumed—' Suddenly my face felt hot and I didn't know where to look. What exactly had I assumed? It occurred to me that although I'd been in the company of these women countless times over many years, I didn't *know* them. The thought left me breathless. What else had I missed? But then you only ever see what you're looking for, don't you? My head pounded.

Lorraine cleared her throat. The others shifted uncomfortably in their chairs. The cards were dealt but my mind was elsewhere and Lorraine and I barely took a trick. All my fault.

'I'm sorry,' I said to her when we were packing up.

'Never mind,' she said. 'We can't all be winners all of the time.'

I always stayed for the wine and nibbles afterwards, partly to see what the hostess had come up with, so that when it was my turn I could outdo her. But today I was overcome by an inexorable urge to leave as soon as the cards had been returned to their boxes. Get as far away from these women as I possibly could. Nothing had been said but I'd had the distinct impression that the girls at the other two tables had overheard our conversation and there was no sympathy coming my way. Or suggestions of who I could recruit to do my cleaning. With or without references.

It was my turn to host the next bridge afternoon and I'd planned to plead off until I'd found another cleaner, thinking everyone would understand. But after what had transpired, I hadn't had the courage.

By the time I'd driven home I'd worked myself into quite a lather. Had any of the women at bridge been the people who'd advised against working for me? That I was an old cow? And mean. If so, what else had they been saying about me? And for how long?

I tried to get angry but discovered I didn't have the energy. So unlike me—self-righteous outrage was a default setting. It annihilated any opportunity for useful introspection. Dennis had pointed that out to me once, or twice, upon a time. He'd been a taciturn man, but with rare bursts of profound insight. Of course, the times he'd voiced the observation, I'd been outraged.

Dispirited to the point of malaise, I washed down two paracetamol with a glass of wine, drew the drapes in the bedroom, kicked off my shoes and lay down on the bed. It wasn't even five o'clock and I never had a lie-down in the afternoon. Not until today.

I woke at nine forty-seven feeling cold. The room was dark. Thirsty and thick-headed, I got up and shuffled to the kitchen. Moonlight filtered in through the window over the sink. It was bright enough to cast shadows in the backyard, and for me to see my way about without turning on a light.

I filled the electric kettle and switched it on. I didn't feel the slightest bit hungry. While I waited for the kettle to boil, I went back to the bedroom, peeled off my rumpled clothes, threw them into the laundry hamper and pulled on a nightie. No shower. No removal of makeup or jewellery. No teeth cleaning. No light. No looking at myself in the mirror.

After I'd made tea—with a bag not leaves—I took it and a glass of water back to bed with me. But not before I'd rummaged in the medicine cabinet and found the sleeping tablets the doctor had prescribed for me in the immediate aftermath of Dennis's death.

I didn't want to think. I didn't want to pretend everything was all right, that *I* was all right, when I knew damned well that I wasn't. I did not want to worry about who was going to clean my house. Or how I was going to get through the rest of my life. I just wanted to sleep.

5

Daisy

Sleep was a precious commodity, especially if you were a shift worker. While Georgia was on night shift, Jess and I made ourselves scarce so she could sleep. We'd both lost weight because we were going for long walks everyday. One day, if my pedometer was to be believed, we'd walked a grand total of twelve kilometres. No wonder we were both sleeping well.

I tried not to feel resentful because, after years working nights, I understood how difficult it was to sleep during the day. Apart from the weather warming up, the walls of Georgia's rental were paper thin. Sound carried and I was conscious of even the slightest noise I made. Jess didn't know not to bark, so we went out and pounded the pavement and when we were exhausted we sat in the shade in the park. A drive out would have been a pleasant change and there were plenty of interesting places to visit. But with petrol the price it was, I couldn't afford to fill the car's tank too often. Spending money on a new pair of sneakers when I wore out this pair would be a more practical investment.

And while I wouldn't have called myself a worrier, after a recent conversation with Gareth about the progress of his project—that is, the tearing down of my home—I'd worried. The more he'd blustered and tried to reassure me everything was on track, the less reassured I'd felt. Hence the shut down of all unnecessary spending. That irked me. At my age, why couldn't I have a new pair of sneakers and go for a drive when the mood struck me?

'What are you doing today?' Georgia said, and snapped me out of my cogitating. She smothered a yawn. After five night shifts, her gorgeous blue eyes were smudged with shadows, her face pale and drawn. The perpetual tiredness of night shift: I remembered it well.

'I'll go to the library this afternoon. It's cool in there. There's plenty of shade outside for Jess. Someone puts out a bowl of water for dogs.'

Georgia screwed up her face. 'Isn't there someone you could visit? Spend the day with? Someone who has air conditioning. You used to live here.'

Already dressed and breakfasted, I was at the sink filling water bottles ready for the day's trek. I'd packed my lunch: a cheese and Vegemite sandwich and a muesli bar. Coolish morning air wafted in through the front door. A magpie carolled from a nearby gum tree. Jess had her nose pressed to the screen door, watching my every move.

'Thirty years ago, love. And the only person I kept in touch with died a long time ago.' Dorothea Gilchrist. She'd been old enough to be my mother, dear woman that she'd been. I'd done a stint relieving as a community nurse. Thea had been caring for her elderly mother. She'd had leg ulcers that had required redressing three times a week.

Thea and I had become firm friends. There'd been a connection I'd never felt with my own mum. When Thea's mother's health failed further, I'd helped them through the palliative phase, as a friend, not a paid employee. Much to Charlie's disgruntlement, I might add, especially on the nights he'd had to watch our boys to free me up to sit with Thea's mother so Thea could get some much-needed sleep. On top of the night shifts I worked at the hospital. Thea's mother had wanted to die at home, and she had.

'Gosh,' I murmured. I hadn't thought about Thea Gilchrist in ages. Perhaps Jess and I could walk out to the cemetery one day and I'd pay my respects.

'What about your old nursing friends? I can't imagine not keeping in touch with a few of the girls I trained with. Lisa's the best.'

I stowed an apple and an orange in the day pack with the other supplies and zipped it closed. The bag was a bit like me: worn and faded but still useful.

'There were a few of us, once upon a time. We'd do like you: sit around and drink and talk shop. The wine wasn't as fancy as the stuff you drink, but I'll bet the chat was similar.' I shrugged. 'Life happens, people move on, friendships come and go—' I paused, suddenly assailed by a string of vivid memories: playing Scrabble; swimming in a waterhole; drinking wine in a farmhouse kitchen; lots of laughter and chatter … Me and Kate Hannaford and sometimes her husband Dennis in the frame.

Close on the heels of the memories came a tightness in my chest, enough to squeeze the air from my lungs. What was that about? I hadn't thought about Kate and the demise of our friendship in such a long time. What had become of her? Thea's death had meant my conduit to local gossip had been severed.

'Gran?' There was a note of concern in Georgia's voice.

'I'm all right,' I said. 'I was just thinking back to a friendship of my own, one that came and went.' I frowned. 'It just sort of faded away. Friendships need to be constantly nurtured because you're right, there's nothing more special than a dear woman friend.'

Georgia tilted her head to the side. 'Do you think it's inevitable that one person always puts more effort into a friendship than the other person does? It's just that with Lisa and me it sometimes feels a bit one-sided, especially when there's a bloke involved,' she said, and then yawned so widely I was surprised the corners of her mouth didn't split.

'Go to bed,' I said.

She stood and stretched. 'I think I will. One more night to go and then two days off. Thank goodness. I don't know how you managed to work nights for as long as you did, Gran.'

In the early years it had been the most workable option. There'd been no money for childcare and Charlie usually came home before I went to work. When the boys were older and more self-sufficient, day shifts became manageable, but over time I found I preferred working through the dark hours. The silent, dimly lit corridors; most patients asleep.

'No one around to bother you at night,' I said. 'The gossip and petty bitchiness during the day used to irritate me. Before I knew it, I'd be gossiping with them and I wasn't good at it.'

'They prefer not to have permanent night-shift workers any more. Reckon it creates an "us and them" culture.'

'It always was easier to blame the night shift for anything that wasn't done.'

Georgia laughed. 'Still is. That's it for me. Bed. I am sooo tired.'

'Sleep well. I'll keep out of your way until … four? Same as usual?'

'Three-thirty today. Lisa and I are playing squash at four.'

★★★

The kids were still on school holidays. After an early lunch, we sat under a tree by the skate park and watched a group of them take ridiculous risks on their scooters and skateboards. Then Jess and I walked to the library. She was content, tied up in the shade with a doggy treat, the bowl of water in reaching distance.

Billowy white clouds were building off to the northeast and I'd swear the humidity had increased with them. When the air-conditioned coolness of the library enveloped me I sighed with pleasure. It was easy to browse away a couple of hours and it hadn't been difficult to get a library card. But I limited myself to three books. That was all I could cram into the day pack, the weight offset by the empty water bottles.

Almost back to Georgia's, Jess toiled loyally along beside me. We were both feeling the heat and humidity. I was in a bit of a daze, thinking of home and a glass of cold water and wishing I hadn't borrowed any library books at all. Next thing I knew, Jess's lead slipped through my fingers and she bounded off and disappeared down the driveway of a newish ranch-style brick house. We'd walked past the place every day and I'd thought how neat and clipped everything looked, not a weed to be seen. Today there were leaves blown about and a newspaper in its plastic wrapping languished on the lawn. A ute and a trailer were parked in the driveway. A young bloke, mid-twenties with a mop of sun-bleached curls, was down on his haunches giving Jess a vigorous tummy rub. What a tart that dog was, rolling over for the first good-looking male to come her way.

'Your dog?' he said in an attractive baritone.

'Jess!' I admonished, and she scrambled to her feet, not quite making eye contact with me.

The young man grinned and stood up. 'Do you know the lady who lives here?'

I shook my head and took a firm grip of the dog's lead.

'I was here earlier to do her swimming pool, but the gate's locked and when I rang the doorbell there was no answer.'

He frowned when he glanced towards the house. 'I've phoned three or four times over the day, left messages and sent a text. Nada.'

'Oh,' I said. 'Maybe she forgot you were coming and she went out. Come on, Jess.'

He shook his head. 'Car's in the garage,' he said. 'I looked. There's a window along the side. And we've been seeing to the pool every week for the past year and she's never missed. Something feels off.'

'Oh,' I said again, because what else could I say? 'Neighbours? Friends? Family?'

'Neighbours. Good thinking,' he said. 'You do that side and I'll do this side. My nanna lives over the road but she never sees anything, too busy watching her soapies or surfing the internet.'

He powered off and left me with little choice other than to do his bidding.

'Come on, Jess,' I said, and we headed for our allocated driveway.

6

Kate

Kieran Hall hadn't given up as easily as I'd hoped. When he'd arrived early this morning to clean the pool, I'd ignored him and he'd eventually driven off. Then he'd phoned several times during the day and left messages. But now his ute and trailer were parked in the driveway. Why couldn't he have stayed away? If he rang the doorbell again I'd have to answer and tell him to come back next week … next month … Never, for all I cared. I'd get the damn swimming pool filled in.

Returning to my observation point, I surreptitiously parted the slats of the blind and peered out. At this rate, I'd be wearing the shine off the floorboards. His ute hadn't moved but of the man, there was no sign. I stepped away from the window. Where had he gone? Surely he hadn't scaled the six-foot-high back fence because the gate was locked? Well, if he had, the shed where all the pool gear was kept was padlocked and he would have wasted his time. But he'd know that.

Then I got a whiff of something stale and sour smelling and, with a start, I realised it was me. I hadn't showered for three days! I was still wearing the same nightie I'd dragged on on Wednesday evening and here it was, late Friday afternoon. There were dirty dishes in the sink, toast crumbs on the counter and I hadn't taken out the garbage or dumped the empty wine bottles in the recycle bin. What's more, I had no immediate plans to clean up either the kitchen or myself.

The doorbell chimed and I jumped. *Shit!* I don't usually swear, not even to myself. During the trip through the entranceway to the front door I quickly rehearsed what I'd say to Kieran. I took a deep breath and cracked open the door not more than a foot wide and, without looking up, I spoke through the mesh of the security door.

'Kieran, I haven't been feeling the best. It won't matter if we leave the pool until next week. No one's swimming in it just now.' I looked up with what I hoped was a smile and found myself face to face with Daisy Miller, not Kieran Hall.

'Kate? Kate Hannaford, is that really you?' she said, leaning in closer, almost pressing her nose against the screen door. 'I was only just thinking about you this morning, wondering where you were these days. Is there anything I can do to help?'

'You can go away, that's what you can do to help,' I snapped. Heart beating a rapid tattoo in my chest, I started to close the door.

'Mrs Hannaford,' a deeper voice said, and that's when I noticed that Kieran was standing behind her. 'I don't think it'd be wise to leave the pool too long. If you unlock the gate and the shed I can see to it now and I won't need to disturb you again.'

Indecision momentarily paralysed me. He was right, but ... My gaze darted from him to her, then back to him. I'd swear I only looked away for a nanosecond but before I knew what was happening, Daisy had wrenched open the security door, which I'd forgotten to lock, and there she was with her blasted dog, nothing at all between us.

'You look dreadful!' she said, and wrinkled her nose.

I wanted to slap her, to shake her, to shout at her to go away, but most of all I yearned for her to gather me into her arms and hug me. Tightly.

That was the bit that alarmed me the most. I swallowed hard against the bitter ball of tears forming in my throat.

'You don't look so good yourself,' I said.

'The gate, would you please unlock it, Mrs Hannaford?' Kieran reminded me again of his presence.

'Oh, all right,' I said. That'd at least get him out of my face. I flounced off. Yes, I flounced. Then I heard Daisy tell the dog to stay put right before the security door clicked shut.

She was standing in the middle of the living area when I came in from unlocking the gate, one of those cotton bucket hats in her hand. Her short salt-and-pepper hair was sweaty and pressed flat to her scalp. She was wearing the same ridiculous pink T-shirt. Over shorts this time, not lycra. And dusty sneakers with the sort of socks people who played sport or walked a lot wore.

I must have been staring at her T-shirt because she gripped the hem between thumb and forefinger and said, 'I have four, all the same colour. They were on special at Target. They just won't wear out.' She threw me a tentative smile. I'd guarantee that right then, she was wishing she hadn't stepped over my threshold.

'This place is huge,' she said. Without any encouragement from me, she scanned the family room. 'And it's all so—' She flapped a hand around in a circle and frowned, then gave up and said, 'When did you move in off the farm?'

'Several years ago,' I said, grudgingly. 'And it's all so what?'

Her frown deepened. She rolled her lips together and then slowly turned 360 degrees, taking in the family room with its monster television screen and matching leather recliners. Her mouth opened and closed.

'I'm surprised you managed to get Dennis away from the farm. Is he about?' she said.

'No. He's dead.'

Her gaze swivelled to mine, her eyes wide as her face drained of colour. Good. My intention had been to shock.

'I'm so sorry,' she said. 'I didn't know. You must miss him terribly.' Her brow pinched with concern.

I looked away. Did I miss my husband? If ever I could find the wherewithal to work my way through the anger and resentment—and the guilt—I might know if the gaping hole inside of me meant that I missed him.

'You live here all by yourself,' she said and nodded, as if that explained something. 'After Thea died—you'd remember her, Dorothea Gilchrist? Her mum was in and out of hospital ...'

I stood rigidly, my arms folded.

'Well, after that, I lost touch with this town, until Georgia, my granddaughter, moved here last year. How long ago did Dennis die?'

'A year or thereabouts.'

'Oh, Kate. That's not very long at all. How are you coping?' She moved towards me and reached out with both hands.

Seemingly of its own volition, my body leaned towards her. It had been so long since anyone had touched me for anything other than necessity. The hairdresser when she cut and coloured my hair. The physiotherapist when I'd sprained my wrist. That was it.

But this was Daisy Miller. I straightened and my hostile expression halted her in her tracks. 'As if it's any of your business,' I said. 'We're not friends any more.'

She winced. 'We were, once upon a time. The very best of friends.'

'And hasn't there been a lot of water under the bridge since then. Now, I don't remember inviting you in. You know which way is out.'

She did not dissemble, hurt and disappointment apparent in her expression. Daisy always did wear her heart on her sleeve. It's one of the quirks about her that had irritated me, but which I'd also envied. That had irritated me even more. She never shied away from *feeling*. I experienced a moment's remorse for being rude. But only a moment.

She turned and made for the entranceway. I didn't follow her. The second before she disappeared from my line of sight she paused, then slowly turned to face me. All I could read in her expression was compassion. Damn her.

'Please accept my condolences, Kate,' she said, her voice steady. 'I'm sorry they're a year late. Dennis was a decent man. You lost him too soon.'

My lips curled with derision. 'You only ever mocked him for being bland and boring, you and that good-for-nothing husband of yours.'

Daisy blinked and swallowed hard. 'Not intentionally,' she said, her voice not as steady as it had been. 'And if I ever came across as mocking, I deeply regret that. And I apologise. Dennis was always kind to me and I'll remember him as a friend, and a loyal and steadfast husband to you. Over the years, I lost count of the number of times Charlie up and left me and the kids high and dry, until the time he went and didn't come back at all.'

'But he didn't die, did he?'

'He might as well have.'

I squeezed my eyes shut and didn't open them again until I heard the front door close with a dull thud then the clatter of the security door. Unable to resist, I hurried to the window, parted the slats of the blind and looked out as she walked down the driveway past Kieran's ute. Not such a spring in her step now. She had a day pack slung over a shoulder and was talking to her dog. About me, I supposed. Unlikely to be anything nice. The dog glanced at her and wagged its tail.

I dropped the wooden slat and snapped the blind completely shut. Then I locked the security door and tried to ignore the headache pounding at my temples. When had I last eaten anything? Or had anything other than wine to drink? I couldn't remember. This would not do.

But after Kieran had finished with the pool it took all the reserves I had to scrape together enough energy to have a shower and put on clean cotton pyjamas. I didn't wash my hair. Afterwards I drank a glass of water and forced down a handful of dry crackers and sat in Dennis's recliner until night time came and filled the house with more darkness.

I had no conscious memory of crying, but the damp patch on my pyjama coat and the salty stiffness of the skin on my face told me otherwise. I went to bed and slept for ten hours without even a glass of wine or a sleeping tablet.

Saturday morning, when I scuttled out to pick up the newspaper off the lawn, there was a bunch of roses propped against the door. Gorgeous, fragrant pink blooms. And a note: *If you need anything, I'm just around the corner. Regards, Daisy.* She'd included her address and mobile phone number. Double damn her. I put the roses in a crystal vase of water, but I screwed up the note and threw it in the bin with all the other garbage.

7

Daisy

The roses I'd left on Kate's doorstep were from Max Purdue's garden. The kind gesture of leaving the flowers for Kate had fundamentally been his idea. He was Georgia's elderly neighbour. There was a vacant block on one side and Max's house on the other. He lived on his own and took great pride in the garden, especially noteworthy because of its stark contrast to Georgia's barren swathe of gravel and dead weeds.

If Max was out tending his garden when I walked past he'd always wave and call out a greeting. Sometimes I'd stop and we'd comment about the weather and the lack of rain. He'd never miss saying hello to Jess and I'd wondered if he'd once been a dog owner.

When I'd walked past Max's place late Friday afternoon, I'd been preoccupied by the heat and humidity and my recent and unexpected encounter with Kate Hannaford. I'd let Jess off the lead at the corner. I hadn't noticed Max in the garden until he called out a greeting. Needing no more encouragement, the dog had taken off up his driveway, tail wagging.

When I called for her to come back, Max said, 'She's all right.'
He'd stooped to pet her. I worried because she could be boisterous,
even for her advanced years, and Max was old and frail. It wouldn't
take much to topple him over and then for him to break a bone
when he hit the ground.

'You're a sweet old thing,' he said. Initially I thought he meant me
and I didn't know whether to laugh or be offended. I wasn't *that* old.
But no, he was talking to Jess while he gave her tummy a scratch. She'd
roll over for any male, not only the young and good-looking ones.

I hovered at the gate and hefted the book-heavy day pack from
one shoulder to the other.

Max gave Jess a final pat and pushed himself upright. 'I wonder if
I could ask a favour?' he said, dusting his hands on his trousers. He
needed someone to witness his signature on a document.

'Happy to oblige,' I said. 'Now?'

He squinted towards Georgia's place. 'If you don't mind. It is a
tad early for your granddaughter to be up.'

I made no attempt to mask my surprise.

Max's smile was wry. 'My late wife Eileen was a nurse and me
and the kids spent many a weekend tiptoeing about the place. In the
end, we'd usually go out.'

Jess plopped down on the grass when I told her to stay. Then I
followed Max to the house and rested the day pack on the verandah.

'The harder you try to be quiet, the more noise you make. But I
know what it's like to be the one trying to sleep. And to be chronically sleep-deprived.'

'You were a nurse yourself?' he said. I nodded. 'Then you'd
understand one hundred per cent.'

He ushered me in through the front door and we went down
a dim passageway into a cool, bright and tidy kitchen. A bread
machine sat on the bench and the room smelled of baking bread.

'Sit down,' he said. 'I'll fetch the papers and my glasses.'

I sat and took in the room while I waited. The house was old and built of stone. A relatively modern electric range stood in place of what would have once been a wood stove. A set of Bakelite canisters, cream-coloured with red lids and labels, sat on the mantlepiece. I guessed the pressed-tin ceiling would be original and the Laminex-topped table and chrome chairs with red vinyl upholstery were reminiscent of my mum's kitchen, which had become my kitchen.

Fussy lacy curtains hung at the window above the sink, which was devoid of dishes. The dishcloth was folded neatly and draped over the tap. There was an upturned milk carton draining on the rack. My breath caught on a powerful pang of nostalgia.

Max returned clutching a large buff-coloured envelope. He had reading glasses perched on the end of his nose. 'I really do appreciate this, Daisy,' he said. 'I was going to ask Pamela, my daughter, but she's not coming again until next week and I wanted to get this away.'

We did the deed and Max sealed the signed document into a stamped and addressed envelope.

'Will you stay for a cuppa?' he said.

One look at his expectant expression and any deferral faded before fully forming. 'Lovely,' I said.

His pleasure was palpable. He filled the electric kettle and switched it on.

'Real tea!' I said with delight as he set out a pot and a caddy of tea leaves. 'Georgia doesn't own so much as an electric kettle and microwaved hot water on a tea bag ...' I shuddered. 'Have you always lived here?'

'Eileen and I were tree-changers, long before they coined the phrase. She was a city girl but I spent my formative years in the country, and always had a hankering to return.'

'Whereabouts in the country?'

'Peterborough.'

'You don't get much more country than that.'

'Dad worked for the railways,' he said, pensive. 'They scrimped and scraped to send me and my brother to the city for an education. I never went back except to visit. When I retired, Eileen and I decided to move here. It's country, but wasn't too far from the city and grandchildren.'

The kettle had boiled and Max made the tea. While it steeped, and for want of anything else to say and because the encounter was still playing on my mind, I said, 'Do you know Kate Hannaford? She lives around the corner, in Wattle Avenue.'

'Huge brick house? Relatively new? More lawn than a bowling green?'

'That's the place.'

Max poured our tea and pushed a cup towards me. I doctored it with milk.

'She was the director of nursing at the hospital when Eileen went into full-time care. My wife had Parkinson's disease. It was a difficult time. Kate Hannaford was a no-nonsense sort of a person, but competent and compassionate in her own way.'

'How long ago did your wife die?'

He frowned and pulled at his right earlobe. 'Eileen will have been gone eleven years this April.' He lifted his shoulders and let them drop with a tired sigh. 'Did you know Kate Hannaford? From your nursing days?'

I focussed on the trio of mini cacti in colourful pots on the window sill. Prickly, much like Kate had been earlier that afternoon.

'Yes, but it was many moons ago.'

'Here?'

I nodded. 'But up until I ran into her this afternoon I hadn't seen her in over thirty years.' I looked down at my hands. Fingernails blunt and pared back. The redundant thin gold wedding band. Joints thickening with age and arthritis. And I needed to moisturise more.

'That would have been a surprise.'

'It certainly was. Did you know her husband died not twelve months ago? Dennis Hannaford.'

'Didn't know the man.'

'This afternoon, when I ran into her, the whole situation was peculiar,' I said, more to myself than to him. 'Her rattling around on her own in that huge house. I wondered if she might be ... unwell.' I rubbed my face with my hands. I felt distracted and unsettled. I finished the tea and stood up. 'That was perfect, thanks. I'd better get going.'

'I know what,' Max said. He slapped both palms onto the table-top. I jumped. He grinned. 'I'll pick you a bunch of roses and you can take them to her tomorrow morning. Eileen used to say that flowers were the best thing ever to cheer up a person.'

Max was true to his word and that's how it came to pass that I left flowers on Kate's doorstep. When I put them there early Saturday morning, I hadn't had the nerve to knock, as silly as that might sound. Intuition told me that all was not well with Kate and she wouldn't answer the door, especially if she suspected I was on the other side.

Now a week had elapsed since I'd left the flowers and I hadn't heard a peep from her, not that I'd expected to. That's not to say I hadn't hoped. Over the past seven days, I'd rewound our chance encounter countless times and worried at it like you do a missing filling or a broken tooth. Each time, I cursed Kieran Hall's conscientiousness. When we'd had no luck with her neighbours, I was all for butting out but he'd been adamant about trying the door one last time. His genuine concern that something was wrong prompted me to accompany him to the door. Strength in numbers and all that.

The shock I'd received when the door had opened and there was Kate Hannaford. An older, thinner Kate. Her bobbed hairstyle was much the same as she'd worn it back when I'd known her; artful streaks now covering the grey. Like they had with me, the years had taken their toll. However, I would have recognised her anywhere.

Her home had been warm and fusty when I'd barged my way inside uninvited, like it'd been closed up for a week with dirty dishes on the sink and the garbage not put out. Her appearance could only be described as dishevelled; so out of character for the Kate Hannaford I remembered. What was with the nightie in the middle of the afternoon? And she'd smelled of stale alcohol and body odour. Something wasn't right, of that I was certain. Could it be because it was the anniversary of Dennis's death? Or was there more to it?

Her antagonism towards me had been too blatant to ignore, although I'd tried to disregard it. If she needed help, and outward appearances screamed that she did, she'd made it abundantly clear that I was the last person she'd accept it from. So where were her friends? Her family? Folk she could lean on in a time of need?

Incrementally, over the course of the week, I'd padded out each rewind of the encounter with memories from the past. Her antagonism? Did that mean she hadn't forgotten or forgiven me, not even after all these years? And here's me, still not clear on what it was I'd done that needed her forgiveness. But there was something, because we'd been such close friends, until we weren't.

Don't get me wrong, whatever had happened hadn't happened overnight, because if it had, I'd have had more of an idea what I'd done that was so unforgivable. But the friendship had begun to fall apart insidiously. We hadn't talked as much or as often. We'd made an effort, but the mutual offers of 'You must come over for a meal, a drink, a coffee', were never followed through. No comparing of rosters and setting dates and times. I'd put it down to us both being busy, me with a young family and her with a full-time job and her commitment to the smooth running of her own household. No one could ever accuse either of us of not working hard.

Then Kate took the promotion that should have been mine, and the Monday-to-Friday day-shift roster that went with it. No evenings and night duties for her after that. The rift in our friendship had widened. Inevitable, really.

To say that up until now I'd never thought about Kate and what had happened to our friendship would be an untruth. But it's not as if over the past thirty years I'd spent hours dwelling on its demise either. Like I'd said to Georgia, friendships waxed and waned, and they came and they went. Very few were forever.

When I'd left this town I'd had three boys under twelve, plus a husband whose approach to parenting and providing could only ever be described as casual. Out of necessity, I'd put the life and friends I'd had here behind me. All except Thea Gilchrist. Without prompting, we'd kept in touch. It had never occurred to me not to. Funny that.

I will admit that when I knew I was coming back to this town for a spell I had wondered what might have become of Kate Hannaford.

8

Kate

It was Valma Parrish's phone call that jolted me out of the blue funk I was in and halfway back into the land of the living.

When the phone rang, as with every other phone call I'd received in the past week, I didn't pick up, but let the call go through to the answering machine. You might ask why I'd have something as antiquated as an answering machine in this techno age? The simple answer: I considered myself a bystander to the digital revolution, even more so since I'd retired. The job had required a level of technical literacy and competence, however, when I walked out the door on my last day, I left it all behind me. A mobile phone and an eReader were as much as I wanted to handle. Dennis's collection of remote controls for the smart TV lay dormant on the occasional table beside his recliner in the family room. The television hadn't been turned on since the day Dennis went out and didn't come home.

'Kate,' Valma said, when the answering machine picked up. 'We'll be late. It'll be closer to eleven than ten thirty. See you soon.' Clunk. *Beep, beep, beep.*

What? Head spinning, I rushed to the calendar in the kitchen. When I worked out what day it was, I howled with dismay. Weeks ago I'd offered to host a fundraising morning tea for the women's and children's hospital later in the year. Today, in one hour to be precise, Valma and representatives of the fundraising committee would be here to nut out how we'd manage the event given the size of the area and the need for social distancing.

How could I possibly have forgotten? It was testament to where my head had been this past week. I glanced back over previous days to see if there were any other engagements I'd missed. Then I wasted precious minutes vacillating about what to do next.

I went with the quickest shower and hair wash ever, and slacks and a slinky knit that didn't need ironing. Wet hair into a barrette. A slick of makeup and jewellery that didn't clash with what I had on. I was surprised I cared. But I did and that gave me a sense of cautious optimism that whatever had had me opting out of life for a week was passing.

The house was a mess, but not as bad as it could have been. Since Daisy Miller's visit I'd at least been stacking the dirty crockery into the dishwasher and wiping up my toast crumbs. And putting the empty wine bottles into the recycle bin. I threw open a few doors and windows and whipped the brush around the toilet bowl in the guest bathroom. Put the garbage out and swept the kitchen floor.

At ten forty-five I was as ready as I could be. The electric kettle was full and a tray holding six of my second-best bone china mugs was ready on the kitchen bench. I'd found an unopened packet of biscuits in the pantry.

But when I went to the fridge, to my horror, there was no fresh milk. I'd used what was left on the cornflakes I'd had for dinner the night before. It'd take fifteen minutes I didn't have to slip to the supermarket. I grabbed a carton of long-life milk off the pantry shelf. Thank goodness for old habits learned of many years living out of town on a farm.

After I'd ushered the four women into the family room at ten fifty-three, Valma followed me into the kitchen to help with the drinks. 'I wondered if you'd even remembered,' she said, sotto voce. 'I was going to remind you at book club but plain forgot.' She studied me with forensic intensity. 'You look a bit peaky, Kate. Have you been unwell?'

With a vague lift of a shoulder, I turned away and busied myself with the kettle and the jar of instant coffee. Valma loitered on the other side of the island bench. I could feel her watching me.

Valma Parrish wasn't someone I'd call a *close* friend, but I'd known her for many years. She'd worked in hospital reception, back when there'd been receptionists in country hospitals. Her hair was snowy white and she always had rosy-pink cheeks that matched her lipstick and carefully colour-coordinated outfits. She was older than me by about five years and we were in the same book club.

The three women who waited in the family room I barely knew at all. In a town this size and living and working in the district for as long as I had, we'd crossed paths occasionally in the course of other community endeavours. Two of them could be a bit hoity-toity, in their pearl earrings and designer polo shirts with the collars turned up. But then 'people' thought I was a mean old cow. I sighed.

'Shall I pour the milk into the jug?' Valma said, startling me so I spilled coffee granules onto the bench. I'd forgotten she was there. She reached for the carton of long-life milk. *Home brand* long-life milk.

Oops. I'd meant to pour it into the jug and put the carton away in the fridge before they came.

Our eyes met across the expanse of kitchen bench. 'Thank you,' I said. 'I haven't been out to the supermarket for a few days.'

She smiled. 'They won't know the difference if it's in a jug.'

But they did, because I overheard Gaye, one of the women with the pearls and turned-up collar, say as they were leaving, 'Lovely place, especially the patio and pool area. I think it'll work, but let's hope she serves more than instant coffee and long-life milk on the day. Perhaps you could have a word with her, Valma?'

I didn't hear Valma's reply. I didn't want to. From my vantage point at the window, I watched as they drove off in Gaye's white Mercedes. Right then I could have slashed her tyres. Extreme, I know, but I was still a bit all over the place emotionally. Their visit left me feeling exhausted, my earlier optimism a mere memory. I slumped into Dennis's recliner. For some reason it was more comfortable than mine.

If Dennis had been alive there was no way I would have been hosting a fundraising morning tea here. He jealously guarded his right to privacy. My ambition had been to entertain more after I'd retired and we'd moved off the farm into town. When I'd suggested a house-warming party, he'd been totally against it.

'What was the point of us building this lovely home if we can't show it off?' I'd said.

'We built this home to live in, not so you could show it off to other people,' had been his response.

I'd been angry and hadn't spoken to him for the rest of the day. That night in bed, Dennis had been reading when I'd rolled over and feigned sleep without even saying goodnight. He'd sighed and I'd heard him put his book down on the bedside cupboard.

'Katie,' he'd said gently, 'I know you're not asleep. It doesn't matter how fine your home is, showing it off won't make people like you more.'

I'd spun over to face him, tangling myself in the bedclothes in my haste and outrage. 'Who said I wanted to have a house-warming party so people would like me? That's an awful thing to say. It implies that no-one likes me. I thought when we moved into town we might have a social life. God knows we never had anything of the kind when we lived on the farm.'

Dennis's mouth had tightened and he'd carefully taken off his reading glasses. 'Let's not go back over old ground, Kate, or neither of us will get any sleep.' He'd flicked off the reading lamp and said goodnight. Only minutes later he was snoring softly and I was lying there wide awake, staring into the darkness. It was no secret that if life had gone the way Dennis had anticipated, we'd have stayed on the farm. And our son or daughter would be working the land with him.

Hot tears had coursed down my cheeks then, as they did now for all the things lost and all that hadn't been. And never would be.

9

Daisy

Max had a cat. A feisty ginger thing that delighted in tormenting Jess. Max was off to the eye specialist followed by a weekend stay over at his daughter's place and I'd agreed to feed the cat. Jess gave me the stink eye when I told her to stay home before I went next door to Max's to get the lowdown on feeding the feline.

'The cat was Pamela's idea,' Max said, and showed me where the cat food was kept. A bowl of dry food and one of water sat on a placemat on the back verandah. 'I'll put food out before I leave so there's no need to come back until tomorrow morning.'

The backyard was as well groomed as the front. There were fruit trees, a grape vine and a couple of raised garden beds containing a selection of vegetables.

'I was a bit down a while back and Pamela thought a pet would be company for me.' He snorted. 'The cat probably would be, if she ever came near me.'

'What's her name?'

'Pauline.'

'Ha! Someone has a sense of humour.'

'That would be Pamela. They have a bullmastiff called Gough and a flightless galah named Tony.'

Max sent me home with a container filled with tomatoes and apple cucumbers. 'Help yourself to whatever's ripe when you come to feed the cat. Don't worry about the chooks. There's only two left and they don't lay often. I won't replace them when their time comes.'

That was a bit sad. But I understood what Max meant. You get to an age where there's a high chance your pets will outlive you. Jess was eight years old and I liked to think I'd have enough time left in my life for one more dog after she'd shuffled off her mortal coil.

Georgia was home from work, her car parked behind mine. Jess looked the other way when I walked past.

'Where have you been?' Georgia said when I went inside. She eyed the container in my hands.

'Next door.'

'Again?' She winked and nudged me with her elbow. 'Cups of tea. Flowers. Home-grown tomatoes. What next?'

'I'm feeding the cat while Max is away for a couple of nights is all.'

'Yes, but you're both—'

'Old?' I said, and there was a definite tone to my voice. 'So that automatically means we're made for each other?'

'Well, you're both on your own and I just thought—'

'Don't, Georgia. The flowers were for someone else and he has more tomatoes than he can eat. He's a kind man who is a decade and a half older than me, and I don't think he's changed one thing in that house since his wife died. Besides, I am just fine on my own. I can hardly believe we're even having this conversation.'

Her eyes narrowed and I braced myself for whatever was coming next. With Georgia it could be anything.

'Dad told me that you and Granddad have never divorced. Mum says she can't understand why. Is it because you guys might get back together one day?'

'You can't be serious. I don't even know where he is! The last time I saw him was when Adam got married, the first time.'

'Do you miss him?'

'He left twenty-three years ago, Georgia. You'd only just been born. I try not to think about him at all.'

'That must be hard when you have children. Mum says Uncle Jay's the spitting image of Granddad. Why haven't you divorced him?'

'Honestly? I've never given it any real thought,' I said.

But why hadn't I? I guess because at my end there'd never been any need to. Hell would freeze over before I'd let myself get tangled up with another man, so what other reason would there be for a divorce? And from Charlie's point of view? If he'd wanted another woman, would still being married to me have gotten in his way? The hurt that came with that thought pinched with its usual intensity. And I pushed that hurt aside the same way I always did.

When Charlie left for what turned out to be the last time, the only real emotion I'd felt then had been relief. One less mouth to feed. We hadn't communicated much in the years since. He hadn't even sent condolences when Mum died, and she'd doted on him. He kept in touch with Gareth and Adam. I know Jay had had a fair amount to do with his dad over the years. Charlie's grandchildren? From what I observed, only if they contacted him first. And they did. Another generation without immunity to Charlie Toogood's charm.

'Now, shall I use some of these tomatoes and cucumbers and make us a salad for tea?' I said firmly, and met Georgia's wide-eyed curiosity with a stony expression.

'You go right ahead, Gran,' she said. 'I'm meeting Lisa and a few others at the pub. We'll most likely grab something to eat there.'

She breezed out of her room an hour later in a cloud of perfume, dressed in a short colourful skirt and a skimpy black top. She looked lovely. So young and fresh. Her skin smooth and blemish free. My eyes stung. I put it down to the onion I was chopping to add to my salad.

'See ya, Gran.' She gave me a one-armed hug.

'Enjoy yourself,' I said, biting my tongue on everything I wanted to say: don't drink too much, and if you do don't drive; be home at a reasonable hour; don't take unnecessary risks; and so on.

'I won't be late, I'm on morning shift tomorrow,' she said.

I ate out on the verandah, balancing the bowl of salad on my lap. Jess sat at my feet. She'd gotten over her hump. In the end, a hug and an extra doggy treat was all it'd taken. If only people were as easy.

The conversation about Charlie left me feeling disgruntled and vaguely melancholy. How could I answer Georgia's questions when I hadn't come up with any answers to my own? Divorce? Did people my age divorce? The bottom line was that my marriage had become the biggest failure of my life. Not all of the blame could be placed squarely at Charlie's feet. That wouldn't be fair. There were two sides to every story.

How different my life might have been if I hadn't married him. But I was pregnant. There'd never been any consideration given to other options because, funnily enough, Charlie was as adamant as I was about not having a termination. Single parenthood? Not as frowned upon in the late seventies as it had been in earlier generations, but to me at twenty-three? Daunting nevertheless. However, it hadn't taken long after the vows had been said for me to realise that not only did I have a baby on the way, but the man I'd married had barely made it through adolescence himself. One of us had had to grow up, and fast. It wasn't Charlie. With the wisdom of hindsight, I now know I could have managed single parenthood with one hand tied behind my back.

Max's cucumbers were crisp and tasty, the tomatoes sweet and juicy. Tomorrow morning I'd fry some tomatoes for breakfast, with a couple of eggs. If I had a frying pan. I closed my eyes and sighed. Jess shuffled closer. I reached down and threaded my fingers through her coat. She sighed, but with pleasure.

'When do you think we'll have a place of our own again?' I said, and my voice cracked. The dog lumbered to her feet and rested her nose on my thigh. She gazed at me with what I interpreted as love. At that moment I wished with all my heart that I'd given a resounding no to Gareth, right back when he'd first suggested buying the house. But I had been struggling to meet the mortgage repayments along with everything else. So when Gareth had proposed buying the house and letting me live there for the duration, much like I'd done for Mum, all I'd felt was gratitude. Right up until recently.

My whole life had been about making ends meet, and too many times they hadn't. The boys had gone without: school excursions; holidays; new bikes; extra tuition; anything other than hand-me-down clothes. The list went on. None of which seemed to overly bother Gareth or Adam, but Jay had suffered because he couldn't keep up with his peers.

I went inside and watched the news on the television. The weather girl was at the beach reporting in her sing-song nasal tone that we were in for a string of hot days. I sat like a zombie and watched the current affairs program. Not because I was interested but because what else was there to do? I'd cleaned the house earlier and it was too early to make up my bedroom. What if Georgia came home and wanted to watch TV? If I'd been in my own home

I would have gone to bed and read a book until I dropped off to sleep with the light on. If I woke at two am and felt like a cup of tea, I got up and made one. These days I wouldn't risk disturbing Georgia. I needed this arrangement to keep working, for the time being at least.

Jess growled, followed by the scrabble of claws as she gained purchase on the verandah's wooden floorboards. Then came a cat's yowl followed by Jess's frenzied barking. Something went thud and I wondered if I should go out and investigate. While I was deciding, the screen door rattled and Jess plonked herself back on the mat. That was my excitement over and done with for another evening, and I didn't even have to get up.

Ten pm came and went. At eleven I made up my bed. Georgia didn't come in until after midnight. She made a lot of noise, the kind a drunk makes when they're trying so hard to do the opposite. I pretended to be asleep. When the light went out in her bedroom I set my alarm for six am because I had a feeling that Georgia might have forgotten she was on a morning shift the next day.

10

Kate

My commitments were few and the second Friday afternoon of the month was always book club. I hadn't had a second thought when I'd reneged on the previous fortnight's bridge afternoon, leaving them in the lurch: at the last minute they'd had to find someone else to host. I'd had no desire to face Lorraine and the other women, and was considering giving up the game altogether. But when it came to book club, I always went along even if I hadn't read the book. There were about a dozen of us and, for whatever reason, I felt the women in this group were more my tribe.

For this month's get-together we were meeting at Evelyn Roberts' home. Around the same time I'd married Dennis, Evelyn had married Reece Roberts and into a family of well-established vintners. She lived in a stately old stone home nestled among the vineyards about ten minutes past the caravan park south of the town. Her youngest daughter was following in the footsteps of her father and competently carrying on the family tradition. Evelyn's wealth and circumstances intimidated some, me included. But she was a generous host and afternoon tea always included wine, plenty of it, for those who chose to partake.

This month's book had gathered dust on my coffee table without even being opened, but after a glass or two, I enjoyed the afternoon regardless. I'd had an extremely difficult couple of weeks and looked forward to the outing—I was fed up with my own company. Perhaps that's why I stayed longer than I usually would have, and why I drank more of the copious amounts of wine on offer than I should have. It hadn't seemed like *that* much over the course of an afternoon.

Not so, the policeman confirmed after I'd blown in the bag.

It had played out like this: On my way home from Evelyn's, I'd glanced in the rear-view, surprised to find a police car behind me with its lights flashing. Not considering for a moment the red and blue display was on my behalf I'd dutifully pulled over to let the vehicle pass. But it hadn't. Instead it had pulled onto the verge behind me.

Apparently, I'd been speeding: eighty-six kilometres an hour in an eighty speed zone. At first I was more annoyed than anything, and anxious a passerby might recognise my car. I'd quickly discovered that was the least of my worries. One whiff of my breath and Constable Whoever forgot about the speeding infringement and whipped out an alcotest. In a daze, I followed his instructions and to my dismay, discovered I was over the limit.

'You'll have to come to the police station, Mrs Hannaford. Please step out of the car,' the officer said, his voice, devoid of any emotion, coming at me as if through a tunnel.

How I managed the next hour or so I'll never know. He drove us back to the police station and, in a state of stupefied supplication, I did whatever he directed me to do. Then he was saying, 'You mustn't drive, Mrs Hannaford. Is there someone you can call to come and pick you up? Collect your car? Or would you like me to drop you home?'

I couldn't think. It was as if my brain had ceased to function. I stood there clutching the paperwork he'd given me, still struggling to absorb what he'd said about fines and demerit points.

'Mrs Hannaford?' he prompted. 'Or I could ring you a taxi.'

'I can walk home. It's not far,' I said, as much to reassure myself as him. I glanced down at my footwear: low heels, but they were comfortable enough. I'd risk blisters rather than the humiliation of asking someone to come and pick me up. Or worse, having my neighbours witness me being dropped home in a police car. And a taxi was out of the question: I knew several of the drivers, or rather, they knew me.

'If you say so,' he said. Of course he'd know where I lived. It was on my driver's licence. 'But I wouldn't leave a valuable car like yours on the side of the road for too long.'

'I'll see to it,' I said.

I set off, head high and back straight, my handbag slung over my shoulder. It was as heavy as a brick. The day had been hot but not overly so and in different circumstances it might have been a pleasant stroll. But all I could do as I trudged along was think about was how much my life had unravelled in the past couple of weeks. Granted, the first anniversary of Dennis's death was never going to be easy, but for heaven's sake, what had I done to deserve all this?

One thing continued to nag at me, and I let it because, for a brief span, it distracted me from the reason I was on foot and hundreds of dollars poorer. It was a simple thing, but I couldn't explain it away: when I'd visited Dennis's grave on the morning of the actual anniversary, there'd been fresh flowers beside the headstone. A huge florist's bunch that had already begun to wilt in the mid-morning heat. There hadn't been a card or any clue as to who'd placed them there. For the life of me, I couldn't fathom who might have been responsible.

Neither Dennis or I could ever have been deemed local. You had to be born and bred in a place for that to happen. My roots were at least in the general area; Dennis was originally from the Eyre Peninsula. His parents had long predeceased him and his eldest brother Lewis had taken on the family property and managed to scratch out a living. Dennis had inherited the land he'd farmed from a bachelor uncle, long dead. Dennis had always been a bit of a loner and there was no family nearby that I knew of.

Derek, the middle brother, lived in Sydney and we hadn't seen him in decades. He was unwell and hadn't come to Dennis's funeral. He'd sent condolences and flowers but nothing as extravagant as the arrangement by the grave. Locally, there were several farming friends, but I couldn't imagine any of them visiting the grave, let alone leaving flowers.

I was about halfway home when my right heel began to burn— the beginnings of a blister. I already had a sour mouth, a raging thirst and the start of a thumping headache. Feeling extremely sorry for myself, I toiled on and tried not to think at all, especially about who I could ask to pick up my car. I wouldn't leave it there all night. Maybe, if I drank lots of water, in a few hours I'd be okay to hike out there and get it myself. But the idea of wandering around town on my own in the dark made me shudder.

Within cooee of home someone called my name. Daisy Miller. I cringed. Of course *she* had to be out walking her dog right at this time. Footsteps sounded behind me, crunching on the gravel path and then she was beside me, she and the dog both breathing heavily.

'You look a bit flushed, Kate. And you're limping. Is everything all right?'

'No, it's not,' I snapped, without forethought.

She fell into step beside me and we continued walking for several minutes without speaking. Sweat trickled into my eyes. I swiped at it with the back of my hand.

'We've been to the library to return books. Did something happen to your car?'

I came to a sudden standstill, drew in a sharp breath and said through gritted teeth, 'The car is fine. I'm fine.' *Now butt out*, I thought, but didn't say.

Daisy and the dog were a couple of steps in front of me before they realised I'd stopped. When it clicked, they turned and I had two pairs of soft, enquiring brown eyes regarding me with concern. Before I knew it, I was blurting out the whole sorry tale.

All Daisy did was nod, once. 'What if I go and get my car, and Georgia. She can drive your car home for you. You mustn't leave it out there all night.'

How typical of Daisy to go straight to the nub of a situation. It's one of the attributes that'd made her such a practical and competent nurse. I'd sometimes dither. At times, I still did. Worse as I'd aged.

She glanced at her watch. 'Shall we pick you up in about twenty minutes?'

I tried to swallow over a throat that felt like sandpaper. 'Here,' I said and rummaged through my handbag for the car key. I shoved it towards her. 'It's a white Peugeot SUV.' I rattled off the registration number and described where it was parked and how to get into it.

'You don't want to come with us?'

'Nope.' I felt disgusting. All I wanted to do was go home and never venture out again. 'I'll raise the garage door. Drive straight in and leave the key in the cupboard. The car will lock itself.'

'Okay. If you're sure.'

'Thank you,' I said, but I had to force the words out and I couldn't quite look her in the eye. Funny how I'd had no qualms about giving her my car key. And she hadn't hesitated to take it.

'I had three sons, Kate,' she said. 'And Charlie. Between the four of them ... Let's just say, there was never a dull moment.'

Three sons. As if I could have ever forgotten that. Three gorgeous babies who'd grown into boisterous, good-looking boys. Dennis and I had only ever wanted one son. We would have settled for a daughter. How unfair life could be. I wondered what Daisy's boys were doing with their lives now, but I would never ask.

'You go on home and have a long drink of water, take a cool shower, then swallow a couple of paracetamol and lie down. We'll see to the car.'

I didn't speak. I couldn't.

She smiled. 'And Kate, don't beat yourself up. What's done is done, and life's too short. Come on, Jess, up off your lazy backside.' She tugged at the dog's lead and together they crossed the road at a brisk pace.

At home I did most of what Daisy had suggested. Not because she'd suggested it, but because it was the sensible thing to do. I was flat out on the bed when I heard them come back with the car. I didn't get up. The painkillers were yet to work and my head throbbed if I lifted it more than an inch off the pillow. I could hardly believe what I'd done. Me, who'd never had a speeding fine or a bingle in all my years of driving. If Dennis knew, he'd be spinning in his grave. He'd always been such a careful, conservative driver. Under the speed limit, not over. That's why I would never, ever understand how he'd died the way he had: swerving off the road and slamming head-on into a tree.

★★★

I woke next morning feeling hungry, until I remembered what I'd done the afternoon before. That was enough to take away my appetite. Forever. *Don't be so melodramatic*, I told myself, and dragged myself out of bed to stand under a hot shower for ten minutes.

The landline rang when I was on my second espresso. I almost didn't answer and when I did, I wished I hadn't.

'Kate? How are you?' It was Evelyn Roberts.

'Fine.' Coffee roiled in my otherwise empty stomach. 'Why do you ask?'

'It's just that when I took out the empties to the recycle bin after book club, I was gobsmacked by how many there were, and how few of us there'd been. Then Reece said he thought he saw your car parked on the side of the road when he came back from town late yesterday afternoon.'

'Really,' I said, sounding positively perplexed, even to my own ears. 'How strange.' I let the silence lengthen.

'Well, then, if you say everything is okay?'

'It is Evelyn, and thank you for enquiring. And what a lovely afternoon it was. You always do the group proud.'

'You're so very welcome,' she said, but there was something in her voice that made me think I hadn't quite convinced her that all was well.

When I put down the phone, my hand was shaking. Four shots of coffee on an empty stomach could have had something to do with that. But drat and double drat. Surely Reece Roberts had better things to think about than seeing a vehicle that looked like mine abandoned on the side of the road?

In the meantime, I'd keep my fingers crossed that Evelyn wouldn't mention to her husband how much we'd had to drink. Or that someone else they knew didn't comment in passing that they'd seen a woman who looked like me getting into a police car. Heaven help me if that did happen and they all started to join the dots. The propensity of most people to gossip was one of the things I hated about country towns.

11

Daisy

'What an awesome car,' Georgia said several times between Kate's place and ours. 'Who does it belong to, and how come we had to go get it?'

'It was a favour, Georgia. The woman who owns the house was a colleague once, and a friend. She got herself into a bit of strife earlier today and we kindly helped her out.'

'Drunk, was she?'

I rolled my eyes.

'Flash house. And a swimming pool. When I put the key in the cupboard I had a squizzy through the garage window. Not a lap pool either. Why don't you rekindle the friendship, Gran? Access to a free swimming pool would be excellent.'

Her phone pinged and her attention shifted. I tried not to show my relief. I drove in through the gate and up Georgia's drive. It was my drive as well, I supposed. The more weeks that passed, the more resigned I'd become to that. After all, I was paying a third of the rent. Inadvertently, I'd discovered her father was paying another third as compensation for me living there. That left her with only a third to pay herself. It was unlikely she'd throw me out while she was on such an extraordinary wicket.

My old home had finally been demolished. Gareth had sent photos. All that remained was a huge pile of rubble and a snarl of torn-out trees and shrubs. The birdbath was a tangle of twisted wire and fractured cement. That night in bed I'd cried silently into the sheet. The number of times I'd cleaned out that old birdbath and filled it with fresh water. Then experienced the joy of watching the honeyeaters and parrots settle on its edge to drink.

I opened the car door and Jess jumped out. She didn't much like riding on the back seat. Never mind. Georgia was still in the car, glued to her phone. I went inside. Jess followed me in through the front door. That had happened a few times lately and Georgia hadn't commented. I'd concluded the rule about no dog inside was my granddaughter's, not the landlord's.

A few things had changed in the six weeks I'd been living there. The secondhand twin-tub washing machine residing on the back verandah was the most innovative, along with an electric kettle and an electric frypan. They both sat proudly on the kitchen bench. Georgia hadn't ordered Lite n' Easy for several weeks and the freezer stock was almost depleted. She was enjoying my cooking, and me doing her washing and cleaning up after her. Did I mind? Not really, because I had to feed myself and the house was small and it didn't take much for it to get in a mess. But I continue to dream of a day when someone might cook for me and clean up after me.

★ ★ ★

Saturday morning I was at the op shop on the main street browsing for anything I could find to bulk out my sparse wardrobe. I was sifting through a rack of skirts and capris, in the mood for something preloved, when someone tapped me on the shoulder. I nearly jumped out of my skin.

'Daisy Miller! I'd heard you were in town for a while.'

'Glenys Carlisle … what a surprise,' I said, pasting on a smile. Glenys had been a Toogood. Charlie's cousin actually. She'd had a long-suffering soft spot for Charlie.

'Why haven't you been out to visit? We haven't seen you since Joe Toogood's funeral.'

That long ago. Charlie's dad had died suddenly in the late nineties, not long before his seventieth birthday. It had been a dreadful time. We were living in Adelaide in what had been my mum and dad's house. Where I'd grown up. Charlie had been 'between jobs' and he'd taken his dad's death hard. Adam was fifteen and still in high school and Mum was living with us. I'd been working full-time shift work. When Charlie wasn't at the pub or sleeping off the night before, he was getting under my feet or picking on Adam. When he said he was going to head north and look for work, I hadn't tried to talk him out of it. I'd even helped him pack.

'How did you know I was back in town?'

'Lorraine Sheriff. You remember her? She's long retired now, but she would have been a kitchenhand at the hospital in your day.'

'I remember her.' And how well the grapevine worked in a country town.

'She saw you in the supermarket. Said your granddaughter was an RN and working at the hospital.'

'That's right. So how are you, Glenys? How's Trevor? And the kids? Grandkids?'

Glenys and Trevor had two girls and a boy. Do you think I could remember their names, never mind the grandchildren? When I met

Charlie he'd been working as a farmhand for Trevor. Charlie wasn't from around here and if Glenys hadn't talked her husband into giving him a job, I might never have crossed paths with Charles Toogood.

'We're all good. Would you believe Martha, she belongs to Kaylene and is our eldest grandie, well, she got married a couple of months ago. I wouldn't be at all surprised if there's a great-grandie on the way before too long.'

'Nooo!'

She puffed out her chest, but then her self-satisfied smile slipped. 'Trev had a bit a scare with his prostrate last year. Turned out it wasn't cancer but the doctor's keeping his eye on it just the same.'

Imagining the doc with his eye on Trevor's 'prostrate', I had to roll my lips together so I wouldn't laugh. Glenys didn't deserve that. Except for the misguided adoration of her cousin, there wasn't an unkind thing that could be said about her. She'd always been decent to me and the boys when we'd lived here. Somehow she'd known when things were extra tight. She'd show up at our place with a couple of dozen eggs, a leg of mutton or the likes, and whatever surplus produce she'd harvested from her garden.

'Now then, when are you and that granddaughter coming out for a meal? No time like the present to firm up a date.'

I slipped the pair of canary yellow capris back onto the rack. They really weren't me. 'Let me ask Georgia first. She's the one working shift work, and the one with a social life.'

'What about lunch next Sunday? Midday?' Glenys ploughed on as if I hadn't spoken. 'I'll do a rolled shoulder of lamb. Home killed. Vegetables from my garden. Trev will be thrilled to see you, and I'm dying to meet Georgia.'

'Can I get back to you, Glenys?'

'Of course.' She plucked a white business card out of the pocket of her handbag and offered it to me. 'In case you've forgotten our phone numbers.' Said without even a hint of reproach.

I slipped the card into my pocket. 'I'll let you know as soon as I've talked to Georgia.'

'It's been wonderful to see you, Daisy. I'm so glad I bumped into you.'

Catching me completely off guard, she hauled me against her ample bosom and hugged me firmly. She smelled of Johnson's Baby Powder. I floundered for a moment, then returned the hug.

★ ★ ★

'Lunch with relatives?' Georgia wrinkled her nose. 'I didn't know we had any relatives around here.'

'They're your granddad's relatives. Glenys is your granddad's cousin. Their fathers were brothers. It would be good for you to meet them.'

'Distant relatives …' She shrugged. 'But I like the sound of a lamb roast.'

'Not that distant. So you'll come?'

'Why not? I'll be on a day off. What time?'

'Midday. I'll let Glenys know.'

Glenys was chuffed. 'Don't bring anything except your dear selves,' she said. 'And you'll be all right finding your way out here?'

'I will,' I said, and felt a moment's remorse for only ever keeping in random contact. These past few years, I hadn't even bothered with return Christmas cards. Shame on me.

★ ★ ★

The dirt road out to their farm was as corrugated as I remembered. As usual, Georgia was engrossed by whatever was happening on her phone, leaving me to drive and reflect in silence. Even though I fought hard against them, memories of my last visit to Glenys and Trev's place wormed their way in.

It had been for Glenys's fortieth birthday. Me and Charlie and the kids hadn't long moved back to Adelaide and we drove up for the day. A Saturday. I'd worked a night shift the night before and the only sleep I'd had was what I'd snatched in the car on the trip up. Of course Charlie drank too much at the party and I'd had to drive home. Jay threw up in the back seat of the car when we were about halfway home. Although he'd been barely thirteen, to this day I'll swear there'd been alcohol mixed with the party pies and birthday cake. Charlie laughed, clapped his son on the back and called him a chip off the old block. Adam, at eight, had been goggle-eyed, and Gareth, fifteen but going on twenty-five, had been disgusted.

I must have sighed loudly, because Georgia looked up from her phone. 'What's up, Gran? Are we nearly there?'

'Yep.'

I indicated and slowed to turn into a rutted driveway. The same old rusted-out fridge stood beside the gatepost, *Carlisle* slashed across the door with black paint. I glanced in the rear-view mirror, expecting to see Jess on the back seat grinning back at me like a loon. I couldn't see her. My heart lurched. Then I remembered I'd left her with Max, not knowing how friendly the farm dogs would be.

We went to the back door, Georgia clutching a bottle of red wine and me the packet of Lindt chocolates. Georgia knocked and called out. As we stood there, I wondered if this was such a good idea after all. But then Glenys was at the door, bustling us inside. A colourful apron covered her black slacks and top. Her cheeks were flushed. We went into the kitchen and my mouth watered: the rosemary-seasoned meat smelled divine.

Glenys made such a fuss of Georgia it was easy for me to put aside any misgivings I'd had about being there.

'I was about to make the gravy. Daisy, you go on through to the dining room. First on your right, in case you've forgotten. Georgia can give me a hand here. And take your wine with you. Trev should have changed by now and he'll pour you a glass.'

I heard muted voices. I headed in that direction. Then Trev appeared.

'Daisy!' he boomed. 'I thought I heard a car a while ago. It's been bloody ages. Good to see you, girl. Come on through.' He reached for the bottle of wine in my hand. 'Let me pour you a glass of that.'

I followed him into the dining room. The table was immaculate: gleaming silverware on a cream-coloured damask tablecloth; fresh flowers as a centre piece. So taken by the table setting and the trouble Glenys had gone to, I didn't notice the other person in the room until Trev spoke. 'Daisy, you might remember Glenys's dad, Bill Toogood? He lives with us now. Since Mavis passed away.'

Bill was wearing a shirt and tie tucked into a pair of baggy grey track pants. Slippers on his feet, tartan-coloured and the style that came with velcro closures. He stood braced against the back of a dining chair, his mouth open. There were drool stains on his tie.

'Hello, Mr Toogood,' I said.

I did remember him from Charlie's dad's funeral and before that, Glenys's fortieth. Both memorable occasions, for all the wrong reasons. If Charlie's dad Joe had lived to be ninety-five I imagined he would have looked a lot like Bill did now. Although, Joe living into his nineties had never been on the cards. Well before Joe's death I'd determined from which parent Charlie had inherited the good-time gene.

Bill stared at me but spoke to Trev. 'Who did you say she was?'

'Daisy is, er, your nephew Charlie's wife?' Trev said, tentatively, and threw a questioning glance my way.

'Wife, you say? Where's Charlie then? Haven't seen the lad in years.'

'That makes two of us,' I muttered, and the old man scowled. His mouth moved in and out while his brain worked on what it was he wanted to say.

This was awkward and I defaulted to my earlier position: we should never have come. Georgia could have met *her* relatives all by herself. Then Glenys bowled in through the dining room door with a laden tray and I wanted to shout hallelujah. Whatever Bill had been working up to, my guess was it wouldn't have been very complimentary towards me.

'Trevor, don't stand there nursing the wine, open it and pour everyone a glass, and Dad, sit down before you fall down.'

In Glenys's wake came my granddaughter bearing the gravy boat and a basket of warm bread rolls, a bemused expression on her face. We sat where we were directed. Georgia was next to me.

'There are golden syrup dumplings for dessert and that's the only reason I'm still here,' she whispered, barely moving her lips.

'That's my girl,' I said, and accepted the glass of wine Trev passed me.

Here we were. As the meal progressed, I repeated to myself that it was important for my grandchildren to know their Toogood relatives. If Georgia decided to visit again, keep in touch, that was up to her. But well before the golden syrup dumplings, I'd had enough of Bill Toogood's leery stare and Trev's forced bonhomie.

As we drove off down the driveway a couple of hours later, Glenys waving in our wake, I decided that *I'd* never need to come out here again.

12

Kate

Any elation I'd felt over quitting the bridge group was short lived. I'd freed three hours every fortnight to do exactly what? When I rang Lorraine Sheriff to say she'd need to find another partner, she'd taken the news with equanimity.

'You've always given the impression you didn't really enjoy the game,' she said.

Had I? But she was right. Why had I persisted with it for so long? Dennis's opinion was that I'd liked the *idea* of the game rather than the game itself. That belonging to a bridge group had seemed a suitable pastime for a retired professional woman. My goodness, how I hated it when Dennis turned out to be right, even from the grave.

It was Sunday afternoon. Over a week had passed since my run-in with the police. I'd paid the fines: well over a thousand dollars. Boy, had that stung, and it continued to do so, as did the fact that I'd broken the law. Twice. As a result, I was keeping an extremely low profile. To the point where I'd done the grocery shopping first thing that morning because it was the hour and the day I'd be least likely to run into a friend or acquaintance.

Deep down, I knew I couldn't keep going on like this, existing from one day to the next, avoiding any kind of a real life. It's basically what I'd been doing since Dennis's death. Probably even before that, if the truth be known. But a person needed purpose to go on. Something to get them out of bed each morning. Some sort of belief that this day would be better than the day before. Or at least different. What that difference might be, and how to conjure such things, continued to elude me.

From where I sat in Dennis's recliner I had a clear view out to the swimming pool and the redundant outdoor furniture on its flank. The wood needed re-oiling. Dennis had suggested we chose anything other than wooden outdoor furniture because of the maintenance required. I'd insisted on wood.

Kieran had been on Friday and cleaned the pool.

'It's going to be a hot weekend,' he'd said. 'I'll leave off the cover in case you want to take a swim.' I hadn't contradicted him, even though I knew I'd not go near it.

Now the water sparkled in the sun. It wouldn't be cold—I'd dipped my hand in after he'd gone, surprised by how warm it had been. I closed my eyes and imagined sliding into the water, feeling its silky glide over my skin; letting myself float, drift, until I sank like a stone, right to the bottom, the last of my breath effervescing above me ...

One of the girls in my nursing group had drowned in a back-yard swimming pool. Christine Fisk. It happened about halfway through our training. We'd all been stunned. More so when it'd come out that she'd had alcohol and other drugs in her system. And she'd been thirteen weeks pregnant. Back then, the depths of her despair had been incomprehensible to me. Not so now.

My eyes drifted to the newly replenished liquor cabinet in the corner of the room and then away again. Unlike Christine Fisk, whose body had been found on the bottom of the pool by her brother, my body would rise to the surface again long before anyone came looking for me. That was a fact, not just me feeling sorry for myself.

When had imagining death become preferable to reimagining life? Like anyone, I'd had my share of low points; mornings when I'd wake and wish that I hadn't. Back after I'd had miscarriage number three and the doctor advised me to give my body a break and not attempt to fall pregnant again for at least a year, I'd been at a very low ebb. We'd taken the doctor's advice and stopped trying for about a year. When we'd decided it was time to give it another go, I hadn't been able to conceive at all.

Then Dennis's mother had been diagnosed with advanced breast cancer. After a traumatic six months, she'd died. His father was bereft. He'd come to stay with us, sometimes for weeks at a time. Not exactly conducive to marital intimacy and making babies. Dennis had been distracted, torn between what his father needed and what I needed. And of course what he needed himself. After all, his mother had died.

Back then I'd had a job and work colleagues to take my mind off what was happening, or not happening, at home. Eventually my father-in-law went home and life returned to a semblance of its former self. When I didn't fall pregnant, we had more tests. Dennis's results were always normal; I had cysts consuming both of my ovaries.

'Kate,' Dennis would say when I was blubbering with grief and self-pity, 'it doesn't matter. We will make a life without children. It'll be different than the one we'd planned, but it'll be okay just the same.'

But it had mattered.

Daisy, once my closest friend and confidante, had not under-stood my predicament at all. She hadn't had to do much more than look at her man in order to fall pregnant.

The afternoon she came out to the farm and told me she was pregnant, and that she and Charlie had decided to get married, I'd already been upset because I'd just got my period. Around the time Daisy was having her tubes tied after baby number three, I'd been trying to come to grips with my fate: that I would never be a mother, Dennis would never be a father; we would never parent a child together.

In the end, I'd sunk all my energy into my career. Although Daisy and I remained friends, we hadn't shared our inner thoughts and secrets any more, the way we had in the beginning. Perhaps that's what happens in friendships that span many years: they change and adapt to the circumstances. I do recall clearly feeling extremely bitter and resentful when Daisy and Charlie's third son was born. I hadn't visited her in hospital. I couldn't.

Dennis had plodded along pretending everything was hunky-dory. Maybe he'd already resigned himself to not having a family. There was no denying we'd had a satisfactory life, but I knew I'd been a huge disappointment to him. And I'd been a huge failure to myself.

'*Enough*,' I said out loud, and levered my body out of the recliner. In eleven days I'd be seventy-two years old and, of late, I'd been feeling every one of those years. With effort, I put on my shoes and went outside. Afternoon heat shimmered off the deck. It was a challenge, but I managed to roll the cover back over the swimming pool all on my own.

★★★

Monday morning, Valma Parrish dropped in without ringing beforehand. It was after ten and I was ashamedly still in my dressing gown. Quiet a common occurrence these days. That and the thick-headiness from one too many glasses of wine.

Valma was carefully colour coordinated in a pretty pink floral skirt and knit top. She came in bearing a large ice-cream container filled with white-flesh peaches off her tree and the rolled-up *Advertiser* she'd picked up from the front lawn.

'I didn't ring because I wasn't certain you'd answer,' she said. 'I've been worried about you, Kate, and then Lorraine mentioned at church yesterday that you'd quit the bridge group.'

'I never really liked the game,' I said flippantly and took the newspaper from her. The plastic wrap was damp from when the pop-up sprinklers would have come on earlier.

'Can't say I was enamoured of it either, the couple of times I went along. You're not going to quit book club as well, are you?' A frown gathered her eyebrows together. 'It wouldn't be the same without you.'

She put the peaches down on the kitchen bench. I picked one out and lifted it to my nose, drawing in the sweet smell and shivering at the fuzzy feel of the skin. 'These look delicious. Thanks. We had a white-flesh peach tree out at the farm.' I transferred them to the glass fruit bowl on the bench and wiped out the ice-cream container.

'Not much you can do with white flesh peaches other than binge on them while they're fresh.'

'Coffee? I have real milk,' I said.

She nodded and her eyes twinkled.

We sat opposite each other at the table in the breakfast nook.

'About book club,' she said after stirring a spoonful of sugar into her drink.

'I have no plans to quit that group, even though I haven't read the last couple of books. I've been—'

She reached across the table and laid a hand on my arm. 'No need to explain, Kate. It's only a year since Dennis passed away. And in such tragic circumstances.'

'These last twelve months have been difficult. It's like I've been stumbling my way through uncharted territory.'

'That's exactly what you have been doing. I might whinge about Bob and all his tiresome habits, but I'll be devastated if he goes before me. Rational me knows it will, but I can't imagine my life going on without him.'

'I'd convinced myself that Dennis would outlive me. I'm the one who's had a few health issues over the years, but apart from the occasional sniffle, he was never ill in all the years we were married. Blood pressure normal, cholesterol normal, no signs of diabetes. And he was always such a careful driver.'

'We never know do we, how it's going to end,' Valma said.

For several minutes we sat and sipped in quiet contemplation.

'I took flowers to his grave on the day. Someone had been there before me and left a huge bunch. There was no card. I have no idea who to thank. That bothers me.'

Valma finished her coffee with a satisfied sigh. 'Why don't you ask the girl in the florist shop? She's a nice kid. Tell her what you just told me. If the flowers were purchased from her she might be able to tell you who it was.'

'I hadn't thought of doing that.'

'It's worth a try. She can only say no.' Valma stood and took her mug to the sink. 'Bob has a doctor's appointment in half an hour. I'd better get going. I'm surprised he hasn't rung already to ask how long I'm going to be.' She rolled her eyes and picked up the empty ice-cream container.

I followed her through to the front door. 'Thank you, Valma,' I said. 'It was very kind of you to drop in.'

'I'll do it again if you serve me another cup of that delicious coffee. You take care, Kate. And don't forget, there are people out there who care about you. We're only ever a phone call away.'

I watched her drive away and wondered if she'd still care as much if she knew I'd been booked for drink-driving on my way home from the last book club. Valma had been an apology that day. She was teetotal. If she'd been there my guess is we wouldn't have imbibed as much as we had.

Later that day when I finally got dressed, I drove down the street to the florist shop, only to discover it was closed on Mondays.

13

Daisy

Georgia came out of the bathroom towel drying her hair.

'Who are the flowers from?' I said. A beautiful bouquet still in its cellophane wrapping sat on the kitchen bench, an empty envelope beside it. No sign of the card. 'They're lovely.'

'I don't have a vase,' she said. 'Or a big enough jar.'

'Yes, but who are they from?'

'Some guy … I did him a favour. And that—' she said, pointing to a cardboard box that took up almost all the coffee tabletop, '—I found it on the verandah when I came home from work. Read the note.' She slung the towel over the back of the sofa.

The box had been opened and a single sheet of paper rested on top of the newspaper-wrapped items inside. I scanned the note. 'Keepsakes for you from Nanna Toogood? Well, I never.'

'That'd be my great-great-grandmother, right?'

'Yes, and how kind and thoughtful of Glenys.'

'I made such a fabulous impression when we were out there,' she said, with a self-satisfied smirk. 'But why give them to me and not her own daughters or granddaughters?'

I picked up the topmost item and peeled off the newspaper: green Depression glassware. Georgia joined me and we unwrapped several more to find assorted crockery and tarnished cutlery. No vases.

'There were only two brothers, Joe and William, the old fella you met at Glenys's. Joe had two boys: Colin and Charlie. Colin never married, and to my knowledge he has no children. He's older than Charlie and a Vietnam veteran. I have no idea whether he's still alive. And as you know, Charlie and I had all boys. You're the first girl in that line of the family for several generations.'

'Whoopee-do,' she said, and studied a plate with gilt-edging. 'Do you think they'd be worth anything?'

'In monetary terms, probably not a lot. But sentimental value? That's up to you to decide.'

'Did you ever meet her?'

'Once. Not long after we were married your granddad took me to visit her. She was frail. I don't think she had a clue who we were. She died before Gareth was born.'

'What about Great-Great-Granddad Toogood?'

'Fought in World War One. By all accounts, not the same man came home from the war as the one who went. Common enough story. From memory, he died around the time I would have been born. Charlie would have been a toddler.'

Georgia carefully placed the glassware back into the box. 'You have it. By rights it should have come to you from Granddad's mother. I wonder why it didn't?' she said and inched the box towards me.

I pushed it back. 'I wasn't a Toogood. I even refused to take the name. It might not mean anything to you now, but when you have children of your own you might think differently.'

Georgia snorted. 'That won't be happening any time soon, Gran, if ever.'

'And isn't that just what I said, way back when.'

Georgia's mouth dropped open. 'You didn't want children?'

'I hadn't thought past getting more nursing experience so I could travel. I had dreams of doing midwifery training in England and then working in a developing country.'

'Why didn't you?'

'I met Charlie.'

'You fell in love?' she said, her eyes wide.

'I fell pregnant. We got married. Your dad was born six months later. Jay? I was still breastfeeding Gareth. And Adam? I was on the pill. I had my tubes tied after he was born. I wasn't taking any more risks. And I did my midwifery training in Adelaide.'

'Dad's never told me any of this.' She flopped down onto the sofa.

'He probably doesn't know, at least not about Jay or Adam. But don't get me wrong, Georgia, I love my children and I've always tried to do my best for them. But that doesn't mean I didn't envisage a totally different future for myself when I still had choices.'

She didn't reply, just sat there staring into space. I went outside and fed Jess. Max called hello from over the fence. He was watering his garden. Even this late in the afternoon it was hot. Every plant and blade of grass in the backyard was tinder-dry. For some reason I thought of Kate Hannaford's swimming pool. What it'd be like to have such a thing only steps away, always available for a cooling dip.

I collected the dry washing off the clothesline. It smelled like sunshine and crackled with static electricity. While I folded it into the laundry basket, I mulled over why Glenys had given a selection of Nanna Toogood's things to Georgia. I'm not saying she shouldn't have, only that I was surprised she had. Charlie had never talked much about his family, the living or the dead. In all the years we'd been together I could count on one hand the number of times I'd seen his brother Colin.

When I went inside, the cardboard box of keepsakes had disappeared from the coffee table. I could hear Georgia rummaging around in her bedroom. Half an hour later she emerged in shorts and a tank top, her hair pulled tightly into a high ponytail.

'I'm going around to Lisa's place. She's in a mess. Another *boyfriend* drama.' Said like someone twice her age.

'I thought they'd broken up? That he'd moved out? Did I get that wrong?'

She shook her head. 'Sadly, they hooked up again at the pub on Saturday night. I truly don't know what she sees in him. I will admit that at first Jake was fun, but it didn't take me long to work out what a loser he was. No real job, never has any money, sponges off Lisa all of the time.'

'Ah, but it takes all kinds … She must see some redeeming qualities in him.'

Georgia folded her arms, her expression contemptuous. 'That's just it, Gran, in my opinion he doesn't have any and she doesn't think she deserves anyone better, when she totally does.' She swept up her car keys and phone. 'Don't worry about a meal for me, I'll eat with Lisa. I might be able to talk her into going out for Indian food.'

With that, the screen door clacked shut. I heard her say goodbye to Jess. I stood stock-still as memories so real and raw took me back to the morning after Kate and Dennis had been out with Charlie and me for the first time.

'Are you sure, Daisy?' Kate said, and although we were of a similar height, she managed to look down her nose at me. 'I suppose he is good looking in a rugged kind of a way, but he doesn't have a proper job, and by the end of the evening he was *very* drunk … I'm sure you could do a lot better than him.'

I don't recall what my reply had been. Probably nothing. But I did know why I'd gone out with Charlie in the first place: he'd been fun, and he'd looked at me as if he'd really seen me and liked what he saw. That had been a new and heady experience for me.

It was all right for Kate, she was gorgeous. Nice clothes, money and a man who'd worshipped the ground she stood on. I'd been to their wedding and there'd been no expense spared. A bun in the oven and a registry office celebrant was what I'd got. Was it because I'd believed it was all I deserved? Not in the beginning. Oh, what plans I'd had for my future.

My dad had been a stern and sullen man. A workplace accident had left him with a limp and chip on his shoulder the size of Uluru. Always harassed, Mum had scurried around the house doing what-ever was expected of a fifties housewife. Me and my brother and sister had always kept our heads down. Dad had never been physi-cally abusive to us, just emotionally absent. Mum had tried hard to make up for it but her rubber band had only stretched so far. From an early age I'd known that I wanted a different life to the one that had been my mother's lot.

I laughed, a single harsh sound that echoed around the silent room. Not so different to Mum's life after all. A car drove past and its exhaust backfired. It jerked me back into the present. Jess was scratching at the front screen door. It didn't need any more holes. I let her inside.

'What's up, sweet pea? Lonely out there, were you?'

She wagged her tail and then sat and watched while I toasted bread and sliced tomatoes for my tea. I'd been going to do an all-in-one spaghetti, but couldn't be bothered now that there was only me to cook for.

★★★

By the middle of the week the temperature had hit forty degrees. Georgia had happily gone to work an air-conditioned afternoon shift. The weatherboard house was like an oven. An ancient ceiling fan in the living area barely stirred the dense, suffocatingly hot air. Jess found the coolest spot: flat out on the bathroom tiles.

Try as I might, I couldn't stop thinking about the swimming pool in a backyard not far from where I sat. At four o'clock, when I couldn't bear the heat for a moment longer, I pulled on my bathers, wrapped a colourful sarong around my waist and bundled Jess into the car. The least Kate Hannaford could do after I'd rescued her car was let me take a dip in her swimming pool.

14

Kate

'Aren't you coming in?' Daisy said, squinting into the sunshine. She breaststroked to the side of the swimming pool and splashed water at her dog. The dog barked and bounced around like a puppy, pretending to get out of the way but really asking for more. Daisy laughed and sent another slice of water in the dog's direction. 'It is heavenly in here, Kate. Go get your bathers and come on in.'

I shook my head, but not quite as resolutely as the first time. The water did look inviting. Together, it'd taken only minutes for us to roll back the pool cover. With a pang of something I couldn't quite pinpoint, I'd moved away. Dennis had been alive the last time I'd swum in the pool. It'd been a hot, dry day much like today. He'd splashed water at me until I'd given in and donned my bathers.

'Stay as long as you like,' I said to Daisy. 'I'm going back into the air conditioning.' The sliding door rumbled shut behind me.

No-one could have been more surprised when I'd opened the front door twenty minutes earlier and there had stood Daisy and the dog. I was beginning to think one didn't come without the other.

'I've come for a swim,' she said, 'and I will not go away until you let me have one. I might die of heatstroke otherwise.'

A most definite no and directions to the public pool had been on the tip of my tongue but then I noticed how flushed her face was, perspiration beading on her top lip. The dog panted heavily beside her. I shouldn't forget how kind she'd been about the car on that dreadful afternoon.

'You can swim but the dog can't, not under any circumstances.'

'Of course not. She'll understand,' she'd said. 'Won't you, Jess?' The dog wagged her tail.

I'd opened the side gate and let them through. Daisy hadn't seemed the least put out that I hadn't invited her inside. Or offered her a cool drink.

I watched them from where I sat in Dennis's recliner. The dog was wet through. She shook herself, a silvery halo of water droplets, before flopping down in the shade. Daisy swam lazy lengths, back and forth. Then she'd float for a bit, followed by a couple of laps of backstroke. I'd forgotten what a confident swimmer she was. My limit was an awkward attempt at freestyle and dog paddle.

Out at the farm there'd been a waterhole thirty minutes' drive from the house and in the hot weather we'd sometimes trek out there to cool off. Daisy and me. Then Daisy, Charlie and me. Occasionally Dennis would come for a swim. Charlie always brought beer. Daisy would plunge in, never minding that the bottom was murky with weeds and submerged tree branches. I'd paddle at the edge, rarely getting wet above my thighs.

The last time I'd been out to the waterhole was after the farm had sold and we'd had the clearing sale. We were in the process of moving into our brand new house in town. It'd been an emotionally topsy-turvy time. We were both physically exhausted. Dennis had been more reserved than usual: although he never spoke of it, I knew he hadn't wanted to sell up and move into town.

The waterhole was a place of mixed memories. Up until then, I couldn't remember the last time I'd driven out there but I'd known I wanted to return to the waterhole again before we left. I wanted to revisit what had sadly become dispensable dreams of family picnics and children's laughter. When I'd asked Dennis to come with me he'd said he was too busy. I'd hidden my disappointment and driven out on my own.

All that had been left was the hole; years of drought interspersed with years of low rainfall had seen to the water. What I'd remembered as a green and cool oasis was a dried-up gouge in the rocky landscape, choked with a tangle of scrub and weeds …

Daisy tapped on the sliding door, rousing me from where I'd drifted. Her hair stood in glistening spikes and she'd rewrapped herself in the sarong, the wet patches darker-coloured than the remainder.

She cracked open the door. 'Thanks so much, Kate. You saved our lives. I've put the cover back on the pool.'

I scrubbed at my face with my hands and stood up, swaying slightly. 'Oh, thank you. Would you like a cool drink before you go? Shall I get water for the dog?'

I sensed her hesitation, not that I could blame her. So far I hadn't exactly re-extended the hand of friendship.

'Tea? Coffee?' For some reason I persisted.

'Real tea, made with leaves?'

'If you like.'

'All right, but I'm wet through.' She glanced down at the half-saturated sarong. 'I didn't think to bring a towel.'

'We can have the tea out there,' I said, halfway through to the kitchen and feeling relieved. By serving the tea outside I could keep her at arm's length. Inviting her inside was a much more daunting prospect, and she might have got with the wrong idea: that I wanted to be friends again.

While the kettle boiled I took out a plastic bowl and Daisy filled it at the outside tap and put it down for the dog.

Daisy was sitting in the love seat on the patio when I returned with the tea tray. I switched on the overhead fans. The potted palms and other plants rustled in the artificial breeze.

'I couldn't remember if you took milk and sugar in your tea.'

'Only milk when it's made with real tea leaves.'

I poured the tea, added a dash of milk to Daisy's and passed it to her.

'Do you swim in the pool much?' she said, tipping her chin in the direction of the water.

'Not often. Dennis used to swim every day, all year round. In the cooler months he said the solar cover took the chill off the water.'

There was no pretending this wasn't awkward, for me anyway. Daisy appeared relaxed. I tried to stop myself second-guessing why I'd asked her to stay in the first place. As she sipped her tea, her gaze swooped around the yard, not missing a thing.

'It's very different from your old house at the farm,' she said. 'That place had such character.'

'And salt damp and wood rot, and don't forget the vermin. It didn't matter how much steel wool I plugged into holes, the little so-and-sos still found their way inside.'

'There must be something you miss about that place. You lived out there for a long time.'

Since the day I was married. Dennis carried me over the threshold. I'd felt as if my life was just beginning.

'Sometimes I miss the peace and quiet, and the fruit trees. But by the time we moved, the house was falling down around our ears. It was either spend another small fortune renovating or do what we did and build in town.'

'I so envied you back then,' Daisy said, wistfully. 'Having your own home to do with what you liked. No landlord breathing down your neck.'

'I lived there for forty-five years. The house was as old as I am now when we first moved in. No-one, except the vermin and the bees in the chimneys, had lived in it for five years. But you can only plug up holes and paper over cracks so many times.' My tone was clipped. On how many occasions had I had a similar exchange with Dennis? Me always justifying why I thought we should move into town. In the end, exasperated with his intransigence, I'd used my own money to buy the block of land we'd eventually built this house on.

'Of course,' she said, the tiniest of frowns puckering her brow. She gulped down what was left of her tea and stood up. 'Let's go, Jess,' she said. 'We've taken up enough of Kate's time. Thanks for the swim, and the cuppa.'

The dog slurped more water and they left through the side gate, the same way they'd come in. It was as if she couldn't get out of the place fast enough and by then I was in no mind to stop her. Along with Daisy Miller, popping up in my life again were things I hadn't thought about in an age. Things I probably wouldn't have thought about, ever, if she hadn't shown up.

I loaded the tea tray and took it inside. While I stacked the cups into the dishwasher my mind wandered back over our recent conversation. I could understand why Daisy felt the way she did about the farmhouse. Her first home had been a rented prefab in a far from salubrious section of town. She'd been six months pregnant, working full-time shift work and sleeping on a mattress on the bedroom floor because they couldn't afford a bed.

'Getting what we'll need for the baby when it comes along is our first priority,' she'd said. Out at the farm, I'd fully furnished and stocked a nursery but hadn't managed to conceive the baby to put in it.

When I'd offered to loan her money so they could buy a bed, she'd refused. Not nastily, but definitely. 'We'll manage,' was all she'd said, and somehow she had managed. How, I'll never know. I'm not sure I would have in the same situation. What I do know is that she always gave polite thanks for the gifts I gave when the babies came along. However, she had never asked me for anything, not even to babysit or swap a shift when she couldn't find a baby-sitter. Had she sensed that I would have refused? That I'd been so consumed with jealousy and resentment because she'd borne three children and I hadn't been able to successfully bear one?

See what I mean about memories? Why did I need to dredge up any of that? I understand how unreliable memory can be but I don't think I'd gotten any of those particular details wrong.

I wandered through to the living room wishing for something. That I could turn back the clock? But by how much? Or that I could experience just one emotion at a time—anger, sadness, despair—not be suffocated by the lot of them all at once. And would I ever find happiness again? How cliched that one sounded.

Oddly, even though Daisy hadn't been inside, the house felt emptier than it had before she'd visited. I ran a finger along the sideboard. Dust. Thicker by the day. The night before, I'd noticed cobwebs dangling from the downlights in the kitchen. I hadn't found a replacement cleaner yet. The fundraiser morning tea was creeping closer by the day. I couldn't seem to make myself care.

Another empty evening stretched out in front of me. *You could always do the vacuuming,* said the voice inside my head. *And don't forget the dusting and the bathrooms ...* Or I could open the bottle of pinot gris in the fridge. Tough choice.

15

Daisy

By the weekend the weather had cooled, bringing a sprinkle of rain that did nothing more than raise our hopes. Georgia was on another stretch of night shifts, sending me and Jess back out onto the streets. We set off on Monday morning grateful for the milder conditions. By now we'd developed a night-shift routine: a long walk and then I'd splurge on a coffee mid-morning. We'd have my packed lunch by the skate park, wander the main street window-shopping and then spend the rest of the afternoon in the library. Plenty of time for woolgathering and contemplation.

As time ticked by I'd found it best not to think too much about what the future might hold for me, and instead found myself dwelling interminably on the distant, and not so distant, past. I began prodding and poking at old and dim memories, long since archived and never thought to see the light of day again.

The swim at Kate's had been wonderful, but Kate herself? I know she was grieving the death of her husband but she seemed troubled, unhappy—angry even. There was a brittleness about her that hadn't been there when we were younger. Was she angry with Dennis for leaving her? With me for coming back here? Or was she sour on life in general?

The more I thought, the more I realised that there'd always been something buttoned-up about Kate; a part of her that was inaccessible. Had Dennis ever wormed his way in? I knew they'd desperately wanted children. She'd had miscarriages, not that she'd ever talked about them much with me. But as my family had expanded, so had the distance between Kate and I. When I knew I was pregnant with Adam, I'd put off sharing the news with her for as long as I could. When I did tell her it was more about what she didn't say rather than what she did: the yearning in her expression; the shimmer of unshed tears in her eyes and the silent withdrawal further into herself. Although I hadn't thought about any of this for years it was still there, tucked away at the back of my mind. I blinked and gave myself a shake in an effort to dislodge the image of a distressed and much younger Kate the memory had conjured.

Jess tugged on the lead, reminding me she was there. And where we were: so lost in memories I'd come to a standstill in the middle of the road. Not a busy road, luckily. By now it was Monday after-noon and school had been out for a long while, so the traffic was sparse. We were on our way home. I'd been dawdling along, being a bit like Alice and following memories down rabbit holes.

I quickened our pace and shifted my thoughts to more practical things. Gareth had rung earlier. He'd had no news to share about the building project. The pile of rubble that had once been my home remained where it was.

'You can't get any bugger to do anything,' he'd said. 'Every-one is short-staffed, or they're crook themselves. And I'm flat-strap because, at any given time, a few of my crew are still off sick.'

On the weekend I'd FaceTimed Adam. We hadn't talked for a week or more and I'd been shocked by how tired and gaunt he'd looked.

'Have you lost weight? You're not sick are you?'

'Nah, just tired, Mum. The double shifts are wearing us all down, and there's no end in sight. I don't give a damn about the extra money any more, just give me the time off that I'm entitled to.'

'How are Bec and the kids?'

'Bec's frazzled. Nadine and Stella have both had colds, luckily not Covid.' He gave a harsh laugh. 'But then again if they had tested positive, being a close contact would have given me some time off work.'

'Shall I come down for a few days and help out?'

'Thanks, Mum, but no. Hate for you to get sick. We're doing okay. Bec's sister lives around the corner now and she's been great. Have you heard from Jay?'

'Not lately. I'm going to ring him when we hang up.'

'Good luck with that. He hasn't returned my calls of late.'

'Is he in Adelaide?'

'Dunno. He was when I talked to him last, but that was before Christmas. You never know with Jay, he could be anywhere.'

If Adam hadn't heard from his brother then no-one else in the family would have, except perhaps his father. As his mother, I was always the last in line for news of his wellbeing or whereabouts. Rarely was it from him directly. I'd given up wondering where I'd gone wrong with my middle child. That's not to say I'd ever stop worrying, but Jay was over forty and he'd made his own choices. Fortunately, there wasn't a partner or children to bear the brunt of them.

Adam and I had said our goodbyes and, without putting the phone down, I'd scrolled through to Jay's number. As Adam had predicted, it went straight to voicemail. I'd left the standard message: *Hello,*

love, Mum here. Trust all's well. Give me a call back when you get a minute
… So far he hadn't. But then it was only Monday afternoon.

Georgia was up when we got home. She hadn't slept well and
was grumpy. I considered backtracking out of the house and going
for a drive. It was pension week and I'd filled the car's petrol tank.

'Sorry, Gran,' she said. 'Crap shift followed by a crap sleep.'

'Anything you want to talk about?'

She shrugged and sprawled out on the sofa; closed her eyes. 'Just
busy. There's never enough staff these days.'

'Is there ever?' Not enough staff had been a resounding lament
throughout my whole nursing career.

'Probably not, but more so now because there's always someone off sick or in isolation. And I suppose I shouldn't tell you this,
patient confidentiality and all that, but Glenys's dad was admitted
during the afternoon shift yesterday.'

'A fall?'

She shook her head, didn't open her eyes. 'The doc's not sure. A
funny turn of some kind. The family want to take him home again,
as soon as they can.'

'Oh.'

'But you didn't hear any of it from me.'

Glenys and I hadn't spoken since a brief conversation the Monday after we'd been out for Sunday roast.

'I'll ring her. Caring for an elderly parent is tough, especially the
closer it gets to the end.'

Georgia opened one eye. 'Of course you'll act surprised when
she tells you?'

'Of course I will! When she takes the old fella home again there
might be something I can do to help. Trev would tell it differently,
but he'd be about as much use around the home as a hip pocket on
a singlet.'

Georgia laughed. 'Mum says she has you to thank for how domes-
ticated Dad is. Aunty Bec says the same thing about Uncle Adam.'

'Charlie was clueless in the kitchen, and I blamed his mother.
When we'd visit she'd fuss over him, make him cups of tea while
the rest of us had to fend for ourselves. I swore my boys would be
different.'

'Yeah, Dad's take on it is that you were always at work and if he
hadn't learned how to cook they would have all gone hungry.'

'Silver linings,' I said matter-of-factly. 'But your dad was a good
kid. Savvy from a young age. Not much of what went on at home
slipped past him, and I relied on his help more than I probably
should have.'

Georgia swung her legs to the floor and sat up. She scrubbed at
her face with her hands and yawned widely. 'He's never sounded
bitter or twisted about it, Gran, just takes every opportunity to
remind us how lucky we are to have had the upbringing we've had.
I get it now, but I'm not sure the sibs do yet.' She stood up. 'I'm
going back to bed. I might even drop off to sleep.'

'Jess and I will be as quiet as mice. I won't get tea until you're up
and about again.'

After I heard the snick of her bedroom door closing I stepped out
onto the front verandah with my phone and called Glenys.

'Daisy!' she said, and sounded out of breath. 'I'm so glad you
rang. I suppose Georgia told you—'

'Told me what?'

'That Dad took a turn yesterday. Splat! Face first into his mashed
potato and peas. Thank goodness Trev was there to ring the ambulance. The doctor doesn't know what's wrong and they're doing
tests.' I heard the wobble in her voice before she dragged in a for-
tifying lungful of air.

'I'm sorry to hear that, Glenys. How's Bill today? And how are you?'

'Apparently, Dad's already giving the nurses the run-around. I suppose that's a positive sign. I was worried he'd had a stroke. And I'm all right. Trev's out fencing.'

'If he's got the nurses hopping he can't be too bad. Any idea when you might bring him home?'

'They haven't said yet but I hope it's soon. I know he's old and he can be a cantankerous bugger, but he's my still my dad and I promised dear old Mum that I'd look out for him right through until the end. I don't want him catching that awful virus.'

How like Glenys to make such a promise. I'd seen my mum through to the *very* end because we'd lived in the same house and I was a nurse, after all. You might think that sounds pragmatic, but it was how it was. There'd only been the two of us after all the boys had gone. Gareth was the first to leave, then Charlie, followed closely by Jay and lastly, Adam. Mum and I had been on our own for about five years before she died. She'd had emphysema and to me, her primary carer, it'd seemed worse than death by a thousand cuts.

'Are you still there?' Glenys said, dragging me back to the present.

'I'm still here, taking in all of what you've said, and when you bring him home, Glenys, please let me help out in whatever way I can.'

'I'm thinking I might need some help, so I do appreciate your offer, Daisy. The kids are all busy with their lives, and Trev means well, but you know ...'

I chuckled, because yes, I did know.

'And Daisy, I do understand how generous your offer is, with Dad being a Toogood and all. It broke my heart how careless Charlie was with you and the boys, and with his own responsibilities. I love him dearly, but over the years I have found it difficult to reconcile his behaviour. I'll keep in touch.'

I must have murmured an appropriate reply because she disconnected, leaving me sitting there staring blindly at the phone. People observed and understood more than you thought they did. My earlier resolve to never visit Glenys and Trevor again had become redundant. Offering to help seemed like the right thing to do, given the changed circumstances. If the situation were reversed I knew Glenys would be there to help in whatever way she could. I'd ask Max if he could spare a bunch of roses for me to take to her when I went out to the farm again.

16

Kate

The next time I visited the florist shop the girl behind the counter admitted that she had a hazy memory of a middle-aged man she didn't recognise buying a lavish bouquet around the date I'd specified.

'The reason I remember him at all is because he was very well dressed. Flashy, in a city kind of a way. He had an older woman with him who might have been his mother. She looked sick.'

'What made you think that?' I said.

'Because she wore one of those turban thingies on her head and he called her Mum?'

'Fair enough. Did you see the car they were in?'

'No. Sorry.'

I sneezed. She smiled apologetically. 'It's the flowers,' she said in a hushed voice.

I mentally rolled my eyes, thanked her and left. Back in the car I sat for a spell and wracked my brains for who it could possibly have been. A long-lost relative? An old girlfriend? I thought I'd known all of Dennis's friends and family, not that there'd been many. At the funeral and then the refreshments afterwards I'd been able to place everyone who'd attended. His eldest brother Lewis and his wife Molly had travelled from the Eyre Peninsula, as had a school friend who'd introduced himself after the service. There'd been a cousin I'd never met. She said she was representing the other cousins who couldn't make it. Of course, they'd all been around Dennis's age.

Was I obsessing over this? Was it another symptom of what was ailing me? Whatever that was. And did it really matter who'd put the flowers on the grave? I drummed my fingers on the steering wheel. *Yes, it did matter.* I needed to thank them. But more than that, I needed to know who it was. The flowers had been expensive. Someone had gone out of their way to put them on the grave. It wasn't a random act of kindness. Two people out there had a connection with my dead husband that I knew nothing about.

Had they been at the funeral and I'd missed them? Had they not come to the refreshments afterwards? Then that uncomfortable thought again: Did whoever it was not want me to know who they were?

I started the car, put it into gear to reverse out of the car park only to slam on the brakes a second later amid a cacophony of alarms and flashing lights. I glanced in the rear-view mirror horrified to discover that, if not for the vehicle's warning system, I would have reversed into a woman pushing a stroller.

Heart racing, I dropped my head into clammy hands and shuddered. What was the matter with me? It was as if I was turning into a flake.

When my heart rate settled, I checked and re-checked before reversing out at a snail's pace and driving home. My plan had been to pick up fresh fruit and vegetables while I was out. I'd make do with what I had.

★★★

When I let myself in I went directly to the cupboard in the study. Stowed on the shelves were several cardboard boxes. They contained Dennis's personal belongings: books; papers; farm records and a few cherished childhood possessions. They'd previously been crammed into an old wardrobe in the sleep-out at the farm. Before we'd moved, I'd asked him to sort through the boxes and get rid of anything he didn't want. That hadn't happened; he was always too busy, he'd said. The boxes had been moved holos-bolus into town, stacked into the cupboard and not touched since. Anyone's guess what I might find in them. Perhaps a clue to who the mystery man and woman might be.

In a burst of frenzied activity in the days immediately after Dennis's funeral, I'd cleared out his clothes, shoes and toiletries. I'd loaded them all into the car, without taking shirts off coat hangers or handkerchiefs out of trouser pockets. Off to the op shop they'd gone. There were no children or close friends to assist or remonstrate with me that it was too soon, that I'd barely given his body time to cool before I was disposing of his belongings. But if I hadn't done it then, each passing day would have made it harder to do at all. Acute loss and the associated grief temporarily blinds you to what came before the loss and what might come afterwards. You can't see past the potency of your bereavement.

I opened the cupboard door. Naphthalene-scented air wafted out. My nose prickled. I never looked in this cupboard. The study had been Dennis's domain. Stacked on the shelves were the original three boxes I remembered from the farm, plus a newer, sturdier-looking cardboard carton that I didn't recognise. According to the label on the side, it had once held tinned fruit.

The top flaps were well sealed with packing tape. I reached into the cupboard and tilted it forward and into the light. It was heavy. *Uncle Frank's journals, diaries etc.* was written across one corner in Dennis's careful hand. And a date: roughly eighteen months previously.

Frank Hannaford had been Dennis's uncle, his father's eldest brother. Frank, a bachelor, had left his land and rundown farmhouse to Dennis—along with his journals and diaries, apparently. The first I knew that any such records existed.

Frank had died several years before I'd met Dennis. There were a handful of photos of him, somewhere. Black and white prints mostly, of an unsmiling man on a tractor or standing beside an ancient-looking piece of farm machinery. No denying the family resemblance between the two men, particularly in stature. Dennis had been very fond of his Uncle Frank and he'd recounted to me the stories behind the photographs, but I'd long since forgotten them. There hadn't seemed much point to remembering, then or now. I'd never met Uncle Frank, and who was I going to pass on the stories to?

That was the thing about being without progeny: what did you do with those precious items collected over a lifetime? Irreplaceable to you, but without the memories attached to them those treasured mementos became nothing more than clutter and junk for someone else to jettison.

I closed the cupboard, turned off the light and shut the study door, and went in search of my brother-in-law Lewis's phone number. He might want Uncle Frank's journals. He might even like Dennis's childhood keepsakes. After I'd been through them of course.

Alas, Lewis didn't want any of it and he didn't beat around the bush telling me so. 'Molly would have my guts for garters,' he said. I could hear her chuckling in the background. Lewis had married later in life and Molly was a decade or so younger than him. 'She sends her love but says there's more than enough of Mum and Dad's stuff still here clogging up cupboards, we don't need anything more to deal with.'

'What about your kids? Grandkids? Aren't any of them interested in family history?'

He hooted with laughter and nearly ruptured my eardrum. 'Not likely! The kids don't have time to scratch themselves, working and running about from one thing to another. And the grandkids? Always glued to those damned *devices* … Can't even be bothered to give an old bloke the time of day.' He wasn't laughing now. 'I'll ask them. But don't hold your breath, Kate.'

Disappointing, not that I'd really expected anything else. It was such a shame. I'd probably end up burning the lot.

'What about the local history group? I'll bet there is one. They might be interested in old Frank's journals. Have you had a read of them?' Lewis said.

'Until about fifteen minutes ago I didn't know the journals existed. And there was a local history group, once upon a time. I'll ask around.'

But that still left Dennis's papers and keepsakes, and I didn't know what I'd do with them after I'd been through the lot. Repack it into the boxes and return them to the study cupboard, I surmised. What else was there to do with them, other than burn or shred them?

We didn't chat for much longer. I could hear Molly telling him to wish me a happy birthday for the following day.

'Thanks,' I said. 'These days they come around much too quickly.'

'I bet last year's would have been a bit of a blur, given it was so soon after Den died,' Lewis said with his usual bluntness. 'Molly says to do something extra special for yourself this year.'

He sounded so much like Dennis that when we disconnected I felt inordinately bereft. And he'd been spot on: I'd missed last year's birthday all together. I put down the receiver, thinking I should ring them more often, but knowing I wouldn't.

★ ★ ★

'The local history group?' Valma said when I telephoned her a few days later. 'Eric Sanderson would be your best bet. My Bob used to be involved but he gave it up a couple of years back. He got fed up with being bossed around by a couple of the women in the group.' She laughed, right from her belly.

'I know Eric,' I said. 'I'll give him a call.'

In the early years of my appointment as director of nursing, Eric Sanderson had been on the hospital board. People said he could be a bit pernickety, but I'd valued that about him. He noticed things others didn't. I'd always liked him. He'd come to Dennis's funeral.

I rang him and he popped in later that same day and collected the box, without me even bothering to open it and look inside first. As I handed it over, I wondered if I should have. But I had no interest in Uncle Frank's journals and, according to Lewis when he'd rung back the night before, neither did anyone else in the Hannaford family.

'All I can promise is that we'll take a thorough look at the journals. On the off-chance they double up with the type of records we already have in our collections, I'll have to return them to you,' Eric said. 'As you can imagine, we don't have surplus space to store things.'

'Of course not,' I said, my earlier relief tempered slightly.

He whisked away the box. Another piece of Dennis's life relegated to history. In the end, who would remember him? Who would remember any of us? More than likely no-one. And Uncle Frank? He was as good as forgotten already.

17

Daisy

Jess and I were out walking Tuesday morning when we happened past Kate's place at the very moment she came out to collect her newspaper from the front lawn. It wasn't that early. Georgia was back on day shift.

'Kate! Good morning,' I called, because how could I not? She would have seen us. 'Seems like we're in for another run of hot days.'

She froze. Just when I thought she was going to scuttle off without acknowledging me, she tucked the newspaper under her arm and stepped closer to the fence.

'How are you?' I said. She was in her dressing gown, with serious bed hair. I hadn't seen her since I'd invited myself for a swim in her pool. She hadn't exactly welcomed me with open arms that day. The swim had been worth it.

She lifted one shoulder and let it drop. 'Does it matter?'

'I wouldn't have asked if I didn't care, Kate.'

'Sorry,' she mumbled.

'So … how are you? And if my memory serves me correctly, didn't you just have a birthday?'

'Seventy-two,' she said, flatly. 'Hip hip hooray.' Her eyes were red, the lids puffy; her complexion sallow. She pressed her finger-tips to her lips, looked left and then right and then directly at me. 'I thought I was all right, you know … coping,' she said. 'Getting on with life after my husband died. But everything has started to unravel. Some days I manage "normal" remarkably well, and on other days it's a struggle to get up and keep going.'

I was momentarily lost for words. To be so forthright about her own personal struggles, vulnerable even, was so unlike the Kate I'd once known. The Kate I remembered was all about control—of everything, if allowed.

Then her lips twitched. 'You asked,' she said, with irony. 'And for some reason you're the first person with whom I've shared even a semblance of the truth.'

I swapped Jess's lead from one hand to the other. 'What about your family? Your mum? Your sisters? Friends?'

'Not all of us have family who're willing and able to be leaned on. Mum's not here any more and my sisters both live interstate. Mum's funeral was the last time I saw either of them. And friends … Well, they often turn out to be a bitter disappointment, don't you think?'

I let the last bit slide, not sure if she was having a go at me or her friends in general.

'I'm sorry, Kate,' I said, not exactly sure which part I was sorry for. You could be surrounded by family and still have no-one to lean on. I knew that better than most.

'Don't be sorry,' she said. 'It is what it is.' She hugged the news-paper close to her chest, her gaze cast downwards.

Jess was restless. She'd wrapped the lead around my shins. I untangled myself and looped the end over a fence picket.

'Have you thought about talking to your GP?'

She sighed. 'He'd probably tell me to get a grip and get over it, and then give me a script for happy pills.'

'Have you thought about finding another GP?'

'He's been my doctor forever,' she said.

'But if you're not satisfied—'

She stared at me with what could only be described as consternation. 'But he was Dennis's doctor. He came to his funeral.'

'Yes, but if you're not satisfied with the care you're receiving ...' My words tapered off.

We stood on either side of the fence for a bit, saying nothing, looking everywhere but at each other. It began to feel awkward, but I couldn't think of anything to say, except that I'd thought she was much smarter than that. The Kate I'd known wouldn't have settled for anything other than the best. Jess whined. Her breakfast beckoned.

'You'd better be on your way,' Kate said, briskly now. 'That sun has a bit of a bite to it already and you don't have a hat.'

'Come on, Jess,' I said. 'You take care, Kate. You have my phone number, if there's anything I can do to help.'

She moved away from the fence, her expression closed.

'Bye,' I said, and reached to unhook Jess's lead. When I looked up, Kate was already walking away, across the lawn towards the front door. No doubt regretting that she'd exposed her most vulnerable self to me only minutes before.

We dawdled home. I was disappointed with myself for not offering more support, something with substance. Pigs would fly before she'd *ring me* to ask for anything. For all I knew she'd thrown away my phone number.

Lingering over an after-breakfast coffee an hour or so later, I tried to tease out why I'd become friends with Kate in the first place. She'd been Kate Smith when we'd met, before she married Dennis, and it'd been the circumstances, really, that had nudged us in the direction of friendship.

When I'd moved to a country hospital after finishing a staffing year at the Royal Adelaide I'd been out of my depth. Chucked in at the deep end, for sure. While I'd been confident in my nursing knowledge and skills, I'd been accustomed to help being a shout away, or at worst a phone call away. I'd soon discovered that in a moderately-sized country hospital there was no such thing as a crash team to come rushing to your assistance and very few experienced colleagues to mentor you through first-time decision making. You and whoever else was on duty were the crash team, with or without a local GP. If you made the wrong decision, you learned from it, hoped you didn't kill anyone, and never made the same mistake twice.

It was against this backdrop that I had met Kate. She'd been given the task of 'orientating' me to the hospital. We were of a similar age and not constrained by husbands and families, although Kate was already engaged to Dennis. I hadn't known a soul in the place; I'd lived in the nurses' home because I couldn't afford anything else, and everything was different than it had been in the city. Fertile ground for the forming of a new friendship.

At first I'd driven back to Adelaide on my days off. Mum was always pleased to see me and it was good to catch up with friends and familiar things. But gradually, as Kate and I became friends outside of work, I'd stopped going home so much and my friends in Adelaide had fallen by the wayside. As friendships do if they're not attended to.

The coffee finished, I pushed aside the past and tidied the house. I was about to set the washing machine going when my phone rang. It was Glenys. She sounded distraught.

'We brought Dad home yesterday afternoon and he's being so damned difficult. I can't seem to do anything right and the minute I leave the room he's yelling out for me. Trev's had to go to the city for tractor parts—'

'I'll come out. Give me an hour. Do you need anything from the supermarket? The chemist? Anything at all?'

'You're a lifesaver! A loaf of bread and two litres of milk, thanks. And a bottle of brandy … Not for Dad but for me,' she said, and laughed.

We disconnected. The washing would wait. Days ago I'd briefed Max on the possible need for more roses, if he could spare them. I rang him.

'Good timing. I have the secateurs in my hand. I'll go and cut a bunch. Pick them up on your way past.'

I showered, dressed in something more respectable than my walking garb and bundled Jess into the car. She was ecstatic to be going for a drive. Max was waiting at the gate with a generous bunch of blooms.

'Glenys will love these. Thank you so much, Max.' We carefully placed them in the back of the station wagon.

'The weather's been kind,' he said. 'But I reckon this'll be the last of them for the season.'

When we were underway I quickly opened the car window. 'Jess, you pong,' I said. 'You need a bath.' Her ears flattened at the word bath. Since the advent of the twin tub washing machine, the regular trips to the laundrette, and inadvertently the dog wash, had ceased.

We arrived at the Carlisles' in a whisker over an hour.

'It's worse than having a baby *and* a toddler,' Glenys said when she opened the door to my knock.

'From my neighbour,' I said, handing her the roses.

'How thoughtful of you both,' she said, and angled her nose towards the blooms.

'I've brought my dog with me. I hope you don't mind. I've parked in the shade and she'll be okay in the car.'

'No, no, you mustn't leave her in the car. Let her out. She'll be fine in the yard. There's water in the bucket by the tank. Trev's dogs are with him.'

I saw to Jess and went inside to the kitchen.

'Dad wasn't the easiest man before this setback,' Glenys said as she arranged the roses in a gorgeous cut-glass vase. 'And he was positively awful to the nursing staff at the hospital. I'm sure they were pleased to see the back end of him.'

I lifted the green grocery bag onto the counter, took out the milk and put it in the fridge. When I unloaded the bottle of brandy, Glenys grinned. 'I was half-joking,' she said. 'But it won't go astray just the same. How much do I owe you?'

'On the house,' I said. 'I haven't forgotten your kindnesses when my boys were little and I was up to my neck. Now, what do you want me to do?'

She wrinkled her nose. 'Would you mind sitting with Dad while I catch up on a few chores? I've made him a cup of tea and cut up a banana. He has one of those feeder mugs now but he needs help with it. He's much less able than he was before his funny turn.'

Right on cue, a holler came from somewhere deeper in the house.

Glenys winced. 'And he hasn't even been home for twenty-four hours.' Her eyes glistened with unshed tears. 'It's just everything,' she said. 'The kids are all so busy and they don't come near the place, not since Dad's been here. He just doesn't cope at all with the grandkids … they're noisy and boisterous. Trev thinks we should have left Dad at the hospital until a bed came up in the nursing home. I just couldn't do that.'

I squeezed her hand. 'He'll settle down and you'll find a new routine that works. I can come out and help whenever you need me. And I'm sure there's a local community services organisation that'd offer respite of some kind. Did the hospital staff tell you about anything like that?'

Another holler, louder this time and spiced with a few choice swear words.

Glenys scooped up the feeder mug and bowl of banana. 'Follow me,' she said, 'and brace yourself.'

'Glenys, I worked in a nursing home for many years. Not one of those posh ones either, where you get wine with your dinner. And don't forget, I have three sons.'

'You're an angel, Daisy,' she said, and swept off towards the front rooms where the shouting was getting louder by the second.

I did brace myself before I trailed off after her, but not for a moment did I ask myself why I was there.

18

Kate

Towards the middle of that week I decided it was time to revisit Dennis's boxes, the ones that were in the study cupboard. Thursday morning I'd lain awake in the early hours contemplating what I'd do with the stuff. First and foremost I needed to look and see what there was, even if I did end up shredding or burning most of it. Another middle-of-the-night decision I'd made was that, after I'd sorted through Dennis's things, I would make an effort to put in order my own personal papers and keepsakes. Pare them back to the few things I didn't want to live the remainder of my life without, and then get rid of the rest.

In an old brown suitcase on the top shelf of my wardrobe were the journals I'd kept when we'd been trying to start a family. Over those years I'd written down everything, from the days I'd thought I'd been ovulating to the number of times we'd had sex; when my periods started and finished; the tests and treatments; the disappointments and grief; and finally the despair when I reached my early forties and accepted that I was destined to be childless.

I hadn't reread any of them since I'd written them, and I wondered how prudent it would be to put myself through that episode of my life all over again by reading through them now. The best thing would be to shred them. They were of no relevance to anyone else. If I dropped dead suddenly, or slammed my car into a tree like Dennis had, I'd hate for anyone to find them and read them. They were too personal. I'd never shared the contents or the fact that I'd written them with anyone. Dennis wouldn't have known they existed. Fleetingly, when I'd been packing up at the farm, I'd considered burning them. It would have been easy out there, but something had held me back.

After I'd made those momentous decisions I'd dropped off to sleep and slept until seven. When I woke I rose with a sense of purpose; something that had been lacking from my life of late.

Dressed and breakfasted, I'd already hefted out two of the boxes from the study and put them outside on the patio when my sister-in-law, Molly, surprised me by telephoning.

'How are you?' she said when I picked up.

First Daisy and now Molly wanted to know how I was.

Without waiting for an answer she continued. 'It's just that after you spoke to Lew last week, he sensed that you were a bit down. Not that we blame you, but we got to thinking … Why don't you drive across and stay with us for a few days? A change of scenery might do you the world of good.'

Not what I'd been expecting. I thanked Molly for the invitation and wondered at Lewis's perceptiveness. 'Perhaps when the weather cools a little,' I said. All the while thinking it was unlikely that I would go and what other excuses could I quickly cobble together. I didn't know Molly well, probably because I'd had very little to do with her. A combination of the physical distance that separated us and the all-consuming nature of farming. But what I did know of her, I liked. The few times Dennis and I had visited them, they'd been welcoming. Now there was nothing to stop me taking up their offer except my own prejudices and singularities. Hard to admit but true nevertheless. In the past I'd determinedly shied away from families with children and grandchildren.

We chatted for ten minutes about the usual things: how mild the summer had been; how desperately we needed rain; and how fed up everyone was with Covid restrictions. Then I enquired after her family, because it would have been strange if I hadn't. It was as if she'd been waiting for me to ask.

'They're all fighting fit, but like Lew said, they don't have much time in their lives for us old fogeys, unless of course it's to babysit or ferry kids to and from sport. And I truly don't mind helping out. These days it's increasingly difficult for the young ones to buy a home and raise a family, not that I'm saying it's ever been easy.'

Then she shrieked and said, 'Is that the time?' She had to go because she had canteen duty at the high school. Later in the day she volunteered as a friend of the local library. We said our good-byes and promised to keep in closer touch.

I listened to the dial tone for several seconds after she'd hung up, thinking how empty my life was. Too much free time on my hands to be miserable and become more self-absorbed than was healthy or normal.

But on a positive note, it was shaping up to be another gorgeous summer day and I was quietly chuffed with myself because the day before I'd vacuumed and dusted the family room. And I'd mopped the kitchen floor. Not monumental in the scheme of things but it was a start. It hadn't been as onerous as I'd imagined.

What had finally spurred me into action was the strange over-the-fence conversation I'd had with Daisy. Standing there on my side of the fence, I'd glimpsed how I must appear to her, and I didn't like what I saw. I needed to do something with myself and the long overdue housework.

As I carried the third cardboard box through to the patio I wondered if my antipathy towards housework and all things domestic stemmed partly from my inability to have children. From as young as I could remember, my plan for when I grew up had been to find a husband and devote myself to being a good wife and mother. I'd chosen nursing because it was a profession that offered women flexibility after they'd had a family. When the time was right I would have been able to supplement the household income with a few shifts at the hospital. Unfortunately, I hadn't made it past the first base. I'd found the husband but the family never eventuated, and I now had serious doubts as to whether I'd been a *good* wife. Instead, I'd poured all my energy into a career. Had it filled the void in my life? To a degree. An unexpected and positive consequence had been that the job kept me out of the house, the place that constantly reminded me what a dismal failure I'd been in doing my part to transform it into a family home.

Then with a promotion had come a higher salary and I'd felt justified and entitled to having a person come in and clean the house, distancing me even further from it. The old place at the farm had been huge and not easy to keep clean. Housework was loathsome and thankless and, after all, I was a career woman. I'd convinced myself that I deserved it.

As time passed, eating, sleeping and preparing for the next week of work was, for me, all that happened in that house.

After I'd retired it'd been harder to justify having someone clean for us and Dennis and I had argued about it. Hotly. But I hadn't backed down, not even when we'd moved into town. I'd glared at him and said, 'Paying a cleaner is a small concession to make given the contribution I've made to the farm coffers over the years.'

There was no arguing with that because in times of drought, my regular and generous income had been the only income until it rained again. We—I—wouldn't be in such a comfortable position now if not for the security and benefits arising from my career and the income that went with it. See what I mean about me having too much time to dissect and analyse, and always being left with a feeling of disquiet?

By now I had the boxes lined up in a row on the outdoor setting. I dusted them off. One of them looked much older than its counterparts and had been markedly heavier. I opened it first. The packing tape had all but lost its stickiness and flaked away in my fingers. I folded back the flaps and was assailed by the musty smell of old books and newspapers. I lifted out the sheets of newspaper on top. They were fragile and yellowed with age; an *Adelaide Advertiser* dated 23 March 1970. I scanned the front page, not surprised to see doctors and the AMA had been making headlines even back then. I would have been twenty in 1970, living away from home and yet to complete my nursing training. Dennis would have been twenty-five; around the time he went to work as a farmhand for his Uncle Frank. What had he been thinking as he'd packed up his precious childhood belongings? Or had his mother done it for him? Is that what mothers did when their bachelor sons left home for good? This particular cardboard box had been in the wardrobe in the sleep-out at the farm for as long as I'd lived there.

Under the newspaper there was a stack of books, including a 1960 Adventure Story Book for Boys, and a couple of Boy's Own Annuals. Bound with string were several bundles of Meccano magazines and instruction guides. Underneath these I found a well-used Meccano set in what appeared to be its original cardboard packaging. Any wonder the box had been heavy. I picked up several of the faded red and green metal pieces and examined them. By the state of the paintwork, they'd been well used. No doubt they'd be classed as vintage by now, and the magazines were probably collector's items. I groaned out loud. What *was* I supposed to do with this stuff? Next thing I knew, my eyes burned with unshed tears as I imagined a twenty-five-year-old Dennis selecting his prize possessions to pack away and someday pass on to his own sons.

I dropped into the closest chair and fossicked in my pocket for a handkerchief. This was more difficult than I'd anticipated, and there were two cartons still to go. Who could I talk to about what to do with this childhood memorabilia? Or did I just repack it into sturdier boxes and put it back into the cupboard? Let it be someone else's problem when I was gone? Tempting. But more to the point, why hadn't I ever asked Dennis what he wanted done with his keepsakes? We'd never talked about it, except for me to tell him to sort through it. Which he hadn't done. Was that because he hadn't been able to bring himself to do it?

Of course we'd both had wills, but in hindsight I'd blithely meandered along, never for a moment consciously considering that the odds were stacked in favour of one of us dying before the other, and what then for the one left behind? If only we had discussed all this while he was alive. I wouldn't be sitting here now, not knowing how to move forward. I repacked the items into the box and then went inside and made myself a coffee. It was that time of the day and I needed caffeine to fortify myself before I could even think about opening the other two boxes.

While I sipped the aromatic brew I flicked through this month's book club read. Of course I hadn't read it and it was book club again tomorrow. Hard to believe a month had slipped past since the last get-together, and that same afternoon's disgraceful finale. I sighed, long and loud. Here I was with my life whizzing past in monthly increments, and all I could do was flail about and feel sorry for myself.

19

Daisy

Since Bill Toogood's discharge from hospital I'd been out to Glenys's every day. Glenys had been grateful to have me sit with her dad for a couple of hours each day in order for her to catch up on housework and other chores. Trev was always conspicuously absent. Not that I could or would censure him for that. Bill Toogood was a difficult man. He didn't have a kind word to say about anything or anyone. I suspected he was in pain but he refused to take any medications. Glenys tried grinding the tablets and mixing them in his food, but he knew and he'd spit it out. I don't know how Glenys put up with him, father or not.

'Stay home tomorrow. It's Sunday,' she'd said to me when I was leaving Saturday evening. 'Trev can spend some time with Dad, even if I have to tie him to the chair—Trev, that is. I did enough for his parents when they were alive.'

Bill was deteriorating. I'd noticed it over the handful of days I'd been visiting. In the process, he was making his daughter's life miserable and I don't know if he realised, or cared. He was becoming more dependent by the day. That said, occasionally I'd catch him managing a task well enough if he thought no one was watching, leaving me to wonder if the level of his helplessness wasn't slightly contrived. For whatever reason, he didn't like me. I don't think he remembered who I was or where exactly I fit in, but his antagonism towards me was clear.

Back home from the Carlisles' and there was a Holden ute in the driveway behind Georgia's car. I parked on the street, let Jess out, collected the eggs and home-grown vegetables Glenys had sent me off with, and dragged my feet to the front door. A shower, food and an early night was my plan. Who cared if it was Saturday night.

I was tired and felt dispirited. My heart went out to Glenys. I could walk away but she couldn't and I remembered what that had been like with Mum: I'd been stuck there, though I wouldn't have wanted to be anywhere else if given a choice. But it was no fun watching an elderly parent die increment by increment. It was a constant reminder of your own fragile mortality.

When I let myself inside it took me a moment to register that Georgia had company. As if the unfamiliar car in the driveway hadn't been a dead giveaway. Duh.

'Oh,' I said. 'I'm sorry … Am I interrupting something?'

Georgia was lounging on the sofa, aka my bed, with her bare feet in the lap of a man who was vaguely familiar. He was massaging my granddaughter's feet! The atmosphere was thick with what my addled brain finally identified as sexual tension. Whoa! A long while since I'd been around any of that. I glanced from one to the other. He had the grace to look embarrassed. Not so Georgia.

'Gran, you're back. How was the old boy? And this is Kieran.'

Kieran looked askance at her before shifting his attention to me. I frowned.

'I remember you,' he said. 'It was you at Mrs Hannaford's place. She was acting pretty weird that day.'

'The pool cleaner,' I said as the penny dropped.

'Hall Handyman and Pool Maintenance, Kieran Hall at your service,' he said, and pushed Georgia's feet off his lap to stand up. He extended his hand. 'Nice to meet you, Mrs Toogood.'

'That'd be *Miller*,' I said, 'but please call me Daisy.' I shook his hand.

'Nice to meet you, Daisy,' he said. 'And I understand you had a swim in Mrs Hannaford's pool. How was it?'

Georgia raised her eyebrows. I hadn't told her I'd invited myself around to Kate's for a swim. 'We're talking about the same woman whose car we—'

'The swim was lovely. The water perfect. You do a good job,' I said with a slight shake of my head. Kate didn't need her dirty laundry aired here.

He beamed at me.

'You didn't tell me you'd been for a swim in her pool.' Georgia pouted and pushed herself to her feet. 'Why didn't you invite me?'

'Because you were at work.' I unloaded my armful of goods onto the kitchen bench. 'Glenys sent eggs. I thought I'd do an omelette for tea.'

'That'd be awesome,' Kieran said.

Georgia nudged him in the shin with her toe. 'You were taking me out, remember?'

'Yeah, but we don't have to go out. We can stay and keep your gran company.'

'You don't mind, Gran?' Georgia said.

How was I supposed to answer that? I did mind but I wasn't going to say that. I peered at her to see if there was anything extra she was saying that she hadn't said, if you get my gist.

'What about a frittata?' I said eventually. 'That might work better for three. And we have mushrooms.'

'All right, but next time you're taking me out,' Georgia said to Kieran. He raised his eyebrows and then nodded enthusiastically. My guess was he hadn't been sure there was going to be a next time.

Cooking for three and then wedged at one end of a two-and-a-half-person sofa watching a movie on Netflix that I had zero interest in was not how I'd planned to spend my evening. But then Georgia probably wasn't thrilled with having her grandmother on a first date with her either. Jammed in the middle between the two of us, Kieran just seemed to be enjoying himself.

It was my non-stop yawning that finally brought the evening to a close. Tactfully, I withdrew to the bathroom to have a shower, clean my teeth and give them space to say their goodbyes. The moment I heard Kieran's ute start I shot back to the living area and began assembling my bedroom.

When Georgia came inside again I said, 'Was he the one responsible for the flowers?'

She nodded.

'He seems like a nice bloke.'

'At least he has a job,' she said. 'He's in business with his dad. They have more work that they can handle.'

'I didn't cramp your style, did I?'

'Nah,' she said and laughed. 'I don't think Kieran was the least bit put out by having two women fussing over him. He lives with two of his mates and they're not exactly house proud.'

'Are you going to see him again?'

She paused to reflect for a moment. 'Yeah, I think I will. I like him. He makes me laugh.'

'Always a good start,' I said. I pecked her on the cheek. 'Night-night, sweetie. Are you working tomorrow?'

'Afternoon shift. I'm meeting Lisa for breakfast. She's been on nights. I suppose I'll get the next instalment in the Jake saga. Do you think a man can change?'

'In theory anyone can change, if they want to badly enough. From what you've told me, part of what this Jake needs to do is grow up.'

'That's what I keep telling Lisa.'

'And what does she say to that?' I said, rummaging around in the cupboard for a dog biscuit to give Jess.

Georgia folded her arms and her mouth turned down at the corners. 'She gets a bit bent out of shape ...'

'Aha!' I said, brandishing the last bone-shaped biscuit in the bag. 'No-one likes being *told*. Back when I wasn't much older than you, Kate Hannaford and I were friends and she was always *telling* me what to and what not to do. Come to think of it, I'd usually do the opposite.'

'Were you friends like me and Lisa are?'

'I suppose we were. We did a lot of things together. Although Kate was already engaged to Dennis when we met.'

'And was he a loser?'

'Quite the opposite, actually.'

Georgia obviously wanted to talk when all I wanted to do was go to bed. My mind and body felt weighed down by fatigue. 'Can we finish this conversation in the morning?' I said, and punctuated it with a yawn that made my eyes water.

'No worries, Gran,' she said, but I could see she was disappointed. She was wired and if I hadn't been there she would have sat up for a while watching television or playing with her phone. Surely Kieran wouldn't have stayed over, not after a first date?

She filled a glass with water. 'See you in the morning,' she said, and reluctantly wandered off to her bedroom.

★★★

Sunday, around lunch time, Georgia breezed in looking flushed and sparkly eyed, and with barely enough time to change into her uniform and get to work on time.

'How was breakfast?'

'Excellent. Kieran showed up. We had fun.'

'Had he met Lisa before? Does he know Jake?'

'No, and Jake didn't come. He was still in bed with a hangover, apparently.' She rolled her eyes. 'I think Lisa liked Kieran. What's there not to like?' She smiled like the cat that got the cream.

I couldn't help but feel a pang of sympathy for poor Lisa. She couldn't help being attracted to the 'wrong' man. It might have been well over four decades ago, but I hadn't forgotten what it was like to have a close friend who outshone you in everything. Not that I'd ever considered Dennis to be a better or worse man than Charlie; they were just so very different, and I'd been attracted to Charlie. Kate, on the other hand, had always been outspokenly certain that she'd made the far superior choice. Not that it mattered now, because we'd both ended up on our own.

'And guess who else was at the cafe? Sitting all on her lonesome? Your friend Kate,' said Georgia. She secured her hair into a messy bun, not the sort of style that would have passed muster in my day.

'Well I never.'

'Yeah, and quite frankly, I thought she looked as if she was a bit spooked.'

'Did you say hello?'

'Kieran waved to her. That's how come I knew who she was. I'd never clapped eyes on her before. Lisa knows her and said she's always been a bit strange.'

'None of us know what's going on behind the scenes in other people's lives, Georgia. Always best to keep an open mind.'

'Just telling it how I saw it.' She sat down on the sofa and reached for her shoes. 'Why don't you go and have another swim in her pool this afternoon? See if she's all right?'

I could feel Georgia's gaze. She was waiting for an answer. But what answer to give her?

'Kate and I have baggage,' I said. 'It goes back a long way. I'm not certain she'd welcome any interference from me. Besides, I've given her my phone number and she knows where I live.'

'Gran! How dare you tell me something juicy like that right before I have to go to work.'

That made me smile. 'And that's about all I will tell you.'

She dropped her bottom lip. 'Not fair!'

I went to the fridge. 'I packed you a salad for tea, with the left-over frittata. And there's fruit.'

'You didn't have to, Gran, but I'm glad you did. Thanks,' she said and gave me a one-armed hug. She grabbed the food and her bag and was gone, leaving me alone to reflect on what she'd told me about Kate.

20

Kate

Sunday morning I had a sudden and inexplicable urge to go to church. I'd never been a regular church-goer, and I'd never before looked to religion for answers. Dennis hadn't been overtly religious, although we had been married in a church because we'd both wanted it that way. But I hadn't darkened the doorway of a house of worship since Mum died, and had no idea why I felt compelled to do it today. Was it all the thinking I'd been doing about death and my own mortality? Did I think I'd be closer to Dennis in a church? Or was it because I was feeling a bit lost? As if my life's foundation wasn't as firm as I'd once thought and subconsciously I was searching for something to shore it up with.

Whatever it was, it took all of fifteen minutes, stumbling my way through one hymn and then listening to the minister drone on, to know that I'd been right: I wasn't a bit religious and it was unlikely I'd find answers here. Being there felt so odd that I crept out again, relieved that I'd sat in the second-to-last pew from the back. I scurried through the foyer and out to my car, crossing my fingers that no-one I knew had witnessed my coming or going. Because if any-one asked, I wouldn't have been able to explain exactly why I'd been there in the first place.

So there I was, all dressed up and with nowhere to go. The newsa-gent didn't deliver on Sundays so I stopped in at Foodland and bought a *Sunday Mail*. A few doors away a cafe was bustling with patrons and energy. Before I could talk myself out of it, I'd stepped over the threshold and into the cafe, and walked up to the counter and ordered coffee and a croissant. The lad who took my order directed me to the only vacant table: a two-seater near the window. If I sat so I could see out the window I'd have my back to the room. I chose the other chair. After I'd made myself comfortable I scanned the busy space and who should be sitting a couple of tables away other than Kieran Hall. He was with two young women, one of whom I was almost certain was Daisy's granddaughter, Georgia. Although I'd never met her, there was something about the young woman that reminded me of Daisy when I'd first known her. Back when we'd both been young.

The girl laughed and tossed her glossy, shoulder-length dark hair. She wasn't exactly pretty but there was an arresting quality about her appearance and demeanour. She was very sure of herself. Kieran couldn't take his eyes off her.

The other girl I recognised as Lisa Collins and I knew she was a registered nurse at the hospital. Her mother worked at the chemist, had done for years, and Lisa's grandmother was my vintage and had been a receptionist at the doctors' surgery. She hadn't long retired. She'd come to bridge several times but hadn't liked it so she stopped coming. How clever of her. It'd taken me several years to reach the same conclusion. In the end, leaving the group had been as much about the women as it had been about the game itself. I hadn't felt as if I'd belonged. Had it been the same for Lisa's grandmother?

The waitress came with the coffee and croissant. She put it down, smiled and hurried off. They'd put butter and jam on the side, and the barista had swirled a heart into the creamy-topped latte. All I could do was stare at it. What on earth was I doing here when I could be at home, eating breakfast in the privacy of my own breakfast nook. I looked up, preparing to flee, but Kieran had spotted me. He waved. I acknowledged with a nod and, I hoped, a smile. It would look odd if I left now, without drinking the coffee or touching the food. I shifted my attention back to it, but not before I noticed Georgia lean in towards Kieran. I just knew she was asking him who he'd been waving to. Ridiculously, heat rushed to my cheeks. What was he saying? And what was her response? I told myself to get a grip and took a sip of the coffee. It wasn't too bad. The croissant was rich and buttery.

They were still there when I left, chatting and drinking coffee, although I got the impression Lisa was tired and would rather have been some place else.

Instead of going straight home I drove around town, out past the hospital, the place I'd spent most of my working life. I slowed to a crawl as I drove past. They'd recently cut down the huge gum tree by the carpark. What a shame. But it'd been a hazard, dropping a limb from time to time. Over the years I'd had plenty of complaints and dutifully taken them to the CEO and the hospital board. They'd always baulked at the expense, not at the loss of a tree and its heritage value. Or that someone could have been squashed by a falling branch.

I sped up, turned right and made for home. In a way, it was a relief that Dennis had died at the scene of the crash. The paramedics said, and the doctor later confirmed, that he would have been killed on impact. It would have been too much to bear if my last memories of him were tangled up with all my other memories of that hospital.

The road home took me along the street where Daisy was staying with her granddaughter. Her station wagon was parked in the driveway; her dog sitting on the verandah by the front door. Daisy had been staying there for quite a few weeks now. Did she have no other place to go? How long had to elapse before a stay turned into something else?

The house was a poky, rundown-looking place, much the same as the house Daisy and Charlie had rented when they'd first married. She'd come the full circle. If it had been me, I would have found that confronting.

Back home, the garage door rolled soundlessly shut behind me. It was so easy to take all that I had for granted. I know I'd worked hard through my life to get where I was. But then so had she. She'd worked hard all of her life, and raised a family.

★★★

Early afternoon that same day I lifted down the old suitcase from the top shelf in the walk-in robe. It wasn't as difficult to shift as I'd expected. The suitcase wasn't large. It had once belonged to Mum. One of the few things I had that'd been hers. She'd loaned it to me to use when I'd gone nursing and later said I could keep it. And I had kept it, for all of these years. In it I'd packed my journals, not knowing what else to do with them when I'd run out of space in the bedside cupboard drawers. I didn't think of them as diaries because they weren't a day-by-day account of what had happened in my life, more a chronicle of my infertility and disappointment. My biggest failure.

Before we'd moved in from the farm, the suitcase had been stored in the same wardrobe in the sleep-out as Dennis's possessions.

Fitting in a bizarre way: the precious things Dennis had kept to pass on to his son alongside the record of my failure to bear him that son.

After book club the previous Friday I'd returned Dennis's boxes to the cupboard in the study. They could stay there for the time being. I'd expected to have at least reduced the contents enough for them to have fit into the two sturdiest cartons but I hadn't been able to bring myself to get rid of any of it.

The two other boxes held an eclectic mix of memorabilia accumulated throughout Dennis's lifetime, plus a swag of farm records. I'd recognised a few of the things: a battered, flattened Akubra hat; a conservative-looking tie emblazoned with an agricultural bureau logo; and the Swiss Army knife I'd given him before we were married. He'd said it was too flash to use. I hadn't realised he'd kept it.

The most surprising find was the bundle of birthday cards trussed up with a partly perished rubber band. Cards I'd given to him. Every year at first, and then for the milestone birthdays. Once again, I'd expected him to have thrown them out. Was it possible that I hadn't known my husband as well as I'd thought I had? Had I assumed that I'd known all there was to know about him and stopped looking for anything I might have missed? Like a mile-wide streak of sentimentality.

The rest of the space had been taken up with farm diaries: notebooks filled with details written in Dennis's precise handwriting. Some evenings after dinner he'd sit at the kitchen table at the farm and write in the notebooks. What had been planted, when it had been planted and where; sheep bought and sold and the husbandry that went with them; wool clips; windmills, troughs and fences; machinery, new and old; the good years and the bad. And rainfall records, and calendars with pictures of tractors on them.

The most recent of the notebooks was a thickish tome dated 1 July 2001 to 30 June 2005. When the computer age arrived,

Dennis had effortlessly upgraded from a notebook and pen to a spreadsheet the way he did everything: without comment or complaint. Those years of records had stayed with the farm.

Dennis had loved being a farmer. He'd put so much of himself into the farm's success. I would have been blind not to have seen that. When we'd moved into town it was as if he cut himself off completely from that huge chapter of his life. He rarely went anywhere, not even to the pub to have a beer with one of his farming mates. I'd wondered if it was because those men still had a hand in the running of their farms, now being worked by their sons or daughters.

He'd loathed living in town, but I'd kept telling myself that he'd eventually get used to it. But in my heart of hearts I'd known that he probably wouldn't and I hadn't had the courage to talk to him about any of it because, underneath it all, I was to blame. I'd been wilfully blind to his unhappiness. It was all so clear to me now. And so irrelevant, because there was nothing I could do to change any of it.

I spread a towel on one end of the formal dining table and placed the old suitcase onto it. Then I took a deep breath and flicked open the two rusty latches.

21

Daisy

By late Sunday afternoon my conscience got the better of me. I put aside my reticence and walked around the corner to Kate's place. I would do what my granddaughter had suggested, and see that she was all right.

There was a doorbell. I pressed it and waited. I hadn't noticed the bell that day with Kieran.

Just as I was preparing to make myself scarce, the front door opened. Kate blinked at me from the other side of the security door. She looked as if she'd been asleep. Or something.

'Daisy,' she said and opened the security door.

We stood looking at each. I found myself at a loss for words, which wasn't like me at all. Why hadn't I rehearsed what to say on the walk?

'How are you?' I said, because wasn't that why I was there?

She regarded me for several seconds and then said, 'Would you like to come in?' She opened the door wider and stepped aside.

I slipped past her and into the house.

'No dog?' she said, with one last glance from whence I came.

'With the neighbour. I don't like to leave her on her own and Max enjoys the company.'

She closed the doors. 'Come through.' She led the way through to the kitchen. 'Shall I put the kettle on? Or would you prefer a glass of wine? The sun's well and truly over the yardarm.'

'Tempting, but I'll stick with tea, if you don't mind. Don't let me stop you.'

She waved her hand at the empty wine glass and unopened bottle of red on the island bench. 'I was going to have a glass earlier but changed my mind. I've been sorting through personal papers and the likes, and thought it better to do so with a clear head.'

She flicked on the electric kettle. It was one of those kettles you could see through. A blue light lit up when you turned it on and you could watch the water boil.

'Back to your earlier query ... I'm much better, I think, than I have been. I've managed to go through some of Dennis's things.'

'What are you going to do with all his clothes?'

'Oh, I've already dealt with them. I did it not long after he died. It was such a waste to hang on to clothes and shoes that others could be benefiting from. Or at least that's what I told myself. This is more his personal bits and pieces, and books. Records from when he was farming.'

'Be hard to know what to do with it. Funnily enough, I've kept an old duffel bag of Charlie's. There's books and the likes in it.'

'Had you hoped he might come back?'

'It's not as if I haven't seen him at all since he went. He's been back to see the boys, when Gareth and then Adam got married the first time, the births of grandchildren ... Not Mum's funeral, though, and I'll never forgive him for that. She thought the sun shone out of his backside. I should just chuck out whatever's in the bag and be done with it.'

'What about your children and grandchildren? Wouldn't they want any of it?'

'Perhaps, but it's not guaranteed.' I recounted the anecdote of Glenys leaving Nanna Toogood's glassware for Georgia. 'At first she didn't appear interested, but she might end up keeping it. Who knows? I can't even decide whether it really matters.'

'Then there are those of us who don't have children or grand-children ... It somehow highlights the insignificance of our lives, doesn't it? Just lately I've thought a lot about that. We traverse our mortal coils bent on accumulating experiences and possessions, knowing but ignoring that in the end all that's in store for each of us is death. That's if we've lived long enough to have accumulated those things. And because life is fragile and death is inevitable why are we so shocked and surprised when it actually happens to some-one we care about? Not meaning to sound too grim.'

'Kate, I didn't work in aged care for as many years as I did not to have considered those very questions. After his family dumped him in the nursing home, an old fella said to me that he knew all his friends were getting old and past their used by dates, but he hadn't expected it to happen to him. Do most of us live our lives in a state of denial? And if we do, I don't know if that's a positive or a negative thing.'

'I just know that when you're young and you lose someone pre-cious it's so sudden and acute, but it's as if you're better equipped to get over it, and to a certain extent move on.'

'I guess because the older we get the more relevant death becomes to us. Our bodies are wearing out and starting to fail. When Mum died I felt as if it was as much about me coming to grips with my own mortality as it was about her dying.'

'Good grief,' Kate said, and her eyes widened melodramatically. 'We are getting into the deep and meaningful. Perhaps we should have opened the wine after all.'

I laughed; it felt good. The kettle boiled. Kate warmed the tea-pot before she added the tea leaves and the boiling water. The skin on her arms and the back of her hands was smooth and creamy, her nails professionally tended. The state of her hands had me wanting to sit on my own to hide the sun spots and other blemishes.

'Georgia said she saw you at the cafe this morning,' I said.

'I thought it was her there with Kieran Hall and Lisa Collins. Georgia reminded me of you at that age.'

'Gareth says that, but I can't see it myself.' I propped my right buttock on one of the barstools alongside the island bench. 'Kieran seems like a nice enough lad, and Georgia and Lisa are friends.'

'You'd remember Lisa's grandmother—Patricia Ellis. She was an enrolled nurse and after she'd had her family she went back to work at the doctor's surgery. She was there for years; part of the furniture.'

'Pat Ellis. I vaguely remember someone by that name.'

'She was a smoker back then. If you couldn't find her, and you often couldn't, she'd be out the back smoking. She used to try and cover the smell with that minty fresh-breath spray. A dead giveaway as far as I was concerned.'

'Oh, yeah. Now I remember her. She was a bit older than me.'

'Pat's my age. How long are you going to stay with your granddaughter?'

'Until she throws me out or her father reneges on his share of the rent. It's how he's bribing her to let me camp on her sofa.'

'Don't you have a home of your own?'

'It feels like I don't, but let's just say I'm between homes,' I said. I couldn't help but sweep my gaze around the spacious kitchen and tastefully decorated breakfast nook. The window looked out onto the patio and its jungle of potted plants and palms. Georgia's whole house wasn't much bigger than this space.

'Let's sit over there, shall we?' she said, and took our tea across to the breakfast nook. 'Would you like something to eat?'

I slid into the booth, my backside whispering across the satiny-smooth upholstery. The tea service was bone china, the cups delicate enough to see through. My heart almost leapt out of my chest as I had a Hyacinth Bucket moment: what if I gripped the handle too hard and it came off in my hand? I shook my head. Food meant crumbs.

Kate slid into the opposite side of the booth. 'This is my favourite spot in the whole house,' she said wistfully and poured the tea. 'I designed the breakfast nook myself.'

'Lovely,' I said, wishing I'd said no to tea. But then the wine glasses were probably Waterford crystal. The room was cool but I broke into a sweat. When I picked up the cup to take a sip I did my damnedest not to grip the handle too tightly. The tea tasted perfect. Just the right amount of milk.

'Is Georgia enjoying working at the hospital?'

'She doesn't complain about going to work so I suppose that means she enjoys it. She always wanted to be a nurse.'

'Things have changed a lot since our day, Daisy. It's all about the numbers these days … Balancing the budget. No such thing as a social admission any more. You have to be able to make money from the patients or at least break even. When the time came, I was glad to retire.'

'In the aged care sector it was all about accountability and compliance to the standards, but there was never enough money to comply. Never enough staff. Never enough anything, really. The poor residents didn't get anywhere near the care they needed or deserved. I ran out of steam trying to advocate for them. You were bashing your head against a brick wall. You're right, it has become all about money, or the lack of it.'

'I found that, by the end of my time, the younger nurses hadn't the same commitment as we'd had. It was just a job to them, they weren't interested in doing that extra little bit to make the patient comfortable. Or am I just looking back through rose-tinted glasses?'

'I dunno … We used to say the same about the first uni-trained nurses when they came on the scene. Remember? All they wanted to do was sit at the desk and chat with the doctors, and tell us what to do. We reckoned they were allergic to giving out bedpans and cleaning up messes.'

'Do you ever miss it?' Kate said. She propped an elbow on the table and leaned forward as if she were keen to hear my answer.

'I missed the pay packet,' I said flippantly.

'Yeah, well, we all missed that. What else?'

'The friendship of the other nurses. There was something special about that. You could feel like crap when you went to work but someone always managed to jolly you out of it. Not too many shifts where you didn't have a laugh somewhere along the line.'

Her expression turned waspish. 'Have you never been in management? Because that camaraderie evaporates when you become the boss and you're not one of the girls any longer. And some of them don't ever forget that, once upon a time, you were their boss.'

'I relieved in a senior position once. The incumbent was on extended sick leave. That was more than enough for me. By the end of the three months I was well and truly ready to move back to my usual position.'

We finished the pot of tea. Although it was comfortable sitting there, I began to feel antsy. I wasn't sure why, but I suspected it had something to do with age-old feelings of envy. Kate's home was everything I'd never had or ever would have.

'Thanks for the tea, but I'd better get going,' I said, and awkwardly edged my way out of the booth to stand up. It was on the tip of my tongue to invite her to Georgia's place for a cuppa one afternoon but I stopped myself just in time. Why would she want to slum it there when she could drink properly brewed tea out of bone china cups in the breakfast nook she'd designed herself?

I toiled home feeling quite miffed, mainly with myself. You'd think at nearly seventy I'd be able to handle the fact that there'd always be people who'd have more than I did. A lot more than I did; possessions that would inevitably be out of my reach. I might not have been so aggrieved if I'd been returning to my own home, to be comfortingly surrounded by my own things. But I didn't have a home of my own, only the promise of one sometime into the future. I'd been around long enough to have experienced how easily and carelessly promises could be broken. How depressing. I thought I might cry, but then there was Jess, waiting at the top of Max's driveway. She must have sensed my melancholy because she didn't stray far from my side for the remainder of the evening.

22

Kate

After Daisy left I couldn't bring myself to go back to the suitcase of journals. I'd bogged myself down in the past for as long as I could tolerate, at least for the time being. I needed something different to occupy my thoughts and energy for a while.

The dirty laundry basket was overflowing, so I started there. Then I cleaned the two bathrooms, scrubbing the shower recesses from top to bottom and mopping the floors. Being physically active was something I hadn't done much of in recent times, and it showed. By the time I finished the floors I was red-faced and breathless.

For dinner I grilled a piece of fillet steak, microwaved a potato and tossed a salad with my favourite dressing. A glass or two of red went down smoothly with the meal. After the third glass I stopped pretending I was enjoying myself; that I was luxuriating in the solitude and ability to do just as I pleased. The truth? It was lonely. I was lonely. I missed Dennis. It was a hollowness inside me that couldn't be filled. He should be sitting here, opposite me. Then

I could look at his dear face, instead of my own reflection in the window. That was no company at all.

Resisting a fourth glass of wine, I made a cup of hot chocolate and took it through to the family room. It struck me again what a misnomer that was. I settled in Dennis's recliner with the new book from Friday's book club. Which, I might add, had been a much more sedate event this month because it'd been at Valma's place. The strongest beverage on offer had been a heaped teaspoon of instant coffee. It had been a pleasant afternoon nevertheless. Valma's scones were to die for.

★★★

Monday morning at the usual time I looked out for Daisy and her dog, thinking I'd invite her in for a coffee when they walked past. Only they didn't. Maybe they'd taken a different route this morning. For all I knew, they didn't walk every day.

After I'd pegged out the basket of washing I stripped the sheets from my bed and put them in the machine. It was a lovely autumn day: clear and warm with a gentle breeze. In the front yard the leaves on the Chinese Pistachio tree had started to fall, making a bright yellowy-orange carpet on the lawn, which needed mowing.

A lawn mower languished in the shed. Lawn mowing had been another of Dennis's task. He'd appeared to enjoy it. Now Rob Hall, Kieran's father, did it for me. He'd mow, trim the edges and do whatever else I asked him to do. Generally, when it needed doing he'd show up and get to it. I assumed Kieran let him know when the time came. Or he'd notice himself when he visited his elderly mother across the street. If he didn't show up soon, I'd have to ring him about the leaves. Alternatively, I could rake them up myself. Now there was a novel idea.

I hadn't been inside the shed since Dennis's death. It wasn't a huge shed; cream-coloured Colorbond to match the house roof and with a whirlybird vent because it was where the pool chemicals were stored. Kieran regularly accessed the shed for the pool gear, but the Halls had their own mowers and garden maintenance equipment.

Before unlocking the padlock and opening the door, I steeled myself. This had been Dennis's domain and I'd rarely ventured in. The few times I had, I hadn't been surprised to see that he kept it how he'd kept his sheds at the farm: a place for everything, and everything in its place. Except for the cupboard with the pool gear in it, nothing would have been touched since the last time Dennis was in there. I shivered, as if someone had walked over *my* grave.

It was warm inside the shed. Dust motes danced on a shaft of morning sunlight. The whirlybird creaked above me. Everything was neat and covered by a layer of dust, the roof laced with cobwebs. To be expected in a place that had remained relatively undisturbed for over a year. A bit like I'd been: undisturbed for a year. On a superficial level, I'd functioned from day to day, unwilling or unable—or a bit of both—to peel back that thin veneer of perceived normalness to see what lay beneath. Then an altercation with the cleaning lady and a few sharp comments from women I'd thought friends had been enough to strip away the facade.

The leaf rake stood alongside the other garden tools. I grabbed it and hightailed it out into the sunshine and fresh air. The atmosphere in the shed was thick with all things Dennis, from the shadow board of carefully arranged tools to the oil-stained rag left folded on the corner of the small bench.

With the green waste bin parked at the ready on the driveway and my gardening gloves and straw hat in place, I set about raking up the leaves. I'd been at it for barely five minutes when the neighbour on the town side of me reversed out of his driveway and nearly took out his gatepost gawping at me. Can't say that I blamed him. Me outside in the garden working was a rare sight indeed. I waved. He gave me a feeble but encouraging smile and tootled off.

It didn't take long before my arms and shoulders began to ache, but I mopped my brow and soldiered on. If I hadn't I wouldn't have witnessed the drama unfold across the street.

When the white late-model sedan barrelled into old Mrs Hall's driveway I didn't take too much notice, other than a passing thought that it'd been travelling faster than it should have been. But before the single occupant had leapt out and cleared the driveway I heard the unmistakable wail of a siren. Oh no. I sidled closer to my front fence. It was the ambulance coming from the other direction, red and blue lights flashing. It stopped in front of Mrs Hall's house. By now I was leaning on the rake and avidly watching what was playing out on the other side of the road.

Two paramedics alighted, grabbed their gear and took off along the driveway and down the side of the house. I didn't recognise either of them. Nothing else happened for some minutes so I went back to the leaves, but with an ear out for any further action across the street. Alas, I finished the job before the paramedics emerged, other than to collect the stretcher. I fetched the broom and swept down the paths and cement driveway. Still nothing. Perhaps the poor old dear hadn't made it. Using a bucket of hot soapy water, I scrubbed away the oil stain left on the cement by the erstwhile cleaning lady. Next thing, Rob Hall's ute pulled up in front of my place with the garden maintenance trailer in tow. Rob emerged from the cab.

'Is Mrs Hall okay?' I called, hurrying to the end of the driveway like a true busybody.

'She's refusing to let the ambos take her to the hospital, so my guess is she can't be too bad,' he said. 'Margie's there and she asked me to come and talk Mum into going with them and at least getting checked out.' Margie was his sister. He glanced across the road to his mother's house. 'Not sure that I'll have any more pull than they're having.'

'Would her doctor do a home visit? I know these days they don't make a habit of it, but they will do it.'

'No harm in asking,' he said, and scanned my leafless front lawn before his gaze shifted to the green waste bin and rake sitting nearby. 'You're not trying to do me out of a job are you, Kate?'

'No risk of that,' I said. 'The weather was too nice to be indoors.'

'It's good to see you out and about. I've got your lawn down to do this week. Probably Wednesday. I'd better get over there and sort them out.'

'If you need someone to check on your mum for a few days, I'd be happy to oblige.'

'I'll keep that in mind,' he said, his expression thoughtful. 'Thanks. Catch you later.'

He loped across the road. He was a fit, lean man about a decade or so younger than me. His mother was ninety. They'd had a family get-together to celebrate in the lead-up to this past Christmas. One of the party-goers had parked across my driveway. Not that I'd been going anywhere that day.

Now I knew what was going on over the road my interest waned. Green waste pickup wasn't until next week so I wheeled the bin back to its spot, put the rake away and went inside, all the while thinking about the plight of old Mrs Hall and imagining myself in a similar situation. Who'd rush to my aid, the way her children had rushed to hers? And did she have every right to refuse to go to the hospital? The last time I'd talked to her, a brief conversation over the fence some weeks ago, she'd sounded mentally on the ball. At the time I'd thought she'd been more on the ball than I had.

As I got older myself I'd noticed how often we use a person's age as a measure of their capacity to be self-determining—way more than we should. But did a person ever get too old to make decisions about their care and what happened to them? A decade ago I would have answered with a resounding yes, they did, and at that point families needed to step up and take on the responsibility. At seventy-two, I wasn't as certain. Ask me again at eighty-two. I had a feeling I might give an entirely different answer.

★★★

Tuesday morning came and went and still no sign of Daisy and her dog. When they didn't show Wednesday morning I experienced a moment's concern. Ridiculous. There were a dozen reasons why she hadn't walked past my place. Besides, it was none of my business; she could walk wherever she liked.

Just before lunch, Rob came and mowed the lawns as he'd promised. It was another glorious day. When he'd reloaded the mower and the edge trimmer into his ute I went outside to pay him.

'How's your mum?' I asked.

'Coming home this afternoon. Two nights is as long as I could coax her into staying in the hospital and the doc has given her a clean bill of health.' He shrugged. 'Who am I to argue?'

'So what happened?'

'Says she stood up and felt a bit dizzy, and doesn't remember anything until she woke up lying on the kitchen floor. In the meantime, when the Telecross volunteer couldn't raise her on the phone she contacted Margie and it went from there. At least we know that part of it works.'

'Will she be on her own when she comes home?'

He shook his head. 'Eleanor, my wife, will stay with her tonight because Margie can't. Knowing Mum, she won't want anyone there for long. She gets Meals on Wheels and other services, and the community nurse drops in every now and then. Not much more we can do than that.'

'Take it a day at a time, Rob, that's about all any of us can do. I'll pop over this evening and say hello.'

'Mum would appreciate that,' he said.

Weeks later, I'd reflect on that conversation with Rob and my decision to visit his mother, and how, in a roundabout sort of way, it had a profound effect on my life.

23

Daisy

Georgia had two younger brothers: Ryan and Mitchell. Mitch was the youngest at fifteen and Ryan a surly seventeen. Gareth and Tess had married young, within weeks of discovering Georgia was on the way. Never once had I offered a word of reproach—I knew how easily these things happened. Luckily, from years observing his own father, Gareth had learned a lot about how not to be a parent and they'd carefully planned the arrival of their subsequent children. Not to say there hadn't been the usual bumps in his parenting journey.

One such bump presented himself on Georgia's front doorstep late Wednesday afternoon. Unable to slough off the melancholy plaguing me since having afternoon tea with Kate on Sunday, the sight of a sullen Ryan, duffel bag slung over his shoulder, had my mood plummeting even further. Not that I wasn't pleased to see my grandson.

He gave Jess a cursory scratch behind the ears. 'George said I could stay for a few days,' he mumbled. He'd always called his sister George.

'You've talked to her?'

'Dad put me on the bus and rang her.'

'And where exactly did she tell your father you could sleep?' I opened the door and he came inside. Georgia was on an afternoon shift. 'Your sister has the only bed. I have the sofa, and I'm not budging. I don't think Jess will share her bed either.'

He dropped his duffel bag onto the floor and looked around. 'What a dump,' he said, going to the fridge. 'Anything to eat? I'm starving.'

I was too busy speed-dialling my eldest son to answer. Gareth picked up straight away. I took the call out onto the front verandah. There were no greetings from either end.

'It's just until the weekend, Mum. I'll drive up Saturday and fetch him, but we all needed some time out. Especially Tess, what with Mitch breaking his arm and needing surgery to sort it out.'

'And when was someone going to fill me in with *those* details?'

Gareth's sigh was long and deep. 'Mum, life here hasn't exactly been all beer and skittles of late. Mitch is fine now, but Ryan getting himself expelled from that posh private school I bust my gut to afford was the last straw.'

'Expelled? What on earth for?'

'Smoking dope. There were three of them. Interestingly enough, only two of them were expelled. I don't know what the matter is with the ungrateful little shit. I'd started my apprenticeship and was making my own way in the world by the time I was his age.'

'I'm sorry, son, truly I am, but have you seen the size of this house? There's barely enough room for Georgia and me. We can't both be in the kitchen at the same time and there's only one sofa to sit on, and that sofa doubles as my bed.'

Silence pulsed for several seconds.

'It's only for a couple of days, Mum,' he said. He sounded defeated. 'I need you to have a talk to him. You were alway good with me and Jay, Adam, any time we stuffed up. You just knew the right type and amount of discipline to dish out.'

'Trial and error,' I said. 'And you and Adam were never too bad. Jay, well, I doubt he'd have the same to say about my discipline as you do. And what's happening with the building project?'

More silence. My heart lurched.

I closed my eyes. 'Don't tell me nothing's happened since we last talked.'

'All right then, I won't tell you,' he said.

Ryan poked his head around the screen door. 'The cake in the fridge ... all right if I have a piece? And there's not much milk left.'

I waved an affirmative hand and he disappeared.

'Did you send anything for his keep? He's only been here five minutes and he's already started eating us out of house and home.'

'I'll transfer a hundred bucks into Georgia's bank account.'

'Why not my bank account? After all, I do the shopping and the cooking, and the washing and cleaning. Don't worry about me not earning my keep, even though I'm paying my way.'

Another one of those long and deep sighs. 'Don't be like that, Mum. It'll all work out in the end. You'll see.'

That was the problem: I was finding it harder by the day to see how it was all going to work out. All of a sudden, having a home of my own became much more urgent.

Gareth promised to collect Ryan Sunday afternoon at the latest and said goodbye and I half-heartedly agreed to talk to him. Already his stay had been extended by a day. I don't know why Gareth hadn't just said at the start that he'd pick him up Sunday afternoon.

When I rang Glenys and asked if she had a blow-up mattress or something I could borrow for Ryan to sleep on, she generously offered the loan of a folding camp bed and a sleeping bag. It was autumn and the nights were cool.

'Okay to drive out and collect them now?' I said.

'Yes, of course, and you'll stay for tea. I've made a lasagne and I'd love to meet Ryan. He's Gareth's middle one, isn't he?'

'That's right, but you certainly don't need extra mouths to feed,' I said. I'd spent a chunk of the previous day helping Glenys with her dad. He was failing fast and more cantankerous along with it. She'd looked to be at the end of her tether.

'There's plenty of food, Daisy,' she said. 'And your company would be wonderful.'

In the time it had taken me to make those two calls, Ryan had finished the chocolate cake and the milk and worked out how to use the remote for the smart TV. I'd been there for weeks and hadn't mastered that one yet.

'Come on,' I said. 'We're going out to collect a bed for you to sleep on.'

'Can I drive, Gran? I've got my Ls.'

'With you?'

He shook his head.

'Not happening then.'

His shoulders slumped and his bottom lip jutted, a facsimile of his sister when she didn't get her own way.

'Get over it,' I said, 'and let's go.' I scooped up the car keys and slipped the phone into my trouser pocket.

'Do I have to come?'

'They've invited us both for tea so it would be rude if you didn't come. And you'll get a much better meal there than you'll get here.'

He snorted. 'Who are these people?'

'They're your relatives,' I said brightly. 'Your granddad Charlie's cousin and her husband. They live on a farm about twenty minutes out.'

'I've never met them.'

'Now's your chance.'

Ryan slouched into the front seat of the car. Jess wasn't impressed at being relegated to the back. I would have preferred not to have been in the car at all. I was getting to know the road out to the Carlisles' like the back of my hand and was relieved that Trev had taken to filling my petrol tank from the farm supply.

'Can we at least get a bottle of Coke on the way?'

I started the car and glanced at him. He was the picture of misery: arms folded, face set in a scowl.

'What's the magic word?' I said.

His expression turned downright fierce and I had to press my lips together to hold back the amusement.

'Please,' he grumbled, as if he were giving up a state secret to an interrogator.

We stopped at the service station and he sloped off to get the soft drink. I didn't offer to pay.

When he got back to the car, I said, 'Ryan, please look at me.' It was an effort but he did turn towards me and eventually made eye contact. 'You're here until the weekend. I get that you'd probably rather be elsewhere, but you're not. I promise not to judge you for what you allegedly did at school and in return I expect to be treated with respect. Glenys is looking forward to meeting you and I will not tolerate any disrespect towards her or Trev. Got it?'

He looked away and mumbled something that I took to be agreement. From the back seat, Jess yipped, her way of telling me it was time to get moving. I put the car in gear and we were on our way. Ryan took out his phone and began that relentless scrolling the younger ones did. Georgia was the same. It must be a mutant gene they'd all inherited.

★ ★ ★

'Mate, are you stupid or what? If you're going to smoke dope, don't get caught.' Georgia threw down her bag and toed off her shoes.

Beside me on the sofa, Ryan rolled his eyes, but I could tell he was pleased to see his sister. We'd been watching TV since coming home from the Carlisles' an hour or so earlier. We'd bought milk on the way home. The camp stretcher was made up as far from my 'bedroom' as was possible, which wasn't much more than an arm's length.

'How was your shift?' I said.

'Not bad. A chest pain who ended up being retrieved. No-one was off sick for a change. I saw Lisa. She was on the morning shift. Jake's taken off again. Reckons he's gone to find work.' She raised her eyebrows. 'That'll be the day.'

'You know, Georgia, you're awfully cynical for someone of your tender age. There's always the chance that Jake's doing exactly that and he will find a job.'

'Whatever,' she said. 'I'm starving.' She went to the fridge. 'What happened to the chocolate cake?' She nailed her brother with a malignant stare.

'Gran said I could have it,' he said, with a casual roll of his shoulders.

'You asked if you could have a *piece* of it,' I said, and the tone was set for the remainder of Ryan's stay.

That night I lay awake until the wee hours, listening to Ryan snore on one side and Jess on the other. She'd been sleeping in since the nights began to cool. Even with the privacy screen I could feel the heat emanating from Ryan. It was like having a radiator in the room. As I lay there I asked myself how come I'd ended up in the situation I was in? There were no ready answers. There never was. Life was like a row of dominoes: you push one over and the rest follow suit; every action had a knock-on effect. My last thought as I drifted off to sleep was of Kate, ensconced in that huge house, five minutes' walk and as many empty bedrooms away.

Life wasn't fair, but then I'd always known that.

24

Kate

Daisy and her dog were back Friday morning, but walking on the opposite side of the street. In a hurry, by the way they were striding it out. She was wearing the usual pink T-shirt and lycra shorts. The dog trotted along beside her. I didn't rap on the window and wave, or make any move to go outside and call out hello. Even at this distance she appeared preoccupied. Besides, I wasn't up to facing her, not after what I'd read in my journals in the small hours.

I yawned. I'd stayed up reading until very late. First the book club read and, when I'd finished that, buoyed by a satisfactory ending, I'd moved on to the first of my journals. They'd been packed in chronological order in a shoebox inside the suitcase. Now, the morning after finishing the first slim volume, I was in two minds as to whether I should continue reading or just burn them and be done with it. Not all things that happen in our lives need to be, or should be, revisited. The jury was out on whether I'd be doing myself a favour or a disservice if I persisted with reading the journals.

Of course I hadn't dropped off to sleep straight away after I'd finished the first journal. Memories of that episode of my life so many years before had weighed heavily on my mind. Daisy had been a consistent and significant presence at the time. On one page of the journal I'd described that shocking afternoon when she'd come to the farm and told me she was pregnant. Anger, jealousy and resentment had poured out of the tip of my pen. I'd pressed so hard as to score the page in several places. The volume had ended with the birth of her first son in the wake of my first miscarriage. Not wanting to jinx myself, I hadn't told a soul other than Dennis that I was pregnant. But I'd been jinxed regardless.

I moved away from the window. Daisy had long since disappeared around the corner. It was early, not yet eight. Mrs Hall, or Rhonda as she insisted I call her, would be expecting me soon. I'd popped by yesterday afternoon and offered to return this morning to assist with her morning routine. She was doing remarkably well. She was mentally sharp, with her iPad and smart phone on the couch beside her. But she was ninety and as frail as you might expect. We'd both enjoyed the company.

This morning Rhonda answered the door minus her walking frame. She was dressed in navy blue track pants and a soft lavender-coloured knit top, her silvery-white hair neatly coiffed in its usual French twist. I don't know how she did that. If ever I tried it my hair looked like a bird's nest held together with twenty bobby pins.

She beamed at me and bragged about not needing the frame.

'But is that wise? It's quite a way down the passage.' I said. 'What if you tripped? Lost your balance?'

'At my age, must I always be wise, Kate? I slept so well and I wanted to see if I could do it, and I did. Don't worry, I wouldn't venture outside without the dratted thing. Come in. Is that the strawberry conserve you mentioned?' She eyed the jar in my hand.

'The very same. I hope you enjoy it. Now, what do you need me to do?'

'Breakfast. Have you eaten?'

'Not yet.'

'Join me then, and we'll chat over tea and toast.'

'Tea would be lovely,' I said.

'Oh no! You must have some toast with it. Eleanor buys me this most wonderful sourdough bread. I could eat it three meals a day.'

I glanced at the strawberry conserve in my hand. Why not? It's what I'd be eating if I was home.

We were on our second cup of tea when I found myself telling Rhonda about Dennis's boxes.

'I have no idea what I should do with the contents. They were special to him. An op shop or secondhand dealer doesn't feel like the appropriate place for them. But what to do? Tell me what you did with your husband's belongings. Those special things that were a part of what made him who he was.'

'They're all where Stephen left them, God rest his soul.' She laughed with genuine mirth and her eyes twinkled. 'After the funeral the kids took whatever memento they wanted. Rob took his watch, an old Swiss timepiece that had been Stephen's father's, and Margie wanted his shaving set, of all things. When I die they'll get the whole kit and caboodle to sort through and do with what they so choose. They're only things, I tell myself. But they were precious to Stephen and he was precious to me and I haven't had the heart to clear them all out.'

'That's the dilemma I'm faced with. And what do you do when you don't have any children?' I said, embarrassed by my plaintive tone.

'Nieces, nephews?'

I shook my head. 'I've been down that pathway already. Not interested.'

'And your late husband hadn't been married previously?'

'Not to my knowledge,' I said, taken aback. What an odd thing to ask. And why would she? 'Do you know something I don't?'

Her eyes widened. 'No! Of course not, my dear,' she said. 'If my daughter Margie were here now she'd tell you that I watch too many soap operas on the television and that I never know when to mind my own business. That said, and in my experience, fact often is stranger than fiction and life is a bit of a soap opera.'

'We tried to have a family but couldn't,' I said. 'All my fault, as it so happened.'

'Luck of the draw, I'm afraid. Nothing to be gained from blaming yourself. Back then there was no IVF or other treatments readily available, not like there are today,' she said matter-of-factly. 'My dear sister wasn't blessed with children and it broke her and her husband's hearts, but they picked up the pieces and moved on. It was all you could do.'

'And you think you've all the time in the world and then suddenly your time's up: no more eggs left. On top of that it's easy to forget, or gloss over, the impact it has on the male half of the equation, isn't it?' After reading only one journal it had become painfully clear to me that I'd been so caught up in my own self-absorbed grief that I hadn't been as attentive to Dennis's emotional needs as I should have been. He'd wanted to be a father as desperately as I'd wanted to be a mother. Very confronting, the idea that I'd carelessly ignored him and made it all about me.

'What about someone else's children or grandchildren?' Rhonda said, and I tuned back into our conversation. 'Is there anyone who might appreciate the sentimental value of his belongings? Someone who knew your late husband, and liked and respected him?'

For some reason I thought of the man with the flashy city clothes the florist had described. Was he someone who'd known and respected Dennis? But from where? And how would I ever find out?

'I've put everything back into the cupboard for the time being,' I said.

Rhonda reached across the kitchen table and patted my arm. 'And I'm sure that's the best place for now, Kate. One day you might find it a comfort knowing they're there, close by.'

I went home soon after that. With all the service workers that came in, Rhonda didn't really need my help at all. She'd been the one to set the breakfast table and make the toast. But when I left she said, 'I'll see you in the morning. Same time? I have a jar of cherry jam I've been saving. Food always tastes so much nicer when you share a mealtime with another, don't you think?'

I didn't have the heart to refuse. She was right. I didn't enjoy my solitary mealtimes as much as I'd once imagined I would.

★ ★ ★

On the weekend Eric Sanderson returned the box containing Uncle Frank's journals.

'I'm sorry, Kate,' he said when I didn't try to hide my disappointment. 'I've had a good look through them and we have a lot of very similar documents in our collections. Rainfall records and crop rotations are something farmers are diligent at notating. And as I said, we don't have the space to store excess documents. But you could try the Miners Ridge history group, given the property detailed in the journals is in their neighbourhood. They had disbanded but I hear there's a handful of interested younger ones … When I say younger, I mean retired but not in their dotage yet.'

He carried the box through to the family room and set it down where instructed.

'Oh, and Kate,' he said, wiping his hands fastidiously on his handkerchief, 'there are several diaries and a few photos in the box that are a much later vintage than Frank Hannaford's journals. I think they might have belonged to Dennis. When I realised what they were I put them straight back into the box.'

'Oh, dear,' I said. 'How embarrassing for you. And me. I should have looked in there before I gave it to you.'

He waved aside my apology. 'Not the first time something like that's occurred. You'd be amazed at what we find between the pages of old books or journals, behind framed photographs ...'

'I thought that only happened in the movies.'

He smiled. 'If you do decide to pass on the journals, best you flick through them first, is what I'm saying.'

'I hear what you're saying, Eric. And thank you.' I saw him out.

He paused as he was leaving. 'By the way, if you're at all interested in local history, Kate, we're always looking for new members. It'd be a real disappointment to see the group fold.'

Hell might freeze over first. When I'd retired, I vowed I'd never join another committee or working party, or ever go to another meeting. Even now, years later, that resolve remained firm. Every week I read the local rag and one service club or another was on the verge of going under because they no longer had enough members. The ambulance and the CFS were always on the lookout for new volunteers. Younger people just weren't interested. That's not to say Eric's comment didn't get me thinking, flirting briefly with the idea of volunteering for something that didn't require being on a committee or going to meetings. I could do that. Because how else was I going to fill in the days? I took in the spotlessly clean family room. There was only so much housework I could do. Once I'd given the family room and kitchen and then the bathrooms a complete going over, the remainder of the house had been easy. It's not as if I'd ever forgotten *how* to clean.

Now that I had all the time in the world to do whatever I wanted to do, I suddenly couldn't think of anything I had a burning desire to do. Was it too early to have a glass of wine?

25

Daisy

Ryan didn't want to go home with his father. The tension between the two of them was palpable from the moment Gareth arrived to collect him. This was about more than Ryan being caught smoking a joint in his school uniform in the parklands opposite the school. Self-preservation warned me to keep well out of it.

'Tess and Mitch didn't come?' I said.

Gareth shoved his hands into his pockets and shook his head. 'Adam says howdy. We had a beer a couple of days ago. They finally gave him some time off. He said to tell you they're all doing okay.'

'And Jay?'

'Dunno. No-one's seen or heard from him,' he said. 'Ryan, grab your gear, I need to get back.'

Slouched on the sofa, phone in hand and earbuds in his ears, Ryan acted as if he hadn't heard his father.

'You'll at least stay for a coffee, won't you?' I'd already filled the electric kettle and turned it on.

He'd been going to refuse, I could see the words forming on his lips. His gaze travelled from me to the hissing kettle and the mugs set out on the sink, and back to me.

'All right,' he said. 'But we won't stay long. Where's Georgia?'

'Working. Day shift. She should be home soon.'

He leaned against the kitchen cupboard and surveyed the living area. 'This place really is a dump,' he said. 'I'm being robbed.'

'Then we all are, given we're all paying an equal share of the rent. At least Georgia gets her own room,' I said.

He grunted.

'Ryan, do you want a hot drink?'

'No thanks, Gran,' he said.

Gareth looked at me and raised his eyebrows. Ryan stood and went outside. Moments later I heard him talking to Jess. I made the coffee.

'How's he been?' Gareth said.

'Pretty good once I set the ground rules. You remember Glenys and Trevor Carlisle? Glenys is your dad's cousin. I've been helping her with her elderly father, and while I did that, Ryan was out on the tractor with Trev, doing jobs around the farm.'

Gareth's eyebrows shot up even further. 'This is the same Ryan we're talking about?'

'Yep.' I handed my son his coffee. 'He hates school, Gareth. Reading between the lines, I think he's being bullied by a couple of older, wealthier boys. You know how they can be, think they're entitled because Mummy and Daddy have got money. I heard him talking to Georgia about it.'

Gareth blew on his coffee, took a tentative sip and then added another glug of milk. 'He won't have to bother about that any more, will he? As luck would have it, Tess and I had already made the decision to take him out next semester and send him to a public school.'

'Had you talked to Ryan about that?'

'Not yet. This happened before we had a chance to. It's not as if academically he's ever going to set the world on fire. We're just throwing away money sending him there. At least Mitch knuckles down.'

'How's Mitch's arm? I'd thought you'd bring him for the drive.'

'Yeah, sorry about that. His arm's healing. The doctor's happy. And he wanted to come but he had some school project to finish.'

I studied my eldest son. 'You look worn out. Have you lost weight? Is everything all right?'

He pursed his lips and then gave a tired sigh. 'Just the same old, same old, Mum. Tess had a lump in her breast—'

'What?' I gasped.

'It's okay. Turns out it's nothing to worry about, but we did for a while.'

'Why didn't you tell me?'

'We would have if it'd turned out to be more than a benign lump.'

'Do the boys know? What about Georgia?'

'We had to tell the boys. They knew something was up. Tess told Georgia when she first felt the lump. Before she told me, as a matter of fact.'

'Oh, Gareth, why didn't any of you tell me all of this earlier? Perhaps I could have helped in some way. And Georgia, knowing and not telling me!'

'Tess asked her to keep it confidential. She didn't want anyone to know until after she'd had the lumpectomy and we were certain all was well.'

I heard a car and then the slam of a car door. Jess yipped; a happy sound. Georgia was home.

Gareth downed his coffee and put the mug in the sink. 'I'll say howdy to the girl and then we'd better get going. What should I do about Ryan, Mum?'

'Tread softly. Remember how you were with your dad at that age. All those raging hormones. Ryan's becoming a man and it's quite an upheaval for everyone, including himself. He's not sure where he fits any more. And Trev said he can come back any time and help out on the farm; work off some of that excess energy. Maybe next school holidays?'

Gareth gave me a one-armed hug. 'Thanks, Mum,' he said. 'I sometimes think none of us deserve you.'

'Just get the building project back on track, son. I need my own home again. I'm too old to be bunking on a sagging sofa bed. And it's not fair on Georgia either.'

He swallowed but didn't say anything. Intuition told me that whatever he had to say I wouldn't want to hear, so when Georgia chose that moment to burst through the front door, I stepped back and didn't press the issue any further. For now.

'Dad! You're here. What's happening? Why didn't Mum come too?' She dropped her car keys and bag and threw herself into her father's embrace. His shoulders visibly relaxed.

'She sends her love but she wanted to catch up on a few things, and aren't you driving down on your next weekend off?'

That was news to me, but then I hadn't been privy to Tess's recent lumpectomy or Mitch's surgery, either. Feeling like a spectator, I turned my back to them and ran water into the sink to wash the few dishes and coffee mugs. I blinked away the foolish tears that welled in my eyes. Almost seventy I might be, but that didn't mean my feelings couldn't be hurt.

Gareth and Ryan took off about fifteen minutes later. Ryan had chucked his duffel bag into the back of the LandCruiser and climbed into the passenger seat without speaking a word to his father. We waved them off from the gateway. Max's cat Pauline

eyed us disdainfully from the top of the fence post. Jess pretended
to ignore her.

'Wouldn't want to be in the car for that trip,' Georgia said as
we walked up the driveway to the house. 'And I promised Mum
I wouldn't say anything to anyone about her lump. Turns out it's
not the first one she's had and as the only daughter, she thought I
needed to know.'

'That's fair enough, Georgia. We're all entitled to our secrets and
our privacy. As long as Tess's okay.'

'She is now. It's Dad we're worried about,' she said, with a quick
sideways glance my way. 'Mum says he's under so much pressure
with the business and all this crap with Ryan.'

'The business? In what way?' I said, my mouth suddenly dry. I
opened the front door and we went inside. I headed straight for the
electric kettle. I know I'd not long had a coffee but I needed a cup
of tea.

'What a day,' Georgia said and flopped down onto the sofa.
'Apparently, there's plenty of work but the materials Dad needs to
do the jobs are in short supply or not available at all, and there's
always one of his workmen off because of Covid. People who owe
him money aren't paying because they have similar problems to
deal with. I said for him to stop his share of the rent, that we'd
manage.' She had her head resting back and her eyes closed. 'I hope
you don't mind.'

'Busy shift?' I said, because paying extra rent was the last thing I
wanted to think about.

Unbeknown to my family, I had a small amount of savings squir-
relled away for a rainy day. Was I getting closer to that day? The
plan had been to use it to buy a better car, or furnish the new townhouse when that eventuated. A modest holiday even. Not more

rent. The savings were what was left of my superannuation, and it wouldn't buy me a house. It wouldn't come close to being a deposit on a cheap house in a back-water country town. Besides, who'd give a pensioner a loan for the remainder?

Another alternative was to spend the money on a caravan and live in that. The mere thought made me feel physically sick. What of Jess? I could not part with her. I *would* not part with her. There were caravan parks that accepted pets, but a lot didn't. And there was limit to how long you could stay. But a caravan? Shared amenities? Comprehending that I had to think about such things was almost beyond me. What had I worked my whole life for? To end up living in a caravan?

'Gran?' Georgia said, not quite shouting. She was standing an arm's length in front of me, her face creased with concern. I hadn't noticed her get up from the sofa.

'What?'

'Where did you go there for a minute?' she said.

'Just thinking. Not happy thoughts. Do you want a cup of tea?'

She regarded me for a moment. 'No time,' she said. Funnily enough, I felt as if I'd been given a small reprieve. 'Kieran's cooking for me and Lisa, and we were going to eat early. And Gran, I don't expect you to pay any more rent than you already are. Don't forget I was managing it on my own before you came.' She began unbuttoning her blouse. 'I'll shower and go.' She gave me a peck on the cheek. 'You can have the place all to yourself for a change.'

About an hour later Jess and me were back from the takeaway with fish and chips for tea. We were ready to settle in for the evening when my phone pinged with a message from Gareth: *We're home. Thanks for taking care of Ryan. He's ok with public school. More relieved than anything. Talk soon. G.*

I flicked back a thumbs up. The fish and chips were getting cold, and besides, what could I say? They'd sort it out or not.

★ ★ ★

It was after ten when I heard Georgia's car in the driveway. I was watching a very B-grade movie on Netflix. Jess was asleep, flat out in the narrow space between the television and the coffee table. When Georgia came in, the dog lifted her head briefly and swept her tail back and forth across the floor a couple of times. Georgia had a rosy flush to her cheeks and a sparkle in her eyes.

'Good time?' I said, pausing the movie.

'Yep.' She yawned. 'The two blokes Kieran shares with were home. We had such a laugh. Even Lisa, which was excellent.'

'Jake still away?'

'Permanently, if my wish came true.' She filled a glass with water and came and sat down beside me. 'Would you believe Kieran's bought a house? He's only three years older than me and he's already saved enough for a deposit. The place needs work he said, but he'll do as much of it as he can himself. And his dad will help—he was a carpenter.'

'Really? So why does he mow lawns for a living?'

'Dunno. Probably got sick of being a carpenter. He does handyman stuff as well as garden maintenance. So does Kieran.' She finished the glass of water. 'Did Dad message you to say they got home okay?'

'He did, and apparently your brother doesn't mind the idea of a public school.'

'No surprises there.' She leapt to her feet. 'I'm going to bed. Do you want a hand to make up yours before I do?'

'Thanks. This movie is garbage, anyway,' I said, heaving myself off the sofa. 'Had you noticed that the tap on the basin in the bathroom is dripping? And the toilet needs a new washer. Who do you tell? The landlord? So he can fix it?'

'Good question,' she said. 'I just pay the rent into a bank account.'

'Don't you have a rental agreement?'

'Nope.'

'Who gave you the bank account details?'

'They came in an email.'

'Let's go back a step: how did you know the house was for rent in the first place?'

She frowned. We shifted the sofa and unfolded it. 'Dad told me. Said it belonged to a friend of a friend, or some such thing. When I first looked at it I thought, nah, what a dump. But I definitely didn't like living in the nurses' home and there was nothing else around in my price range.'

'Sounds a bit suspect to me. So what do we do about the dripping tap?'

'I've been here over a year and the rent hasn't gone up so I'm happy. Lisa's unit is through an agent and her rent's increased every six months. I can ask Kieran to fix the tap,' she said, as if that were a no-brainer.

We finished making the bed and she went off to use the bathroom. I let Jess out to do her pre-bedtime business. I sat on the edge of my bed and waited until Georgia finished in the bathroom. Here it was the end of another day. After Gareth's blow-through visit and Georgia's revelations, I was feeling even more powerless and unsettled than I had before. One thing I knew for sure, I didn't like feeling the way I did: old, and ashamed that I hadn't provided better for myself.

26

Kate

By the middle of the following week I couldn't pretend any longer that I was visiting Rhonda because she needed my assistance. The few chores I did for her were inconsequential. I'm sure she thought them up to keep me coming over and I found that I didn't mind that at all.

'There you are, my dear,' she'd say on opening the front door to my knock, the greeting alway accompanied by a broad smile. 'What shall we have on our toast this morning?' If she was leaning on the walker I'd know she hadn't had the best of nights and was feeling a wee bit wonky.

This morning we'd miss our tea and toast together because she had a doctor's appointment. Her daughter was picking her up. Margie's car was already parked in Rhonda's driveway when I went out to collect the *Advertiser* off the front lawn. 'I don't know what the poor man's going to tell me that I haven't worked out for myself: I'm old and I'm wearing out,' Rhonda had said the previous morning. 'Not one of us lives forever.'

I took my toast and coffee out to the patio with the newspaper and journal number four. I was halfway through this volume. Had I known all along that I would eventually read them and that's why I'd kept them?

They hadn't been what you'd call *easy* reading and I will admit, but only to myself, in some places I sounded downright whiny. Ashamedly, the further along I read only reaffirmed what I'd said to Rhonda: I'd never given more than a cursory thought to what Dennis might have been going through at the time. He'd had my misery to deal with along with his own disappointment.

I was up to was 1980; four and a bit years of trying to conceive and then maintain a pregnancy past the first trimester. I'd turned thirty that year. My periods had been hopelessly irregular. How many times had I thought I was pregnant, only to be devastated a day or a week later? I'd put on weight and couldn't shift it, no matter how much I monitored what I ate. My GP kept telling me to relax, that I was too uptight and if I just loosened up, it would happen. Of course it was always the woman's fault. And did I mention that Daisy had given birth to her second child by then? Another bouncing boy. Jay. Barely two years after their first son, Gareth.

I rested the journal on the table beside the half-eaten toast, butter and jam congealing on its surface. I sat back in the chair and exhaled a long, slow breath as I remembered vividly what an emotional wreck I'd been back then. Life had been a rollercoaster. My primary focus: was I ovulating? If I thought I was: where was Dennis? In the beginning it had been fun, but as the months multiplied into years, conceiving became my obsession; an unnatural obsession which had nothing to do with lovemaking and intimacy. To Dennis's credit, he'd taken it all in his stride. Every now and then he'd mumble something about stud fees, but he had never complained.

For several minutes I sat and shut out everything but the gentle warmth of the sun, the occasional flurry of breeze and the rustle of the potted palms on the patio. Magpies warbled from the neighbours' trees.

Inevitably, as I'd progressed through my thirties, the obsession to have a child had burned itself out, and a part of me went with it. I didn't need to read the journals to know that. Daisy's third son was born only months before I'd turned thirty-five. Adam. Like I mentioned earlier, I'd been so twisted up with bitterness and resentment, I hadn't even visited her in the hospital.

Truly, my predicament had had nothing whatsoever to do with Daisy. Not her fault, not in the slightest, but in my mind I'd blamed her just the same. I reached for the journal and flicked to the page where I'd written in thick, black capitals that I LOATHED her, because at that point in time she'd had two healthy babies and I'd had none. But then in the very next sentence I'd written: *Saw Daisy M today. She's back working full time and she looks exhausted; almost ill. I wouldn't be surprised if she was anaemic. I told her to get the doctor to check her haemoglobin. Someone should shoot that good-for-nothing husband of hers!!!*

There it was, mention after mention of her, all with a recurring theme: me worried about the state of Daisy's health, but jealous and angry along with it. It's almost as if there'd been two Kates: one the caring and concerned friend, the other an embittered and irksome foe. Had I managed to always keep a lid on the second Kate? To the external world perhaps, but I know I hadn't with Dennis. To him I'd ranted and raved ad nauseam about the unfairness of it all.

It struck me then and there, and it was like a physical blow, just how awful I would have been to live with. How thankless it would have been to be my friend. And it wasn't only for a month or two, it'd been for *years.* How had Dennis put up with me? But he had. If he'd faltered along the way I hadn't noticed, nor would I have blamed him for it if he had. Would it have been better for us both if, just once, he'd been the one to sound off about the unfairness of it all?

I clutched the journal tightly to my chest and whispered, 'I am so sorry, Dennis.'

That he wasn't there to hear my long overdue apology was nothing more than I deserved. He'd hung in there when a lesser man might have jumped ship. What wisdom came with hindsight. If you let it.

What was left of my coffee was cold. I stood up with purpose: I'd make a fresh cup and read the newspaper. Don't think for a second that I was ready to give up on reading the journals. Now that I'd started I would finish all eight of them. However, I made myself a promise: I wouldn't dwell on what I read there. The past weeks of unhealthy introspection had given me an insight into where that path might lead: nowhere but self-destruction, by one means or another. Nothing would bring Dennis back or change the past. The only way to go was forward. One day at a time.

★★★

Molly and Lewis surprised me with a whirlwind visit on Friday afternoon. It was just what I needed. They were on their way to Adelaide and it was quite a detour for them. The pleasure I experienced when I opened the door to them was heartfelt.

'It's my sister's sixtieth birthday celebration tomorrow,' Molly said. 'She actually turns sixty-one on Sunday, but because there was no getting together last year, she's having the bash on the last day of her sixtieth year.'

'Not that your sister ever needs an excuse to pop a champagne cork,' Lewis said.

Molly elbowed him in the ribs. 'You always have a good time, and don't deny it,' she said.

They hadn't eaten lunch so I offered to make them a sandwich while the pot of tea brewed.

'Uncle Frank's journals are through there in the family room, if you want to have a quick glance,' I said to Lewis, eyebrows raised. 'The local history group didn't want them. I might try one further afield so if you want to look, now's your chance.'

Lewis nodded and wandered through to where they were.

'It's lovely to see you, but it's a bit out of your way,' I said when there was only Molly and me in the kitchen.

'We haven't seen you since Dennis's funeral, and that's far too long to leave between visits,' she said. 'Losing him so suddenly hammered home how precious life is, and none of us is getting any younger.'

She was perched on a stool on the opposite side of the island bench, smiling, her chin resting in her hands. She watched as I gathered the sandwich ingredients. I'd always thought of her as a tad bohemian, with her halo of greying curls and cheesecloth skirts. She'd cut through the prattle and say what needed to be said, but never in an offensive manner.

'We stopped at the cemetery on our way here,' she said. 'Although they didn't see each other, they talked often and Lew misses him.'

'How often did they talk?'

'Weekly, sometimes more often … Depending on what was happening on the farm.'

The butter knife stilled. I swallowed. 'I'm learning all these things about my husband after his death that would have been nice to know while he was alive.'

Molly lifted her shoulders. 'It's always the way. And sometimes the information is available but we're so caught up with our own stuff we just don't see it.'

I nodded, sharply, and went back to buttering the bread.

'I learned things about Mum at her funeral that I hadn't ever known. It annoyed me that the celebrant knew more about my own mother than I did,' I said, half to myself. I layered roast beef onto the bread. 'Tomato sauce?'

She nodded. 'We'd love you to come and stay with us, Kate. For as long as you like. It'd be nice to have another woman around the house for a while.'

'It's kind of you to offer—' I said. I knew I was frowning when I said it.

She laughed, an infectious tinkle of mirth. 'I didn't mean to put you on the spot. I just wanted you to know the offer is there, and will remain so indefinitely.'

I arranged the sandwiches on a plate.

'I'll go get Lew,' she said, sliding off the stool.

'No need, I'm here,' he said. 'Frank's journals are similar to the old man's records. Only difference is there was more rain over this way.'

He pulled up a bar stool and needed no encouragement to start on the sandwiches. I poured the tea. Molly tucked in. With the best part of two hours left to travel, they ate and ran.

Molly said as I saw them off, 'It was so good to see you, Kate. And you sound a lot better than you did when we talked on the phone.' She hugged me tightly, and so did Lewis. It was all a bit overwhelming.

The house felt lonely after they'd gone. Molly's energy and quirky sense of humour had brightened the place for a moment. Back in the family room I noticed Lewis had left several of Uncle Frank's annals stacked on the coffee table in front of Dennis's recliner. It was the sort of thing Dennis would have done. With a pang of nostalgia, I let them sit there over the weekend.

Sunday evening, not even the tiniest bit curious about the contents, I returned the journals to the box. There on top were the notebooks Eric Sanderson had mentioned. In an attempt to lift them out with one hand, they slipped out of my grip and slid onto the floor, spewing out a dozen or so photos on the way down. I bent to retrieve them. There were several colour photos taken around the farm, and the missing black and white snaps of Uncle Frank posing with various farm implements. Plus one other: a smiling teenage boy with a shock of sandy-coloured hair. Dennis, I thought, and smoothed my fingers across the print. I flipped over the photo to see if there was a date written on the other side. No date, just: *Tom, Year 7.*

27

Daisy

For over a week now Jess and I had been taking a different route for our walks. A change of scenery was all, or so I told myself, but I knew part of the reason was because I didn't want to bump into Kate. If she was out in her front yard when we walked past I'd feel obliged to stop and make conversation; she'd ask me in for a cuppa and, knowingly or not, flaunt all of what she had and I didn't. Kate would have joined the dots by now and worked out that although my situation was different, it was certainly no better this time around.

While I wasn't thrilled about my current circumstances, up until I'd run into Kate Hannaford, I'd been thankful for what I had and optimistic about the future. But that optimism and gratitude were being slowly chipped away by the day. Not Kate's fault entirely, but the part that had me dwelling morbidly on the past could be dumped fairly and squarely at her feet. What was it about her that could still make me feel ashamed of who I was and what I had, or didn't have? I thought I'd long ago outgrown those silly feelings of insecurity.

What irritated me the most was that Charlie Toogood, the person I'd painstakingly relegated to the periphery of my consciousness, was back in my thoughts, front and centre, and in a way that had me feeling twitchy. To a degree, the frequent contact I was having with Bill Toogood could account for some of that unease. Bill was a lot like his brother Joe, and Charlie had been a dead ringer for his dad.

Today's walk had become a trudge. Jess glanced up at me when I sighed deeply. It was early, because I'd promised Glenys I'd be out at the farm by nine, and I hadn't slept well. Glenys was keen to do her grocery shopping and other errands. My guess was she desperately needed respite from Bill, if only for a while. I know I wasn't looking forward to spending several hours alone with him. The physical care didn't bother me in the least, but he had little tolerance for what needed to be done. I'd come to the conclusion that he didn't have a tolerant or grateful bone in his body. Glenys's infinite patience with him was worthy of a medal.

It was Monday morning and Kieran's ute and trailer was parked out the front when we got home from our walk. He'd come to fix the leaky washers. Georgia had a day off and I heard voices and laughter as we came up the drive. You would have had to have been blind not to see what was going on there. My level-headed granddaughter was falling hard. Not too old to have forgotten what it was to be young and in the first flush of attraction, I knocked loudly on the door before I went inside.

Georgia poked her head out of the bathroom door. 'Oh, it's only you, Gran.'

'Only me,' I said. 'Has Kieran nearly finished?'

'Yep,' he called from the bathroom. 'Packing up the tools now.'

'After breakfast I'll shower and be on my way. Glenys is expecting me by nine.'

'Are you going to be out there all day?' Georgia propped herself against the kitchen cupboard while I filled the kettle and spooned instant coffee into a mug.

'Not if I can help it. What shall we have for tea tonight?'

Kieran emerged from the bathroom carrying a toolbox. 'I'll bring around some whiting if you like. Me and the boys went fishing a couple of weekends ago and the freezer's full.'

'Inviting yourself to tea, are you?' Georgia said with a cheeky smile.

'Sure am. You two do the chips and salad and I'll provide the fish.'

'Sounds fair,' I said, and tried to inject a modicum of enthusiasm into my voice. No-one liked being the third wheel. 'I'll do potato chips in the oven, and there's salad stuff in the fridge.'

I made coffee and left it to cool while I took a quick shower. When I came out of the bathroom I could see Georgia on the footpath, leaning in the ute's passenger-side window, talking to Kieran. I'd finished my coffee and muesli before I heard him toot as he drove off.

'What have you got on your agenda for today?' I said when she came inside.

'Getting my hair trimmed at ten, and then I might have a coffee and a sandwich with Lisa before she goes to work.' She glanced around. 'Perhaps I'll tidy up this afternoon and run the vacuum over the floors.'

'What a good idea,' I said. 'And the laundry basket's full of your clean clothes ready to be put away.'

'Okay.'

Jess was waiting by the door, tail wagging. When I picked up the car keys she knew a drive was on the cards.

There was no sign of Trev's ute and his dogs when we arrived at the farm. I let Jess out of the car and she zoomed off, nose to the ground. Glenys met me at the back door. She must have been on the lookout for my car.

'I'm not sure if I should go,' she said. 'Dad seems—' She frowned and shrugged simultaneously. 'Different?'

'How so?'

'Quieter. He's hardly said boo this morning. And he refused to get out of bed.'

'Did he eat breakfast?'

She nodded. 'Porridge.'

'I wouldn't worry then. He could be tired.'

'I suppose so,' she said, not sounding totally convinced. 'I know he's not going to get better, Daisy, but I'd hate for him to be suffering.'

'Let me go and say hello,' I said. I put my bag on the kitchen table and we went to see how he was.

Crowded into the doorway of his room, we held our breath. There, the gentle rise and fall of the mound beneath the bedclothes.

'Still asleep,' Glenys whispered, wide-eyed.

'He doesn't appear to be suffering,' was my hushed reply.

She nodded. We tiptoed back to the kitchen.

'Should we have a cup of tea before I go?' she whispered, and then laughed. 'Why am I still whispering?'

'Go while the going's good would be my advice,' I said, shepherding her towards the door. 'Have you got your green bags for the groceries?'

'In the car. Trev should be back in an hour or so. He's checking stock. Ring me if you need me to come home.'

'Go,' I said and gave her a gentle shove.

She didn't budge.

'What?'

'I think I might have given Dad too much of the pain medication last night. He spat some out so I crushed up another two tablets and mixed them with jam. He gobbled that down.'

I pursed my lips. 'Just the two tablets?'

'Yes.' She was on the verge of despair. 'Will it kill him?'

'I doubt it. It's probably the best rest he's had in ages.'

Without any warning and a chance to step back, she'd pulled me into one of her breathtaking baby powder-scented hugs.

'I don't know what I would have done without you, Daisy,' she said, with tears in her voice.

'You would have managed. Now, off you go. And don't worry, he'll be fine.'

He slept the whole two and a half hours she was gone. Nevertheless, I crept into his room every twenty minutes or so to check he was still breathing. In between observations I pegged out a load of washing and threw a chewed-up old tennis ball for Jess. I boiled the kettle and when Bill didn't rally, I drank tea on my own. Trev didn't put in an appearance at all.

★★★

'Guess what?' Georgia said when I arrived home mid-afternoon. 'Lisa's pregnant.' Her expression was one of horror.

The news pulled me up in my tracks. 'Jake?'

'As far as I know. She didn't say anything to suggest otherwise.'

'How is she?'

'That's the thing, she's excited.' Georgia's horror morphed into disbelief. 'Says all she's ever wanted is to have a family. First I knew of it, and I'm her best friend.'

'Friends, even the best ones, don't tell each other everything, and neither should they. And it is all some women want, though I've never quite understood that. Then there are those of us who get lumped with it even if it's not what we wanted or when we wanted it.'

'It takes two to tango,' Georgia said.

'So it does, and don't you forget that when you make your own choices, my girl.' I sounded churlish but I didn't need to be reprimanded by my own granddaughter. I was tired and my back ached. Bill had made a mess in the bed and when he'd woken up enough I'd helped Glenys haul him out of bed, onto the shower chair and into the shower. The community nurse wasn't due until the next morning so we'd had no other option. It hadn't been the easiest of tasks, even with the two of us. There was a time when I would have managed the job on my own.

Glenys had sent me home with jars of zucchini relish and bread and butter pickles. All home grown. I put them in the fridge. There was a ziplock bag of fish fillets thawing on the second shelf.

'Where did the fish—' I started to say, but then with a sinking feeling I remembered: Georgia's boyfriend was coming to tea.

'I ended up having lunch with Kieran,' she said, peering over my shoulder and into the fridge. 'That's why the fish is there. Lisa slept in and was under the pump to get stuff done before she went to work.'

'Are there enough potatoes?' I said.

Georgia rummaged around in the pantry cupboard. When she turned around she held a potato in each hand. 'We'll need more than this.' She put them on the sink. 'I'll go. Do we need anything else?'

After a quick inventory of the salad ingredients I said, 'Not unless you want a special dressing.'

She bounced out with her purse and car keys. All I wanted to do was swallow some painkillers and lie down with a hot pack on my lower back. For at least two hours. In the peace and quiet. But where was I going to do that?

There were women out there who were older and frailer than me, and who were far worse off than I was. But then and there I found no consolation in that thought. Although I'd been doing it a bit of late, I let myself wallow in self-misery for a good few minutes. Then I half-heartedly squared my shoulders and told myself it was time to quit the pity party. I had a roof over my head and a yard for my dog. I'd take the painkillers and semi-recline on the sofa with a hot pack on my back for as long as I could. That would have to do for now.

28

Kate

After scouring the contents of Uncle Frank's box and reading every word of Dennis's diaries, several times, it'd been late Sunday night. Dennis's diaries had been dry reading, primarily about the farm. Occasionally there'd be a personal comment and that'd been enough for me to keep ploughing through them. In the end, I'd had no more idea who Tom was than when I'd first stumbled upon the photo. I'd even dragged every last album off the bookshelf and pored over Dennis's family photos. What I found was a black and white school photo of Dennis at around the same age and the resemblance to Tom was undeniable. Any wonder I'd assumed it was Dennis. Although it should have clicked that it wasn't, because Tom was in colour.

Before I went to bed I'd piled everything, except the photograph of Tom, back into the box. I'd shoved the box back into the cupboard in the study and wished that I'd never seen the damn thing. The photo I'd slipped between two books on the bookshelf: *Vintage Tractors* and *The Encyclopaedia of Modern Aircraft*. More of Dennis's books that'd need re-homing.

Over the course of that evening an uncomfortable feeling had settled in the pit of my stomach. Now, a day later, it had solidified into a lump, and all the while my brain played hide and seek with the likely identity of the teenager in the photograph. It was as if I knew who he had to be, but would not let myself believe it possible. Because if he was who I thought he was, I didn't know how I'd ever recover from that blow.

By Tuesday morning, after another poor sleep, I felt over-the-top agitated. And annoyed, because I had been doing so well. I begged off visiting Rhonda, saying I had a headache and the sniffles.

'Do one of those tests, my dear,' she said when I rang. 'Make sure you haven't got that awful virus. I only have to sneeze and Margie has me poking one of those dreadful swabs up my nose.'

But my headache was because I hadn't slept or eaten anything nourishing since Sunday lunch-time. And there on the bench was another empty wine bottle ready to go to the recycle bin.

I'd spent Monday reading and then rereading all of my journals. Searching for a hint of anything I might have written that would substantiate the likely identity of *Tom, Year 7*. Trying to read between the lines I'd written decades earlier.

I'd even returned to Uncle Frank's box and shaken out every one of his journals on the off-chance another photo of Tom had been slipped—hidden—between the pages. There'd been nothing.

While I lingered over a second espresso, not that I needed more caffeine in the state I was in, I tried to gather my thoughts and make a plan of where to from here. What would be the best way to discover Tom's identity? And did I even need to know?

Of course I did.

There were people I could discuss it with, such as Molly and Lewis and others who'd known Dennis and me back when. But I didn't dare do that because then I'd feel as if I had to explain lots of other things, and my infertility wasn't a subject I'd ever talked about with Dennis's family. Had he? He'd given no reason for me to think so, but then again, posthumously, my husband continued to surprise.

What if I did mention it to Molly and Lewis and they didn't know anything more than I did? Then they'd be left wondering as well. Every course of action explored led to the same conclusion: me looking incredibly foolish because I hadn't known my husband had a son, and I wasn't his mother. Besides, there was always the slim chance I was completely wrong. It was to that premise I'd cling and somehow manage to get through.

Coffee in hand, I went to my spot by the window. Someone I could ask, who'd known me back then and better than most, was Daisy. She'd known how much I'd wanted a family. I couldn't believe that she'd never asked why we hadn't. A journal entry I'd read the night before from early 1979 sprang to mind: *Daisy came out to the farm today to tell me she was pregnant. AGAIN!! I cannot believe it. It's only weeks ago that we went to Gareth's first birthday party. Don't they know about contraception …*

What I hadn't journaled then and what I remembered clearly now was how apologetic she'd been when she'd told me. And how rude I'd been in return. I hadn't offered her a cup of tea or even a glass of water. She'd left again not long afterwards. The wedge splitting apart our friendship had been driven in even further.

I refocussed on the familiar view outside the window. No sign of Daisy again this morning. She was either taking a break from walking daily or she was going a different way. Which she had every right to do, but I felt snubbed just the same, as absurd as that might sound.

She was still with her granddaughter. I'd gone out of my way to drive by on the way back from the supermarket several days ago, and her station wagon was parked in the driveway. I couldn't account for the immense relief I'd felt at seeing the dusty old vehicle sitting there. What was *that* about?

I took the empty coffee cup and put it into the dishwasher. I'd have something to eat later.

★ ★ ★

Hard to believe another week had almost passed and it was book club again. Another month gone, just like that. For once I'd read the book and enthusiastically joined in the discussion. When I looked around at the familiar faces, I wondered if any of these women would be able to shed any light on the identity of Tom. They'd all lived in the district most of their lives. Undoubtedly, they'd have come up with something. But I would never dream of asking them. My insides shrivelled at the very idea.

We'd been at Rose Timms' place that afternoon and as we were leaving, Valma bailed me up to ask how I *really* was.

'I dropped by one morning last week,' she said, 'but you weren't home, and then Rhonda Hall's daughter Margie said you'd been popping into her mum each morning, since she'd had that last turn.'

'Rhonda's doing remarkably well,' I said.

'The company will do you both good,' Valma said, and patted me on the arm.

I'm sure she didn't mean to sound patronising, but she did. I'd been clumped into the lonely old widow cohort with Rhonda, who was nearly twenty years my senior. Irritated was how that left me feeling.

'I'll see you later,' I said. I walked away before my tongue got the better of me and I said something I might later regret.

I drove home. It wasn't far and I should have walked because I needed the exercise. Why, I don't know, but on the way home I detoured and drove past Daisy's granddaughter's place again. The station wagon was in its usual spot and this afternoon there was no sign of the snazzy SUV I'd seen parked on other occasions. The dog was sunning herself on the front verandah.

I pulled into the kerb and stopped the car. Before I could think twice, I climbed out and walked across the street and up the gravel driveway. The dog stood up, stretched and met me at the edge of the verandah, her tail wagging. It was almost as if she was smiling at me.

'Hello,' I said, and awkwardly reached out to pet her. Her coat was short, the hair coarse but oddly smooth, and warm from the sun. I wasn't a dog, or a cat, or any kind of an animal sort of a person. My discomfort around the farm dogs had always left Dennis slightly bemused.

The screen door rattled open and Daisy came out onto the verandah.

'Kate,' she said, her face devoid of expression. 'I thought I heard someone walk up the driveway.' She wore three-quarter length denim jeans and a baggy orange T-shirt that had seen better days. Thongs on her feet. She needed a hair cut.

'I was just passing,' I said. 'And I saw your car. I haven't seen you out walking and I wondered if you were all right.'

Her mouth turned down at the corners. 'We've been going a different way,' she said, bright spots of colour appearing on her cheeks.

We stood and looked everywhere but at each other. The dog nudged my hand, wanting another pat.

'Jess,' Daisy said firmly, and the dog ambled across the verandah to her. She stooped to scratch it behind the ears. 'Shall I put the kettle on?'

'That would be lovely,' I said, although she didn't sound enthusiastic. I followed her inside. The dog stayed put on the verandah.

'Tea or coffee?' she said, her back to me as she filled the electric kettle at the sink. She took out two mugs: chunky, ceramic things. Ugly.

'Coffee. Black, thanks.'

She turned around and caught me scrutinising the living area. It was neat and spotlessly clean. A saggy sofa offered the only place to sit. Her expression dared me to comment.

'It's very cosy,' I said. Poky, was what I thought.

'Most people just call it a dump, but we manage.'

'These old workers' cottages have a certain ... charm ... about them. There aren't many left standing. Most have been pushed over to make way for new homes. Who owns this one?'

'No idea,' she said. 'Georgia's been very vague about it all.'

The kettle boiled and she made the drinks.

'Grab your coffee and let's go out the back,' she said. 'There're a couple of folding chairs out there.'

We walked down a short passage with the bathroom on one side and a bedroom on the other.

'Only the one bedroom,' I said. 'Where do you sleep?'

'On the sofa bed, behind the screen.'

'Oh.'

The back verandah was old and dreadfully dilapidated. One end had been built in and doubled as a laundry by the look of the twin tub parked in the corner. There were several large pots with an assortment of herbs growing in them. It was all very tidy, not a cobweb to be seen. Daisy unfolded two drooping canvas chairs and we sat down. Clothes flapped on the clothesline. A ginger cat wandered across the backyard. The dog gave it a malevolent stare but didn't budge from where she'd plopped down beside Daisy.

'I wanted to ask you something,' I said after I'd taken a sip of coffee. Instant. Made with tap water, but not *too* bad.

'Ask away,' she said. She tilted her head to one side. 'But I can't promise I'll have any of the answers you're looking for.'

I rested the coffee on the arm of the chair, not exactly certain where to begin. And then I thought, *what the hell*, and started from the beginning, the moment I'd first stumbled upon the photograph of *Tom, Year 7*.

29

Daisy

You could have knocked me over with a feather when I stepped out onto the verandah and there was Kate, patting Jess. The manners my mother taught me were so ingrained that instead of ignoring her and going back inside, I asked her in.

From what she was wearing, a French navy–coloured shirtwaist dress, heels and pearls, she'd obviously been out and was on her way home. Had stopping here been an impulse? But then she said she wanted to ask me something, suggesting the visit had been premeditated.

'Wow,' I said, after she'd recounted her story of finding a photograph of a twelve- or thirteen-year-old boy named Tom, who happened to be the spitting image of Dennis at a similar age. Or so she said. She hadn't brought the snap with her.

'I don't know who he is,' she said, frowning and staring into what was left of her coffee.

'And what made you think I'd know? Especially if there's no clue to when the picture was taken. Or who took it. It could have been ten, twenty or even thirty years ago.'

She sighed. 'Clutching at straws, I suppose. I thought because you knew me and Dennis way back, there might have been something you remembered … Gossip you'd heard …' She crossed her legs and then straight away uncrossed them. I could see she was uncomfortable, and not only with the chair she was sitting in.

'Oh,' I said, drawing the word out as it dawned on me what she was implying. 'You think Dennis might have strayed and this Tom was the result?'

'It had crossed my mind,' she said. I had to strain to hear.

'I can't imagine Dennis doing something like that,' I said, because I couldn't.

She laughed, a harsh, bitter sound. 'We went through some challenging times, Daisy, when we were trying to have a family and couldn't. I've been rereading the journals I kept back then. I wouldn't have been the … easiest person to live with.'

Her tortured expression told me how difficult it was for her to admit that. Always so proud. So Kate.

'I'm sure Dennis would have had his moments along the way.'

'You knew him, Daisy. Can you imagine him having *moments*?'

'No, not really. I don't recall Dennis ever getting cross, or raising his voice or anything. Not while I was around, anyway. But that doesn't mean he didn't. You're the one who was married to him.'

'For forty-five years. But do we ever really know anyone? He wasn't an overtly emotional man, and he was always stoic about us not being able to have a family. But I know now, after reading the few diaries he kept, that he was as heartbroken about it as I was.'

'You must have hated me,' I said. 'I only had to look at Charlie and I was pregnant.'

She met my eye briefly and then looked away again. 'Jealousy, resentment, bitterness, ambivalence, I've felt all of those things towards you, but I don't think I ever actually *hated* you. I wasn't blind, Daisy. Your life was far from plain sailing, and I knew what you ended up with wasn't what you'd wanted for yourself.'

'It does take two to tango, or so Georgia reminded me the other day,' I said, and snorted at the memory. 'Charlie charmed the pants off me, literally. If only I knew then what I know now, or even a half of it.'

'Don't we all wish that,' Kate said. 'What do you think I should do?'

'You could try a private detective. Is it a school photo? Is the lad in school uniform?'

'Yes, he is, but it's quite generic. Grey jumper; striped tie. I've studied it with a magnifying glass and I can't find anything distinguishing to suggest a school, and there are no other markings on the back of the photo. And you don't remember anything?'

I shook my head. 'I was friends with *you*. Dennis was there, but only on the periphery. Didn't Dennis have brothers? Maybe they'd know something?'

She screwed up her face. 'Yeah, I thought of that but I'm not sure I want to ask them and then have to explain why I'm asking. It's not really any of their business.'

'Unless he's their nephew … However, I can see why you might hesitate. I suppose I could ask Charlie. He'd sometimes run into Dennis at the pub and they'd have a beer together. He might remember something.'

'You still talk to him?' Her eyebrows disappeared under her fringe.

'Of course, if ever the need arises. We share three sons and six grandchildren, Kate. We need to talk from time to time. Besides, our parting wasn't acrimonious. Charlie just couldn't bear being hemmed in, especially in the city.'

'Hemmed in? He had responsibilities,' she said, appalled. 'When you marry it means you commit to the bad times as well as the good.'

'I couldn't physically tie him down, could I? And in the long run, this way probably worked out better for both of us. It's like I had four boys and eventually they all left home.'

'Has he been happy?'

'You'd have to ask him that. We talk but not often and *never* about our inner lives. But if you want me to ask him if he recalls anything, I will. It would be awful to have something like that nagging at you, indefinitely. I'd have to know, if it were me.'

I could see she was curious about Charlie and our relationship, and I was relieved when she held back, because I'd had enough of a trip down that memory lane. I didn't have the stomach for any more probing about why my marriage had been such a dismal failure. I just knew that it had.

She left a short while after that. On the way out, she said, 'I know it's a big ask, but I would appreciate it if you could talk to Charlie. It's not unheard of for men friends to be privy to facts their wives aren't.'

'All right. I'll message him, but be warned, it might take a few days for him to ring me back. He could be anywhere. Last time we spoke he was mustering in the Pilbara.'

'What if it was something urgent?'

'Kate, if Charlie wanted to be available to his family for any urgent situations, he wouldn't be in the Pilbara mustering in the first place, would he?'

'No, I suppose not,' she said. 'Not at his age.'

'Not at any age,' I said.

She opened her mouth to say more, but instead she briefly closed her eyes and gave her head a slight shake. 'Some things continue to burn, don't they?' she said. No answer was required.

'I'll be in touch if what you suspect about the lad in the photo rings any bells for Charlie,' I said, and walked with her down the driveway. We exchanged phone numbers. She mumbled something about misplacing the note I'd left with the flowers.

She waved as she drove off in her flash car. Jess and I stood at the gate long after she'd gone. I don't know what Jess was thinking about but I'd drifted off, lost in thoughts about Kate and Dennis and the past, and the conundrum that had dropped into her lap the moment she'd found the photograph of Tom.

'Daisy, how are you?' Max called, nudging me back into the present. 'How's that precious dog?'

'Max, hello.' I followed Jess next door. 'She's fine, as you can see. And I'm okay. How are you?'

'Plodding along,' he said, and leaned forward to pat the dog. 'Some days I feel as if I'm not doing much more than marking time until it's my turn to meet my maker. Today's been one of those days.' He straightened again and smiled. 'But I'm all the better for seeing you both.'

'Your garden's looking amazing,' I said. The lawn was newly mown, the edges trimmed. He'd been dead-heading roses; a basket and secateurs sat on the path where he'd left them to greet us.

'The lad came yesterday. Unbelievable what he gets done in a couple of hours. It's all part of one of those aged care packages. Pamela organised it for me ages ago. Worth her weight in gold, that girl. Have you got time for a cuppa?'

'Why not?' I said. All I had to do was get the washing in off the clothesline. Georgia was on an afternoon shift. 'Why don't I go in and make it? I know where everything is. You sit yourself down and let me see to it.'

He didn't argue. There were cane chairs on the verandah and he sat with a satisfied sigh. Jess sidled up and let him pet her some more. That dog was too spoilt. I went in and made the tea and we wiled away the next hour chatting about anything and everything, and none of it important. I'm sure we both felt better for it.

★★★

Later that same evening, Charlie made a liar of me and rang back less than a minute after I'd messaged him.

'What's up?' he said. I could hear laughter and voices and country and western music in the background.

Annoyingly, I still experienced a flutter of something whenever I heard his voice. What a nuisance. I didn't ask where he was or how he was; that smacked of normalcy and Charlie didn't do normal. I explained why I'd been in touch.

'Ah, so old Dennis popped off the perch and Kate thinks he might have been spreading it around beforehand.' He chuckled. 'How is she? Still as vinegary and prudish as she always was?'

'She's mellowed, like most of us have, Charlie. She's grieving. It's only been a year since Dennis died.'

The music faded away. He coughed and cleared his throat. 'Let me give it some thought, Daisy. Can't say I can put my finger on anything right now, but who knows what a bloke might remember at the oddest of moments. How are you?'

'Sorry … What did you say?' I'd heard him the first time but I wanted to hear him say it again.

'I asked how you were. I'm allowed to do that, aren't I?'

'I suppose so, it's just that you never have before. And I'm fine. How are you?'

'Fine,' he said. 'Everyone else okay?'

I took the phone away from my ear and stared at it.

'Hello? Daisy? Are you still there?'

'I'm here. I've spoken to Gareth and Adam recently. Usual ups and downs of life. If you want more information than that, talk to them. Is Jay with you?'

'Nope. Haven't seen him.'

'Then he's gone to ground somewhere. We thought he might have been with you.'

'Right,' he said, and I could visualise perfectly the puzzled expression he'd have on his face as he scratched his head.

'Don't stress, Charlie. I'm sure he'll resurface again. And if he doesn't, we'll deal with that when it happens.'

'You always were excellent at that Daisy, dealing with whatever came up. I'll call you back if I think of anything that might hint at what Dennis was up to. Take care,' he said, and disconnected.

My goodness! Had my estranged husband just paid me a compliment? And asked how I was? I flopped back on the sofa and lifted my feet onto the coffee table. I replayed the conversation in my head, and yes, he had complimented me and asked after me. I thought about it some more and decided to take his comments at face value. It would be foolish to read anything more into them.

30

Kate

Over the weekend I hadn't let my mobile phone out of my sight, but come Monday there'd been nothing from Daisy. Scruffy grey clouds scudded across the sky, however no rain was forecast. If Dennis had been alive and we'd been on the farm he would have been getting fidgety about now, wondering when and if the season-breaking rain would come and crops could be sown.

Here it was Monday lunch time and since my conversation with Daisy late Friday afternoon on the way home from book club, I hadn't spoken to a soul. Rhonda's granddaughter had driven from Adelaide to stay with her over the weekend, making any visit from me superfluous. Rhonda was such a bright spark and I'd missed her company. The need to get across the street to see how she was faring also helped propel me out of bed each morning. How was I going to fill in the rest of the day? The week? I'd finished this month's book club read already. I had too much time on my hands to sit and brood.

With a burst of energy, I set about planning what I'd do for the women's and children's hospital fundraising morning tea. It wasn't until mid-May—five weeks away, to be precise—but it'd be here before I knew it.

The day Valma and her associates had come we'd agreed that if guests spilled out onto the patio there'd be enough room for at least thirty-five. It could be cool by the middle of May, but there were two outdoor gas heaters in Dennis's shed. If I could find someone to get them going. I added that to my growing list, with a note to ask Kieran if he'd see to it on the day and check the gas bottles were full beforehand.

By the time I'd counted the cups and plates and crockery I'd need and drafted a menu, I felt as if I'd achieved something, and kept the brooding at bay. The menu would need tweaking; I'd yet to ask Valma if she'd do the scones and Evelyn the jelly cakes. My contribution would be assorted sandwiches, mini quiches and a lemon curd slice. The slice recipe was an old one and a go-to favourite. I couldn't tell you the number of times I'd made it for various work functions and fundraisers. And the odd family occasion.

I flicked through my recipe book and came across another slice I hadn't made for years: Wanganui slice. A no-bake recipe. Dennis had loved the cornflake, coconut and caramel concoction, but I'd never liked it. Too sickly sweet and gooey for me. The last time I could recall making it had been for an Australia Day barbecue lunch we'd had out at the farm. The reason I remembered it was because it was the day that in my mind I'd terminated my friendship with Daisy.

I'd wanted everything to be perfect. The weather obliged and Dennis had promised to take the whole day away from farm work and cook the barbecue. There were a dozen or so friends coming, and Daisy. She'd be on her own. Because I found it so difficult, I'd specifically requested that there be no children, and Charlie had agreed to stay home and look after their boys.

Then on the day who should show up—and late—but Daisy, with her three ratbags in tow. I'd been incensed when I'd clearly said *no* children. Gareth would have been about nine years old, making Jay around seven and Adam about four.

Daisy's only explanation was: 'No idea where Charlie is. I wasn't going to come, but then I'd already baked the cheesecake.'

Which everyone enjoyed, except me. I'd wished she hadn't come at all. I would have made do without her dessert. The Wanganui slice, assorted chocolates and fruit platter would have been plenty.

The boys had been total ... boys. My afternoon had been ruined. I'd spent it chasing around after them making sure they didn't go into the sheds or get into any other trouble. That's the thing about farms: they are dangerous places for the uninitiated. Dennis had ignored them, and in a way so had Daisy, leaving it all up to me.

Later, when everyone had gone home and we'd been cleaning up, I'd had a meltdown. 'They all left early and it was wholly and solely because *she* brought her *bloody kids* with her when I'd explicitly said, *no children*!'

'Kate, it's after five and they came for lunch,' Dennis had said, unperturbed. 'I don't think any of them left early.'

But I just knew I'd been right. That had been it. For me, the friendship had well and truly run its course. From that day onwards I'd struggled even to be civil to Daisy. I hadn't sought her out; I'd requested opposite shifts. All invitations had ceased. If I happened to see Charlie, I'd cross the street to avoid him.

But now, propped on a barstool at the island bench, chin resting in my hands as I stared down at the recipe until it swam in front of my eyes, it all seemed so trivial. Slumping deeper onto the barstool, I folded my arms on the bench top and rested my head on them.

I closed my eyes. All I could see was the haunted expression on Daisy's face when she'd said, 'No idea where Charlie is. I wasn't going to come, but then I'd already baked the cheesecake.'

I must have drifted off or something, because the next thing I knew, I jerked awake and nearly slipped off the stool when someone rapped loudly on the door that led to the patio. It was Daisy. Had I conjured her up from my dreams?

'It's unlocked,' I called, slightly bewildered.

She came in through the sliding door and I heard her telling Jess to stay. She was wearing her walking clothes and she toed off her sneakers and left them by the door.

'I rang the doorbell first,' she said. 'Then I saw the side gate was open so I came through. Is everything all right?'

'I didn't hear the doorbell and I must have left the gate open earlier.' Not like me at all. Never mind.

I stacked the recipe book and notebook I'd been using to make lists for the morning tea and sat the pen on top. 'Have you heard from Charlie?'

'He doesn't remember anything. Sorry. He said when he and Dennis occasionally had a beer at the pub, all they'd do is pass the time of day or gripe about the weather. Are you sure you're all right? You look a bit pale.'

I put a hand to my face. My skin was dry and cool. 'Taking one too many trips down memory lane. It can be detrimental to one's health,' I said with forced levity. 'I'm hosting a fundraising morning tea in mid-May and I was jotting down notes and flicking through my recipe book.'

'I see,' she said, with a wry smile.

I moved the pen and picked up the recipe book; the pages were tatty with age and stained by use. It fell open at the Wanganui slice. I showed her. 'Remember that Australia Day barbecue?'

She frowned. And then she remembered. 'Charlie promised to look after the kids, but went on a drinking spree with his mates instead. I spent money I couldn't afford on a spring-form cake tin and the ingredients for a baked cheesecake. Then I'd stayed up half the night to make it, after I'd put the boys to bed. That's a long time ago, Kate.'

'Isn't it.'

'And if my memory serves me correctly, we ruined the afternoon for you, didn't we? You had everything so perfect, even the weather, and then I arrived with the boys ...' She snuffed out a humourless laugh. 'I hadn't thought about that day in forever, but now I can see vividly the look on your face when the boys tumbled out of the back seat of the car.'

'Like you said, it's a long time ago.'

'But you obviously haven't forgotten.'

'No,' I said.

'I'd wanted the sitter to come, but I had a night shift that night. If she came in the day she wouldn't come back for the night, and I knew I'd need her if Charlie didn't come home at all. I'm sorry, but I couldn't afford to take the night off. Charlie wasn't working at the time.' She folded her arms, her mouth a severe line.

'I'm sorry, too,' I said. 'For a lot of things.'

'I don't want your pity, Kate. I didn't then and I don't now. You said the other day that you were jealous of me, bitter, resentful because I had children and you didn't. Well, you had everything else. Money, your own home, an attentive husband, a nice car and a career. From where I sat, *you* had the perfect life.'

'Appearances can be deceiving.'

'Can't they just. You say you desperately wanted children, well, I don't remember you ever being user-friendly with mine, or anyone else's, for that matter. Kids are far from perfect, Kate. The ways they can mess up your life are inexhaustible, even when they've grown up. But you love them regardless.'

She backed away and started putting on her shoes again. Jess was peering in through the sliding glass door. She had a look of concern on her doggy face and that wasn't me being fanciful. It was as if she felt Daisy's distress and was telling her she was there for her.

'What are you doing?' I said.

'I'm leaving. I've told you what I came to tell you.'

'Stay. I'll make tea. With leaves.'

She paused, standing on one foot, one shoe on and the other in her hand. I envied her balance. 'Why do you want me to stay?' she said.

'We were friends once. We knew each other well.'

'So we did, but like we've agreed, it was a long time ago. What do we have in common now?' She gave an all-encompassing sweep around the room with the hand not holding the shoe.

'The fact that we were friends once, and that we knew each other well.'

Standing on two feet again, she lowered her arm and regarded me, her expression unreadable. In that moment she looked all of her sixty-eight years. Life hadn't always been kind to her, in so many ways. But then that was life, wasn't it? We'd all had our ups and downs.

'All right,' she said. She dropped the shoe in her hand and slipped off the one she'd already wriggled into. Jess eased herself down onto the mat outside the door, but she glanced back over her shoulder several times.

I let out a breath I hadn't realised I'd been holding.

31

Daisy

Georgia went home to her parents' place for three days over the Easter weekend and Jess and I had the house to ourselves. It was pure bliss. Georgia left early Saturday morning, and I went back to bed the second after I'd waved her off. I drank tea and ate breakfast in bed, and read until my back couldn't bear the sag in the sofa bed any longer. Only then did I get up. We went for a leisurely walk down to the shops and I treated myself to a cappuccino and slice of carrot cake with thick, creamy icing. It was a gorgeous day and I sat at a table outside, Jess at my feet, both of us content to people-watch away what was left of the morning.

Late Saturday afternoon, after leaving Jess with Max, I drove out to the Carlisles' farm. Glenys and Trev had been invited to dinner with friends and I'd offered to sit with Bill. Trev's dogs would be roaming and Jess would be happier with Max. He'd give her the run of the house and treat her like an honoured guest.

When I arrived, Glenys was flapping about in a satiny purple dressing gown with curlers in her hair.

'Dad's miserable,' she said. 'I'm wondering if I should leave him?'

'Of course you should leave him. Go and have a nice time. You deserve a night off.'

'Do you think so?' she said. 'He's had his tea. Scrambled egg. Although he hardly ate a bite. I can't seem to tempt him with anything, not even his old favourites.'

'What do you want me to offer him for supper?'

'He likes his cup of warm Horlicks. Sometimes he'll dunk a biscuit. It's all there on the cupboard, ready to go. And I've put you up a meal. It's in the fridge. All you need to do is zap it.'

I kept insisting that she didn't need to feed me, and she kept on feeding me. This evening's offering was meatloaf and four veg, smothered in gravy. Apple pie and cream for dessert.

They left twenty minutes later, Trev looking spiffy in slacks, white shirt and navy blue tie, and Glenys in a floral frock and a cloud of Lily of the Valley perfume. Bill was dozing when I looked in. I didn't disturb him, and went out and heated the meal left for me. The size of the serve was fit for a shearer and I wrapped a chunk of the meatloaf in aluminium foil to take home for Jess.

The second time I went in to check on Bill, he was awake.

'Oh, it's you again,' he said, and turned his head away.

Guess what? I would have loved to reply, *You're not exactly my favourite person either.*

That's the sum of what he said to me the whole evening. At supper time, I propped him up and he drank half the Horlicks. I took the lid off the feeder cup and he dunked a Scotch Finger. Without comment from him, I provided the necessary personal care and he cooperated as best he could. In the end we both did our best because although we didn't care for each other, we cared about Glenys. By eight-thirty, he was snoring his head off.

Bored, I wandered around the lounge room. I browsed through a few of the books on the bookshelf and then perused the extensive display of family photos. There'd never been time before, and it fascinated me how every horizontal surface held as many framed photographs as could possibly be crammed there. I was surprised by how many of the faces I could put names to. The vintage of the photos made it somewhat easier. On the walnut chiffonier sideboard, right at the back, I found an ornate frame with a faded 35mm photo behind the glass. With a jolt, I realised it was me and Charlie, outside the registry office after we'd been married.

'Good grief,' I said to the empty room.

Kate had taken the photograph. We hadn't owned a camera, not even a Kodak Instamatic. And there was Charlie, as handsome as ever in a borrowed suit, grinning broadly with his arm slung around my shoulders; me with a stunned expression on my face. I remembered the dress and the gold platform sandals. Mum had given me the money for the outfit, and made me swear not to tell Dad. To this day I'm positive they were more relieved than anything when I'd married without asking for a formal wedding. The question of who'd pay had never had to be asked.

When I'd told Mum I was pregnant and we were getting married, she'd closed her eyes and said, 'Oh, Daisy, I'm so sorry, love. I know that's not what you wanted for yourself. Whatever you do, don't tell your father you're in the family way. And if we're lucky, he won't work it out for himself, because if he does, you'll never live it down. And I mean *never*.'

She hadn't asked if I loved Charlie, or how I felt about the sudden change to my 'plans'; to my whole life, as things turned out. Dad never did work it out; he died not long before Gareth was born. But then, on the odd occasion we ever visited them, he'd throw a supercilious glance my way and I remembered wondering at those times if he had known, or suspected, that I'd had to get married. I don't recall him ever mumbling more than a few words to Charlie. One of the few people who'd never succumbed to the charm of Charlie Toogood.

How had Glenys come by a copy of this photo? I had the original somewhere. Kate had given it to me. As far as I knew, I'd had the one and only copy. Without a proper wedding or a reception, there'd been no need for a wedding album.

Picture in hand, I moved closer to the light. We'd been so very *young*. Charlie at twenty-three and me a year younger. Too young and immature to be married, and with a family on the way. At least I'd cottoned on to that, which probably accounted for my stunned expression.

Headlights swept the driveway just before eleven and the dogs barked. Glenys and Trev were home. Lost in memories, I was sitting still as a statue right where I'd plonked myself in one of the plush lounge chairs. The framed photo rested face-up in my lap. I quickly returned it to its place and went out to greet them, checking Bill on the way past. Sound asleep.

'We had a lovely time, but the food. So much of it. *Three* desserts and after-dinner mints! That woman always over-caters,' Glenys said, and yawned. 'How's Dad been?'

I told her. She yawned again.

Trev was red-faced and glassy-eyed. 'I'm off to bed,' he said, and sounded slurry. Glenys rolled her eyes. There'd obviously been ample alcohol to accompany the plentiful food.

'You'll stay for a cuppa won't you?' she said, when Trev had disappeared.

'I'll let you get off to bed. You look about done in. Yell out when you need me next.'

Forever gracious, she saw me out and waved me off. I collected
Jess and was home and tucked in minutes before midnight. What a
treat not to have to make the bed first.

On the verge of sleep, I realised I hadn't asked Glenys where the
photo of Charlie and me had come from. I'd ask her the next time
I went out to help her with Bill.

★ ★ ★

While we're on the subject of photographs, Kate had shown me the
one of Tom the afternoon I went around to tell her that Charlie
had nothing new to offer. We'd taken it out into the sun and, with
an extra set of eyes and the magnifying glass, we'd discovered the
remnants of a faded and smudged stamp on the back. Ink that had
once been red was now pink and totally indecipherable.

'My guess is it was taken in the early nineties,' I'd said. 'I've a
bundle of photos that are a similar vintage from when my boys
were at school. Year seven would make Tom barely a teenager.'

On my reckoning, Tom had probably been born somewhere
between Jay and Adam. Kate nodded but hadn't said a word.

It'd occurred to me, when I was driving home from the farm
on Saturday night, that Glenys might be a good person to ask. She
was closer to Kate and Dennis's age and she'd lived in the area since
before she'd married Trev. Their property was in the vicinity of
where Dennis used to farm, and farmers generally had an affinity
for other farmers, and often knew their business. Which they might
choose to share with their wives. Added to that, Glenys had a keen
interest in her fellow man; she noticed things other people didn't.
Perhaps I'd mention it to Kate the next time I saw her.

Easter Monday I went out walking with Jess much later than
usual. It'd been my last chance for a lie-in. Georgia would be back

some time that afternoon, and was on a night shift. That meant Jess and I would be out early tomorrow, pounding the pavements for the remainder of the week and into the weekend.

Being a public holiday, the streets were eerily quiet. The sky was overcast, a solid mass of steel grey, and the wind had picked up since we'd set off. We'd taken to walking along Kate's street again and I wasn't surprised to see her scurrying across the road. I was about to call but she saw me first and waved. She waited on the footpath.

'Have you been out walking?' I said when we caught up to her.

She laughed and it was such a happy sound I found myself smiling. 'I've been visiting my neighbour, Rhonda Hall. Kieran's grandmother,' she said.

'Oh, yes, I do remember him mentioning his grandmother lived there. And Georgia said something about her having a fall, or a funny turn. How is she now?'

'Very sprightly. My wish is that I'm as sprightly when I'm ninety. Did you want to come in?'

'Thanks, but no. Georgia gets home this afternoon and the place looks like a bomb hit it. My housekeeping's been a bit lax while she's been away. But I've thought of someone who you could ask about Tom: Glenys Carlisle. She's lived here forever and they farm out your way, and you know how farmers can gossip. Do you know her?'

'I wouldn't say I know her, but we have bumped into each other over the years.' Kate folded her arms as if she was hugging herself. Her happy demeanour of minutes before had disappeared. She gazed off into the distance. 'I don't know, Daisy. The more I think about it, the more convinced I am that I should put the photo back in the box and forget all about it. Probably the wisest way to go.'

'But will you be able to forget? I know I wouldn't. When I was young, what with Charlie being the party animal he was, I'd sometimes wonder what I'd do if another woman showed up on our doorstep claiming Charlie was the father of her child.'

Kate frowned. 'I don't think you had anything to worry about back then, Daisy. Charlie married you because he wanted to. You didn't force him; he insisted. You told me that. I wrote it in my journal. I can show you the entry, if you like.'

'You wrote down stuff like that?'

'It has been interesting reading, believe you me.'

'I'll bet.' Jess tugged on the lead. 'I'd better go. But think about talking to Glenys. She's a caring person and I'm sure you could trust her.'

'You haven't said anything to her, have you? Isn't she Charlie's cousin?'

'Yes, she is, and of course I haven't mentioned anything to her. It's not my business to do that. But she was always very kind to me when the boys were little. Now she's looking after her elderly father and I've been lending a hand.'

Kate continued to hug herself tightly. 'I'll think about it,' she said and rolled her lips together. 'Probably the best thing is to forget all about it. Because what if I do find out that he definitely could be Dennis's son? What then? It'd open a whole different can of worms.'

She was right. And she'd be no closer to finding him. Even if she wanted to.

'Life never gets any easier, does it? I thought by this age it would have, but no.'

'I can certainly vouch for that,' she said. 'I'll see you later. Pop in any time for a coffee. I'm home more often than not.'

'All right, thanks. Georgia's on nights this week and I make myself scarce so she can sleep.'

Kate smiled and dropped her arms to her sides. 'Ah, how I hated night shift. I would not wish for that time of my life over again. Forever sleep-deprived.'

'I learned to sleep standing up,' I said. 'Come on, Jess.'

We ambled our way home. I chewed over the conversation with Kate as we went. Simply put, I'd had no choice but to learn how to grab sleep whenever I could. Being chronically sleep-deprived was part of being a mother and a full-time shift worker. After Gareth came along, my aim was *not* to get pregnant again, and night duty did have its upsides in that it offered a vague sort of contraception: a lack of physical proximity. For Kate, desperately trying to conceive, it would have been hard. I could see that now.

32

Kate

Valma and Evelyn were sitting with me in the breakfast nook. We were having coffee and discussing the women's and children's hospital fundraiser. It was four weeks away. Valma had offered to do the scones before I asked and Evelyn the jelly cakes. Evelyn would be away on a holiday in sunny Queensland but she'd make and freeze them before she went. They agreed that their contributions plus my slices, mini quiches and assorted sandwiches would suffice. Until Valma said, 'Should I ask Lorraine Sheriff to do several of her sponge rolls?'

'You think there won't be enough food with what we've planned? It's only morning tea.' This from me.

'Tickets are twenty-five dollars,' Valma said. 'Granted it's a fundraiser, but you know how people are: they want value for money. And we know the ones who'll be very vocal if they don't think they're getting their money's worth. And then there are those who'll make it their breakfast and their lunch.'

'What if you offered a glass of bubbly along with morning tea?' Evelyn said, directing the question to me.

'At ten thirty in the morning!' Valma's eyes bulged.

Evelyn didn't miss a beat. 'You'd only need half-a-dozen bottles, and Reece would happily donate them. A mix of pink and white.'

'But alcohol, for morning tea?'

'Valma, you just said you want them to get value for money. I guarantee there will be no complaints about value if we offer a glass of bubbles in the ticket price.'

'It'd save you asking Lorraine for sponge rolls,' I said. 'And I wouldn't have to put out cake forks.' Personally, I'd rather bubbles over Lorraine Sheriff's jam- and cream-filled sponge rolls any day.

'But you'd need champagne glasses,' Valma said triumphantly. 'Where would you get those?'

'We have dozens of the things. We use them for cellar door.'

Valma blinked several times and sat back in her seat.

'And thirty-five people aren't going to get rolling drunk on six bottles of sparkling wine.'

Had Evelyn really needed to press the point any further? To me, Valma seemed convinced—or resigned.

'Would anyone like another coffee?' I said, cheerfully.

'Not for me, thanks, Kate.' Valma slid out of the booth. 'I'll be on my way. No need to see me out.'

I did, all the same.

'I promise there'll be no long-life milk,' I said to her on the way through, hoping to get a smile. No such luck.

'I can't be sure what Gaye and Maureen will have to say about serving wine at morning tea,' she said. 'And I will have to mention it to them, seeing as how they're organising the tickets.'

'What if we gave guests the option of having orange juice with the bubbly?'

Valma's countenance brightened. 'I suppose that could work. Please don't think I'm being a wowser, Kate. It's just—'

'You don't have to explain, Valma. I'll make sure there's orange juice.'

Valma trekked off down the driveway to her little buzz-box parked on the street. It was a dreary day. There'd been a sprinkle of rain earlier. I closed the front door and went back to the kitchen. Evelyn was gazing out the window.

'Another coffee?' I said.

'How about a glass of wine instead?' she said, and raised her eyebrows.

It wasn't quite midday, but what the hell. I had nothing on for the rest of the day. Or the next day. Or the day after that.

'Sauvignon blanc okay?'

'Perfect. Poor old Valma.'

'She's hardly old, Evelyn. Believe it or not, she only has five years on us. And she means well.'

'The funny part about it is, back in the day, old Bob was a real soak. Just ask Reece.'

'Could be why she doesn't drink at all.'

Evelyn scoffed at that and wandered off to use the bathroom. I took down wine glasses and fetched the bottle from the fridge.

When we were seated again with brimming glasses in front of us, Evelyn said, 'I'd better just make it the one. I wouldn't want to get pulled over and have to blow in the bag on the way home.' She winked.

I wanted to slap her. A fleeting impulse, thankfully. 'Why don't you say what you mean, Evelyn?'

'All right, I will. It was your car, wasn't it? Parked on the side of the road after book club that day? One of the blokes who works for us recognised it, and you, getting into the police car.'

'And your point is?'

'Why couldn't you have just admitted it when I asked you? I thought we were friends. I might have been able to help.'

'How? You'd had as much to drink that afternoon as I had.'

'I could have asked one of the workmen to pick up your car. Did you leave it there all night?'

I shook my head.

'I hope you waited until you'd sobered up. You could have lost your licence.'

'Well, I didn't,' I said, without admitting that I hadn't been the one to retrieve the car. 'Rest assured, it won't ever happen again. I'd never so much as had a speeding ticket before that. Now, can we talk about something different?'

She laughed. 'You should know, Kate, after all the years you spent working at the hospital, there are no secrets in a country town. Someone *always* sees something, and don't they love joining the dots.'

'But they don't always get it right, do they?'

She raised her glass and clinked mine. 'What would be the fun in that?' she said.

At that precise moment I made the decision: as soon as Evelyn went, I would return the photograph of Tom to the box containing Uncle Frank's journals and I'd pretend I'd never seen it. There'd be no more dots to join with that one.

★ ★ ★

Daisy didn't say so outright, but I gathered she was disappointed when I confirmed that I'd no need to talk to Glenys Carlisle. We were out walking, believe it or not. She'd invited me to come along with her and Jess one morning. See if I liked it. I knew the exercise wouldn't do me any harm, if I could keep up with them.

'I'm not going to pursue the matter any more,' I said, huffing and puffing along beside her. 'Tom's identity can remain a mystery.'

'Fair enough,' she said. 'Glenys's dad has gone downhill fast in the last few days, and she's pretty focussed on him right now.'

'What's wrong with him?'

'I don't think the doctors know exactly, apart from him being well over ninety.'

'That'll do it.'

'She might flap about a bit, but when it comes down to it, Glenys is extremely level-headed. There have been no futile tests and treatments for old Bill, the tests that make everyone else feel better.'

It was only a gentle incline, but my lungs were burning and I could hear my heart pounding away. Without a word, Daisy modified her pace. Jess glanced at me. Was that scorn on her doggy face?

'You really are unfit, Kate,' Daisy said. 'But if you keep at it, gradually build up, you'll be amazed by how quickly your fitness improves.'

'I used to go to the gym and do pilates,' I said, between gasps.

'Of course you did,' she said with a smirk.

There was a seat coming up on the side of the trail. I didn't hesitate, I just flopped down, chest heaving. 'You go on. I'll wait here.'

'You're not having a heart attack, are you?' she said, sort of jokingly.

'Go,' I said, and they went.

I'd barely caught my breath before they were back. Daisy sat down beside me.

'Are you sure you're all right?' she said. 'You don't look as flushed as you did.'

'I'm unfit. I didn't realise how unfit.'

'You were a nurse. You know how these things work. Do you at least get your cholesterol and all that stuff checked regularly?'

'Of course I do,' I snapped. At the last count my total cholesterol was on the upper end of normal and my blood pressure had been borderline elevated. I'd visited the GP not long after Dennis had died and we'd put it down to the stress of that. Getting a bit fitter would be good for me, that much I knew for certain.

The return journey was all downhill and much easier. My legs felt like jelly nonetheless.

When we reached my front gate, Daisy said, 'Do you want to go again tomorrow?'

'Maybe the day after? I'll need tomorrow to recover.'

'Wimp,' she said, but she was smiling when she said it.

She peeled off to her place at twice the speed we'd been walking. I went inside and flopped into the nearest chair.

33

Daisy

When I arrived at the Carlisle farm there were several unfamiliar vehicles parked alongside Trev's ute and Glenys's wagon. I pulled in at the end, in the shade.

'You'll have to stay in the car, Jess, until I see what's happening. I've got a pretty good idea, though.' She hunkered down on the seat beside me. 'You are such a good dog.' I grazed the backs of my fingers along her snout. She sighed and closed her eyes.

With a heavy heart, I walked along the path to the back door. When no-one responded to my knock, I went inside. The kitchen was empty. Dirty mugs and plates cluttered the sink and surrounds, along with spilled sugar, coffee granules and used teabags. Glenys's cake tin had been abandoned on the kitchen table, the lid off. This was the first time I'd ever seen it empty.

The murmur of subdued voices emanated from the passageway. I rolled up my sleeves, put the plug into the sink and filled it with hot water and detergent and set about doing the dishes.

I'd almost finished when a woman burst into the kitchen. I knew at a glance it was Kaylene, Glenys and Trev's eldest. If not for several decades and a more contemporary fashion sense, she was her mother all over again.

'Aunty Daisy! Mum said you were coming out.'

'Hello, love. Long time no see,' I said. We hugged. 'How is he?'

Her expression sobered. 'Not good. That's why we're all here. Mum said it was unlikely he'd see the day out.'

'How is your mum?'

'Holding up. Between you and me, I'll be glad to see the end of Granddad. He's always been a miserable old sod. Mum's a saint for putting up with him and running around after him. When she said she was having him here ...' She groaned, closed her eyes briefly. 'Just the same, Uncle Ross could have helped out more. I suppose we all could have, but you know how it is.'

I did know, more than Kaylene could ever imagine. As Mum's health had failed, my brother and sister had rarely put in an appearance. They'd left the bulk of the caring to me—and then acted put-upon when they'd had to take a day out to help with the funeral arrangements.

'It'll be your turn one day, Kaylene,' I said, with a smile that might have been a tad sickly. 'And don't you forget that your mum deserves the best.'

Her eyes narrowed slightly but she didn't get a chance to reply because Glenys bustled into the room.

'Daisy! Thank goodness you're here. I think Dad's gone.'

Her eyes were wide. She grabbed my arm. I threw the tea towel onto the cupboard and let her propel me through the house to Bill's room. She closed the door behind us. All I could hear was our breathing; not his. And there was that smell. One a nurse never forgets.

Glenys tip-toed over to the bed. She still had a firm grip on my arm so I went with her.

'Dad?' she said, in a hoarse whisper. She poked him. 'Dad?' she said again, louder this time.

'I don't think he'll hear you,' I said gently. He was as white as the sheet; eyes open and already cloudy. 'Were you going to ring the doctor? Did he say he'd come?'

'In a while … He was here late yesterday. He didn't think Dad would last out the next twenty-four hours. That's why I called everyone, so they could come and say their goodbyes.' She gave a dry laugh that morphed into a sob. 'Not that they haven't had long enough to come and say their goodbyes.'

I squeezed her hand. 'We each make our own choices, and you did everything humanly possible to make his last days comfortable, Glenys. And then some. Don't let anyone dare suggest otherwise.'

She nodded, tears tracking silently down her cheeks. 'I know better than most what a difficult old so-and-so he could be, but he was still my dad.'

I laughed, swiped at the tears on my own cheeks and held Glenys close in a brief and fierce hug.

Someone tapped on the door. It opened a fraction and Trev's head appeared. 'What's happening?' Then he saw his wife's tear-streaked face. 'Oh, dear,' he said. He came into the room and gathered Glenys into his arms.

'I'll leave you to it,' I said, and left.

A man around my age loitered outside the door. It took a minute but then at the same time we recognised each other.

'Ross Toogood,' I said to Glenys's younger brother. 'It's been a long time.'

'That it has, Daisy. Decent of you to help Glenys out with the old man,' he said, looking down at his feet. 'Is he, um—'

'Your dad's not with us any more,' I said. 'I'd give Trev and Glenys a minute or two before you went in.'

He stepped back and he had that deer in the headlights look. 'I, er, said my goodbyes earlier,' he mumbled.

'Is Barbara with you? I'll go and say hello if she is.'

'No, unfortunately Barbie couldn't make the trip. Her health's not the best.'

'I'm sorry to hear that. Please pass on my regards. And how are your kids? Grandkids?'

'Three grandchildren, and they're all doing very well. Glenys said you're staying with your granddaughter. Do you ever hear from Charlie?'

'Not often, and before you ask, I haven't a clue where he is, how he is, or what he's doing. Now, I must get back to the dishes. Let me know if Glenys needs me.'

'Right-o,' he said, and squared his shoulders and fixed his gaze on the door like a sentry.

The loungeroom door was closed when I sped past on the way to the kitchen. I could hear the television or a radio. Kaylene was standing at the sink, staring out of the window. She turned when I came into the room.

'Is he dead?' she said.

'Yes, he is.'

'I'd better go to Mum.'

She hurried off. After I'd dried the dishes, I filled the kettle and left everything laid out ready for when they'd want their next cuppa. There was a packet of biscuits in the pantry and I put it out. Then I went outside to check on Jess. She had a leg stretch and a drink of water and happily jumped back into the car.

'Should we just go?' I whispered close to her ear. 'Leave them to it. Not much I can do here now.' I straightened and peered across the roof of the car towards the house.

Kaylene's husband Darren came outside, to smoke, as it turned out. I hadn't seen him since he'd married Kaylene, but I easily identified him from the plethora of family photos around the house. They lived in Adelaide. Kaylene was the eldest; then came Garry, who worked up north in the mines and hadn't been home to see his granddad in an age, according to Glenys. Bridgette, the youngest, lived locally with her husband and was a regular visitor at the farm. Hers was the only car I'd recognised in the lineup.

The smell of tobacco smoke drifted over. I wrinkled my nose. Trev came out of the house. He spoke to Darren, glanced my way and then walked towards me.

'Glenys was asking where you'd got to. Are you coming in for a brew? The kettle's on.'

'I thought I might go home. Leave you all to it.'

'Don't you dare,' he said, affronted. 'You're family, Daisy. Come on inside. Glenys said there's more cake in the freezer. And lamingtons.'

Was I family? Better still, did I want to be family? I didn't think of myself that way, not any more. Never really had thought it even when Charlie and I were together. My children were a mix of Miller *and* Toogood genes and I'd always acknowledged that other part of their heritage. But I'd never gone out of my way to maintain a Toogood connection, not ever. Sad, really, that Charlie's whole family had born the brunt of his misdemeanours and irresponsible behaviour.

'My dogs are penned up so you can let your dog loose. Mind you, she looks mighty comfortable where she is,' Trev was saying, while I had my mini epiphany.

Jess jumped out when I reopened the car door and scooted off, nose to the ground. Trev and I walked towards the house. Darren was lighting another cigarette as we passed.

'You know those things'll kill ya,' Trev said.

'I'm here for a good time, not a long time,' Darren replied and coughed a phlegmy cough.

'Yeah, right.' Trev shook his head. 'Not much happening upstairs with that one,' he added when we were out of earshot. 'Beats me what Kaylene ever saw in him. But Glenys tells me he was her choice, not ours, and that's how it should be.'

He paused at the back door, turned to me and frowned. 'How's young Ryan getting on? Damn good worker that lad, keen as mustard. Picked things up just like that,' he said, and snapped his fingers. 'I hated school myself, so I know where he's coming from.'

'He's settling into the new school, so I believe. Gareth and Tess won't consider letting him leave school before the end of Year 12. And they're right. No matter what he chooses to do in the future, he needs a solid academic foundation.'

Trev nodded sagely. 'End of next year. I can wait that long.'

'For what?'

'I offered the lad a job. I need help here. I'm no youngster and Garry's not interested in farming, and neither is that drop kick,' he said, and jerked a thumb in Darren's direction. 'Bridgette's husband is a copper ... No interest in the land.'

'What about your grandkids? One of them might be interested.'

'Only the one grandson, the rest are girls, and he's a bit of a pansy if you ask me. Wants to be an architect! I thought Martha might be the one, but she's got herself married to a teacher and all she wants to do now is pop out a bundle of babies.' He shook his head, genuinely perplexed. 'Makes a bloke wonder why he's busted his gut all these years.'

'Yeah, but what else would we have been doing, Trev?'

He clapped me on the shoulder. 'True, mate. Let's go in and get into that cake before everyone else gobs it.'

★★★

On the drive home, I considered what Trev had said about Ryan. Who knew what the future held? The sun slanted right into my eyes and reminded me how late in the afternoon it was. Georgia would have had one whole, uninterrupted day to sleep. With three nights left to work, I hoped she had.

Glenys had wanted to clean up Bill before the undertaker arrived, and I'd helped her do it. We'd dressed him in a fresh pair of pyjamas, and she'd insisted on bed socks. 'Because he always complained about having cold feet,' she'd said.

Martha and her husband had shown up around lunch time. Kaylene and I had made sandwiches for everyone. Never once had I felt like an intruder.

Before I'd left the farm, I'd said to Trev, 'Regarding Ryan, should I mention anything to Gareth?'

'Wouldn't hurt. And give Gareth my phone number, tell him to call me, and we'll chat. Down the track, Roseworthy Agricultural College might be an option for Ryan, but he'd need to pull his weight at school, if that's the direction he decided to go.'

'Thanks, Trev,' I'd said, but it'd felt inadequate. In a word, I was humbled by the kindness and generosity shown me by Glenys and Trevor. Over the years, I'd given them no reason to continue considering me, or my offspring, as family, but they had regardless.

Kate's garage door was open when I drove past, but the garage was empty. While I was glad she was out and about, because in my opinion she spent way too much time on her own moping about and wallowing in the past, I was disappointed that she wasn't home.

My day had been huge. One of those days you rewind and wonder how everything that happened did so in that amount of time. It would have been nice to stop by and debrief with her.

Fancy that, I thought, and indicated to turn into Georgia's street. Not much surpassed the company of an old friend. Maybe it was possible to breathe new life into an old friendship, one that had been let fall by the wayside. Only time, and a bit of effort, would tell.

'Oh, no,' I said to Jess and let my shoulders slump. Kieran's ute and trailer were parked out the front of Georgia's. The last thing I felt like was putting on a smile and being the third wheel, again.

34

Kate

It was a sound decision to forget about Tom. Dwelling on the issue would get me nowhere, and there wasn't much to forget: a photo and a name that didn't even include a surname. That was it.

Why, then, couldn't I forget about him? He was never far from my thoughts and that I didn't know who he was continued to plague me. So much so that I retrieved the photo and propped it on the bookshelf in full view. Every time I walked from the family room to the kitchen, I glanced at it. Did I hope that might shift a deeply buried memory? A hint to the identity of the boy in the photograph? So far, it hadn't.

Glenys Carlisle's father had died the previous Thursday and his funeral was tomorrow, a week after his death. Of course Daisy was going, but I wouldn't. No point. While I knew of the Carlisles, I didn't know them. Nothing more hypocritical than attending a funeral when you could only claim a flimsy connection with the deceased and their family. In my opinion.

I glanced at the clock. Almost nine. I'd better get a move on. I was taking Rhonda to the podiatrist by ten and I was still in my walking clothes. That's right, my walking clothes. I'd even invested in a quality pair of gaudily coloured sneakers. But I refused to even consider switching my cotton cut-offs for lycra.

Rhonda was her usual cheerful self, but I did notice her white-knuckled grip on the walking frame. And the food stain on the front of her powder-blue twinset. After the podiatrist, I suggested coffee and cake and she agreed enthusiastically. Instead of a main street café, I took her to a nearby cellar-door restaurant and cafe that boasted the best of everything.

'Isn't this special?' she said. 'And it's not even my birthday.'

We stopped to peruse the cake cabinet on our way past. Then a waitress showed us to a table by the window and the view of the valley, resplendent in autumn colours, was stunning. My breath hitched remembering the last time I'd been there with Dennis: his birthday the previous year. I'd been impatient with him for dithering over what to eat. I was snapped back to the present when the thoughtful waitress whisked away Rhonda's walking frame and asked to take our order.

'Were you thinking about Dennis?' Rhonda said, after we'd sat for a while and taken in the view. 'The last time you came here? It's never easy, is it? The places look the same, except the person's no longer in the frame. I still look for Stephen. I sometimes turn to him to share an anecdote, and I'm reminded afresh that he's not there. He's been gone seventeen years now … and I share the anecdote with him anyway.' She laughed and, still smiling, said, 'Life's hard, Kate, and we do whatever we can to ease our way through it.'

The waitress came with our morning tea, saving me a reply.

'Ooh, decadent,' Rhonda said to the authentic-looking puff pastry and cream mille-feuille the waitress placed on the table in front of her. 'It wasn't that big in the cabinet!'

'My cholesterol goes up just looking at them,' the waitress said.

'When you get to my age you stop worrying about a trivial thing like cholesterol,' Rhonda said. She poured her tea, milk in first, picked up the dessert fork and elegantly tucked in.

On the drive home, out of the blue, she said, 'You know, Kate, soon after Stephen died, I found myself worrying less about my own death. He passed peacefully in the night. He hadn't been unwell, and I thought, death happens, whether we're ready or not. No point stressing over it.'

'What about all those things you wish you'd said, or not said, to him? And the things you'll never be able to make right? To say you're sorry. To take more time with him. To listen. Appreciate him more.'

We were home. I pulled into her driveway and stopped the car. When I turned to her, I knew there were tears in my eyes.

'Oh, my dear,' she said gently, and took my hand in both of hers. Her hands were warm, the grip firm, but so very fragile. 'You must forgive yourself, Kate, for all those things you could have or should have said or done differently. And never forget the good times; I'm sure there were many. I try to live each day as if it's my last, that way I'm not leaving the door open for new regrets.'

'Wise advice,' I said. No small task, forgiving myself. There was so much to forgive.

A car door slammed. I glanced in the rear-view mirror. A silver sedan was parked in front of Rhonda's place and a slim, dark-haired woman was walking through the gate.

'Are you expecting anyone?'

Rhonda shifted in the seat to look. 'My goodness. Ellen. She does my cleaning. I'd forgotten today was her day.' She fumbled with the seat belt. I leaned over to help her.

'I've had a lovely morning,' she said. 'I'll book you to take me to get my toenails cut next time, and morning tea's on me.'

Back at my place, I closed the garage door and went inside. Would Rhonda's cleaning lady be interested in more work, I wondered. The next time I saw Rhonda, I'd ask her to ask Ellen. Or not. Cleaning gave me something to do. I went into the kitchen and put the kettle on, then changed my mind and turned it off. The house was quiet; a lonely kind of quiet. It had gone twelve but after scones with jam and cream for morning tea I wouldn't be needing any lunch.

I wandered aimlessly into the family room. If we'd been living at the farm when Dennis had been killed, would his presence have lingered there for longer than it had here? After all, he'd lived in this house a mere two years, but over four decades in the farmhouse. And while this house was everything I told myself I'd ever wanted, now that Dennis was gone, there was a perpetual emptiness about it that no amount of bespoke furniture and limited-edition prints would ever fill.

The doorbell rang after I'd been home about an hour. My first thought was that Rhonda had left something in the car and she'd sent Ellen to collect it. I could ask her myself if she was interested in more work. Maybe.

With that thought, I smiled and opened the door, only to be confronted by a man I'd never seen before.

'Yes,' I said. 'Can I help you?'

'I'm looking for a Mrs Kate Hannaford,' he said in a pleasant baritone.

'I'm Kate Hannaford,' I said. There was something so familiar about his voice that without hesitation, I unlatched the screen door and pushed it open. I felt the blood drain from my head.

Not Dennis, but close. I felt as if I'd been sucker-punched.

'Hello,' he said, and held open the screen door. 'I'm Tom.' His smile—*Dennis's* smile— faltered.

I made a strangled sound; a noise that came from the very depths of my being.

'Are you all right?' he said, reaching out a steadying hand.

I shook it off.

He stepped back. 'You know who I am? How?'

'A photograph. Among my late husband's belongings. Your resemblance to my late husband was … remarkable. Even in Year 7. Do you go by Hannaford?'

'No, Wilkins. My mother's name.'

So it *was* true. All this time, Dennis had had a son. Rage and bitterness rose inside me; I could taste it in the back of my throat. It threatened to choke me. 'Just tell me one thing, how old are you?'

'Forty-two, last birthday.'

'And when was that?'

'January the twenty-seventh.'

The day Dennis had died.

I saw black spots just before I fainted.

★★★

He must have carried me inside because I woke lying in Dennis's recliner, my feet up. The situation outstripped irony. With an effort, I sat up.

'You passed out,' he said, handing me a glass of water. 'I caught you before you hit the deck. Here, drink this.'

He'd been in my kitchen and opened my cupboards to find a glass. What else had he been doing while I'd been unconscious in *that bastard* Dennis's recliner?

I drank the water, slow sips until the wobbliness passed, then I put my feet to the floor. 'You can go now,' I said.

'Not until I've done what I came to do. Please don't forget that I had absolutely no say in any of this.'

I refused to look at him. I couldn't. It was all too hard to process, and I was so enraged by what Dennis had done, and then not done. 'Why did you come?' I whispered.

'My mother died a few weeks ago, and it was a deathbed request, if you like.' He reached into the inside pocket of his jacket and took out a white envelope, the size that bills come in. 'She asked me to give you this. She said it would explain most things. I couldn't say one way or another because she asked me specifically not to read the letter, at least not until you had. Then you could decide whether or not to give it to me to read.'

'How did you know where to find me?'

'Dennis.'

Tom held out the envelope and, when I didn't take it, he carefully placed it on the coffee table. 'I'll go. I'm booked into accommodation here for tonight. If you want to talk, I'll be there until I check out at ten tomorrow morning. I've written my mobile number on the back of the envelope. Ring any time.'

'Before you go, I have one question,' I said, and my voice cracked. I cleared my throat. 'Was his accident on the way to visit you, or was he on his way home?'

'Home. I'm sorry.'

I heard the front door close in his wake. I scrambled to my feet and waited briefly for the light-headedness to pass before I hurried to the window. He drove a nice car. European, by the looks. I watched until he'd driven away. Then I swallowed back the lump of bitterness that had risen again in my throat and went to get my journals. Forty-two on the twenty-seventh of January this year. What had been happening in late April, early May, 1979? Apart from the obvious.

35

Daisy

It was late. My bedroom had been reassembled for the night and I was ironing what I planned to wear to Bill Toogood's funeral the following day: a dark-coloured linen-mix dress; a lucky find at the op shop earlier that day. If it'd ever been worn at all, it would have only been once or twice. Georgia had loaned me a pair of shoes to wear with it. They'd fit, with cotton wool stuffed into the toes.

I'd put the ironing board away and left the iron to cool on the sink when my phone rang. I was tempted to ignore it. These days there was rarely any uplifting news. It was Kate. I was surprised. She'd messaged me a few times but she'd never rung me before.

'You sound a bit drunk?' I said, after her slurred greeting.

'Not drunk ... just very upset. Could you come around?'

'Now?'

'Please.'

'All right. I'll be there in ten.'

I flicked Georgia a message telling her what I was up to and that I'd leave Jess inside. My granddaughter was with Kieran and would head home soon.

Kate's entrance light was blazing and the front door unlocked. I experienced a shiver of apprehension as I let myself in. I found her standing forlornly in the family room. She'd aged a decade since we'd walked that morning, her eyes red-rimmed and puffy. What she was wearing would have looked smart when she'd put it on. Now it was a wrinkled and dishevelled mess.

'What's happened?'

'He came here. To my house.'

'Who?' I put my car keys down on the coffee table beside a stack of journal-sized notebooks. Then I noticed the photograph propped on the middle shelf of the bookcase. 'Tom?'

She nodded, as if she didn't trust herself to speak.

'When?'

She moved her mouth and licked her lips. 'Some time after lunch.'

'How did he know where to come?'

She pointed to a folded letter and a torn-open envelope lying on the floor beside the coffee table. 'It's all in there,' she said, and swayed.

'Kate!' I grabbed her just in time and guided her into one of the leather recliners. 'Sit. Put your feet up. I'll go and make tea. I don't suppose you've had anything to eat since he came.'

'It would have made me sick,' she hissed.

At the kitchen sink I sucked in a deep breath, filling my lungs right to the bottom, and then let the breath out slowly. That's when I noticed the dirty wineglass on the sink. And the empty wine bottle. *Don't judge*, I told myself. I filled the electric kettle. While it boiled, I went to see how she was faring. She looked old and frail, propped up there, dwarfed by the size of the recliner.

'Is he Dennis's son?' I said.

Without opening her eyes, she nodded. 'It was almost like seeing Dennis standing there. He's a trifle taller, leaner, but he even smiles like Dennis.'

'Oh, Kate. What a terrible shock for you. Did he stay long?'

'I didn't want him to stay at all, but I fainted, and he carried me inside.' She gave a croaky laugh. 'Not like me to be a drama queen.'

I had to agree, it wasn't like her at all. When I'd known Kate before she'd always kept her emotions on a tight rein. Along with her alcohol intake. Things change.

'The kettle will have boiled. I'll make the tea. Do you want something to eat?'

'Just tea.'

After I'd found the two largest mugs in the cupboard, I poured the tea and added milk, and two spoonfuls of sugar to Kate's.

She wrinkled her nose when she took the first tentative sip. 'Too sweet,' she said, but drank it any way.

I sat down with my tea on one end of the ginormous leather couch. It made a rude noise when I sat, but it was more comfortable than I'd imagined it would be.

'Do you want to read the letter?' she said when she'd finished the tea.

'No. Unless you want me to.'

She lifted one shoulder and let it drop. 'Basically, Tom was conceived in late April 1979. Not a one-night stand, but almost. The fling lasted over a weekend and then, supposedly, they each went their separate ways again.'

'Was she from around here?'

'Her letter said that she was in town with a group of girlfriends. For a boozy weekend, would be my guess.'

'I would have been pregnant then. Jay was born on the seventh of July that year.'

'And I'd been *totally* obsessed with trying to get pregnant. Too obsessed to notice my husband was—' She choked back a sob. 'It's all there in my journals. I was just too self-absorbed to see it.'

'How do you mean?'

'The weekend it would have happened, Dennis didn't come home on Friday night. He'd been to an Ag Bureau function and they all went to the pub afterwards. He rang, late, said he'd had too much to drink and was staying at the hotel. I was exhausted after a crying jag because I'd just got my period. I did offer to drive in and pick him up, but I'd taken painkillers for the cramps and wasn't keen on doing that. He stayed at the hotel. Didn't get home until Saturday lunch time.'

'Weren't you worried?'

'I was asleep. The pills must've knocked me out, and I wasn't working that day, so no alarm. I remember waking up about ten am and thinking he must be outside working.'

'That was only a one-night stand.'

She looked down at her hands, clasped in her lap. 'He went back Sunday for more.'

'How do you know that?'

'She says so, in her letter. Reckons they used contraception, and she didn't know she was pregnant until it was too late to do anything about it.'

'Do you think she knew he was married?'

'She didn't say, and now she can't. She died recently, of some kind of cancer. That's why he came. She asked him to bring me the letter.'

'Any mention of a stepfather? Half-brothers or -sisters?'

'Nothing.'

'This is a lot to take in,' I said, suddenly feeling overwhelmingly tired.

'You're telling me.'

'Do you want more tea?' I yawned.

'I'll make it,' she said and pushed herself to her feet. I held out my empty mug. 'Thanks for coming over, Daisy,' she said. 'It means more to me than you'll ever know.'

'We're friends,' I said, and she smiled.

She came back a while later with the teapot, milk and sugar on a tray; two bone china mugs and a packet of chocolate Tim Tams. She dragged an occasional table over to me, put the tray down and opened the biscuits.

'I couldn't be bothered putting them on a plate.'

'Good grief, what an unforgivable catering faux pas,' I said.

'Don't be cheeky.' She poured the tea. 'Can I ask you another favour?' she said, and sat down. 'He left me his mobile number. He's staying in town overnight and said to call if I wanted to talk. I might, but not now. It's all too new and raw. Could you ring him for me, and say I'll be in contact, if and when I'm ready?'

'Now?'

'You think it's too late to do it tonight?'

'Probably, but I'll bet he can't sleep. Not after the bombshell he dropped on you earlier.'

Kate found her mobile phone underneath the stack of journals. 'Do you want to use this?'

'Better I use mine,' I said. 'Unless you want him to have your phone number?'

'It doesn't matter to me. He knows where I live.' She handed me her phone and picked up the envelope off the floor. I tapped the number in as she reeled off the digits.

It rang. And rang. Kate's gaze bored into me.

'Hello, Tom Wilkins,' came a sleepy, deep voice. 'Mrs Hannaford?'

'Her friend, Daisy Miller,' I said. 'She asked me to call you.'

Kate was mouthing *thank you* over and over as she backed out of the room.

'Is she all right?' he said.

'Yes, apart from being extremely upset.'

'I'm relieved she has a friend with her. I didn't like leaving her on her own, but she didn't want me to stay.' He cleared his throat. 'The whole situation is ... awkward.'

'I agree. She asked me to tell you that she might want to talk to you, but not now. It's all too ... new and raw, were her words.'

There was pause. I could hear him breathing.

'Did you know my father ... Dennis?'

'A long time ago. I met Kate before she was married. I was at their wedding. Dennis always treated me with respect.'

'I didn't have the pleasure until I was a teenager, and his visits were only ever brief, and few and far between. Mum did explain that back then they hadn't had a relationship per se, which made it difficult for her as well.'

'And with Dennis being *married*,' I said, because I couldn't help myself.

'That too. I would appreciate talking to Mrs Hannaford. I have questions about who he was, because I am his son, whether she likes it or not.'

'She has your phone number, she'll call when she's ready.'

I'd taken the phone from my ear and was about to disconnect when I heard him say, 'Wait. Before you hang up ...'

'Yes?'

'Advise her to get a check-up. She was out to it for a while and it might have been more than a faint.'

'And how would you know?'

'I'm a doctor. An orthopaedic surgeon, as it happens, but I still remember how to take a person's pulse, and what's normal and what's not.' He was a whisper away from sounding pompous. But that might have been because he was tired. This would have been emotionally demanding for him as well.

'I'll pass on the message,' I said. 'Good night.'

He said good night and, after all that, I think he hung up before I could.

Kate must have been listening for the sound of my voice because she was back in the room moments after I'd disconnected.

'What did he say?'

'You could have stayed and listened.'

'I couldn't, and I needed to go to the bathroom.'

'He said that you need to get your GP to check you out. He thought it might have been more than a simple faint.'

Her mouth dropped open.

'He's a doctor,' I said. 'Orthopaedics.'

She flinched, and then her eyes narrowed. 'I'll bet that's why she contacted Dennis in the first place. To help pay for the boy's education.'

'Did she say so, in the letter? And when did she first tell Dennis he had a son? Tom said he was a teenager before he met his father. Any hints in your journals? You'd think a bombshell like that would have sent even Dennis into a spin.'

'I'd stopped keeping a journal by that time, and nothing springs to mind. The letter made no mention, but it makes perfect sense that she'd want money, don't you think?'

'Hate to agree, but yes, it does.'

'There'd be no easy way of proving it for sure, or how much. I had little to do with the farm books and banking, not enough to know where the money went.'

'You could always ask Tom. To me he sounded like a straightforward sort of person. And honest. It would have been easier for him to just throw his mother's letter in the bin.'

The tea had cooled but I drank mine anyway. I had a Tim Tam but Kate's appetite had deserted her again.

She perched on the edge of the recliner, shoulders hunched. 'What do you think I should do?' she said in a small voice.

'Not make any decisions until you've carefully thought it all through. I don't see how talking to him could do any harm. Even if it's only the once. It might help you both understand a bit more. None of this is Tom's fault.'

'That's the thing, Daisy, I think I do understand why Dennis did it, but that doesn't mean I'll ever forgive him for doing it.'

'He'll never know that. What would be the point of letting yourself get all bitter and twisted about it?'

She glared at me, then a scatter cushion came flying through the air. I ducked just in time.

'I wish you wouldn't always be so practical and annoyingly right,' she said, and dropped her head into her hands with a groan.

With more effort than it should have taken, I stood up. Everything ached. Some days I forgot I was almost seventy. Not today. 'I'm going home. If you're okay enough to toss a pillow at me, you're okay to be here on your own.'

'Leave the tea things,' she said, her voice muffled from behind her hands.

'Unless you want me to stay?' It was close on midnight, but I would have.

She lifted her head and gave it a shake. 'Thanks for offering but I'm going to shower and go to bed. I'm totally drained. I'll give tomorrow's walk a miss.'

'Don't forget to make a doctor's appointment,' I said. 'I'll see myself out.'

36

Kate

The following morning I watched the clock and only let myself relax when ten o'clock, check-out time, came and went. Not that I'd expected him to come back, but I felt better knowing he'd be on his way out of town. *Dr* Tomas Wilkins, Orthopaedic Surgeon. I'd googled him on my smart phone. Nothing about marital status or offspring, but he was in a practice with four other orthopaedic surgeons. One name I recognised: a visiting specialist who used to consult when I'd been the director of nursing at the hospital.

I'd never know how much of the farm's income had gone into putting Dr Wilkins through medical school. Some farmer's wives chose to be actively involved in the farm business, but I hadn't been one of them. Dennis had never asked it of me, and I'd never volunteered. I'd had my own career; my own pay packet. Nevertheless, in a roundabout sort of a way, a portion of my income could have contributed to the good doctor's education.

While I might have insight into why Dennis had behaved the way he had, I couldn't get my head around the fact that he *actually had*. Now that I'd met his son in the flesh, there'd be no pretending otherwise. How could I ever forgive him for that? Had he ever been going to tell me about his son?

Late morning, when I walked across the street to Rhonda's place, I found it near-impossible to assimilate that only twenty-four hours previously I'd craved Dennis's forgiveness for *my* flaws. How contrary life could be.

An hour later, over cups of tea, I'd recounted the whole tawdry tale to Rhonda. Except for the part about Dennis's being killed in a car crash on his way back from visiting his son on his birthday. I hadn't told Daisy that bit either. It was too painful for even me to contemplate.

'How do you forgive someone for something like that?' I said when I'd finished. 'And why would I want to have anything to do with that man? His son.'

Rhonda had listened with rapt attention and now she regarded me with a thoughtful expression.

'Kate, you need to ask yourself, what it is that you can't forgive? Is it that your husband was unfaithful to you? Or is it that he had a son after all, the one thing that you couldn't give him? Or rather that he didn't share the boy with you?'

I gasped. It was if she'd thrown cold water over me.

She reached across and patted the back of my hand. 'At your age, Kate, don't waste any time on unnecessary resentments and recriminations. Dennis is dead. Given what you've just told me, this Tom sounds to be very much alive. Please pardon my poor choice of words, but don't throw the baby out with the bathwater. Besides, he might want his father's keepsakes, the ones you didn't know what to do with the other day.

'Have I been too candid?' she said, with a note of concern when I just sat there. 'I'm sorry if I have. My children tell me I can be quite blunt.'

'No,' I said eventually. 'My friend Daisy said something similar when I told her. I should be grateful I have friends who care enough to give it to me straight.'

But I was still reeling from it all when I walked home a while later. Even after considering other options, the overwhelming premonition I'd had after studying Tom's photo had proved to be correct: Tom was Dennis's son. But that didn't mean I had to like it, or embrace it. That the reality of it hadn't been the biggest slap in the face.

After Daisy had left last night, I had showered and gone to bed, taking my journals with me. I'd read and reread what I'd written in the weeks and months after 'the weekend' and conceded that Tom's mother had most likely been telling the truth: I couldn't find the slightest hint of anything suggesting an ongoing affair. Nothing in Dennis's diaries either.

The more I thought about it all, the more I had to allow that Daisy was right: none of this was Tom's fault. My grievance was with his parents and they were both dead, so there could be no satisfaction found there. As rational as all of that sounded, I couldn't talk to him yet. The mere though of it made my stomach roil, because I knew what he'd want to know and I wasn't ready to tell him what a decent man his father had been.

★★★

That afternoon I went to the hairdresser. My regular cut and colour were long overdue, and I needed a boost. After several failed attempts at making conversation, the hairdresser finally left me in peace and went about her job in silence. My usual girl was on extended leave, but I was pleased with the job this girl did.

Who should I bump into when I left the salon but Evelyn.

'Kate, hello. Your hair looks nice. I was going to ring you later. I've made the jelly cakes. Have you enough room in your freezer?'

'Plenty. Do you want me to pick them up?'

'I can drop them around. Tomorrow? Mid-morning? Coffee?'

After we'd confirmed the arrangement, she said, 'Do you know who died? There's a huge funeral happening. Cars lined up both sides of the road when I came into town.'

'Bill Toogood.'

Her mouth turned down and she gave her head a shake.

'Do you know Glenys and Trevor Carlisle?'

'I don't think I've ever heard of them. Are they in the wine business?'

'Broad acre farmers, out where we used to be. Bill is Glenys's father.'

'Really,' she said, totally losing interest when she discovered they weren't in the *waan* business. 'I'd better get on my way. I'm in the middle of packing the caravan for our trip north and I needed a few things. I'll see you tomorrow.'

Walking back to the car, I decided I didn't like Evelyn as much as I thought I had. She really was quite snobby and gossipy. Imagine what she'd do with the Dennis and Tom story, if she ever found out. That thought stopped me dead in my tracks. Rhonda and Daisy would be discreet with the information, but would Tom? Surely he had no reason not to be tight-lipped about it. He was a doctor; he'd fully comprehend the importance of privacy and confidentiality. Reassured to a limited extent, I kept walking. When I did talk to him, I'd specifically request that he didn't speak about it to anyone. Fingers crossed that he hadn't already.

★ ★ ★

Friday morning, Daisy and Jess picked me up at the corner. It was a bright, sunny morning and the front lawn had been heavy with dew. Daisy's face was pale and drawn. Even the dog was subdued.

'You look as if you've been to a funeral,' I said. My attempt at humour.

She sniffed.

'How was it?'

'A substantial crowd. A reflection of how well liked and respected Glenys and Trevor are in the farming community. Georgia swapped a shift and came with me, which was nice.'

'I suppose they're her relatives, and she wouldn't have met many of them before. Was Charlie there?' It had only just occurred to me that Bill Toogood was his uncle.

'Nope. Glenys said they'd talked on the phone. How are you?'

'Let's not talk about me and my woes! Who else did you know at the funeral?'

She glanced at me then said, 'A few faces looked familiar, but I couldn't put names to them.'

'You sound a bit flat.'

'We went out to the farm afterwards. Georgia wanted to spend more time with her new-found—' She paused.

'Second ... third ... cousins?'

'Something like that. Anyway, I should have encouraged her to go on her own. These days I'm not up for two late nights in a row. And I'd forgotten how rowdy and relentless a mob of Toogoods are when they get together and into the booze. They must have a party gene.'

'How's Glenys coping?'

'She's sad, physically and emotionally worn out, but relieved. He was only ever going to leave the house feet first. She knew that when she took on the role of caring for him.'

We crossed the road and traversed the path that led to the walking trail. Honeyeaters flitted through the scrub and a kookaburra laughed nearby.

'He really was a horrible old man, Kate. I couldn't find anything about him to like. Glenys must take after her mother.'

'Was it difficult being there, with all the Toogoods? Do you feel as if you're still part of the family?'

She laughed. 'I'll be honest, the day Glenys tapped me on the shoulder at the op shop, my first thought was, *Oh, no!* And when she invited me and Georgia out for a meal I went because Georgia needed to meet them. But with Glenys and Trev being the way they are … It's hard not to feel like part of the family.'

I faltered momentarily when a deep and powerful yearning to be part of such a family squeezed at my insides. A family who laughed, argued, partied and grieved together. It was something I'd never experienced. My own family had been reserved and distant. The only arguing we'd ever done had been nasty. None of us could wait to be away from each other, forever.

'Do you think there's a Mrs Tom Wilkins?' I said. 'Children?'

'Quite likely, unless of course he's gay. But then he could still be in a relationship and have children. Why don't you ask him when you talk to him?'

I stopped dead in the middle of the trail. Daisy kept on for several paces before she cottoned on that I wasn't beside her. She spun around. Jess followed suit.

'What?'

'So you think he's gay?'

She held up both hands, palms facing upwards. 'How would I know, after one very brief phone conversation, where he fits in today's alphabet soup of gender identity and sexual preference? But would it matter if he was gay? Now that I've put it out there.'

'It wouldn't matter to me,' I said, and caught up with her again. 'But I don't think Dennis would have coped with it.'

Daisy grabbed my arm. 'Why are we having this ridiculous conversation?' she said.

'I've no idea, except that I was imagining what it would be like to be part of a family like the Toogoods. And then I got to thinking about the likelihood of Tom having a wife and a family ... What they'd be like ... If they'd like me ...'

'I'd forgotten how much you overthink things, Kate. Worrying at something doesn't change the outcome. Not it my experience, anyway.'

'But surely you worry about the big things?'

Daisy laughed. 'In the middle of the night, everything is big. Worrying about it only keeps me awake. It doesn't solve anything, and I feel extra tired the next day.'

'But don't you worry that you don't have a home, except for a sofa bed at your granddaughter's? And what if Gareth's plan to build the townhouses goes awry? Then there's Charlie. Imagine if he showed up one day and asked for a divorce so he could marry someone else? Don't you think about any of those things and worry what the future might hold?'

'Of course I do! I wouldn't be human if I didn't, but what control do I have over any of it? Worrying doesn't change one damn thing. Today I have a roof over my head, a yard for my dog, friends and plenty to eat. Right at this moment, I'm okay.'

'But what if all that changed tomorrow? Or even later today?'

'Then I'd do my best to deal with it,' she said, and looked at me as if her answer was obvious. 'If something's going to happen, worrying myself sick beforehand won't make any difference, will it? It's what I do after it happens that matters.'

'I suppose so,' I said.

We finished the walk mostly in silence, me deliberating on what she'd said. At one stage I must have been frowning, because she nudged me with her elbow. 'I hope you're not overthinking my problems along with your own,' she said.

That made me smile. 'I was remembering how easy you are to be with. How sensible and practical. Should we have made more of an effort back then, to keep our friendship on track? To keep in contact?'

'Not necessarily, Kate. We were young, less mature, there were so many other demands on our time and our attention. Perhaps we could have tried harder, but we didn't, for whatever the reasons.'

'There you go again, pragmatic to the very end.'

'Just for the record, I'm not always sensible and practical,' she said, and bumped me with her shoulder.

For the remainder of the walk neither of us felt the need to fill the space between us with trivial chit-chat. Being in each other's company was enough for now. I hadn't realised how much I'd missed it.

37

Daisy

Laughter drifted in from outside. Georgia and Kieran were out the back, where he was ostensibly patching up the verandah after I'd put my foot through a floorboard. The place had termites. It truly was in a poor state of repair, and I could have done myself a more serious injury than the minor ankle sprain I'd sustained. I shifted the icepack, wiggled my backside into a more comfortable position and went back to my musing.

Although I hadn't said as much to Kate, I wouldn't have been surprised if Charlie had shown up at Bill Toogood's funeral. Over the years there'd been a few occasions where Charlie and me were required to be in the same place at the same time: weddings; the odd funeral; grandchildren. We'd navigated them all with relative decorum. For it to work I'd treated each instance as if I'd run into an old friend; one I'd once shared a house with, but then lost track of. Regardless, each time had been an emotional strain for me. But although I'd wished for many things, I'd never wished him ill.

How it'd been for Charlie, I couldn't tell you. Apart from the superficial, I'd never once enquired and he hadn't ever volunteered the information. He'd always appeared to be his usual easy-going self. That said, considering the likelihood of him being at Bill's funeral had sent me into a minor spin, and I couldn't explain why. Kate's summons the night before the funeral and then the explanation behind it had given me something else to occupy my thoughts for a time. Until those same thoughts had sucked me back into the past again.

I'd meant what I'd said to Kate earlier: I did try not to worry about what life might deal me; a lemons into lemonade approach. Most of the time it worked, but deep down I was beginning to tire of the effort. I was fed up with always being the flexible one, and although I fought against it, a paralysing anxiety about what the future might hold was slowly insinuating itself into my consciousness. I was too old to be living my life on a knife-edge of uncertainty.

Jess barked. More laughter. I returned the icepack to the freezer and hobbled out to check on their progress. The splintered old floorboards had been removed and replaced with two bright and unblemished pine boards. Kieran and Georgia were throwing a tennis ball for the dog. I sat in a canvas chair and put my foot up on the washing basket. Georgia jogged over.

'Are you okay, Gran? Your ankle looks a bit swollen.'

'You don't say,' I said, because right then I felt old and sour.

Kieran joined us and then Jess, panting hard. She flopped down beside me.

'Best I could do, Daisy,' he said. 'I thinks the floor's pretty safe now. But the walls are riddled with termites. The place is a—'

I held up my hand. 'Don't say it!'

They both laughed.

'We're going out tonight for drinks and then dinner, if the drinks don't go on past dinner time,' Georgia said. 'Will you manage all right on your own? You don't need me to pick up a pair of crutches or anything?'

'I certainly do not, but thank you nevertheless. If you could do my bed before you go, I'll take painkillers and go to bed early.'

It wasn't even five, but after they'd gone, I'd be happy to dose myself up and sleep away the next ten or twelve hours, not think about anything; not the past, the present or the future.

Kieran collected his tools. 'I'll see you,' he said, giving Georgia a quick, but proprietary, kiss on the lips. Things had progressed, the chemistry between them unashamedly evident. They did make a handsome couple. What next for them? Anxiety about my own future ramped up a notch. Whatever they were planning, it wouldn't include Georgia's grandmother. Neither should it.

Georgia buzzed around and made up my bed, then showered and changed into skinny jeans and an off-the-shoulder knit. Ankle boots with spiked heels.

'Shall I get you something for tea before I go, Gran?'

'I think I'll manage,' I said. I could see she was bursting to get going. She grabbed her phone and car keys. 'Don't drive if you've had too much to drink.' The words were out before I could soften them. It took me back to the countless times I'd said them to the boys and Charlie. And then responded to their drunken late-night calls to come and collect them.

'Of course not,' she said. 'Besides, I'm on afternoon shift tomorrow.'

I fed Jess and then myself: cheese, crackers and an apple for dessert. The apples were from Max's tree, crisp and tart, just how I liked them. I was in bed and sound asleep by eight.

Some time in the night, a noise woke me. It was pitch black, no moon, the only light the tiny red glow from the television. Jess didn't stir. She must be going deaf. I'd almost dropped off again when I heard a thud from Georgia's room. She was home. That's what woke me. I felt myself relax. Then there was a muffled giggle. Too much to drink, I thought. I rolled over and went back to sleep.

When I woke it was early, the sun not up yet. My ankle felt a whole lot better. I let Jess outside, then I limped to the bathroom, and ran headlong into a naked Kieran on his way out.

'Oh, shit, sorry,' he said, and edged around me and back into Georgia's room. The door closed, followed by smothered laughter.

I went into the bathroom. He'd left the seat up. I had this dreadful feeling of deja vu and I didn't like it one little bit. I could easily have burst into tears.

There'd be no walking for me today, not on this ankle if I wanted it to get better quickly. After I'd dressed, I hobbled outside with my tea. I sat on the front verandah and ruminated. The three of us crammed onto the couch watching a Netflix movie was one thing, but running into Georgia's naked boyfriend coming out of the bathroom before the sun was up was quite something else. The nakedness part didn't bother me one iota. It was the lack of privacy that irked me. My privacy, and theirs. We were all entitled to it.

Max came out to collect his newspaper. It hadn't made it over the fence. He was still in his pyjamas. Each time I saw him it struck me afresh how doddery he was on his feet. He waved when he spied me. Jess toddled down the driveway to say good morning, until she spotted Pauline.

'You're such a brave dog,' I said, when she legged it back to where I was sitting.

Shortly afterwards, Kieran came outside, fully dressed. He yawned. 'I'll see you later,' he said.

'Don't leave because of me,' I said.

'Nah, I'm not. I've got work to do.' He yawned again. 'I'm back staying at Mum and Dad's. My house settles in a couple of weeks and then I'll move in there.'

'What happened to the house you were sharing?'

'A mate of one of the other blokes was looking for a room and they knew I was leaving soon anyway. No biggie.'

'So I suppose we'll be seeing a lot more of you?'

'But you've already seen everything.' He smirked. 'Catch ya.' He scratched Jess behind the ears and loped off down the driveway. No sign of his ute, only Georgia's SUV.

I went inside and Georgia was at the sink making herself a coffee, and yawning.

'A good night?' I said.

'Not exactly the one we'd planned … We tried not to wake you when we came in.'

'What happened?'

'Lisa ended up in hospital, bleeding. She had a miscarriage. They kept her in overnight.'

'Oh, the poor thing. She's not having a very good time of it, is she. Was Jake around?'

'What do you reckon? It is really awful for her, Gran, but probably the best thing that could have happened. She hasn't heard one word from him since she told him she was pregnant.'

'Then that's doubly sad for her.'

I poured muesli into a bowl and dolloped on some yoghurt. Georgia made toast. We sat outside in the sunshine and ate.

'Did Kieran tell you he was back at his parents' place?' she asked.

'For a fortnight until his house settles.'

'You don't mind if he stays over sometimes?'

'It means there's not much privacy. For any of us.'

She screwed up her face. 'The share house was gross, and there's no way I'd stay at his parents' place. They're nice, but—'

'It's only two weeks, Georgia, until he has his own place. Hardly an eternity.'

Her bottom lip jutted and I knew I was on the losing side of this dispute.

'It won't be every night,' she said. 'And it is *my* place.'

'Granted. But I pay my share and I do most of the housework, the meals and the yard.'

'You could always stay out the farm with Glenys and Trev for a few days.'

'I could, but I'm not going to ask them. There's Jess to think of. And after Bill, Glenys needs a holiday, not another houseguest.'

She finished her toast, chewing with attitude. 'Bloody Dad and his grandiose plans,' she said, and kicked at one of the buckled floorboards. 'Big Mr Property Developer. Always saying he's going to be a millionaire.' She stood and stomped off inside.

Breakfast curdled in my stomach. It was the closest we'd ever come to an out-an-out quarrel. If you'd asked me four months ago what we were most likely to fall out over, I'd never have dreamed it'd be a man.

Four months. I'd been couch-surfing here that long already. How much longer would it be? I hated to think.

Georgia came out ten minutes later. She was dressed and had her car keys in her hand. 'I'm going to pick up Lisa from the hospital and take her home,' she said.

'Okay, love. Please tell her how sorry I am for her and wish her a speedy recovery.'

'Don't worry about lunch for me. I'll have something with her.'

'Gotcha,' I said, fully familiar with being the persona non grata.

She sashayed off to her car and I went inside so she wouldn't have to decide whether or not to wave to me. Basically, she was a good kid. She wouldn't relish being in the position she was in: having to choose between her own wants and needs, her boyfriend's wants and needs, and her grandmother. At her age, I wouldn't have wanted my elderly grandmother living with me. The idea of it made me shudder. Next weekend I'd take me and Jess off somewhere and give the lovebirds a couple of days on their own.

But now I needed to ring Glenys and see how she was holding up. Where was my phone? I found it under my pillow. There was a missed call from Jay. I sat down on the sofa bed. He'd left a message: *Dad told me to get in touch to let you know if I was okay. I'm okay.* End of message. I puffed out the breath I'd been holding. I wasn't swamped by relief. He hadn't indicated where he was or what he was doing. But knowing he was at least okay was one less thing left to niggle at my peace of mind. Only to be replaced by a niggle regarding Charlie ... When we'd talked on the phone recently he'd actually asked how I was, and then he'd paid me a compliment. And now he'd done something he'd never done before: he'd intervened between me and one of our children. Just what was he up to?

38

Kate

There was little point to it because guests were unlikely to venture into the bedrooms or formal areas, but in the lead-up to the fundraising morning tea I had all the drapes dry-cleaned. Nowadays, without a local drycleaner, I'd be a week or more with bare windows. That prompted me to ask Daisy to help put up bed sheets at the front windows.

'Tell me again why you took down all the curtains?' Daisy said from the top of the ladder. She was fastening a bed sheet into position on the final window.

'Drapes … and they're at the drycleaners.'

'That must be costing you a small fortune,' she said, coming down the ladder.

'They hadn't been done since we moved in.'

'What, all of three and a bit years ago? I don't think I've ever had curtains—drapes—dry-cleaned. Take them outside and shake them, give them a good airing in the sunshine. That's as good as it's ever gets with me. How much?'

I told her.

'My goodness! That's a lot more than my share of the rent for a month.' She clicked her tongue several times and moved the ladder to the opposite end of the track.

'You're doing well for someone who sprained their ankle a few days ago,' I said, as she nimbly climbed the stepladder again.

'It wasn't a bad sprain and I did all the right things, rest, ice, you know. How on earth did you manage to get the drapes down on your own?'

'The neighbour's grandson helped me on the weekend. I paid him, of course. He's thirteen and saving for a techno-gadget of some kind. He did explain but lost me after the first sentence.'

'Is he going to help you with the re-hanging?'

I nodded. 'But I had to up the price because he'd already worked out it'd be a bigger and more complex job.'

Daisy smiled, something she hadn't done much of late. 'He'll do well in life,' she said. 'Do you want me to put the ladder back in the garden shed?'

'Leave it. I'll need it again in a few days. Come through and I'll make us a coffee.'

The day was cool and it was trying to rain. We sat in the breakfast nook and I put out a plate of lemon slice to have with our coffee.

'This is lovely,' Daisy said, taking a second bite.

'I've been trying out a few recipes for the morning tea. I'd thought to make this one. It's an old favourite but it doesn't freeze well. I took some to Rhonda.'

'Have you talked to Tom?'

'Not yet,' I said, irritated. More with myself than with her.

'Are you going to?'

'I don't know. I don't want to, I know that much.'

'Not easy, whichever way you look at it. Do you think you have a moral obligation to talk to him?' she said, and carefully took another piece of slice. 'Given he *is* Dennis's son, and there are blood relatives who might welcome Tom into the family.'

'I've been thinking about that. What if I sent him Lewis's contact details? Would that suffice? Lewis could tell him whatever he wanted to know about the Hannaford family. Way more than I could. And there's Derek he could talk to if Lewis wasn't enough. Let Tom do the explaining about who he is, rather than me having to do it.'

'Is that what's holding you back? Having to explain who Tom is, and the context of him being who he is and that you didn't know?'

How typical of her to go straight to the crux of the matter. Much like Rhonda had. And how annoying. I didn't answer. Instead I stood and went to the kitchen to make myself another coffee. 'Would you like a refill?' I said, albeit grudgingly.

'I'm only halfway through this one, thanks, and I didn't mean to annoy you. But I can see that you're struggling with this, Kate. Say you do nothing now, and then find yourself looking back in a year or six months and wishing you'd made a different decision? Only more disappointment and frustration down that path.'

I slid into the booth. 'I worry what will people think if it all comes out.'

'But Dennis is dead, and so is Tom's mother.'

'I'm not so much worried about them …'

'But you're worried about what people will think of you.'

'Yes,' I said, but I couldn't meet her in the eye when I said it. 'I've always had a certain standing in this community, because of the position I held, or so I'd like to think.'

'How many years since you retired? Five? I've got news for you, Kate. No-one remembers you, and those who do, probably won't care whether your late husband had a weekend fling that resulted in an unwanted pregnancy forty-plus years ago. I'd bet any one of them would have as bad, or even worse, skeletons in their closets.'

'You're wrong. There are those who'd love to see me brought down a peg or two.'

'Really?' she said, bemused. 'I'm sorry to hear you say that. In that case, you'll have to do what you decide is best for you. That might mean giving Lewis's phone number to Tom so he can contact him of his own volition. Any explaining to be done is left up to him, like you said.'

'But do you think Lew, or his wife Molly, would be satisfied to leave it there? I don't think they'd give up until they'd heard my side of the story.'

'It is a bit of a vexed question, isn't it? And what if Tom does have a wife and children, who now only have one grandmother ...'

I swallowed hard and tried to calm the butterflies fluttering about in my stomach. I had entertained that thought. Many times, until it had insinuated itself into my mind like a grass seed into a sock. I pushed aside the second coffee, untouched. This was what I'd been grappling with since Tom had first shown up on my front doorstep a week ago. Was there a chance, even a slim one, that I could I have the family I'd always yearned for? The grandchildren? Not mine, but the closest I'd ever get. Myriad scenarios flitted through my mind. And something that felt a lot like hope.

Daisy leaned in across the table. 'Talk to him, Kate. Ask him about his family. What harm could it do? You never know ...'

The atmosphere throbbed with anticipation. She'd been thinking along the same lines as I had: a family for Kate. Sounded like the title of a Mills and Boon novel, without the guaranteed happy ending.

'Say I did agree to see him,' I said, carefully. 'To answer his questions and hand over Dennis's keepsakes. What then if he decides he wants nothing more to do with me? He's fulfilled his mother's deathbed request and delivered the letter. And he has no obligation, moral or otherwise, to me.'

Daisy sat back, a tiny frown tugging her eyebrows together. 'I see what you mean. But it works both ways: after you've met with him *you* might decide you don't want anything more to do with *him*.'

'Aargh!' I groaned and squeezed my eyes shut.

'But nothing ventured, nothing gained,' Daisy said. I could hear the shrug in her voice. 'Sometimes you've just gotta take a leap of faith. He sounded very reasonable on the phone.'

We sat for several minutes, each lost in our own thoughts. I was thinking about what I'd say to Tom if—and that was a big if—I spoke to him at all. I glanced at Daisy. She looked sad, like she was someplace else completely. I reached across the table and grasped her forearm. She gave a grunt of surprise.

'Are you all right? For a second there you looked positively bereft.'

Her expression lightened, but it took effort. 'Georgia's boyfriend has practically been *living* with us and it's not always easy to get a good night's sleep. The walls are thin.'

'Kieran Hall? That boyfriend?'

'The very same. Don't get me wrong, I have nothing against him. I like him, he's a decent lad and I do try to keep an open mind, Kate, but I'm Georgia's grandmother, for goodness' sake!'

'Oh, dear,' I said, and tried not to sound too horrified. 'How long has this been going on for? I can't imagine what I'd do in a similar situation.'

'He's back living at home with his parents until he moves into his own house. Georgia won't go to his parents' place.'

'No surprises there,' I said. 'I can't imagine Eleanor, or Rob for that matter, tolerating that sort of thing under their own roof. That said, I can imagine Rhonda not batting an eyelid at it. As strange as that might be.'

'We sound like a couple of old prudes,' Daisy said with a snuffle of amusement. She was blotting up stray coconut flakes and dropping them onto her plate. 'Now, to change the subject completely, how's your preparation for the morning tea coming along? It can't be that far away. Do you need help with anything?'

'Two weeks tomorrow. I don't know how ticket sales are going. Valma said she'd let me know closer to the time, and the numbers are capped at thirty-five, which is fine, because I don't have to borrow or hire any crockery.'

'I've noticed posters around the place: the library; the community noticeboard at the supermarket.'

I was about to ask if she'd bought her ticket, but then thought better of it. Spending twenty-five dollars on a morning tea and then being expected to buy raffle tickets and the like at the event could be considered frivolous and wasteful when you were on a tight budget.

'I could do with some help on the day,' I said, tentatively. 'If you're free?'

'Of course I'll help you. I'd planned to offer. And if you need a hand in the days before to set up, I can do that too.'

'All right, I'd appreciate that. Come now and I'll show you where I thought I'd lay out everything.'

'I can't believe you have enough crockery for *thirty-five* people.'

'Of course, it doesn't all match,' I said.

'No, of course it doesn't,' she said, following me out of the kitchen.

It wasn't until much later, after she'd gone, that her comment about the amount of crockery I owned struck me as being a trifle sarcastic. My chest swelled with outrage. What sort of a friend was she? Then, with an oomph, my chest deflated. Owning that amount of crockery would seem extreme to Daisy. It did a bit even to me, if I were honest, and I hadn't included my best cups and saucers in the count.

But the thing that played on my mind the most, and not in a favourable way, was that after she'd shared the snippet about Kieran sleeping over, I hadn't offered her the use of one of my three spare bedrooms so she could have a few nights of decent sleep. What sort of a friend did that make me?

39

Daisy

We went to Adelaide for our weekend away. Jess had a bath, I packed the car and we drove down Friday afternoon. Friday night we stayed with Adam and Bec. Their house was small and it was a squeeze, but the grandkids were thrilled to see me. Adam and Bec were simply exhausted. They slept in Saturday morning while Stella and Nadine helped me make their breakfast, and then we took Jess for a walk in the park. Will was at a mate's place for the weekend and I'd slept in his bed.

Saturday afternoon we'd all trooped around to Gareth and Tess's for a barbecue. Jess and I would camp with them that night. When I asked Tess how she was, she said she was fine now, but the going had been tough while she'd waited for test results.

'I didn't realise how worried I was about it being breast cancer,' she said, 'not until I was given the all clear.'

Mitch's arm had healed and his life was back to normal. Ryan spent more time with Jess than with me, but he did ask after Glenys and Trev, and the farm dogs.

Sunday morning, I managed to wangle a few minutes alone with Gareth. I'd begun to suspect he was avoiding me. We took our coffee out onto the deck. The sun was peeping through but I was glad I'd pulled on a polar fleece over my T-shirt.

'So how goes the building project?' I said. 'You're being frustratingly closed-mouthed about it all.'

'That's because there's been nothing to tell you. The pile of rubble has gone, but that's it.'

'That's it?'

'Yep.'

'I'm feeling a bit exposed here,' I said, my voice rising with each word. 'Five months, and the foundations haven't even been poured.'

'Yeah, well, no-one factored the long-term consequences of Covid into their business models, did they? Times are tough and getting tougher.'

'What am I meant to read between those lines, Gareth?'

He shrugged, a whole-body shrug, and that's when I knew the project was in trouble. *I* was in trouble.

'You've got a home at the moment,' he said. 'It might not be the most ideal arrangement ...'

'And getting less ideal by the day,' I said.

'Why? What's changed? Georgia hasn't said anything.'

So she hadn't told them about Kieran. There was no reason she had to, and it wasn't my place to tattle. 'Nothing that won't sort itself out eventually, one way or the other,' I said. 'You've seen the place. It gets a bit crowded at times.'

He regarded me steadily for several moments and then, when I didn't elaborate, he said, 'Fair enough.'

We finished our coffee. The atmosphere was uneasy. We both had things that should be said, but neither of us would say them.

'I meant to tell you, I heard from Jay. Adam said he'd had a message as well,' I said.

'What did he have to say?'

'That he was okay.'

'That it?'

'Verbatim. You know your brother. I was lucky to get that much.' I didn't mention that Charlie had prompted him.

Tess came out onto the deck. Her anxious glance took in her husband first, then shifted to me. Her frown deepened.

'You two finished your business meeting? Who got to take the minutes?' she said, attempting humour.

Neither of us laughed, or even so much as smiled.

'Right. I'm making pancakes. I thought brunch, because breakfast time is long gone,' she said.

'Lovely.' I stood and picked up Gareth's empty mug along with my own. 'What can I do to help?'

I preceded them inside and I'll swear I heard Tess say to my son as I stepped through the sliding door, *'Did you tell her?'*

I didn't hear his reply.

Tell me what? My disquiet escalated.

★★★

The drive back to Georgia's went quicker than I wanted it to. Jess, exhausted after such a social weekend, slept the whole way. I couldn't remember a time when I'd ever felt as low as I did right then. When Tess and Gareth had waved me off, I'd sensed it'd been with relief. What was going on and why was no-one telling me all the facts?

To my relief, the house was deserted when I arrived. Jess bounded out of the car and set off on her routine sniff-fest. I took the luggage inside. The place felt, and even smelled, different. I put it down to

Kieran's aftershave. To my dismay, all my belongings and bedding had been piled into one corner of the living room, the privacy screen upended on top of them. I felt like curling up on the floor and crying with frustration, but what good would that do me?

After I'd tidied up, reclaimed my space and put on a load of washing, I sat down on the sofa with a pencil and paper and my most recent bank statements. I'd go over my budget with a fine-toothed comb. If I was left to fend entirely for myself—and instinct told me that time was closer than even I'd realised—I had to have a plan. To make a plan, I needed to know how much I had to spend.

I was in bed and feigning sleep when Georgia came home, alone. She tip-toed around the house. The toilet flushed and then I heard her sort through the bag of shopping her mother had sent. I'd left it on her bed. Before the advent of Kieran I would have stayed up until she came home and she would have unpacked the bag with me and shared her enjoyment of Tess's gift. The dynamic between my granddaughter and I had changed, and I was regretful for that. When she had a bit more life experience under her belt perhaps she'd better appreciate what had been lost.

★★★

Over the next few days, I saw very little of Georgia. When she wasn't working she was doing something with Kieran or Lisa.

On one of the few occasions we did connect over breakfast, she said, 'I'm really worried about Lisa. I think she's depressed.'

'She had a miscarriage, that's bound to make her feel down. Or do you think it's because of Jake's defection?'

'A bit of both, but mainly Jake. She said on the weekend that she'd never wanted to be a single parent. I told her about you and granddad. How you got pregnant and he'd married you and then left anyway.'

'And what did she say to that?'

'That at least he'd married you.'

'Maybe they both dodged a bullet, if all she really wanted was to get married, and he didn't. But that wouldn't make it any easier for her. Did you suggest she talks to someone? Her GP or a counsellor?'

'She's not exactly open to any of my suggestions right now. Actually, she told me she didn't want to see me outside of work, not for a while. Said she needed some space.'

'Oh, dear. How did you feel when she said that?'

Georgia gave a shrug of seeming indifference. 'Her call,' she said. 'Kieran says not to worry about it. About her. But I suppose I am, a bit. We've been friends for a long time. She's the reason I came to work in this town in the first place.'

Georgia was doing her utmost to tough it out, but I didn't miss the tremor in her voice and the quiver of her bottom lip.

'Men are clueless when it comes to the strength, and nuance, of friendships between women. Believe me when I say that when it all boils down, we need those friendships, sometimes more than we need men.'

'Gran! You sound like a feminist.'

'I'm not against men per se, not at all, but the strength and resilience of friendships you have with other women are what'll get you through the rough times. And any friendship requires work for it to survive and flourish.'

'So what should I do?'

'Give Lisa the space she's asked for, and then be the friend she deserves, not the one *you* think she needs. Most importantly, don't let a man ruin a good friendship.'

Jess went and stood at the front door. We'd been for a walk already but she wanted out. I stood and opened the door for her.

'Is that what happened between you and Kate Hannaford?'

I closed the door and considered her question. 'In a way, yes. I just hadn't thought about it like that until now. She didn't like Charlie; didn't think he was good enough for me. She was envious because I had babies and she couldn't. I think she thought she was more deserving than I was, because Dennis was a fine, upstanding farmer and Charlie was, more often than not, an unemployed layabout and always on the lookout for a good time. We lived from one of my pay packets to the next. We couldn't even afford a bed to begin with, never mind thirty-five coffee mugs. And *drapes*! Not curtains.'

'Gran?' Georgia said, watching me intently. 'What's that last bit about?'

'Nothing,' I said, and deflated. 'Just me being envious of what she has.'

'I thought you were friends again?'

'We are, and it's good. But I'm learning that some of that stuff never goes away, no matter how old you get.'

Georgia picked up our empty breakfast bowls and took them to the sink, then switched on the electric kettle.

'Your friendship with Lisa will survive, if you want it to. Put in the effort required, but tread carefully. My guess is she's a tad envious of you because you have a boyfriend who has a job, who's bought a house and has no intention of going anywhere.'

'That's now. I really like Kieran, but anything could happen in a week, or a month … And if it does, I'll be upset, and I can see that's when I'll need my girlfriends.'

'Correct, so don't let the important ones fall by the wayside.'

Georgia made me a coffee and handed it to me.

'Kate asked me the other day if back then we should have worked a bit harder on our friendship. I said no. We were young, immature, had a lot of other things to deal with. I've thought about it since, and what we didn't have was a long history to fall back on when it all started to unravel. You know that saying, *Friendships are for a reason, a season, or a lifetime*? Back then ours was for a reason, and then it became a season. But now, that reason and season have become a shared history, and who knows, we might make it to a lifetime.'

'I totally get that, Gran,' Georgia said, nodding slowly. 'Lisa and I met at primary school. We've been close friends ever since. We went to uni and did nursing together. I'd be devastated if I lost her as friend.'

'Then don't.'

Like old times, she gave me a one-armed hug and planted a kiss on my cheek. 'Thanks, Gran,' she said.

It made my day. Although I was under no illusions that it would last. There was a man in the picture now, and that changed everything.

Georgia breezed out a while later. She was on days off. Kieran took possession of his new house at lunch time. There would be celebrations planned and I wouldn't see Georgia for the remainder of the day. Or night. Her bulging overnight bag hadn't gone unnoticed.

After she went I sat down again with my calculator and bank statements and kept working on a budget. Georgia hadn't even hinted that she might move out; however, my goal was to see if it would be possible to live here on my own until the townhouse was ready, if I scrimped and scraped, and picked up a few hours of casual work.

After an hour's studious calculations, I'd figured it was doable, barely, and only if: the landlord didn't raise the rent; my car had minimal use and I walked whereever I could; I was prepared to live on baked beans in order for Jess to eat and keep healthy; and nothing went wrong or broke down, including me. Otherwise I'd be dipping into my rainy-day savings, and who knew if and when the rain might get much heavier.

40

Kate

My GP relaying the news that my blood pressure was higher than it'd ever been, as was my total cholesterol and blood sugar, probably shot them all up another notch or two. He wanted to send me for a glucose tolerance test and start me on blood pressure medication, but I resisted. It was all too much. The fundraising morning tea was tomorrow.

'Give me a month,' I said, grimly. 'I'll improve my diet and up the exercise.'

'And cut back on the brandy and dry, and the wine you have with dinner every night,' he said.

'No spirits. Always wine and only ever two glasses,' I said, petulantly.

'And that's two standard drinks, is it?'

I didn't answer, only stared down at my hands instead. A bottle lasted me two sittings. That meant I was having three or four standard drinks most evenings. Then there were the days I had a drink with lunch …

'I thought not. You know the score, Kate, there's no amount of alcohol that's totally harmless. Aim for two or three alcohol-free days each week and no more than two standard drinks a day.'

'It's been a difficult time since Dennis died, more so of late,' I said, my attention fixed on my hands.

'Do you need to talk to someone? I could refer you,' he said, surprising me. 'Or there are those you can access who don't need a doctor's referral. Plenty of options. And if you don't want to see anyone locally, it's not onerous to travel to the city.'

'Let's give that another month, too,' I said, and finally made eye contact. 'See how I go. I am coping a lot better than I was. And I've started walking, with a friend.'

'Good.'

The printer hissed and clicked and then he passed me the blood request form. 'One month,' he said. 'Not a day longer. Make the appointment on your way out.'

I did as I was told. Back in the car I sat and reflected for several despondent minutes. My wine consumption had slowly crept up since Dennis's death. After the DUI incident I'd cut back, stretching a bottle out over three nights. But that hadn't lasted long. Living on your own had its positive aspects, but it also had its downsides: you only had yourself to be accountable to, and we all know how easy it is to talk yourself around when it's something you desire.

After picking up groceries at the supermarket, I drove home. It was almost lunch time. Tomorrow was the morning tea and I was at the point of only having a few finishing touches to make. Valma's tiny car was parked out front when I got home. As I pulled into the garage she climbed out and powered up the driveway, like a pack-horse loaded with Tupperware containers.

'Is there anything else?' I said.

'Only the basket with the jam and cream. You don't mind whipping it in the morning? It's always nicer done on the day.'

We carried everything inside, my groceries included. The perishables went into the fridge. Evelyn had brought the bubbly when she'd dropped off the jelly cakes. It was in the second fridge in the garage.

'Have you time for a coffee?'

'A quick one would be lovely. Gaye and Maureen have sold all the tickets, and said they could have sold them twice over if there'd been room.'

'And the guest speaker is primed and ready to go?'

'So I'm told. Now then, I've been meaning to ask you for ages if you ever found out who left the flowers on dear Dennis's grave? Did you ask the girl in the florist like I suggested?'

Heat flashed through me. I fumbled with the lid on the coffee and was grateful I had my back to her. 'She wasn't very helpful,' I said. That wasn't a fib. There's no way I would have tracked down Tom based on her information. That he'd found me was no-one's business but our own.

'Never mind,' she said, and smiled when I put the mug down in front of her. 'Is there anything you need a last-minute hand with?'

'Daisy's been helping me set up and she's coming back this afternoon. The quiches are made and we'll do the sandwiches in the morning. I think we have everything under control.'

She sipped the coffee and sighed with pleasure. 'Isn't it marvellous that you two have reconnected after all these years. How is she?'

'You can ask her yourself tomorrow. She'll be here, helping out.'

Valma peered at me over the rim of her mug. 'You seem very organised, Kate, and so calm. If it was me, I'd be rushing about like a chook with its head cut off.'

'I'm sure there'll be last-minute hiccoughs, but I've had plenty of time to prepare. And Daisy is always *so* practical.' I wasn't as serene as I appeared but that inner turmoil had little to do with how organised I was for the morning tea.

'Whatever happened to that husband of hers? Good-looking chap. Thea Gilchrist always said he was a charmer, but not the most reliable husband or parent.' Valma frowned. 'You remember Thea?'

'Vaguely. Can't say that I knew her well.'

Valma finished her coffee with more chit-chat about tomorrow's event. As she was leaving, she said, 'Should I come a bit earlier in the morning?'

'If you like. You can whip the cream. Might be easiest to spread the scones beforehand.'

'Done! I'll be here at nine.'

Lunch was pasta leftovers from the night before. A glass, or two, of something crisp, cold and calming would have been nice with it, but I left the bottle in the fridge. I had a month to clean up my act.

Daisy arrived. She put Jess around the back and came inside.

Before she could ask, because she always did, I said, 'No, I haven't contacted him yet. Let me get this morning tea out of the way first.'

'Did I even ask?'

'No, but I could see it there on the tip of your tongue.' I didn't mention the three unanswered calls I'd had from him.

We sat down and went through the list of things to do. Some-how, Daisy had managed to get the outdoor gas heaters working so they were ready if we needed them. She even knew how to determine if a gas bottle needed refilling. Many years spent with up to four males about the house at any given time, and yet she knew how to do all of these things proficiently.

I'd put a padlock on the gate to the swimming pool enclosure. The cover was on but I didn't want anyone tipping over and into the pool. I could imagine Gaye and Maureen's hysteria if that happened.

'That's about it, don't you reckon?' Daisy said after we'd set out the last of the chairs. 'It all looks pretty good, Kate. Well done.'

It did look wonderful. Between the family room and the patio there was seating for thirty-five. Morning tea would be served when people arrived. Then the guest speaker, a local author whose latest book was a memoir about growing up in the area, would speak for twenty minutes and take questions afterwards. There was a raffle to draw and a lucky door prize, and Gaye and Maureen were giving a spiel on the women's and children's hospital. It'd all be over in two or three hours, and then there'd be the clean-up.

'I'll be off then,' Daisy said and called out for Jess. 'What should I wear tomorrow?' She glanced down at what she had on: a long-sleeved red T-shirt with bleach splotches down the front and a pair of ratty jeans. 'Not this, of course,' she said.

'Do you have a skirt and blouse, or a frock? Something dark coloured? I have an apron you could wear.'

'You want me to look like the maid?'

Was she joking? There was a rigidity to her expression that suggested she wasn't.

'No, of course not. If you're dressed like that, a sort of uniform, everyone will know you're the go-to person.'

'All right,' she said, after a beat or two of silence. 'I'll wear the dress I wore to Bill's funeral. But it'll be sneakers on my feet, especially since I'll be on them for the whole day.'

With the outfit agreed upon, and that she'd be back by eight the following morning, she left with her dog. She could be a prickly thing. Not often, but often enough for me to have noticed. I watched them go. They were on foot, as usual. With petrol around two dollars a litre and climbing, I could understand why. What must it be like to have to budget for every kilometre you travelled in your car? All those trips back and forward to the Carlisles' must have put a dent in her bank balance.

I shuddered, and sent up a prayer of thankfulness that I wasn't in a similar position. The doorbell sounded. Ah, the courier with my monthly wine order.

He stacked the boxes in the garage for me. I'd sort them out later. After he'd gone, whistling his way back to the van, I eyed the three boxes. Should I cancel the whole order or cut it down by half? Or perhaps a third?

★★★

The following morning, my heart swelled with pride as I took in the crowded family room and outside patio area. The weather had cleared after a sullen start but it remained cool and Daisy had put the heaters on. Everyone sat with rapt attention listening to the guest speaker, coffee or tea and loaded plates balanced on their knees or nearby tables. Quite a few held glasses of bubbly. There hadn't been many takers for the orange juice.

Daisy was at the kitchen sink filling the small urn I'd borrowed. Her cheeks were flushed. She had been such a help. I don't know how I would have managed without her. On my way across to tell her just that, the front doorbell chimed. Daisy glanced in my direction and raised her eyebrows.

'I'll get it,' I mouthed, and changed direction.

I opened the screen door to an attractive woman with a sleek blonde bob and ruby-coloured lipstick. 'Can I help you?' I said.

'You can if you're Kate Hannaford,' she said in a carefully modulated voice. She glanced over her shoulder at the car-lined street. 'I'm not interrupting anything, am I?'

'I won't know until you tell me who you are and why you're here,' I said, with a shiver of apprehension.

She took off her sunglasses and regarded me with a clear blue gaze. 'I'm Helena Wilkins, Tom's wife. I want to know why you haven't rung him, and why you don't answer his calls.'

'Then you are interrupting,' I said, after I'd quickly gathered my wits. 'I have a houseful of guests. Come back in two hours and I may discuss it with you then.'

She stared at me for a moment longer, until I began to close the door and withdraw. Then she glanced at her watch. A huge diamond flashed on her ring finger.

'That'll make it one-thirty. I'll be back here on the dot.' The way she said it made it sound like a threat.

My jaw firmed as I closed the door. I would not be threatened, not by her or by anyone else.

Daisy came through from the kitchen, wiping her hands on a tea towel. 'Who was that?' she said quietly. 'Obviously not someone late for the morning tea.'

'Helena Wilkins, Tom's wife,' I said, and Daisy's mouth formed a perfect O. 'She wanted to talk and I told her to come back in a couple of hours.'

Then came the sound of muffled clapping: the guest speaker had finished.

'I expect there'll be a rush for more cups of tea. I'd better get back,' Daisy said, adding over her shoulder as she scurried off, 'I can be here when you talk to her, if you want me to be.'

'Yes, I think I would appreciate that.'

We went back to the kitchen and for the next hour and a half I was too busy to give it any more thought.

After the last guests departed, and Gaye and Maureen had finished congratulating each other on the success of the morning and left, Daisy and I looked at each other. We stood on either side of the kitchen island bench, which was covered with dirty crockery, food scraps and crumpled paper serviettes.

'So there is a Mrs Tom Wilkins,' she said. 'She must really care about her husband to come all this way to get answers for him. I wonder if he knows she's here?'

'No, he doesn't.'

I spun around. Helena Wilkins was standing in the doorway that opened from the family room to the patio. We'd been ferrying stuff in and out and hadn't closed it.

'I'm a few minutes early. Sorry. I waited until everyone had gone. I've made arrangements for the children, but I need to be back before Tom gets home.'

'Why don't you take Helena through and sit down, Kate, and I'll make tea?' Daisy said, because I was standing there, mute, propped up by the kitchen bench. She turned to Helena and smiled. 'I'm Daisy Miller, a friend of Kate's. How do you take your tea?'

Helena returned her smile. 'Tom said he'd spoken to you. White, no sugar, thanks.'

'Come on through,' I said, and I tried to smile too, but I just couldn't. The effort was too much. Suddenly I felt as old as Methuselah, and so very tired. It was as if a weight had settled on my chest and wouldn't be shifted. We went through and sat down.

41

Daisy

After I'd made the tea I continued with the clean-up. When Kate hadn't asked me to join her and Helena, I'd felt a tangle of relief, hurt and annoyance. I'd wanted to hear firsthand what Helena had to say, not have it skewed by Kate's biases and baggage.

Not wanting to appear as if I was eavesdropping, I went outside, collected the wheelie bin and began picking up discarded serviettes and other rubbish. Unbelievable what a mess a mob of older women could make in less than three hours. When I found a ten dollar note under one of the chairs, it cheered me no end. Finders keepers.

In what seemed like a very short amount of time, Kate came out onto the patio.

'Well?' I said, hands on hips, when she wasn't immediately forthcoming.

'I've agreed to meet with him, somewhere neutral. She assured me that they're not after Dennis's estate, that they have enough money of their own.'

'I hadn't thought about it from that angle. Were you worried they'd want money?'

'It had occurred to me. But in the end, who is there to leave it to? I won't spend it all.'

I should be so lucky. My debts were the only thing I'd have to leave anyone. But I'd be past caring about it by then.

'When she first came in she said something about children?' I said.

'They have four. Two boys and twin girls. Eight, ten and thirteen. The twins are the eldest.'

'Helena would have her hands full.'

Kate looked over her shoulder towards the kitchen. 'Shall we sit down for a bit, have a glass of wine?' she said.

'You go ahead, but I want to get this done. Max has Jess and I don't want her outstaying her welcome.'

'Go and get her and bring her here,' Kate said. 'I don't mind.'

I debated that for all of three seconds, but it wasn't only Jess: I wanted to go home, sooner rather than later. It had a been a full-on day, and then Kate's distress at the appearance, and then reappearance, of Helena.

Kate must have read some of that in my expression because she sighed and began half-heartedly gathering the remaining coffee mugs and plates.

'I'm supposed to be cutting down on the alcohol as it is,' she said, not sounding thrilled by the prospect. 'I've got a month to get my blood pressure and cholesterol down. And as if that's not enough, my fasting blood sugar was borderline.'

'You do have your job cut out then, don't you? All the stress wouldn't be helping any.'

'That's what I said to him.' She bent down. 'Oh, no,' she said, and held up a broken plate. 'It's from the dinner set I bought with one of my first pay packets. How annoying.'

How typical. Only Kate would have bought a dinner set with her first earnings. I returned the wheelie bin to its home alongside the garage. We took all the dirty crockery inside, loaded the dishwasher and set it going. There'd be several loads.

'Did you set a date for this get-together with Tom? Will Helena be there?'

'Saturday, in Adelaide, and she said she'd do whatever he wanted.'

'But what do *you* want? Would you rather she wasn't there?'

Kate nodded, and then sighed. 'I don't want to do this at all, Daisy,' she said. Her eyes glistened. 'It'll just rake over the past even more than it's already been raked over. I've come to the conclusion that some things you do not need to keep revisiting.

'You know, since Dennis died, it feels as if I just get my head above water, that I glimpse dry land and something comes along and pushes my head under again.'

'In my experience, that's life, Kate. What matters is whether you keep bobbing up again each time. There's a lot we have to be grateful for and that's what brings my head up every time.'

She gave a glimmer of a smile and we went back to work. By five everything was shipshape again. The final load was in the dishwasher and the furniture had been returned to its usual configuration. I was exhausted and Kate looked even worse than I felt.

'I can put the bin out as I go. It's chock-a-block.' I peeled off the apron Kate had loaned me. 'I'll take this home and wash it.'

She plucked it out of my hand. 'No, you will not. I'll do it. I don't feel as if I can thank you enough as it is, Daisy. For everything.'

'I had fun at the morning tea. It was a hoot to catch up with Valma. Apart from the wrinkles and her hair being snow white, she's no different. And Bob was always a laugh. He and Charlie got on well, in that I mean they used to drink together. But let's not go there,' I said, and went to pick up the foil-wrapped parcel of leftovers off the kitchen bench. There was a white envelope with my name on it sitting on the top. When had she put that there?

'What's this?' I said.

'A token of my appreciation.'

'It had better not be money, Kate. I came today because you're my friend and I wanted to help.'

'It is money, Daisy, and I'm giving it to you because you are my friend and I want to help. Don't you dare even think of giving it back. That's always been your problem, right from the get-go: you've known how to give but you've never mastered the art of receiving; of gratitude. What you do now is, you take it and you say, "Thank you, Kate, how generous. It was very thoughtful of you."'

I picked up the envelope as if it were a venomous snake. Kate's eyes rolled heavenwards. Then I glared at her and she returned my glare.

'Thank you, Kate, how generous. It was very thoughtful of you,' I said, mimicking her.

'There, that wasn't too hard, was it?'

'You would have made a good mother, Kate. I'm sorry it didn't happen for you. Back then I was too absorbed by how much I didn't want to be a mother, to even try to understand how desperately you wanted the exact opposite. And how shattered you were when it never happened. I should have been a better friend.'

'Like you said, we were young, immature, I was bent on getting what I wanted, and turned into a bitter and resentful bitch when I didn't. I don't blame you for pulling away, although I did blame you for a long time. But you had more than your own fair share to deal with. Valma said how marvellous it was that we'd reconnected, and you know, she was right.'

We'd never hugged. Kate wasn't the huggy type, and neither was I, to be truthful. But we hugged each other then. Firmly. And we forgave, tacitly agreeing we had no time to waste with more acrimony. Life was short, and getting shorter by the day.

'Why don't you have an early night?' I said. 'You've had a whopper of a day.'

'And yes, I promise I won't open a bottle of wine. I know that's what you're thinking, but wouldn't dream of saying.'

'There you go,' I said, and trundled off outside to pick up the wheelie bin.

★ ★ ★

Since Bill died Glenys had messaged me several times, inviting me out to the farm for a cuppa and a chat. Any time, she'd said, and today was the day I'd finally make it. It had been negligent of me not to have visited once since Bill's funeral. But I had seen Glenys a couple of times: she'd popped into Georgia's one afternoon, and another day we'd met for a coffee down the street. She hadn't been her usual sanguine self on either of those occasions.

Jess perked up at the prospect of a car ride. She was pushing past me and onto the front passenger seat the minute I opened the car door. I stopped at the supermarket on the way for milk and bread, and custard tarts. Glenys's favourite.

The dirt road to their place had deteriorated markedly in the past few weeks, the corrugations so bad they almost shook our teeth loose. And the dust! The old car was layered with grime by the time we arrived. The countryside was so very dry; the dams empty and sheep snuffling around in the dirt for what little they could find to eat.

Glenys was at the clothesline, bedsheets billowing in the brisk breeze. No sign of Trev's ute or the farm dogs, so I let Jess out to roam.

'She'll be fine. Trev and the dogs won't be back for hours. Come on in,' Glenys called. 'I'll put the kettle on.'

I collected the green bag with the groceries and we went inside.

I wrinkled my nose. 'Can I smell paint?'

'I've stripped Dad's old room and I'm halfway through putting on a coat of paint. Freshen it up a bit. It got to smell like him. Poor old bugger,' she said. 'I might even make new curtains.'

'What else have you been up to?'

'Not much. Spent a lovely few days in Adelaide with Kaylene. I had a specialist's appointment. Women's stuff ... You get old and everything dries out and starts to sag.'

'Doesn't it just.'

'Is Georgia at work? I thought she might have come with you.'

'She has a boyfriend, Glenys. He's bought a house. He took possession of it a week ago. She wasn't home this morning so my guess is she's at work or at Kieran's place. I've hardly seen her at all this past week.'

We sat down at the kitchen table with cups of tea and one of the custard tarts cut in half.

'I hope she knows what she's doing,' Glenys said. 'The young ones rush into relationships. They're hardly past the hand–holding stage and next thing you know they're sleeping together, and setting up house and home before they've known each other two months. No wonder so many marriages end up in the divorce court.'

'Not like you to sound so down.'

Glenys closed her eyes and slowly shook her head. 'Kaylene says Martha's not having an easy time of it. She's moved back home. And she's pregnant. She was barely out of school when they got married. And they had to have everything straight away ... Ikea this and Ikea that, until they were up to their eyeballs in debt. What's the bet the baby ends up in Kaylene's lap, and she's already got enough to worry about with Darren, the lazy so–and–so.'

'It never gets any easier, does it? No matter how old they are.'

'Trev said he'd throttle Darren, if he could get away with it, and that idiot Martha married. I was so lucky with Trev. He's not perfect, but then neither am I.'

'None of us can make that claim,' I said, and gobbled the last of the custard tart. It was sweet and greasy and it'd sit in my stomach like a stone, but I'd enjoyed every mouthful.

'How on earth did you manage on your own, Daisy? All those years, three energetic boys … Even when Charlie was there I imagine he was about as useful as an ashtray on a motorbike.'

I laughed. 'Couldn't have put it better myself. I figured out pretty early on that, with a baby on the way, one of us had to step up and be the adult, and it wasn't going to be Charlie.'

'No surprise really, his dad was the same. My dad used say Joe was always the life of the party, but life's not always a party.'

'Speaking of Charlie, I noticed you have a framed photo of us on our wedding day. All this time I'd been under the impression I had the only copy. Can you remember who gave it to you?'

'Charlie, but don't ask me when except that it was a long time ago. I put it in the frame.'

'That was the only photo ever taken of the day. I wonder who else he gave copies to?'

'I found one at Mum and Dad's when I was cleaning out the place after they went into the unit. I imagine Charlie gave his parents a copy. Maybe his brother, Colin.'

'How very curious,' I said.

'Not really,' Glenys said. 'He thought the world of you, Daisy. You were always so capable. In part, I think the reason he drank was because he knew he would never measure up. He didn't know how to and that bothered him. As kids, believe it or not, Charlie was very shy and Joe was never any sort of a role model. Charlie's mum tried her best with the boys, I'll give her that.'

'Don't we all try our best? Sometimes it pays off, and sometimes it doesn't.' I thought of Jay and how like the Toogood men he was.

Glenys smiled, as if she knew what I was thinking. 'More tea?' she said. 'And what about that other custard tart?'

It was late afternoon when I put Jess into the car and we left. I'd stayed for lunch and we'd talked and laughed while we'd sorted through Glenys's fabric cupboard and then the linen press, looking for a suitable curtain length for Bill's old room.

Glenys sent us off with the usual eggs and a butternut pumpkin from her garden. She hugged me and said, 'A day of your company was just the tonic I needed, Daisy. I feel so much better. You know you are welcome any time.'

I drove off squinting into the sun, wondering where I'd left my sunglasses this time. The driveway was a single-lane track, and it was the best part of a kilometre from the farmhouse to their gate. Because of the sun, and my woolgathering, I very nearly sideswiped a once-white LandCruiser station wagon barrelling in through the gate and towards me. I had to get right over. The vehicle was filthy, covered in red dust and splatters of mud. I was too busy navigating my way through the gate and all I saw was a dark shape behind the steering wheel. I cursed out loud. Another farmer come to visit Trev. They thought they owned the road.

Back home at Georgia's the driveway was empty and when I let myself in, the house felt eerily quiet. A weird kind of emptiness accompanied the silence. I went straight out to the clothesline to get Georgia's dry washing. It wasn't until I opened her bedroom door to take in the basket of folded clothes that the echoey silence was explained: the room was virtually empty, her bed, the chest of drawers and bedside cupboard gone.

My first thought was we'd been broken into and, with a dry mouth and pounding heart, I rushed out into the living area. When

I'd first come inside I'd been intent on getting to the clothesline to bring the clothes in before they got damp again and I hadn't noticed if anything was amiss. I carefully scanned the room. Everything appeared as I'd left it that morning.

Then it hit me like a brick: Georgia had moved in with Kieran, and she'd failed to mention it to me beforehand.

42

Kate

It was Saturday. The cafe where I'd agreed to meet Tom for coffee was down a narrow alley off Prospect Road. The place surprised me. I'd expected something swanky, not an eclectic mix of retro furniture, galvanised iron walls and polished cement floors. Tom fit right in, wearing distressed jeans and a faded grandpa shirt. He lifted his hand in greeting. I was nearly at his table when I noted his clothes were genuinely aged and well worn, not designer labels made to look as if they had. I felt ridiculously overdressed.

He stood up, his smile hesitant. 'Mrs Hannaford, thank you so much for coming. I trust the drive wasn't too much of an imposition.'

'It's a pretty drive, I never tire of it.'

We sat down. He slid a dog-eared menu across the Formica tabletop. 'The coffee is excellent,' he said. 'And so is the food.'

'Do you live nearby? Is that how you know about the coffee and food?' I perused the drinks menu, ignoring the alcoholic beverages with effort.

'A reasonable walk.'

'An espresso, milk on the side, thank you.'

Tom went to the counter to order. I wanted to stare but I daren't. The situation was uncomfortable enough as it was. He came back balancing a bottle of water and glasses and a piece of banana bread on a plate.

'I haven't had breakfast,' he said. 'Did you want something to eat?'

'No, thank you.' Food was out of the question with my stomach tied in the knot that it was. 'How did you know Dennis had been killed?' The question had been gnawing away at me ever since the day Tom had visited me.

'Mum read it in the death notices,' he said. 'In the *Advertiser*. She always read them. Said they gave her ideas for her own.'

'Oh … But what an awful way to discover your father had died. Was it you who left the flowers on the grave, back in January?'

'Mum insisted we do it. She knew it would be the last time for her to make the trip with me.'

'They were lovely. Thank you. Were you at the funeral? I don't remember seeing you there.'

'Helena and Mum thought it best that we kept away. I agreed.'

'Thank you for that, it would have been too much to take in. And although I regret you didn't have the opportunity to make your final farewell, I deeply resent that you were the last person to see him alive.'

'And I don't blame you for feeling that way,' Tom said, not the least put off by my candour.

A waiter with a sleeve of tattoos, a *Peaky Blinders* haircut and a nose ring brought our coffee. 'Cheers,' he said when he put them down. He winked at me. He must have noticed me staring at his tattoos. My cheeks felt hot.

'Don't be a stirrer, Baz,' Tom said, and Baz blew him a kiss and sashayed off.

I concentrated on getting the right amount of milk into my espresso and not on the table: just a dribble. Then I changed the direction of the conversation because I could easily become too maudlin.

'Do you have a stepfather? Half-siblings?' I said after I'd taken a sip. He was right. It was good.

'No, to both. Perhaps that's why Helena and I have four children. Mum was your stereotypical single parent. She dated when I was younger, but not often and nothing long term. I couldn't have asked for a more devoted mother. But isn't it me who's meant to be asking you the questions?'

'Yes, of course,' I said, embarrassed for the second time in as many minutes.

'I was joking,' he said in a hoarse whisper, leaning across the table towards me. 'And can I call you Kate? I had a primary school teacher called Mrs Hannaford.'

'Kate will be fine,' I said.

He'd almost finished the banana bread when he said, 'I'm sorry you couldn't have children, Kate. Dennis told me what a stressful time it had been for you both, I think mainly to put the circumstances of my conception into context.'

'You refer to him as Dennis?'

'That suited us both. I wouldn't call him Dad, because he'd never fulfilled that role in my life, and Father would have made him sound like a character out of a BBC drama.'

'I see.'

'I found him to be a kind man, once I was old enough to get past my teenage angst and resentment and understand how difficult his situation would have been. Making the surprising discovery that he had fathered a child after all, but then unwilling to openly acknowledge it. And be clear on this, I did not see him very often, and never for more than a couple of hours at a time. He was as hesitant and unsure about our relationship as I was.'

'Did you ever visit the farm?' I'd thought not to ask that question, but it came out of its own accord. Then I fought the urge to block my ears so as not to hear his answer.

'Once, when I was still at uni. I asked to see it, he didn't offer. Mum wouldn't come with me. I didn't go further into the house than to use the bathroom. You were at work.'

I took the answer in as if it were medicine, and tried not to make a face at the unpleasant taste.

'Did you think you might want to be a farmer?'

He smiled and looked down at his hands. 'No, I always knew I wanted to do medicine.'

'You know the part I stumble over the most?' I said. 'Why he didn't ever tell me about you. Was he never going to? And he had grandchildren, for goodness' sake. Did he think so little of me that he didn't … couldn't … confide in me? That cuts deeper every time I think of it.'

Tom filled our glasses with water. He took a long sip of his and carefully wiped his mouth with the paper serviette. 'In the beginning Mum said he didn't tell you because he didn't want to hurt you. You'd been through a lot. Mum said he was concerned about your mental health and general wellbeing. And then the longer it went, the harder it would have been to explain why he'd never 'fessed up. I didn't ever ask him, but that'd be my guess.'

He took another sip of water. My hand trembled when I reached for my own glass. He noticed.

'I'm sorry, Kate. I didn't fully appreciate how painful this would be for you. I grew up knowing who my other biological parent was.

Mum never kept any secrets about it and I had no expectation of Dennis ever being in my life. As a parent or a grandparent.'

'So what changed? Why did your mother come looking for Dennis?' I felt my top lip curl of its own accord.

'When I was twelve I became quite ill. They thought I might die. The doctors couldn't work out what was wrong with me. They mentioned hereditary conditions they wanted to rule out and Mum only knew about her side of the family. So, she went looking for Dennis. He wasn't hard to find, as it turned out. He still drank at the same hotel.'

Inside, I cringed. There was me thinking it had been all about the money. And she'd come looking for him, right under my nose.

'You can imagine his shock: he finds out he has a twelve-year-old son, and in the next breath, Mum tells him I could die.'

Right then I couldn't imagine anything. All I could do was blink.

'Did you wonder if Mum came looking because she wanted money? The child support laws meant that she was entitled to it,' he said, not waiting for an answer. 'Helena's take is that in your position that's what most women would have thought. Mum did okay—she was an accountant and she was determined to manage. And her parents helped out along the way. They could afford it.'

'Did Dennis?'

'Not at first, but as we got to know each other he wanted to contribute. It did help when I was at uni. I only had to get one job.'

'I had no idea about any of this,' I said, unable to keep the bitterness out of my voice. 'And your children? Was he Grandpa or Poppa to them?'

'Neither, Kate,' Tom said, calmly. 'He met Helena but he wouldn't come to our wedding, and right from the very start he refused to have anything to do with our children. He said that would have been the ultimate betrayal of you.'

I closed my eyes and let the storm of emotions sweep through me. What was left was a vacuum. And that weight on my chest.

'I think I should I go,' I said, and fumbled for my handbag. I stood up, the chair legs screeching across the cement.

He reached out and gently grasped my forearm. 'Please sit down, Kate. You're in no state to go anywhere.'

Lightheaded all of a sudden, I plonked into the chair in a most unladylike fashion. He topped up my glass with water and handed it to me.

'Did your see your GP like I suggested?'

I nodded.

'And?'

'Blood pressure is up a bit … cholesterol …' I sipped the water and slowly regained an equilibrium. Patrons who'd turned to stare went back to their coffee and cakes.

'Have you eaten anything today?'

When I didn't answer, he stood up. 'Don't move. I'll get you something to eat.' He came back with another slice of banana bread and put it in front of me. 'Eat,' he said. 'There's more coffee coming. Decaf this time around.'

After I'd eaten I did feel a lot better. The decaf was passable, but barely. I couldn't see the point of coffee without caffeine.

'Can I ask you more questions? And it is okay to refuse,' he said, with a fleeting smile, making it even more impossible for me not to like him.

'Ask away.'

'Whenever we caught up, Dennis always urged me to talk about my life and what I'd been doing. But I don't know anything about his family: parents, siblings, nieces, nephews.'

I filled him in on what I knew of Dennis's parents, which wasn't much; and about Lewis and Molly, their offspring, and Derek. How Dennis had inherited the farm from his Uncle Frank.

'There are a handful of photos and a box of Uncle Frank's journals; they're yours if you want them. And Dennis's childhood memorabilia. I don't know what to do with it all.'

'I'd love to have them,' Tom said, taken aback. 'If you're sure you don't want to keep them.'

'Positively sure. In fact, I'd be thrilled if you took them.'

'Did he enjoy farming? When he talked about the land he had that faraway squint that I've learned to associate with farmers.' He chuckled. 'I have quite a few older farmers as patients.'

'Dennis worked extremely hard and rarely grumbled. He never trivialised the legacy left him by his uncle. There were difficult years—drought, poor commodity prices—but generally he did well and he gained a lot of satisfaction from that. His peers liked and respected him.'

'What did he do in his downtime? Did he play sport? Golf? Bowls? Did you travel? As I said earlier, he'd never talk much about himself at all.'

'Dennis didn't have downtime. An overnight in Adelaide to take in a show or a movie, or a few days to visit Lewis and Molly was about as much of a break as he ever took. It might have been different if we'd had children. But I had a career, and my holidays were usually spent catching up on projects around the home. We went to Kangaroo Island once.'

Tom nodded and I gave a brittle laugh. 'Not a very exciting life, I'm afraid.'

The food had brightened me up but I felt myself beginning to flag again. Most of the previous night had been spent tossing and turning, and this conversation had sapped what little energy I'd had.

'Are you driving back or staying overnight?'

'Driving back. It's only a couple of hours. And there's no bed like your own.'

He smiled again, and there was Dennis. I wanted to reach out and hug him as much as I wanted to shake and slap him. Tears welled in my eyes and I did my best to blink them away.

'I need to go,' I said. Before I had a complete meltdown on the polished cement floor.

'Of course. I'll walk you to your car.'

'There's no need to do that,' I said, flustered. 'I'm all right.'

'I'll come with you all the same,' he said, in a voice that brooked no further argument.

We arrived at my car, parked in a back street. After I'd unlocked it he opened the door for me, then closed it after I was settled. I opened the window.

'Thanks for this, Kate. It's been … wonderful,' he said. 'Would it be all right if I drove up sometime to collect the journals? Bring Helena and the kids with me so you can meet them?'

'You don't want me to send the journals by courier?'

He looked away, and for the first time, he appeared unsure of himself. Then he made eye contact again and said, 'Kate, you're the only link I have to my father, and by getting to know you, I'll get to know him better, and I'd like that. I'd much rather come and collect them, if you don't mind.'

I knew what my response would be but I wanted to be one hundred per cent certain before I committed. There were some aspects of this whole situation that required more time for me to work through. Why Dennis had never told me about Tom was the main one.

Tom thrust his hands into his pockets, stepped back and waited for my answer.

'I would be delighted,' I said, after several minutes. 'You must come for a meal.'

'Good! I'll talk to Helena and we'll be in touch.'

Tom waved me off and I drove home, making a concerted effort not to think about any of it until I'd had a solid night's sleep.

43

Daisy

Thursday evening, after I'd discovered Georgia's empty bedroom, she'd *messaged* me to say she was staying at Kieran's. She'd
forgotten to mention the part about being able to sleep there in
her own bed. I hadn't heard from her since. She'd eventually have
to come back to collect the remainder of her clothes. After I'd
stumbled upon the empty bedroom, I had opened her wardrobe
and there they were. Nana Toogood's box was on the floor of the
wardrobe.

As far as I was concerned, her moving in with Kieran had been
a fait accompli, I just hadn't expected it to happen so soon. What
nonplussed me the most was that she hadn't mentioned her plans
to me. Undeniably, things had shifted between us since Kieran had
come on the scene, but this? Being melodramatic wasn't my thing,
but her sudden—and to a degree secretive—defection had left me
feeling confounded.

There'd been no sign of her on Friday and now Saturday was
almost over with her yet to show up. Jess watched anxiously as I

paced around the living room. I stopped to stare out of the window into the growing gloom of the evening. I hadn't left the place for two days, not even for a walk with Kate. When Georgia did return, I would be here. I wouldn't let her get away with sneaking in to grab her clothes when I wasn't.

I fed Jess, a fraction less than her normal serve. 'I'm afraid we have to tighten our belts, my sweet,' I said. 'It won't hurt either of us one little bit.'

Then I remembered the envelope Kate had given me after I'd helped with the morning tea. It remained unopened in the pocket of my suitcase. I went and fetched it and tore it open: inside were four fifty-dollar notes. 'Oh, Kate!' I said, feeling both grateful and aggrieved. Knowing I was in for rainy weather, I stashed the money back in the suitcase.

I was sitting in the dark when my granddaughter finally came. Her key rattled in the lock and then the door opened. Jess stirred and Georgia said, 'Gran?'

The light came on and I squinted into it.

'Why are you sitting in the dark?' she said.

'Because I won't be able to afford a big electricity bill on my own, will I? Did you think I wouldn't go into your bedroom? I took in your clean washing.'

Her throat contracted as she swallowed. 'I had every intention of telling you,' she said. 'But then it all happened at once. Kieran's mate came, he could help with the lifting ... Besides, I didn't leave you in the lurch. The rent here's paid until the middle of next month.'

'You haven't known him long. I hope you know what you're doing,' I said, echoing what Glenys had said the other day. 'And what furniture were you planning on leaving me?'

'Oh, I'm not taking anything else. Apart from the television and the cupboard it's on. And the coffee table. Mum and Dad gave that to me. Kieran has a fridge and his parents gave him a sofa. He was going to buy a bed, but then we decided that was ridiculous when mine's new and it'd be sitting here empty most of the time.'

'How practical,' I said, icy on the outside but red-hot underneath. 'I could have slept in the bed. It would have been much more comfortable than the sofa.'

'Oh, we didn't think of that,' she said, eyeing me with uncertainty as she backed towards the bedroom. 'I came for the rest of my clothes.'

'It's all right, Georgia. As cross as I am this minute, I do understand that I'm not your problem. I know your father foisted me onto you, but do you think I deserved to be treated like this?'

'Dad said it'd only be for a few months. It's been five already, and with no end in sight. Not your fault, but I need to get on with my own life.'

'Of course you do, as do I, but if the situation were reversed, you would have been the first person to know I was moving out, long before I actually did.'

'I'm sorry, Gran,' she said, and her bottom lip trembled. 'This isn't how I'd planned for you to find out, but Kieran—' She shrugged, looking everywhere but at me.

I refused to bail her out by telling her it was okay, that somehow I'd manage, because I didn't know if I would. When she finally realised I wasn't coming to her rescue, she shrugged again, her bottom lip firmed and she scuttled off to collect what she'd come for.

'Kieran will get the TV and the other stuff tomorrow,' were her parting words about half an hour later. I hadn't moved from the sofa. Jess had stayed put at my feet.

★ ★ ★

The following morning I met Kate at the corner for a walk. It was clear and cold. Not quite a frost. I'd worn a beanie and Kate laughed when she saw me.

'I don't have hair to cover my ears like you do,' I said.

On our way up the trail she recounted her meeting with Tom. 'There were a few awkward moments but overall, I believe it went reasonably well.'

'So he's going to let you know when they'll drive up to collect Dennis's gear?'

'In a fortnight's time. He rang last night to see that I'd arrived home safely.'

'That was thoughtful of him.'

'Yes, I suppose it was.' She looked perplexed. 'It's an aeon since a man showed any overt interest in my wellbeing.'

'What about Dennis?'

'Not as you'd notice. We were definitely at the take-everything-for-granted stage of our relationship.'

'Pretty normal I would have thought, after forty-five years.'

'True, but I wish I'd been a bit less …'

'A bit less what?' I prompted when we'd covered considerably more ground and she hadn't finished the sentence.

'Self-absorbed and self-centred, especially in the early years of our marriage. As hard as it is to admit it. If I hadn't always been so self-focussed I might have been more understanding of Dennis's perspective, and this would never have happened. There would be no Tom. And Dennis might still be here.'

'Don't be too hard on yourself, Kate. What's done can't be undone, and who wouldn't do things differently if they had their time over?'

We walked for a stretch in silence, through patches of dappled sunlight. Kangaroos grazed in a nearby paddock. I took off my beanie and stuffed it in my pocket.

'What would you do differently, Daisy? If you had your time over? Not marry Charlie?'

A kookaburra laughed in a gum tree high above our heads.

'It's only lately that I have considered what I might have done differently. Maybe it's being back in this town, where Charlie and I met, and Georgia asking why I'd never divorced him. The bald truth is I married him because I was pregnant. And I was in love with him. I wouldn't have married him otherwise.

'Not to say there weren't times when I loathed and despised him for his recklessness and immaturity; his total lack of responsibility when it came to his family. But he could always make me laugh, and he loved me, as best that he could. He just didn't know, or want to learn, how to be a husband or a father. To be a grown-up, actually. He loved his boys, but he didn't know what to do with them, or with his own feelings. I have wondered where we would have ended up if I'd never fallen pregnant.'

'And where do you think that might have been?'

'Oh, he would have left, only much sooner than he did. And he would have broken my heart.'

'You're not still in love with him, are you?' Kate said, aghast.

I laughed, right from deep down. 'No, I'm not still in love with him, Kate. I haven't seen him in the flesh since Adam got married, the first time, and his son, Will, is almost sixteen.'

'Have you not ever been interested in another man?'

'No!' I replied without hesitation. 'Why would I ever want *another* man to mother? Four has been plenty, thank you very much.'

★ ★ ★

When we got back, Kate invited me in for a coffee. I declined. We went our separate ways at the corner. I wanted to be home when Kieran came for the television and the coffee table, if he hadn't been already.

As was our habit, I let Jess off the lead and she bounded home, me not far behind. Pamela's silver sedan was parked in Max's driveway. She'd come up yesterday and stayed overnight with her dad and we'd had a brief over-the-fence chat. She was worried about Max's increasing frailty and him being on his own all the time.

Half a scoop of kibble for Jess's breakfast before I let myself in. Luck was on my side. The TV remained in situ on its wood-grain cabinet. The room would be empty without the TV and the coffee table. I didn't have a television stored with my other possessions in Gareth's shed. Mum's telly had been an old monstrosity and I'd never bothered about upgrading. It'd gone to the dump. A new television was out of the question. From now on I'd fill my evenings with other activities. There were more important expenses to suck up my money without even contemplating that kind of purchase.

Kieran and his mate came an hour later. Georgia was at work, or so Kieran said. In a flash the TV, cabinet and coffee table were gone, a rectangle of dust and dog hair the only indication there'd been anything there in the first place.

'Would you mind moving the sofa into the bedroom while you're here?' I said before they left.

No, they didn't mind at all, and in ten minutes it was done.

'You'll be pleased to have the place all to yourself at last,' Kieran said with his usual candour.

'Whatever makes you think that?'

'Georgia said you were used to living on your own. That you had for years, ever since your husband left you.'

'Did she say that?' I said. 'It's not quite the truth.'

He didn't know what to say to that. He shuffled his feet a couple of times and then they went. After I'd swept the floor I brought in the two rickety old canvas chairs from the back verandah and arranged them in the living area. When I plonked down into one of them, it screeched in protest.

Everyone I'd ever lived with had eventually left. Mum had died, but the others had just up and departed when they decided it was time to get on with their own lives. Or whatever. And here I was again, high and dry. What was it about me that made it so easy for people to leave? Rephrase that—to *use* me and then leave me. I wasn't having a pity-party, just facing up to the cold, hard reality.

Jess rattled the front door to be let in. I hugged her and for once she didn't wriggle to get away. She was warm, alive and vital. And she didn't want to leave me.

★★★

If I'd been a drinker, I would have taken to the bottle later that same night after Gareth's phone call.

'Mum,' he said after a vapid greeting. 'There's no easy way to say this, so I'll tell it to you straight: my business is in deep shit and I have to sell the land. In fact, I've already sold it. I'm sorry, but I had no other choice. Is Georgia there? She's not answering her phone.'

'No, she isn't here,' I'd said, like an automaton. I couldn't quite get my head around what had come before the question. 'Did you just say you've sold the land? The land you were building me a new home on?'

'That was the plan, Mum. You knew there were risks. And like most things in life, it hasn't panned out the way we'd hoped. I'm mortgaged to the hilt and the money from the land will give us a bit of breathing space until things improve.'

'But where am I going to live?'

'What's wrong with where you are? You and Georgia get along. You all seemed happy enough when I was up there last.'

'Gareth, don't you ever talk to your daughter?'

'I would if she'd bloody well answer her phone. Can you tell her to ring me?'

'I will if I see her,' I said.

'I really am sorry about this, Mum. But there was no other choice.'

'Fair enough. I'm hanging up now. Goodbye, son.'

He tried several times to call me back but I chose not to answer. I sat in the canvas folding chair in the dark and the cold until my feet went numb and my lower back burned. My thoughts went around in circles. I urgently needed a plan for my future but do you think I could pin one down? Every direction I explored needed money. Money I didn't have. Money I'd never have. I was another step closer to being homeless and the thought terrified me.

I took a scalding hot shower and went to bed. I was tired and achy from sitting in the canvas chair for so long. My throat felt scratchy. It was eleven fifty-three when I turned off the light. With only a small single sash window in the bedroom, it was much darker in there than it had been in the living area. I'd shifted Jess's doggy bed in beside mine.

All the thinking had worn me down to the point of exhaustion and I went straight to sleep.

Next thing I knew, Jess growled and woke me. The bedroom light came on and Georgia was standing beside the sofa bed, shaking my shoulder.

'Gran? Wake up!'

'What are you doing?' I said, squinting into the light. Jess growled again. I levered myself up and shrugged off her hand. 'You're upsetting the dog.'

'Thank goodness you're all right.' She put a hand to her chest.

'What time is it? And why wouldn't I have been all right?' I said, trying to slough off the fuzziness of being woken from a deep sleep.

'A quarter to one. Dad's been going mental because I wasn't answering my phone, but I'd accidentally left it at Lisa's. When she noticed it and saw all the missed calls, she brought it around and I called Dad. He said he'd told you about selling the land, and that you sounded a bit weird afterwards. He was worried, so I came straight around. Are you all right?'

'Fine, but answer me one question, and please, no fibs. Did you know about the land being sold?'

'No, I didn't, Gran,' she said, without pause. 'I knew Dad's business was under pressure, but that's all I knew, and I passed that info on to you. And tonight I told him that I'd moved in with Kieran.'

In the blink of an eye her expression changed from concern to defiance. I didn't utter a word.

'Aren't you going to ask me what he said?'

'You'll tell me if you want me to know.' I snuggled down under the bedclothes and closed my eyes. I was so tired. 'It was nice of you to come and check on me, Georgia. As you can see, I'm all right. You can tell your father that.'

Seconds later the bedroom was plunged into darkness once more, followed not long after by the slam of the screen door. Next time I caught up with Georgia, we'd need to talk about house keys. The ones I'd paid to have cut. I wanted them back.

I was asleep again in seconds.

44

Kate

When Daisy was a no-show at the corner at our prearranged time on Monday morning, I walked around to her house. We'd only made the arrangement the day before and Daisy had been okay then. Her station wagon was parked all on its lonesome in the driveway. I crunched along the gravel and tried to find a redeeming quality in the old house. The block was a good size and it was in a reasonable location, but that was about it. Someday it would be demolished and replaced with new.

Before I'd raised my arm to knock, the door swung open and Daisy regarded me from behind the screen. She was in her dressing gown.

'Stay where you are, Kate. I have a cold or something. Last night I felt tired and achy and my throat was scratchy. This morning my throat is sore and I feel lousy. Georgia's bringing me a Covid testing kit.'

She sneezed, muffling it with a handful of Kleenex. I stepped away from the screen door, as far back as I could without tipping off the verandah. 'Where do you think you picked it up?'

'Who would know?' she said, and punctuated it with another sneeze. 'All those women at the morning tea, hardly anyone wearing a mask, and I took mine off because it was warm in the kitchen. I was with Glenys on Thursday and she's okay, so far. Are you all right? Did you not get my text message?'

Message? It hadn't occurred to me to look at my phone. I didn't even have it with me. I needed to get better at doing that, now I had people wanting to ring me and message me.

'Do you need anything? Milk? Bread? Tissues? I suppose Georgia is seeing to all that.'

She blew her nose. 'I'm sorry, Kate, but I need to lie down. If you're going for a walk, would you mind taking Jess? I'll fetch her lead.'

Could dogs get Covid and pass it on to humans? I hoped not.

'It might only be a cold,' Daisy said, when she came back. 'Or the flu. It does feel worse than a cold.' She sounded more clogged up by the minute. The door opened wide enough for her to reach through with the lead and put it down on the verandah, along with several sanitising wipes. When I'd wiped it over she let out the dog. Jess homed in on the lead in my hand and wagged her tail. She came to me and I clipped it on.

'Good dog,' I said, experimentally. She wagged her tail some more.

'She'll be okay. She's used to you. We're both grateful,' Daisy said, and closed the door. She sounded miserable. Jess and I headed off on our jaunt.

We had a lovely time meandering through the parklands and along the streets, admiring the gardens. Just about everyone we saw said hello to the dog. I don't think they even noticed me on the other end of the lead. An hour later I took Jess back and shut her into the yard.

The first thing I did when I got home was find my phone. Sure enough, there was a message from Daisy saying she felt unwell and wouldn't walk. I laboriously tapped out a message to her, getting more and more frustrated as I went. I'd never thought of myself as having fat fingers.

Jess was good. Shut in the yard. Can take tomorrow if you're not recovered. Sing out if you need anything. K.

Off it went with a whooshing sound. I held the phone for several more minutes but nothing came back. It was awful feeling unwell and being on your own. If I hadn't heard something from her in the next few hours I'd walk around this afternoon to check on her. I had a full box of P2 masks in the linen press, and I knew all about hand hygiene. No excuses.

The last two of Evelyn's jelly cakes were thawing out on a plate on the kitchen bench. They were for morning tea with Rhonda. She'd planned to attend the fundraiser, had even bought her ticket before her daughter Margie put her foot down and said she shouldn't go. Rightly so, especially if it turned out that Daisy had Covid and it'd come from here. Not that we'd ever know for sure. There'd been nothing from Valma to say anyone had come down with it, and she would be all over it if there had been. Fingers crossed. These days, checking yourself for a sore throat, fever, headache or any other symptoms had become routine. Covid had brought about many changes in our lives, most of them unwanted.

★★★

I didn't hear from Daisy so I walked around to her place mid-afternoon. An older woman was unloading bags of groceries from the back of 4WD station wagon parked behind Daisy's car. It wasn't until I was alongside that I recognised her.

'Hello, Glenys,' I said. 'How is she?'

She paused and peered at me with a slight frown. A surgical mask was tucked under her chin. 'Kate Hannaford,' she said, and her face relaxed. 'She's not good at all. She did one of those rodent tests. It was negative, and then Georgia said she'd need another test, and that girl is a registered nurse so she should know. Anyway, I drove her to the clinic at the hospital to have the test.'

By rodent I assumed she meant RAT, and that another test was a PCR. 'Let's keep our fingers crossed that it's nothing worse than a cold.'

'The flu, more than likely. What worries me is that she's here on her own.' She rested the groceries down again. 'It's not right. But she refused point blank to let me take her out to the farm and look after her there. And when I offered—' Glenys was getting herself quite worked up.

I held up my hand and said, 'Whoa, Glenys, back up a step, can you please. Why is Daisy on her own?'

Glenys's eyes narrowed and she folded her arms, propping up an ample bosom. 'Moved in with her boyfriend, didn't she, without bothering to tell her gran. Daisy came home and discovered half the furniture gone.'

I was stunned. From the way Daisy talked about her granddaughter, I'd expected better of her. 'When did this happen?'

'Late last week.'

'She didn't tell me,' I said, sounding peeved.

'Don't think you're special, she didn't tell me neither, but I just happen to be good friends with Eleanor Hall, and she mentioned it.'

'Kieran's mother? I can't imagine her or Rob being over the moon about it. They're quite conservative and Kieran hasn't known Georgia very long at all.'

'My thoughts exactly, but it seems to be the way of the world: the younger generations do things that upset the oldies, purposefully or not.'

'I guess you're right,' I said. 'When you're young you think you know everything. By the time you get to our age you've discovered that you don't know anything much at all.'

Glenys laughed. She pulled the mask over her mouth and nose and picked up the bags of groceries. 'Are you coming in?'

I hesitated. Luckily, Glenys had her back to me and didn't witness my consternation. Talking to Daisy at a distance through the screen door was one thing ...

Before I could talk myself out of it, I took out my mask and put it on, and felt for the hand sanitiser in my handbag. Minimally reassured, I followed Glenys to the front door. After all, I was only going into Daisy's house, and she may or may not have Covid. It wasn't as if I was being asked to step into the reactor soon after the Chernobyl disaster.

★ ★ ★

An hour or so later, Glenys and I debriefed in the driveway alongside her car. Glenys had stood by while Daisy showered herself, and I'd unpacked and put away the groceries and washed the few dirty dishes in the sink. The inside of the house, though spotlessly clean and tidy, was as pitiful as its exterior. How the owner got away with renting out a place in that condition was beyond me.

Glenys let out a pent-up breath. 'That woman is stubborn! I wish she'd agreed to me bringing in the camp bed and staying for at least a couple of nights until she's over the worst.'

'But that's Daisy, isn't it: stubborn. She never expects anything from anyone and she would *never* ask for help.'

'Sometimes to her own detriment,' Glenys said with surprising vehemence. 'She was wonderful with Dad. Never raised her voice to him once, and he could be awful. I put up with whatever he dished out because he was my father, but some days ... truly, even I could have clobbered him.'

'It's a pity Georgia isn't here.'

'She'll be on night duty later in the week, anyway. Now, Kate, I'll come back tomorrow, around lunch time. I'll make a pot of chicken noodle soup. That's nourishing and it'll slide nicely down her sore throat. There's a boiler chicken in the freezer. Can you pop around first thing in the morning? Get her something for breakfast? There's plenty of fresh fruit, yoghurt ...'

'I can do that, and I'll walk the dog.'

'That's settled then. You have my phone numbers and I have yours. Please let me know how she really is in the morning, because she'll tell me she's fine, and we both know that she isn't.'

Glenys drove off and I walked the short distance home. I noticed as I passed that Max Purdue's place appeared all closed up, the garden not as manicured as usual. Then I remembered Daisy saying how concerned his daughter was about his increasing frailty, and that she'd taken him home with her for a while.

Getting old came with relentless challenges, more so if you only had yourself to rely on. What would become of me when I couldn't care for myself any more? No son or daughter to whisk me off for a week of tender loving care. It was an inevitability I chose not to ponder, not for too long anyway. What was the point? My preference would be to go to bed one night, go to sleep and never wake up. Isn't that what most wished for, and very few were granted?

On a lighter note: was chicken noodle soup still fed to invalids? And made out of real chickens? Who did that? Apparently Glenys Carlisle did. I'll bet she'd slaughtered and dressed the bird as well. Perhaps I could make a baked custard ... That would be nourishing and would slide painlessly down a sore throat. With that thought, I quickened my pace home.

45

Daisy

The cat. I'd forgotten all about Pauline. I'd promised to feed her while Max was away for the week, or longer, if Pam could talk him into staying. And the chooks. I was to top up their pellets and water and collect any eggs. My head pounded when I sat up. It was dark. Jess was snoring. I had no idea what time it was, and I felt worse than I'd ever felt before in my life.

Fumbling around for the torch, I woke Jess. My bare feet hit the floorboards with a slap and I shivered. I was clammy and cold.

'I promised to feed the cat,' I croaked. My throat felt as if I'd swallowed a handful of razorblades. Jess climbed out of her bed, ready to accompany me to the ends of the earth if needs be.

The overhead light nearly blinded me so I flicked it off again and searched for slippers and dressing gown in the torch light. Who'd hung up the dressing gown in the wardrobe? It certainly wouldn't have been me ... Ah, Glenys. She'd been here. With Kate. Was that yesterday or the day before? Had Georgia come? How long since the cat had been fed? Had I fed her at all since Max left with Pam?

The glow from the bathroom light was enough for me to find my way slowly through the house to the front door. I felt as if I was doing it all in slow motion. I was in my body, but not. Jess's ears flattened and she turned away when I told her to stay on the verandah.

Stars twinkled overhead. The night was still and cold. I'd made it at far as the end of the verandah, shivering so hard my teeth chattered, when a vehicle wheeled into the driveway. I groaned and threw up an arm against the powerful beam of the headlights. Then it was dark again and white spots danced in front of my eyes. The slam of a car door and the sound of feet on the gravel.

'Daisy? What the hell are you doing?'

The voice came at me like a distant memory. Was I hallucinating? I must be. The floorboards moved and then he was standing beside me. I pointed the torch into his face. He swore and pushed it away.

'Charlie Toogood,' I said. 'I promised Max I'd feed Pauline.'

Next thing I knew I was being swept off my feet. I giggled. I was definitely delirious. This was nothing but a feverish dream. Although I hadn't dreamed about Charlie for a very long time.

'Hang on to me,' he said, and I inched my arm around his neck. He was warm and strong and so solidly familiar. Not a dream.

'Put me down,' I demanded, in as firm a voice as I could muster. 'And you should be wearing a mask. I'm infectious.'

'Stop wriggling about, will you, and who the hell are Max and Pauline?' he said. Somehow, he opened the screen door and carried me into the dimly lit house.

'Max is my neighbour and Pauline is his cat.' I said, my lips moving against the warm skin of his neck. He smelled like soap.

Jess danced around his feet and yipped with excitement.

'Mind the dog,' I said, trying to shimmy out of his arms. His grip tightened.

'Never mind the bloody dog, where's the bedroom?' he said, but was already heading in the right direction. The only direction really.

'Where's the bedroom? That's what you said our very first time.'

'I bet you wish you'd never told me.'

'I don't think it would have mattered. Because if you remember, we didn't get as far as the bedroom.'

He grunted and put me down on the bed, ever so gently. I'd started to shiver again and my head was pounding.

'You've got your slippers on the wrong feet,' he said as he bent to ease them off. 'Now lie down.'

I didn't need to be told twice. I curled into a foetal position and he pulled the bedclothes over me. The shivering wouldn't stop.

'Have you got any more blankets?'

'Nope.' I closed my eyes. I could hear him moving about in the living room, talking to Jess in a low voice. He'd always had a way with animals: they trusted him without reserve.

I must have dozed. Next thing I knew he was nudging me.

'Here, drink this, and I've brought you a couple of Panadol. When did you have the last dose?'

'What time is it?'

'Midnight.'

I elbowed myself up and held out a trembling hand.

'Open your mouth,' he said, and when I complied he dropped the tablets onto my tongue. He held the mug to my lips and I drank greedily, wincing when the first mouthful slid down my throat. The tea was warm, black and sweet. When I'd finished it I flopped back onto the pillow.

There were so many questions swimming around in my head but I didn't have the wherewithal to gather my wits and voice them. I closed my eyes and drifted. Then the room was plunged into darkness again. I strained to hear the front door close. Nothing, except the sounds Jess made shuffling around in her bed. My eyes sprang open when the sofa bed creaked and I felt my side tilt precariously.

'What are you doing?'

'Getting in with you.'

'Don't be ridiculous! Besides, you'll catch whatever I've got.'

'Too bad,' he said. 'You'll get warm quicker this way.'

I lay there, rigid, staring into the darkness, my heart racing a mile a minute, and not just from whatever it was I had. Without explanation, my absentee husband had appeared out of nowhere and now he'd climbed into the bed beside me. Over two decades had passed since that had last happened.

'Go to sleep, Daisy,' he rumbled, half-asleep himself. 'We'll talk in the morning.'

Not long after I must have dropped off, only to wake several hours later slippery with sweat, and with something heavy resting on my chest. I shoved aside the bedclothes, and Charlie's arm, and swung my legs around and sat up. The cotton T-shirt I wore to bed was damp and I was cold; my hair matted to the back of my head in a sweaty tangle. I found the torch and turned it on.

'What's happening?' Charlie said from behind me, wide awake. 'You're not going to throw up or anything like that, are you?'

'I'm saturated with sweat. A hot shower would be wonderful, but I don't have the energy so a wipe over with a warm face washer will do, and then a clean T-shirt.'

He was out of bed and pulling on his jeans in one fluid movement.

'How do you feel?' he said.

'Like death warmed up.'

The bathroom light came on across the passageway and I turned off the torch. He came back with a towel and a face washer. I wanted to protest, to push away his helping hands, but I felt as weak and wobbly as a newborn lamb. Tears blurred my vision. This was all too much. If Charlie noticed I was crying, he didn't comment. He went out and fetched one of the canvas chairs and I sat in it with my dressing gown draped over my shoulders while he remade the bed with the only other set of clean sheets.

'Do you want a drink of tea?' he said when he'd finished the bed and helped me back into it.

'Please. Not as much sugar this time.'

His smile flashed briefly in the gloom. Putting too much sugar in my tea was an old argument.

When he came back he propped me up before handing me the brew. Then he went to the window, parted the curtains and stood staring out into the night while he drank his tea. He wasn't a tall man but there'd always been a muscly strength about him that made him appear bigger than he was. It was impossible to see in the dim light how much nature's clock had aged him. More than likely, not as cruelly as it had me.

'Why are you here?' I said, addressing his back.

He looked over his shoulder. 'It was time,' he said quietly.

'Time for what, and on whose reckoning?'

He shrugged and went back to staring out the window. His head tipped back as he drained the mug. Without a word, he took the empties back to the kitchen and turned off the bathroom light. Then I heard the clank of his belt buckle as his jeans hit the floor, and the bed dipped as he climbed back in.

'Go to sleep, Daisy,' he said. 'I'll see to your neighbour's cat in the morning.'

It wasn't long before he was snoring softly.

★ ★ ★

Raised voices woke me. I felt fuzzy-headed and shaky. Jess's bed was empty. She barked, adding to the din coming from outside. Getting out of bed and pulling on slippers and dressing gown flattened me, but I needed the bathroom. And to tell whoever it was arguing out front to take it some place else.

They didn't. They brought it inside. Kate and Charlie, head to head. What a trip down memory lane that was. Then I saw Georgia on the other side of the screen door, her nose pressed close to the wire. I'd never before seen such a bewildered expression on her face.

'Gran? Are you okay?' she called. 'Have you had a text message with the test results yet?'

Kate and Charlie's argument stopped immediately, as if someone had pulled the plug. They swivelled to look at me, guilt written on both their faces.

'What's he doing here?' Kate said, plaintively.

I closed my eyes to stop the room spinning and leaned heavily on the linen press door. 'You should all be wearing masks,' I said.

'But what's he doing here?' Kate repeated.

'Tell her, Charlie, because I'm not sure myself.'

'Gran, the test results? I need to know if I'm a close contact. I didn't go to work yesterday afternoon, just in case. I'm rostered on again this arvo.'

My phone was on charge, plugged into the powerpoint where the TV had once been. Kate zeroed in on it before Charlie did, but he was closer. If I hadn't felt so awful, I would have laughed. He handed me the phone. Kate glared at him.

There were three missed calls and a message from Glenys: *How are you? Charlie just showed up the other day. Please don't be angry with me for not warning you. Trev told me to mind my own business. I'll be in later. G.*

It hadn't occurred to me to be cross with Glenys. Why would I be? Giving no advance warning of intent was Charlie's modus operandi. I knew that.

'The PCR was negative,' I said when I finally got to the message. There was a collective sigh of relief. Georgia came inside, her expression pinched.

'Must be the flu. You look terrible, Gran. Shouldn't you be in bed? You can hardly stand up. You don't want to end up with pneumonia.' Then she turned to Charlie and, with hands on hips and in a biting tone, said, 'And what the hell are you doing here, Granddad? Does Dad know you're here?'

'Georgia, please …' I said, sinking into the canvas chair Charlie put behind me. It creaked and groaned on my behalf.

Kate's eyes darted between Georgia and Charlie. She cleared her throat. 'Shall I take Jess for a walk?'

'Would you, Kate? Her lead's just there.'

Our eyes met for the briefest of moments. *Will you be all right if I leave you here with them?* is what I read in her glance. I nodded. Her shoulders softened and she took the lead and went looking for Jess.

Georgia was scowling at Charlie. His jaw tightened, and I braced myself on the arms of the chair. Charlie wouldn't stand there indefinitely and take whatever his headstrong granddaughter felt she had the right to dish out.

'With all due respect, Georgia,' he said, 'the reason for me being here is none of your damned business. And just for the record, Gareth does know I'm here. So do Jay and Adam.'

'It is my business if you go upsetting her,' Georgia said, but with less bite in her voice.

'You didn't worry about upsetting her when you moved in with your boyfriend.'

Georgia flinched. 'Yeah, well, I apologised for that, didn't I, Gran?'

'In your own way,' I said. 'You look tired.'

'I didn't sleep that well, but I wanted to make sure you were okay. I'll call you later,' she said in a proprietary manner. After sending a baleful glance Charlie's way, she left.

'Are you sure she's related to us?' he said, and gave his head a slight shake. 'I bet her patients are shit-scared of her.'

'Try looking at it from her point of view, Charlie. She was a baby when you wandered off in search of who knows what, and now, out of the blue, you just show up again. She has no knowledge of *us*, just what she's gleaned from her father and uncles. And from me.

'Because I'd loved you, I tried my damnedest to understand why you had to go, and to accept that none of us would ever be enough to make you want to stay. But you can't expect them to understand the situation the way I do.'

That was it. I'd run out of steam. I needed to lie down again soon.

'You always did have a way with words, Daisy. The truth is, I'd aimed to get back to see old Bill before he died. When I didn't make that, I'd aimed for the funeral, but with one thing and another, and then a breakdown out from Marla Bore … Needed parts and they had to come from Adelaide.'

'So you're not here for long,' I said. I levered myself out of the chair but swayed as the room swam in front of my eyes. If Charlie hadn't grabbed me when he did I would have ended up in a pile on the floor.

'I'm here for as long as you need me, Daisy. And I don't give a damn what anyone else has to say about that, or about me.'

He all but carried me back to the bed. He tucked me in and made me drink more tea with too much sugar. Afterwards, I slept until midday.

46

Kate

Back from our walk, I shut Jess in the yard and left her lead hanging on the front door handle. Charlie's 4WD hadn't moved. I'd got the shock of my life to see him standing on the verandah when I'd arrived to pick up Jess. And the bastard—excuse my French—looked closer to sixty than just shy of seventy. His hair had thinned and he might have been a trifle thicker around the middle, but basically he looked as handsome and vital as he always had. I suppose if you'd shirked all your responsibilities and only ever suited yourself … That's the part I'd said to him earlier, and it had got the ball rolling, good and proper.

With no desire to run into him again today, or ever if I was given a choice, I gave Jess a pat and scuttled off home. On the way I messaged Glenys and asked her to swing by and collect the baked custard on her way to Daisy. No way was I taking it around there on the off-chance that I'd run into him.

Ensconced in my breakfast nook an hour later, second espresso in front of me, I took time to purposefully unpick why I disliked

Charlie Toogood as much as I apparently did, and always had. It was something about the way he regarded me: as if he knew I didn't like him and that it didn't bother him one iota.

Back in the beginning I'd been jealous of the relentless way he'd courted Daisy, and how she'd fallen head over heels for him. The way they'd been together. I'd thought him brash and shallow, a boy in a man's body; always craving to be the centre of attention. But I couldn't deny that he'd been as besotted by Daisy as she had been by him.

The memory of how they'd been as a couple dragged on my insides with potent longing. For a moment I was swamped by an incredible sadness that I'd missed out on something important; that I'd never experienced that undeniable attraction, the helpless yearning, the intense passion for another, no matter how short-lived. And now it was too late.

Dennis, God rest his soul, had tried, but he'd never had whatever it was that Charlie Toogood had—and from what I'd seen of the man earlier, still did. The good looks, the charm, the animal magnetism that meant he always got his own way. How Daisy had looked through that to discover the man underneath and then to let him go because that's what he wanted—or needed—was beyond my comprehension. Was that what love was about? If it was, then had I ever really loved Dennis? Had I ever really loved anybody?

I'd convinced myself that Dennis and I had taken a mature approach to our relationship, to what we wanted from each other and from life in general. To marry, to raise a family and then grow old together. Content. At first our courtship had been tentative, neither of us comfortable with public displays of affection. Or private displays, as it turned out. Dennis had been as shy and self-conscious about showing his feelings as I had. It was easier not to. Then my obsession with having a family had extinguished what passion there

had been between us. And there had been passion, before inter-
course had become a mechanical act that could only happen when I
thought I was ovulating. Or hoped I was. Any wonder Dennis had
succumbed to having sex with an unknown woman purely for the
joy of it.

The coffee had gone cold so I tipped it down the sink. Another
coffee? No. My gaze drifted to the fridge. Here it was not even ten
in the morning and I was thinking about having a drink. I pinched
myself, hard. After I'd put the baked custard in the oven I went
outside to water the plants on the patio.

The question I needed to answer with complete honesty, but
struggled even to consider, was: Did I love myself? Did I even like
myself, just one tiny little bit?

★★★

Glenys rang the doorbell right on midday. I invited her in. The
baked custard was just out of the oven. I wrapped the CorningWare
dish in aluminium foil while she watched me from the opposite side
of the kitchen island. She fidgeted with the hem of her blouse, her
gaze darting around the kitchen.

'Gosh,' she said. 'I wouldn't know what to do with a kitchen like
this.' She smoothed her hand across the granite bench top. 'I didn't
know Charlie was coming here, Kate. Honestly. He just showed up.
Shocked me and Trev as much as everyone else.'

'Never mind,' I said. 'Knowing Charlie, he won't be around for
long.'

'No,' she said with a sigh. 'Poor Daisy.'

Did she mean poor Daisy because he wouldn't stick around, or
because he'd come back in the first place?

I covered the foil-wrapped dish with a tea towel. 'How did the
chicken noodle soup turn out?'

Her face brightened. 'Good! Luckily I had enough egg noodles. And plenty of fresh parsley. It's not the same without them. Trev's having a bowl for his lunch. He loves it and I don't make it very often.'

'I can't say I've ever made it,' I said.

'It's easy. I'll write you out the recipe. A few bowls of homemade chicken noodle soup will perk Daisy up no end.'

I blinked. Slowly. It was if I saw her for the very first time. Past the drab clothes and the awful haircut.

'What a kind person you are, Glenys,' I said.

Colour rose in cheeks. 'She's my dear friend. I hate to see her so poorly. And Charlie turning up like he has …'

'When exactly did he turn up?'

'Late last Thursday. Funny thing was, Daisy had just left and I was outside after seeing her off when who should drive up but Charlie. They would have passed each other on the road, maybe even the driveway. Imagine that.

'He headed off to Adelaide the next morning, to see his boys. He only came back from them last night and that's when I mentioned how worried I was about Daisy, her being sick and on her own.' She paused to draw breath. 'I'd put up a meal for him, lamb chops, veg and the potato bake I know he enjoys. Rice pudding for dessert. Anyway, he had a shower, gobbled the food and then took off. He didn't say where he was going but I just knew, and I wanted to ring Daisy and warn her. Trev said it was none of my business where Charlie went and for me to butt out. They were both adults.' She looked down at her hands and swallowed a couple of times. 'Charlie rang me a while ago to say how she was. I could tell he was worried. She still has a fever. He said you'd been there this morning.'

By the way she carefully avoided eye contact I guessed that whatever Charlie had said about me hadn't been the least bit complimentary.

'We had a robust discussion,' I said, downplaying the stoush we'd had in the front yard. Loud enough to bring the neighbour across the street out onto her verandah. Then we'd moved inside. I don't even remember exactly what I'd said to him, about him, just the general gist of it, and that I'd been so angry at him for being there. Over-the-top angry. Nothing I'd said had been complimentary about him.

'The past can come back with a rush, can't it?' Glenys said gently. 'It can be a shock when someone from back then turns up, out of the blue.'

'I've had a bit of that happening to me of late,' I said, with a hollow chuckle. 'First Daisy, the flowers, then the photo, and now Charlie.'

'Flowers? Photo? I'm not sure I follow you,' she said.

I had wondered if Daisy had told her about Dennis's infidelity; about Tom. Obviously she hadn't. I should never have doubted, knowing Daisy.

'A story for another time, perhaps.' I smiled, a rueful smile, and picked up the tea towel-wrapped bundle. 'I'll carry this out, shall I?'

Glenys put the baked custard in a basket alongside the container of soup. Poised to climb into the driver's seat, she paused and said, 'I don't think he's ever stopped loving her. I think he knew he did nothing but break her heart, so he left and didn't come back. Until now. But then Trev says I'm nothing but a hopeless romantic.' She gurgled with laughter. 'And he might just be right.'

I stood at the kerb for a while after she'd driven around the corner. That last bit had given context to her 'Poor Daisy'. A hopeless romantic indeed. I had to admire how comfortable Glenys was in her own skin; confident about who she was and where she fit in this topsy-turvy world. I only wish I could be half as generous to other people as she was. I envied how secure she must be in the love of her family and friends.

My shoulders sagged. At the end of the day it had little to do with how you looked or what you wore, the car you drove or the flashiness of your kitchen appliances. It was who you were on the inside. And how easy it was for you to be with yourself.

Instead of going back into the house, I crossed the street to Rhonda's place. I didn't have the stomach for my own company just now.

47

Daisy

It was day four of the flu, or whatever it was I had. Certainly more than a cold. When I'd woken this morning I'd felt hungry for the first time. With an omelette in mind, I dragged on my dressing gown and slippers and shuffled out to the kitchen.

Charlie was in the shower, his swag spread on the living room floor. After the second night I'd persuaded him that beside me in the sofa bed wasn't the optimum place for him if he wanted to stay flu free. The bed was comfortable enough for one, but not two, not in any sense. He'd studied me for several seconds, an unreadable expression on his face, before concurring. Then he'd gone out to his vehicle, the one I'd almost sideswiped coming out of Glenys and Trev's driveway, and returned with a well-used swag and a scarred canvas duffel bag. The same duffel bag I'd helped him pack twenty-three years before.

I leaned heavily on the edge of the kitchen sink. All I could hear was the rasp of each breath and the frantic beating of my heart. Getting the eggs, butter, milk and cheese out of the fridge and the pan out of the cupboard had worn me out.

'What the hell are you doing, Daisy?' Charlie said gently from beside me. He smelled of Imperial Leather soap and toothpaste. Achingly familiar, but from another time. How come smell was the strongest trigger for nostalgia? For me anyway.

'I'm hungry,' I said, and focussed on that empty feeling instead.

'Good to hear. I'll get breakfast.' Ready to support me if I stumbled, he guided me to the canvas chair. 'Now sit. Don't move.' He scanned the ingredients spread out on the cupboard. 'Scrambled, or an omelette?'

'Omelette.'

He went to the fridge, opened it wide and started rummaging around in the vegetable crisper. 'Any mushrooms? Tomato? Spring onions?'

'I dunno,' I said. 'You'd have a better idea what's in there than me.' I craned to see around him and into the fridge. I needed to double-check the six pack of beer I'd expected to be there really wasn't. But why did I care?

'I'll do some grocery shopping today. Can't expect Glenys to keep feeding us forever.' He put several shrivelled mushrooms and a tomato onto the bench. There wasn't much space, not with the stack of empty containers that'd held the food Glenys had ferried in daily. The chicken noodle soup had been wonderful. And Kate's baked custard. It was all I'd eaten for the first couple of days.

I watched with something akin to awe as he whipped up cheesy mushroom omelettes, toast and the inevitable sweet black tea.

'When did you learn to cook?'

'It was either learn or starve,' he said. 'When you're out mustering with a few other blokes, someone has to step up and do the job.'

'I thought you took a cook with you. You know, in the chuck wagon.'

He smiled and it sent a wave of warmth right through me. I was none too pleased about it either. The last thing I needed was Charlie Toogood worming his way back into my life, and into my heart. Only to leave again when the urge took him. And it would. I didn't return the smile.

'That's on television, Daisy. Real life is a whole lot tougher.'

'Don't I know it,' I said, flatly.

His smile faded, and he acknowledged my statement with a sharp incline of his head.

Charlie had brought in a camp table and another folding chair from his vehicle. The room looked like an indoor camping site. But if not for the camp table we would have been eating off our laps. The omelette was lighter and fluffier than anything I'd ever made.

'I've had a decent look around, inside and out, and this place is a dump, even to an old bushy like me,' Charlie said. 'How much rent did you say you were paying?'

We'd finished eating and I was considering whether or not I'd go back to bed for a while. I had no strength or stamina, which was disconcerting. Any time now I was expecting Charlie to pack up and go and I'd be on my own again, stressing over how long I could keep paying that rent.

'I don't think I've ever said how much.'

'The place should be bulldozed,' he said, getting up to make himself another brew. 'It's riddled with white ants. At some stage someone must have put their foot through the floorboards out back.'

'That would have been me,' I said. 'Georgia's boyfriend fixed it.'

He stared at me, open-mouthed. 'Why do you stay here? I reckon any building inspector would condemn it.'

'Comparatively speaking, the rent's reasonable. If I'm careful I'll afford it on my own. It belongs to an acquaintance of Gareth's, and there's no rental agreement.'

'So this acquaintance could put the rent up whenever they like? Or ask you to move out?'

The likelihood of either of those things happening hadn't escaped me. I pushed aside my half-finished mug of tea. I'd had enough.

'When I came here, Georgia and I were sharing the rent. Up until a while ago, Gareth had put money towards it too. I never expected to be on my own here, nor for it to be long term. But—'

'Yeah, I heard all about about Gareth's business almost going belly-up. I don't understand why you sold him your parents' house in the first place.'

'There was still a mortgage on it, Charlie. A substantial mortgage. After Mum died I was up to my eyeballs in debt. Gareth offered to do for me what I'd done for Mum: buy the house. It was old, needed a heap of work. He understood the real value was in the land. And losing those mortgage payments helped me a lot.'

He took a deep breath and let it out slowly, all the while contemplating the inside of his empty tea mug. 'Me going when I did meant you had one less mouth to feed,' he said.

'True.' I coughed. It hurt and I winced.

'You need more painkillers.' He grabbed the packet. I took two tablets off his palm and swallowed them with a mouthful of lukewarm tea.

When I had my breath back, I said, 'For the time being I'll stay here. I can afford it, if nothing goes wrong, and most importantly, there's a yard for Jess. Speaking of which, where is she? Did Kate come for her?'

'A while ago. She sneaks in, grabs the dog and goes. I've watched her. It's quite funny.' He went to the open front door and peered out through the screen. The sun was shining. 'I guess she wants to avoid running into me again at any cost.'

'You never did like her, not ever. Why was that? She's not that bad.'

He turned to face me. 'She's a fake. Up herself. Always was and always will be. Dennis was a solid sort of a bloke. I dunno how he put up with her.'

'Like I said on the phone that day, people change, they mellow with age. Hopefully we all learn, gain some wisdom along the way.'

'Some people. Not her. Did you hear the things she called me the other morning? Granted, I deserve some of it. But I don't know how she's figured it was my fault her marriage was a disaster.'

'Did she say that?'

'In a roundabout sort of a way. And who the bloody hell is Tom?'

'Dennis's son.'

'Ah, so he *was* spreading it around. Bugger me. It's always the quiet ones, the one's you'd least expect.'

'Kate's had a difficult time, especially the past few months.'

'And she would have be milking it for all it was worth. It's always been all about her—'

'Stop!' I croaked as loud as I could and held up both hands. Charlie drew back, startled. 'She is my friend. I never expected to run into her again, but I did, and in her own unique way, she's been a kind and dependable friend.'

And she'd be there to continue being that friend long after Charlie breezed off again. That brought to mind what she'd said, how we should have worked harder on our friendship back then. Perhaps we should have. How it might have been if we had. On the lonely days, the difficult days, and I'd had my fair share of them, it would have been nice to have an old friendship to retreat to.

Charlie let it go. I don't know if it was because I'd convinced him, or because I'd started to cough again. I suspect it was the latter. He helped me back to bed, via the bathroom. I could have made it on my own but I'd let myself enjoy the help while it was on offer.

'I'll put on a load of washing,' he said after he'd tucked me in. 'Is there anything else you want me to do? I'll slip out to the supermarket later.'

I shook my head and closed my eyes.

I thought he'd left the room, but then he said, 'You wanna know the real reason I can't stand her?'

I opened my eyes to see that he hadn't moved at all. He was standing beside the bed, gazing down at me.

'When you and I first got together she told me in no uncertain terms to piss off, to leave you alone, that I'd never be good enough for you.' His hand rasped across his mouth and jaw. 'I hated that she was right.'

I squeezed my eyes shut and rolled onto my side, willing myself not to think, just to be.

I don't know how long he stayed in the room, or if he witnessed the tears that oozed down my face and onto the pillowcase. Thankfully, not long after that, I slept.

48

Kate

Saturday morning I went early to collect Jess. I'd been awake since five and there was only so long you could lie in bed and not sleep. Replaying the past, over and over again.

Speaking of the past, Charlie was outside, loading gear into his 4WD, when I got there. He'd washed the vehicle and a hose was coiled beside the tap. Red dirt had silted up the gravel. It'd leave a silhouette the shape of his 4WD.

'You're off then,' I said, with barely controlled glee.

He turned slowly and regarded me coolly. 'Not going far. Daisy's a lot better.' He returned to his task.

I knew how well she was. Thursday afternoon I'd dropped by to say hello when Charlie went to the supermarket. And then again yesterday when he'd driven out to visit the Carlisles. Glenys had messaged me with the inside information.

It would be a few days yet before Daisy was up for a walk with Jess and I, but she'd had colour in her cheeks again, and yesterday afternoon she'd made the tea.

'I'll go in and say hello,' I said. He didn't turn around, just lifted his shoulders in a way that said he didn't care what I did.

Daisy was up and about but still in her dressing gown. Even though well on the road to recovery, the characteristic spring to her step remained absent. I wondered if that was only because she'd been ill.

'How are you?'

'One hundred per cent on what I was, and better by the day,' she said, with a flicker of a smile. 'Charlie's going out to help on the farm for a few days. Trev's hurt his back. Physio told him to rest.'

There were a dozen things I could have said, none of them kind, so I bit my tongue instead. Daisy handed me the dog's lead. Jess wandered over, tail swinging from side to side.

'I think I'll have enough energy to walk to the corner with you tomorrow,' she said to Jess, and then to me, 'Thank you again, Kate. From both of us.'

Charlie and I ignored each other when I walked past with the dog. Now he had his head under the bonnet of the LandCruiser, tinkering. More than likely filling in the time until I'd disappeared with the dog and he could go inside. I threw him a hostile glare.

I couldn't get past the dread that he'd take her away from me for the second time. After all these years, and a tentative and sometimes lumpy start, we were re-establishing our friendship. To me it'd been like being thrown a lifeline: without it I might have gone under, never to resurface.

A cold wind churned up leaves on the footpath. We plodded on. In a way, Daisy having the flu had been good for my health. With all this walking I'd lost a kilo and felt better than I had since forever. My decision to limit wine to weekends only, and open a piccolo instead of a full-size bottle, hadn't proven too onerous, so far. Another reason for my increasing sense of well-being. If only Charlie Toogood hadn't shown up.

As we walked, I planned and then discarded one menu choice after another for when Tom and his family came to lunch. It was a week away and whatever I served would need to be child friendly. I'd thought about a barbecue, but the weather forecast wasn't that promising. Plus, I wasn't exactly a dab hand when it came to cooking outdoors. That had been Dennis's department. Maybe Tom would be willing? But not the first time they visited. Did that mean I was hoping they'd want to come back? Of course it did.

The hulking 4WD had gone when Jess and I returned. I breathed a sigh of relief, until I went inside to use the bathroom. The swag had gone but the camp table and chair remained firmly in place. There was a tablecloth on the table. Obviously he was coming back. I went out the back and threw a handful of dry food into the dog's bowl. She was ready and waiting for her breakfast. Hard not to become fond of her. She was constant and undemanding company. I'd begun to understand the thing about dogs being a man's best friend.

Daisy was sitting on the verandah in the sun. Her hair was damp and her face glistened with recently applied moisturiser.

'Did you want a cuppa? Have you had breakfast?' she said, and went to get up.

'Stay there. I'll have a coffee when I get home.'

'Don't blame you. Your coffee is so much nicer than mine.'

We sat in silence for several minutes and soaked up the morning sun. It was delicious. I was thinking about making a move when Daisy said, 'He hasn't told me why he's come back, except that he'd hoped to get to Bill Toogood's funeral, but had car trouble and didn't make it.'

'What are his plans?' I said, and then wished I hadn't. It really was none of my business and I'd told myself not to pry.

'I don't know. I won't ask. He'll tell me if he wants me to know.'

'How is he?'

'The same, but different. It's as if he's finally grown up. He's taken good care of me. He's a passable cook. He's even put in loads of washing, hung them out and brought them in. God knows I could have done with his help when the boys were little. I try not to feel bitter, but it's hard not to. It's all so weird, so unexpected. I keep thinking I'll wake up and discover it's all been a dream.'

'It would be strange if you didn't feel bitter. Resentful. Just plain pissed off. If I were you I'd want to shake him until his teeth chattered, and then some.'

'He's been to see the boys. His grandkids. Jay even showed up. But has Jay been to visit his mother in the past year? Of course not. And yet who's the first person they come to if they want something?'

There was a thought. 'You think that's why Charlie's here? Because he wants something?'

She gave a harsh, croaky laugh. 'I have nothing left to give, Kate. The well is dry.'

I glanced at her but her eyes were closed, her face an expressionless mask. I stood up. 'I'll go. Shall I bring you back a decent coffee for morning tea? I have several insulated travel cups.'

Her expression brightened. 'Would you? That would be a nice change. Yesterday, Glenys brought a homemade boiled fruit cake. We can have a slice of that with the coffee.'

'I'll see you around eleven.'

On the short walk home I tried to imagine how it would be for Daisy, having Charlie show up without any warning after an absence of over two decades. Sure, they might have crossed paths at the odd family gatherings in that time, but even that would have been tricky for her. An emotional minefield. Here's me thinking about myself and what his return might mean for me, not sparing a second to consider how it might *really* be for her. The more I did think about it the more I realised what an extremely traumatic time she was having. And to be unwell along with it. That would have put the cherry on the top.

★ ★ ★

Valma's dinky little car was parked out the front of my place when I came back from Daisy's for the second time that day. Glenys's boiled fruit cake had been second to none. Valma, looking smart in several shades of pink, was walking down the driveway towards me.

'There you are,' she called. 'I rang the doorbell. How are you? You're looking marvellous. Have you lost weight?'

'A little. Doctor's advice. My blood pressure was up a fraction … I'm trying to do the right thing.' Except for the chunk of cake I'd just scoffed.

'Whatever you're doing seems to be working.'

I unlocked the front door. 'Would you like a coffee?'

She glanced at the travel cups I was holding. 'Lovely, unless you've just had one.' She followed me inside and through to the kitchen.

'Daisy's been laid up with the flu, and I took her a coffee.'

'Is she on the mend?'

I nodded and turned on the coffee machine. I was beginning to feel like a real barista.

'They asked me to give you the final report about the morning tea. It went off very well, don't you think? Gaye and Maureen said the committee have met, and they were very, very satisfied. They asked me to pass on that fifteen hundred dollars was raised, with the tickets, raffles and various other donations.' She beamed with pride.

'It was a lot of work, and I'm pleased to hear it was worthwhile.'

We took our coffees through to the breakfast nook.

'This is such a gorgeous spot,' Valma said, and wiggled her bottom into the booth. 'I've tried to work out how I could do something similar at my place. It wouldn't take much. I've got it all worked out. Our son-in-law is a carpenter and the next time they visit I'll ask him about it. I've even started cutting out cushion covers. Bob thinks I've gone mad.'

All I could do was raise my eyebrows.

Valma didn't linger; she had places to be. Lucky her. Not feeling a bit hungry, I skipped lunch, then moped about the house. Rhonda wasn't even home to distract me for an hour. Her daughter had taken her for a drive and then out to lunch. How nice for them. In the end I pulled out all of my cookbooks and began planning in earnest for the Wilkins family lunch. After all, it was only six days away. But who was counting?

49

Daisy

That envelope hadn't been there when I'd gone to lie down an hour ago. Mid-afternoon. Someone must have shoved it under the door without knocking. Jess hadn't barked.

I picked it up and turned it over. *To The Householder* was scrawled on the front in blue ink. I tore it open and extracted a single sheet of paper. I read it, and then reread it, because at first I could not believe what I was reading. No mistaking it for what it was on the third read: an eviction notice. I had two weeks to get out. The house was being demolished. Turns out everyone had been right: it was a dump and they were going to bulldoze it.

Dump it might be, but it had become my home. In a fortnight, I'd be homeless. My hands shook. I shoved the sheet of paper back into the envelope and rushed to the front window, half-expecting to see an excavator parked in the driveway, engine idling.

Frantic, I called Jess and brought her inside. Irrational though it sounds, I locked the doors, front and back. Jess picked up on my panic and started to fret. Her distress was enough to short circuit my own. I came to a standstill in the middle of the living area and took several slow breaths. Jess pressed her warm body against my legs then tried to jump up.

'It's all right, sweetie,' I said. 'I'm sorry for getting us both into a panic.'

This was a circumstance I'd known could eventuate, but I'd given it little more conscious consideration than the likelihood of an asteroid hitting the earth in my lifetime. More fool me. My main fear had been that homelessness would be a fait accompli when I could no longer afford the rent, not because there'd be nothing here to rent.

A fortnight. Fourteen days and fourteen nights. The rent was paid until then. My legs began to wobble. When they wouldn't firm up, I sat down heavily in the canvas chair. I'd almost fully recovered from the flu but found a rest in the afternoon was still beneficial. Charlie was at Glenys and Trev's, had been there since Saturday and now it was Thursday. Glenys said earlier that he'd been working hard because Trev couldn't do much yet. The physiotherapist was optimistic that if Trev's back continued to improve the way it had, he'd be back at work in no time.

The irony of the situation hadn't escaped me. Charlie had been working for Trev when we'd first met.

How had I let myself get into this mess? Wooed by the idea of a brand spanking new townhouse, and no garden to speak of, that's how. Not like me at all, to be so easily seduced by one of Gareth's money-making schemes. It's not as if I hadn't seen them come and go before. But the idea of a new, much smaller home with gravel and succulents had been irresistible.

Some time later and with no plan, not even a half-formed one, I found my phone and rang Gareth.

'Mum, how are you? Over the flu?'

His voice was echoey and I could hear the hiss and hum of road noise: he was in the car, with me on bluetooth.

'I'm much better, thanks. Are you on your own?'

'Yep. What's up?'

'I'm being evicted, that's what's up. Two weeks and then they're going to demolish this house.'

'Shit. What are you going to do?'

'I thought you might help me brainstorm, seeing as your relentless need to make more money is one of the reasons I'm in this mess.'

Nothing but the road noise.

'In fourteen days I'll be homeless, Gareth. I don't have much money. I'm almost seventy. Any ideas?'

'You can't live with us,' he said, bluntly. 'I won't even ask Tess, because she'd most likely offer and then insist.'

'And do you think for a moment that I'd *want* to live with you? Or either of your brothers? Disrupt your homes and families? Have no life and privacy of my own?'

Adam had three children and a small home that barely housed them. They couldn't afford anything more. Who knew where Jay lived—in his car for all I knew, if he even had one. I suppose we could park next to each other in the lay-bys ...

I felt like howling.

'Just putting it out there, Mum, so there are no false expectations from the get-go. It's not that I don't care because I do, and I'm sorry, but there's not a lot I can do. I'm struggling to keep a roof over our heads.'

'What about your mate? The bloke who owns the house. Couldn't you talk to him, ask him to give me a few more months to sort something out?'

'What'll be different in three months, Mum? Unless we win Cross Lotto, and I can't even afford the tickets. Besides, he's a mate of a mate and I wouldn't ask. You know I warned Georgia way back that this could happen. The owner's plan always was to eventually knock the joint down and build. She didn't ever mention that to you?'

'No, she didn't, unfortunately. Even when I voiced my concern over the state of the place and the lack of a formal rental agreement.'

'Pity. But then she's young and the rent was cheap. No biggie to her if it all went pear-shaped. So, how's the old man?'

Head spinning with just how much of a *biggie* it was to me, it took me a second to catch up with the last bit of what he'd said. I shouldn't have been surprised by the question.

'You'd have to ask him. And what's he got to do with any of this?'

Back to the drum of the road noise, the distant honk of a car horn.

'Dad's not getting any younger. I get the impression he's tired of his solitary, outback life. Maybe you should think about pooling your resources. You might afford somewhere reasonable to live if you did that.'

I didn't answer him. A strange kind of calm descended over me, and I did something I'd never done before in my life: I hung up without so much as a goodbye.

Then the calm evaporated and I did howl, smothering the sound with my fist when Jess joined in.

If it wasn't so totally absurd, one could almost believe that *they*— whoever *they* were—had conspired for this to happen. Just because you were paranoid, didn't mean they weren't out to get you. But how could anyone have predicted this sequence of events?

How long did I have before the news filtered through to Adam and Jay? The phone vibrated in my lap. Not long. Adam's name flashed on the screen.

'Hello, love,' I said.

'Mum. Gareth just filled me in. You must feel like crap, apart from still getting over the flu. Come and stay with us until you can sort something out. Will can stay with his mother and you can have his room. I'll run it by Bec, but I can't imagine why she wouldn't agree.'

No way I'd be doing that. They'd had enough issues with Adam's teenage son as it was. I wouldn't dream of uprooting him again. The occasional night Will slept on a blow-up mattress in the lounge room when I stayed over was an entirely different circumstance. I blinked back tears.

'Thanks, love, but I'll manage, somehow. I have a small amount of savings. Who knows, I might be able to find a live-in position, or something. I could afford to buy an old caravan. Go grey nomading, all funded by Centrelink.'

Who was I kidding? My budget wouldn't get me much further than Port Augusta. I gave a hollow laugh. Adam didn't join in.

'I've got two weeks. Something will turn up.'

'Bloody Gareth and his money-making schemes.'

'It's all right, son. I agreed to it all.'

Then he did laugh, but without humour. 'What choice did you have? He owned the damned place. I wish I could have helped out more, but I was at uni, Will was a toddler and we were always dead broke.'

'You did what you could, and I appreciated that.'

'Yeah, but Gareth swooped in like a vulture when Nan died. Dad had well and truly cleared out and I bet he never sent any money home ...'

'We live and learn, and it seems the lessons keep coming, no matter how old you get.'

He coughed and cleared his throat. 'I know Dad's back. But whatever you do, Mum, don't let anyone talk you into doing anything you don't *want* to do. Dad might have cleaned up his act some, but I've never forgotten how it was before he left. In the meantime, if you're desperate, or you need some breathing space, we'll always find a bed for you, even if we have to pitch a tent on the back lawn.'

My heart clenched with love for my youngest son. He'd always been such a dear boy. The best parts of me and Charlie. I was too choked up to speak.

'I'll go, Mum. But don't forget what I've said. And I meant all of it. I love you.'

★★★

There were only so many times you could hash over the past. Simply put, it was the past and no amount of hashing would change it. What to do now, so that I wasn't hashing over these decisions in a month's time, and wishing I'd made different ones?

While I'd sat and turned it all over again, the sun had set, the day spent. It was June, the daylight hours dwindling. Jess was sniffing about the kitchen, her way of telling me it was tea time. And reminding me that Max was still away and I needed to feed Pauline. He'd be back on the weekend, but for how long was anyone's guess.

My phone rang soon after I'd fed the dog and the cat and was assessing my own appetite, which wasn't quite back to normal yet.

'I just had this awful thought,' Kate said when I picked up. No hello, how are you, her tone becoming shriller by the syllable. 'What if they're all vegetarians? Or worse, *vegans*. I'm doing a roast!'

I winced and shifted the phone away from my ear. 'You didn't think to ask?'

'No,' she said. She deflated like a soufflé. 'They'll be here the day after tomorrow.'

'Ring Glenys. One of her tribe is vegan and she made a lasagne for tea one night after Bill died. Kidney beans instead of meat. It was delicious. I'm sure she'd give you the recipe. Then you'll have something to offer if they are vegetarian, or worse still, *vegan*.'

'I could freeze it if I didn't use it. I don't mind a vegetarian meal every now and then.'

'There you go,' I said. Vegetarian meals were a staple in my diet. Baked beans and other pulses were cheap, you could jazz them up with herbs and spices and they went a long way.

'I still can't decide whether or not to serve wine with lunch. I'll serve orange juice or soft drinks for the children. What do you think?'

'It's a family lunch, Kate. Either Tom or Helena will be driving. If it were me, I wouldn't serve wine, but I'd say it was there if they'd like a glass.'

'Perfect,' she said, 'that's what I'll do. Now then, how are you?'

'I'm ready for a short walk on the trail in the morning.'

'That's wonderful news. I'll look forward to it, but I won't walk Saturday morning. I'll be in too much of a flap,' she said.

'Remind yourself about the fundraising morning tea. You catered for close on forty people with one hand tied behind your back. You didn't get in the tiniest of flaps. Saturday you'll have six, plus yourself. You're a fabulous cook. Don't underestimate your ability to manage.'

She sighed. 'You're right. You usually are. It's just—'

'I get it, Kate. Saturday is special, and complicated, and you want it to work. It will, just trust yourself.'

'Whatever did I do to deserve you as a friend, Daisy? Not once, but twice,' she said. 'Thank you.'

We disconnected soon after. I was exhausted. Emotionally drained. Toast with honey and a mug of hot milk was all I ate for tea. The evenings were getting cold and I'd had a hot shower and was on my way to bed to read when Georgia swept in.

'Gran, Dad told me about the eviction notice. I feel so bad for not mentioning the demolition thing. To be honest, I'd completely forgotten Dad even telling me that's what the owners had planned, they just didn't know when.' She glanced around the room. 'Where's Granddad?'

Another one who expected Charlie and me to just pick up where we'd left off twenty-three years before. Pool resources. For them, problem solved. My hackles rose.

'He's not here. You could try Glenys and Trev's.'

'I don't want to see him. I just thought—'

'Sometimes it's best not to. Or keep the thoughts to yourself.'

She cast a guarded glance my way. 'Fair enough,' she said. 'What are you going to do?'

'Have an early night, and then think on it some more in the morning. And don't stress about offering me a bed with you and Kieran. I'd most certainly refuse if you did. You've put up with me couch-surfing once already.'

'It was fun, and I would have done it without Dad bribing me with rent money. I'm sorry it's worked out the way it has. You shouldn't have to deal with something like this, not at your—' She paused, shrugged.

'Age? Is that what you were going to say?'

'Yes,' she said with a sheepish smile.

'Just promise me, Georgia, that you'll learn from what's happening to me, and that you'll make sensible, considered decisions about the things that really count. Life can spiral out of control in a heartbeat, never forget that, and always have a safety net. Now tell me, how's Lisa?'

Georgia took a moment to digest what I'd said, and then she brightened. 'She's great. One of the blokes Kieran used to share with keeps asking her out. I don't think she's ready for a rebound romance, but he's really nice and she likes him, so who knows?'

I asked her how work was and we chatted about that for a few minutes. Not long after, she left, saying on the way out, 'If there is anything I can do to help, please ask me, Gran. Don't battle on in silence, not like you always do. There are plenty of us who would help in some way, if you'd let us.'

I raised my eyebrows at that, and felt a new respect for my grand-daughter. She *was* growing up.

50

Daisy

In a matter of days, winter set in with a vengeance. Today it was overcast with a biting wind. The house creaked and wheezed and was like an icebox. There was no heating, except extra layers of clothing and the hot water bottle I'd invested in. Over the past few days, Georgia had popped in several times but I hadn't seen Charlie since he'd left to help Trev. He'd rung a couple of times to ask how well I was recovering but we hadn't talked for long. What was there to say? He'd said he was working harder than he had for while, that there was more than enough to do and he was buggered at the end of each day. 'Nothing to do with being almost seventy,' I'd said, and he hadn't contradicted me. That's why I was surprised when he showed up late Friday afternoon.

'Trev gave me the weekend off,' he said. 'You look well.' He went straight to put the kettle on. 'What have you been up to?'

'Not much.' After the walk with Kate I'd had a quiet day, revisiting my budget and my options, trying not to get too despondent. I'd also talked Kate down a couple of times when she'd got herself into a tizzy about tomorrow's lunch. Truthfully, I'd be glad when Tom and co had been and gone. On a positive note, once again her woes had provided temporary relief from my own.

Charlie took in the paperwork spread out on the camp table. 'What's all that about?' he said.

'Working on my budget.' I quickly gathered the bank statements and notes and replaced them into their cardboard envelope, conscious of his scrutiny. He was waiting for me to elaborate, and I wouldn't. He'd know about the eviction notice, of that I was certain. I wondered which one of the boys had told him. Not Jay; he watched the world go by and tried his hardest not to get involved. Gareth or Adam? My money was on Gareth. He'd justify it by telling himself he'd done me a favour.

'Tea?' Charlie said, and I nodded.

When he'd made it he took the mugs and set them down on the table. I collected the other canvas deckchair from the verandah.

'Nice,' I said when I took the first sip. 'Not too sweet.' I wrapped my hands around the warmth.

His mouth twitched and his eyes crinkled at the corners. 'I got the message,' he said. 'Where's the dog?'

'Out the back. She knows where to find the warmest spot, and she's on cat watch.'

'I'd forgotten how damn cold it could be in this neck of the woods. Do you have any heating in here?' He glanced about the room. 'You don't want to get crook again.'

'It's not too bad,' I said. 'I'm wearing several layers.' It wouldn't matter if there was an air conditioner, I wouldn't use it because then I'd have a huge power bill to deal with.

He sniffed and sipped his brew. 'I thought we could go to the pub for tea.'

'I don't think it would be wise for me to go *out* into the cold,' I said. 'There's plenty of food here.'

'It'd be my treat,' he said, having guessed straight up what I was really worried about. Thirty-plus dollars for a meal and a drink … Not on my current budget.

'I don't have anything suitable to wear,' I said, and wrinkled my nose. 'My wardrobe is limited. It had to fit into a suitcase.'

'You look all right to me,' he said, and gave me a slow once-over.

Something tingled in the pit of my stomach and my face felt hot. 'Don't do that,' I snapped.

'Do what?'

'Look at me like that.'

'I'm sorry,' he said. 'My intention wasn't to make you feel uncomfortable. But you do look all right to me. More than all right. That's something that's never changed.'

'For goodness' sake, Charlie,' I said and surged to my feet. 'We're not in our twenties any more.' I paced briskly back and forth across the living area. After all, there wasn't any furniture to impede me.

'So,' he said, after he'd watched me retrace my steps several times. 'Are we going to the pub for tea, or not?'

'Okay,' I said. 'Thank you. It would be nice to go out for a meal.'

He smiled, satisfied. 'I've got a couple of jobs need doing. I'll be back just before six.'

I carried the empty mugs to the sink. The front door closed behind him. I stood at the sink until I heard him reverse out of the driveway. Then I rushed into the bedroom to find something, anything, to wear rather than what I had on: baggy leggings, a long-sleeved T-shirt and a washed-out polar fleece with a broken zip.

★★★

The hotel dining room was far from crowded, but it was early. Charlie had booked a table. I sat down and tried to remember the last time I'd been taken out for a meal. Nothing sprang to mind.

Charlie didn't sit, rather stood with his hands braced on the back of his chair. 'What would you like to drink?'

'Lemon squash, thanks.'

'You look nice,' he said.

Before I could reply or rebuff, he was gone, ambling across to the bar. He looked good in a pair of well-worn moleskin trousers and a bottle-green shirt. I'd showered and washed my hair and put on makeup, which for me meant a dusting of face powder and a smear of lipstick. Mum had knitted the jumper I was wearing, that's how old it was. It'd been the last thing she'd ever knitted and I hadn't worn it often. I knew the colour, a bright cobalt blue, suited me.

He was back with two glasses of lemon squash and a couple of laminated menus tucked under his arm.

'I thought you'd be having a beer.' There, I'd said it. Although there was no evidence to support it, I'd assumed the 'couple of jobs' he'd had to do would have been done in the front bar. It wouldn't have been the first time.

'I don't touch the stuff any more, Daisy,' he said and sat down.

My mouth dropped open in disbelief. 'How long since?'

'When did Adam get married, the second time around?'

'About nine years ago, or thereabouts. Why? You weren't there. Adam and Bec thought you were coming but then you didn't show up. Created a bit of furore at the time.'

He drank a third of his lemon squash and then carefully put the glass down on the table. 'Then it's nine years or thereabouts since I gave up the booze, for good.' He didn't meet my eye. 'I had planned to be at the wedding, had my plane ticket and all. But ...' he said, and then he did look at me. 'I got to Alice Springs, ran into a couple of mates I hadn't seen for ages. We got on the piss and I missed the flight. Simple as that.

'When I got over my hangover, and it was a doozy, I was so disgusted with myself, I have not touched a drop since.'

'I hope you apologised to Adam and Bec.'

'Yep, I did.' He folded his arms but his focus remained on me. 'I don't know where to start, Daisy, in my apology to you.'

I sipped my drink, it was tart and cold and made my salivary glands prickle.

'We were young,' I said. I picked up one of the menus. 'We both made mistakes.'

'Yeah, but the majority of the stuff-ups were mine. You were smarter, savvier, more forgiving than I'd ever be.'

'Don't make me out to be a better person than I am.'

'You were—are—the better person, Daisy, and I've never understood why you didn't throw me out years before you did.'

'Just for the record, Charlie, I didn't throw you out then. You left to find work. You didn't come home.'

'I thought it was for the best. Like I said the other day, one less mouth to feed.'

'Yeah, well I eventually gave up on us too, Charlie. There's a threshold to how much absence a heart can tolerate. I'm sure both of us would do things differently if we had our time over.'

'But not all of it, surely. We had some good times, didn't we? When we came back here after you'd done your midwifery training and I had that job on the station out from Miners Ridge. They were good years.'

'But you lost that job. I had to go back to full-time work. Adam was barely a toddler, Jay had just started school.'

'Times were tough, they had to cut back. They would have kept me on if they could have. I know that.'

Charlie picked up the other menu. I went back to mine. I read without really seeing. The times had been tough. But Charlie had still been able to make me laugh. And the boys had worshipped the ground he'd trodden on. Gradually, over time, Gareth began to notice how hard I worked, how tired I always was, and how much time his father spent at the pub. And Charlie stopped being able to make me laugh as much or as often, and then not at all.

I chose what I'd have to eat and he went to order and buy himself another soft drink. I'd hardly touched mine.

When he came back, he said, 'I reckon it all started to really unravel after my mum died, and we went back to Adelaide because your mum couldn't cope. Be buggered if I know why you ever agreed to buy that house from her. Got into all that bloody debt, and I *hated* living in the city.'

'I know you did, but I'd hoped that buying the house would mean the boys and I would always have a roof over our heads, and Mum wouldn't have to worry any more about how she'd make ends meet the way she had since Dad died.'

Ironical, wasn't it, I thought, bitterness rising in the back of my throat, enough to almost choke me. Mum hadn't had to worry; the boys, including Charlie, had always had a home until they chose to leave. But look at me now. No roof over my head. No nothing. In under a fortnight I'd probably be living in my car.

'Daisy?'

'What?'

'You drifted off there for a minute, and you didn't look very happy,' Charlie said.

I swallowed a mouthful of lemon squash. 'I was just thinking about some of the things I would do differently, if I had my time over ... Buying that house from Mum would be one of them. But it doesn't matter what I wish I'd done or hadn't done, does it? Because here I am, and none of it can be changed.'

The waitress brought our food: grilled fish for me and steak for Charlie. He didn't say anything, or add extra salt to his chips, which surprised me.

Halfway through the meal I put down my knife and fork. 'Have you had a good life so far, Charlie?' I said, unsure if I was aiming for sarcasm, or to wound, or if I was genuinely curious.

Nonplussed, he put down his cutlery and wiped his mouth with a paper serviette. 'It's had its moments. I like what I do now. I'm good at it. I love the outback; the wide open spaces. Marrying you was the best thing I ever did, the boys too. You did an amazing job as a parent, to all four of us. Me not having the balls to step up and be the husband you deserved and the father they were entitled to will always haunt me.'

His words loosened the ball of bitterness in my throat.

'What about you, Daisy? Tell me that some of it has been good. That you've been content?'

I took a sip of squash, considering how best to answer him. 'After Mum died and I was living in the house on my own, I was content. Financially, it's always been a struggle. Gareth bought the house but there were other debts. In the last year of Mum's illness she needed me there all the time. When I'd used up all my paid leave, I took unpaid leave.

'At first it was strange not having anyone at home needing to be looked after, but I got used to it. I liked my job at the residential aged care facility well enough. It kept me busy, I had friends and was left with little time to dwell on the what ifs. Overall, you could say I was content.'

He nodded, picked up his knife and fork again. 'I'm relieved to know I didn't exile myself for nothing.'

He said it lightly, but I'd reflect on his words later and understand that he'd made some sacrifices himself. No-one walked away from a marriage and a family without hurts and regrets, even if they were the one who'd chosen to do the walking.

We finished the meal in silence, but it wasn't uncomfortable. We'd aired things that had long needed an airing.

'You know, we've been apart for as many years as we were together,' I said, just as it occurred to me.

He pushed away his plate and dropped the scrunched-up serviette on top of it.

'Were you ever lonely?' he said.

'Yes, but I got used to it, and having a dog helped. Jess is number two. Lizzie was the first, a border collie. She'd belonged to one of the residents where I worked. He'd come in for respite and I'd take care of her. She was a delight, and when he became a permanent resident she came to live with me. I'd take her into see him at least once a week, right up until the end. He loved her. And so did I.'

'And Jess?'

'She came from a shelter. She wasn't much more than a pup when she was abandoned.'

Charlie chuckled. 'Run out of people to look after so you start collecting stray dogs. Sounds about right. I've got a kelpie called Bruno. He's great with the stock. The best mate.'

'Where is he now? At Glenys and Trev's?'

'Nah, I left him in Alice Springs. Loaned him to a mate. His dog took a bait, and he had work and needed a dog. He treats him well and Bruno likes him.'

'So is Alice Springs your base? I've never been there. I've never been anywhere, really. What's it like?'

'Hot and dusty in the summer, cold and dusty in the winter, but the most magnificent scenery.'

'Have you been to Uluru?'

'Yep. It's awesome.'

A waitress came and collected our empty plates. I finished my drink, the ice clinking noisily in the glass.

'Dessert?'

'Not for me, thanks. You go right ahead and have your nut sundae,' I said. 'Hate to see you miss out.'

'You haven't forgotten then.'

'No, Charlie, I haven't forgotten how much you love a nut sundae.'

The dining room was filling up and we didn't linger after dessert. Charlie dropped me off home. I didn't invite him in. The meal had been nice but our conversation had left me feeling rattled.

'I'll see ya,' he said.

I wanted to ask him when that might be, what his plans were, but I didn't.

I wouldn't have known what to do with his answer.

51

Kate

'How was it?' Daisy asked the moment we met at the corner Sunday morning. The day was grey and grim and showers of rain were forecast. She was wearing her usual walking gear, with a beanie and a yellow raincoat.

'Okay,' I said.

'Only okay?'

'The food turned out. The eye fillet melted in your mouth, and the creme brûlée was perfect. I made Glenys's vegan lasagne just in case, but they're not vegetarians. I sent it home with them all the same. It would have taken me forever to get through it.'

'So what made it just okay?'

'Oh, I don't know. It was all very stiff and formal. My fault, I'm certain of that. The boys wanted to swim in the pool but I said no, and of course that made me the baddie. But it was too cold!'

'Boys don't care, Kate. And doesn't the pool have a solar cover? It wouldn't have been too bad.'

'Yes, but they hadn't brought their bathers, towels …'

'I bet they were wearing jocks, and you'd probably have more towels than the Hyatt. And you have a clothes dryer.'

I stared at her. 'I see what you mean,' I said. 'I'm such an old fuddy-duddy.'

When we made it to the trail there were no other walkers in sight and Daisy let Jess off the lead.

'So what did the boys do?'

'Sat on the lounge in the family room and looked daggers at me. I showed them Dennis's old Meccano set. Tom enjoyed it but the boys weren't the slightest bit interested. But they worked out how to get the TV working in about two minutes, something I haven't been able to do since Dennis died.'

Daisy smiled. She plodded along beside me, her plastic raincoat rustling with each arm swing. The flu had taken it out of her. She'd make the distance today but at a much slower pace than her usual. Another week and I hoped I'd be pushing myself to keep up with her again.

'What about the twin girls?' she said, with a quick glance my way. 'How were they?'

'They didn't come. Apparently, they had other plans.'

Daisy laughed. 'What two thirteen-year-old girls wouldn't have other plans? You know, you might have dodged a bullet.'

'That's the impression Tom gave me, that with the four of them it would have been full-on. But I was looking forward to meeting them, more so than the boys.'

'Next time?' Daisy said.

I sniffed. 'That's if there is a next time. They didn't exactly eat and run, but almost. And we made no plans.'

'With boys eight and ten, and your lovely home with not a thing out of place, they wouldn't have wanted to overstay their welcome. You can trust me on that one.'

A willy wagtail flitted onto the trail and caught Jess's interest. It teased her for a bit and then off it went.

I let a deep breath out on a sigh. 'It was me. I was the disaster.'

'Not a disaster, Kate,' Daisy said, and bumped her shoulder against mine. I liked the way she did that. 'You're a novice at this. Give yourself time. It takes practice, and kids can be scary.'

'You're telling me!'

But I hadn't thought about it like that. I'd assumed that being in the appropriate age bracket meant I'd instinctively know how to act like a grandmother. Not that I was their grandmother, and I knew I never would be. Only in my fantasies had I aspired to that. What had I been thinking? I'd had next to no experience being with young children. Not ever. Given my first real go at it, I'd had no idea how to act, had worried I'd misstep and upset someone. Or everyone. I shuddered. Daisy's glance was questioning.

'It might have been a blessing that I never had any children. What sort of a mother would I have made? More than likely clueless, much like my own mother. I know next to nothing about children and parenting, and even less than that about grandparenting.'

'Because you haven't needed to know, Kate. Don't punish yourself too much. You'll pick it up soon enough. And grandchildren are easy, because generally they like you, and at the end of the day they go home to their parents.'

We'd come to the spot where we turned around and retraced our steps home. There were cyclists coming towards us and Daisy quickly rounded up Jess and clipped on her lead.

'I only ever knew one of my grandmothers,' I said when we'd fallen into step again. 'Mum's mother died when I was a baby and Dad's mother was an old battleaxe. I don't think I ever saw her crack a smile. We used to hate visiting her place. It was dark and dingy and smelled like her cat, and all she did was tell us off.'

'I had a granny like that. She didn't even pretend to like us. Mum's mother was kind. She gave me my first fifty-cent piece; I still have it somewhere. I was twelve when she died. You could say you and I are at the tail end of the generations of children who were expected to be seen and not heard.'

We lapsed into a comfortable silence. The last stretch was a gentle incline and Daisy was breathing hard by the time we made it back to our corner. 'I'm all right,' she said, before I could ask. But she leaned against the fence until she caught her breath.

'Why don't you come around for lunch?' I said. 'I have plenty of leftovers from yesterday.' I felt fragile, and not much like being on my own.

'I'm sorry, Kate, but Glenys has asked me out to the farm for lunch. Granted, we won't be having eye fillet followed by creme brûlée, but she does an excellent rolled shoulder of lamb.'

'Oh,' I said, miffed. And disappointed.

'I'd say come along, I know Glenys wouldn't bat an eyelid if you did, but Charlie will be there.' She raised her eyebrows.

'Tempting,' I said, because I was tempted, and I would have accepted the offer if Charlie hadn't been there. 'Is he back to stay?'

'His dog's in Alice Springs, with a mate.'

'I see.'

'I'd better get going,' she said, with what I thought was forced cheer. 'Georgia and Kieran are coming around to collect her last few bits and pieces before I head out to the farm. I must remind them to take the potted herbs. Thankfully, Georgia said I can use the sofa bed until the sixteenth.'

'Why? What's happening on the sixteenth? Have you bought a proper bed? Some real furniture?'

Daisy frowned and stared down at her feet. Jess pressed into her leg. I experienced an inkling of unease.

'No, Kate, I've been served an eviction notice. I have to be out
of the house by the sixteenth of this month. Ten days away.' She
looked up, her expression set. 'You don't know anyone who'd want
a twin-tub washing machine, do you? I'll happily give it away. It's
not modern enough for Georgia.'

'But Daisy, what will you do until your new townhouse is ready?'

'There will be no townhouse. Gareth's business was in trouble
and he sold the land. I'm about as close to homeless as I've ever
been.'

I was speechless. Not about the washing machine or the townhouse, because I'd had a premonition that it'd never come to fruition
when she'd first told me about it. What had me losing my tongue
was that Daisy could be *homeless* in ten days.

Homelessness was something I'd only ever read in the
newspaper or seen on the television: mostly men with unkempt
beards and mental health problems. Not my friend Daisy. Smart,
attractive, accomplished, a mother three times over.

I must have looked as horrified as I felt because she said, 'Don't
worry, Kate, I can bunk with Adam as a last resort. Currently, I'm
exploring my options. I have a car and a small amount of savings.
I'd thought about a caravan, but with people travelling here instead
of overseas because of Covid, there's little about that I could pull
with my car, or afford. And there's Jess to consider. I will not give
her up. She's been abandoned once already.'

The wind picked up. I felt a drop of rain splat against the side of
my face. And then another. Daisy drew the collar of her raincoat
around her chin and glanced heavenward.

'We'd better get in before it buckets down,' she said. 'What if I
come to lunch tomorrow? The leftovers will be okay until then.'

'Come at midday,' I said. 'Are we walking in the morning?'

The rain drops were coming harder and faster. I wasn't wearing a raincoat. 'Go!' Daisy said, giving me a gentle shove. 'Let's see how the weather is in the morning.'

She scurried off. I watched until she was out of sight and then I hurried home, barely making it before it did bucket down.

At home I shucked off my sneakers and jacket and walked slowly through the house in my socked feet, padding from room to room. As I went, I tried to envisage how it would be not to own a house, not even to have a place to come home to; no haven that was safe and secure. And private. Try as I might, I could not put myself into Daisy's shoes, teetering on the edge of homelessness. The bricks and mortar surrounding me felt too solid, and the money I had invested a substantial buffer between me and poverty. Worrying about keeping a roof over my head wasn't what kept me awake nights.

The rain had settled in. It was cold so I put on the heating and took a coffee through to the family room. What *would* Daisy do? What could she do given her limited resources and, by default, her scant options? It was common knowledge there was a dearth of public housing and private rentals were scarce; *affordable* private rentals even scarcer.

There was so much I took for granted: this house; my generous fortnightly income; a late-model car; private health insurance; a gardener and until recently a cleaner; a swimming pool that I never used … The list went on and on. If I wanted or needed anything I went out and acquired it. Admittedly, there had been the odd occasion during our marriage when we'd had to tighten our belts: sausages instead of steak; a cheaper brand of coffee … No genuine hardship that's for sure, and there'd always been a house to come home to.

But what if Dennis's weekend fling had become something more? What if he'd left me because he wanted to be with the woman who'd given him a son? Who could give him more children? How would I have coped on my own? Without the security of the house and the farm and a steadfast husband beside me?

It was as if my vision cleared momentarily and I glimpsed with perfect clarity how readily everything might have unravelled if Dennis hadn't stuck by me. My mental health had already been teetering on the edge. Dennis had inherited the farm and I'd had no claim to any of it. If we'd separated my right to any significant monetary compensation would have been contestable, compounded by the fact there'd been no offspring.

I gazed around the family room at the plush furnishings, the leather recliners, the gigantic television. If Dennis had left me all those years ago and I'd had to fend for myself, I wouldn't have all this. Who knows what I would or wouldn't have had by now? With a rare and fleeting insight, I let myself slide into Daisy's shoes. It was only for a moment, and I'd never walk a mile in them, but what a difference that moment made.

52

Daisy

It hadn't stopped raining since I'd left Kate at the corner that morning, which was a blessing, but it'd made the track from the farm gate slippery and treacherous. When I let Jess out of the car, Trev's dogs appeared out of nowhere and harassed her. After I'd chased them off, I'd had to put her back into the car, covered in mud. Neither of us were happy in the aftermath. Trev's dogs disappeared from whence they'd come, and I went inside grumpy, only to find Glenys in a flap and on the verge of tears.

'I'm sorry but lunch will be late,' she said, frantically peeling potatoes. 'I'm so glad you're here. Trev and I had the biggest barney.' Her eyes glazed over. 'He stormed off and I haven't seen him since. I don't know where Charlie is.'

I put the kettle on and relieved her of the vegetable peeler. 'You make the tea,' I said, 'and do whatever else you need to do. I can peel potatoes.'

There were carrots, brussel sprouts, green beans and a Queensland Blue pumpkin waiting on the bench.

She made the tea and while it was brewing she launched into a recap of the row with Trev.

'As you know, Bridgette and her husband are building a new home. It won't be ready for months, and as luck would have it they've got a buyer for the house they're living in. They're still paying that one off and getting rid of the mortgage would be a great help. It's just sooner than they'd anticipated.'

'Where would they live?' I said, knowing firsthand the paucity of rental properties available. In the event that you could even afford to pay the going rate.

'That's the thing,' she said, and her mouth flattened. She looked sad. 'I offered for them to live here until their new home was built. They both work, we'd hardly ever see them, and there's plenty of room. Trev said en-oh. A very definite en-oh. He said, "*We've just got rid of your old man. We're not taking in any more freeloaders ...*" Freeloaders! That's what he called them. His own daughter. And my father.'

'Oh,' I said.

'It's my home as well. I should have some say in who stays and who doesn't. Bridgette will be devastated.'

'Maybe Trev'll come around to the idea, after he's thought about it.'

'Oh, no, not Trevor Carlisle. Not this time. He didn't want Dad here but he was an old man and had nowhere else to go.' She poured the tea. 'Now I have to tell Bridgette they can't stay here.'

We were both standing at the kitchen sink. I'd finished the potatoes and started on the carrots. Glenys gazed out the window. A solitary tear rolled down her cheek. She swiped at it with the back of her hand.

'I know I should never have offered without talking to Trevor first. But she's our daughter, for heaven's sake.'

'Does he get on okay with Bridgette's husband?'

'Passably, but Trevor's never been able to get past the fact that he's a policeman.' Her lips pressed together. 'It would have been lovely having Bridgette around for a while, if only in the evenings and weekends. It can get lonely out here. I never see Trevor much in the day and he's always glued to the telly at night. Never mind.' She picked up a large and lethal-looking kitchen knife and vented some of her frustration on the pumpkin.

★★★

It was almost two when we sat down to lunch at the kitchen table. There was only the four of us. Charlie had been fixing gutters on one of the sheds. When he'd stood in the kitchen doorway he'd scanned the room—looking for me, I soon realised with something akin to amazement. He'd smiled when he found me, sending that wave of warmth right through me. Drat the man.

The food was up to Glenys's usual standard: delicious farm fare. Trev was polite but subdued and I noticed him nervously eyeing his wife every so often. Glenys tried her hardest to act as if nothing was wrong. If it had been anyone other than Glenys and Trev, I would have felt uncomfortable, but they were family.

After we'd eaten, Charlie said to me, 'Why don't I take you for a drive? Check that bit of fence, Trev, where the stock got out the other day.'

'If you like,' Trev said, and cracked open another beer.

Glenys gritted her teeth. 'The rain's stopped for now and the sun's peeping through,' she said, forcing a rigid smile. 'Don't you worry about the dishes, Daisy.'

Before I could protest I'd been bundled out of the house and into the front seat of Charlie's 4WD. He'd helped Jess into the back. Charlie didn't seem to notice the mud, or he didn't care.

When we were mobile, he said, 'What the hell was that all about?'

'They'd argued earlier.'

'So I heard. I was on my way inside for morning smoko. What a racket. Didn't know Glenys had it in her. I turned around and went right back to where I'd come from. Had a drink of water instead.'

I told him what they'd argued about.

'Tricky,' he said. 'Glenys is a good soul, but I can understand Trev wanting his home to himself.'

'So can I. Bill was difficult and he was there for months. Wore Glenys out. But she gets lonely. Trev's always busy, or whatever.'

We bumped along the rutted driveway, through puddles and potholes. A loose sheet of iron on one of the sheds flapped in the wind.

'Is the place a bit rundown?' I said. In all my comings and goings I'd never noticed until then how dilapidated some of the outbuildings appeared.

'Not really, not where it counts. I'd say stuff like driveways are pretty low on the priority list. Essentially, this property is too much work for one person to manage, but the farm doesn't make enough income to support two, so Trev takes on a casual labourer every now and then. Always has. That's why I was working for him back when we met. Nothing's really changed since then, except to get a whole lot older. A bit like all of us.'

We turned right onto the dirt road. 'Ryan spent a few days out here helping Trevor and he loved it,' I said, and recounted the reason behind our grandson's visit.

'Yeah, Trev said he took to it like a duck to water. Who knows what the future might hold, and I understand why the lad might hate school. Wasn't my favourite place, but there's many a time since I've wished I'd stuck at it for a bit longer. *Applied myself*, isn't that how they put it?'

'Getting a solid education first gives a person more choices later, there's no doubt about that.'

'Yeah, but someone's gotta do the grunt work. There's always plenty of that.'

He pulled over to the side of the road and left the engine idling while he jumped out and walked along a stretch of the stock fence. Jess and I watched from the comfort of the 4WD. Plump grey and white clouds sped across the sky, letting the sun burst through every so often.

Charlie swung effortlessly back into the cab. 'Bloody sheep,' he said. 'You fix one spot and they start pushing through another.'

He put the vehicle in gear and we drove off. Jess shoved her head between the front seats. She was happy. And funnily enough, so was I. I'd explore that a bit more later.

'See that fence yonder? That's the boundary to what used to be Dennis Hannaford's property.'

'Really? I didn't realise they'd lived so close to Trev's. Kate and Glenys barely know each other. That seems odd.'

Charlie glanced my way. 'Ya think? Farm folk wouldn't have been good enough for Kate. She always was a stuck-up—'

'That's enough, Charlie,' I said. I scowled at him. 'She's not the ogre you make her out to be. I like her. Glenys was pleasantly surprised how well they got on when I was sick. I think they might becomes friends, which is good, because they're both lonely.'

'Fair enough,' he said, and briefly lifted both hands off the steering wheel in acquiescence.

I waited for him to say more, to have the last word, as was his wont. But all he added was how much he'd been enjoying the countryside. 'A welcome change from saltbush and mulga,' he said, squinting into the distance.

We were away about an hour, meandering along the dirt roads and taking in the scenery. The colours were vibrant. It was as if the rain had washed off the dust, leaving everything sparkling clean. Except for that one minor hiccough, I'd enjoyed his easy company. Glenys put the kettle on the second we stepped through the kitchen door. Trev was sitting at the kitchen table reading the *Stock Journal*, a beer in a stubbie holder on the table beside him. The atmosphere was much more congenial than it had been when we'd left. Charlie caught my eye and winked.

It was right on dusk when I left for home. Glenys would have had me stay for the evening meal but I was tired. And another day closer to being homeless. I'd wasted four days already, feeling sorry for myself and paralysed by the awfulness of the situation I was in. Tomorrow was Monday and I needed to take action.

'Watch out for kangaroos,' Charlie said when he walked me out to the car. The clouds had cleared and the sun had set, leaving the horizon limned with gold, the sky above a soft pinkish-grey. He clipped Jess into her seat and gave her head a scratch.

I started the car but before I drove off he leaned in and said, 'This is all I'll say on the subject, Daisy, but you be careful when it comes to your dealings with Kate Hannaford. I agree that people can change, and it is all a long time ago, but I have not forgotten the times that woman hurt you, had you in tears … Her with her high and mighty ways.'

'Believe it or not, Charlie, she was jealous of me. She wanted children but she couldn't have them. I had them easily, and in her eyes, I didn't deserve them because I didn't want them as badly as she did. And we didn't provide for them as well as she and Dennis would have.'

'Our kids did okay,' he said, affronted. He stepped back from the car and folded his arms. 'Jay's had his problems, but I reckon he's sorted himself out. Gareth and Adam make a good livelihood, they treat their partners well, and they're decent parents. I know you had more to do with how they turned out than I did, but what more could we want?'

Indeed.

I spent the journey home listening to the radio and trying not to think about anything; past, present or future. I didn't notice if there were kangaroos or not.

53

Daisy

Wednesday morning I woke to the sound of voices; male voices and right outside the bedroom window. After two gruelling days exhausting any options I might have had, I'd lain awake until the early hours and let my increasing anxiety consume me. The progress I had made had been more about things ruled out than finding a satisfactory solution to my imminent homelessness.

There'd been no walk with Kate this morning. She'd had an early appointment. I felt dull and thick-headed. When I parted the curtains, there were two men in high-vis shirts standing on the back verandah. I'd let Jess out earlier so why hadn't she barked a warning?

After hastily donning clothes, I went outside. They'd moved out into the backyard. The younger of the two was doing all the talking and waving his arms about with it. Currently they were focussed on the old shed and rusted-out rainwater tank.

'Hello,' I called. 'Can I help you?'

They turned in unison, then walked over to where I stood on the verandah.

'Just having a bit of a look around.'

'Who are you?' I said, through narrowed eyes.

'Demolition contractors. We'll need to come inside and inspect for asbestos, and see what there is to salvage.' This from the younger bloke.

'If that's all right with you,' said the older man, with an apologetic smile. 'You're the tenant, right? Moving out next Thursday?'

I nodded.

'Power goes off Friday and we start the following Monday,' he said.

My heart thudded hard against my ribcage and my mouth went dry. 'You'd better come inside, then,' I said. 'And did you see a dog when you let yourself into what is effectively still my yard?'

'She went next door … An old fella was talking to her.'

They clomped inside in their steel caps, tracking dirt. Remonstrating would have been absurd, given the whole place would be a pile of wreckage in a fortnight .

They poked and prodded and looked into every cupboard and behind every door. They fetched a ladder from their ute and the young bloke disappeared through the manhole with a torch in his meaty paw. I couldn't pretend any longer that this wasn't happening to me.

Standing by and watching was bad for my mental health so I went next door to retrieve Jess. It wasn't yet nine. Max had come home on the weekend and we'd talked on Monday morning when I'd handed back the care of the cat.

'I've accepted Pam and her husband's offer and I'm going to move into their granny flat,' he'd said. 'It'll be a wrench leaving this house, but I think it's the best decision for us all. I can't expect Pam to be running up here every time I get into strife.'

Apparently, the granny flat was just sitting there, empty. Their children, now adults, had all flown the coop and it was free for

Max. When he'd told me I'd felt happy for him despite experiencing a stab of envy. And a vicious twist of anger about the unfairness of my own situation.

I knocked on his front door and waited for the sound of his shuffling feet.

'Daisy, come in,' he said, answering the door to my knock. He was dressed in his day clothes, and I could smell burned toast. 'Jess is here. Those men left your gate open. Who are they?'

'Demolition contractors.'

He gasped.

'They're going to knock the old house down and the owners are building a new one.'

'Oh, yes,' he said slowly, and frowned. 'I seem to remember someone saying something about that, months ago now. My memory certainly isn't what it used to be. Have you had breakfast?'

I followed him down the passage and into the kitchen. As I passed, I glanced into the lounge room and noticed a stack of cardboard packing boxes.

'I'm good, thanks. I'll just grab Jess. Has Pauline shown up?'

'Her food's gone so my guess is she's about the place somewhere. But I do worry how she'll manage the transition to the suburbs. Pam seems to think she'll be fine. I'm not convinced. Are you sure you won't have a cup of tea? Plenty in the pot.'

'Okay. Just a quick one.'

His face brightened. He took down another cup and saucer and poured the tea.

'What'll you do with your chooks?'

'Ah, the lad who helps with the garden has taken them. Very keen to have his own fresh eggs. When are you moving out of next door?'

'Out by next Thursday, that's what the letter said.'

'We're all on the move then,' he said with a lift of his eyebrows and a shake of his head. 'The estate agent's coming this afternoon to look at this house. Pam was onto it the second I said I'd move in with them.' He sat down. 'I'm not complaining. I know how blessed I am to have family who actually want me with them. What will you do, Daisy? Until your new townhouse is ready?'

I'd never shared with him how precarious my situation was, that the townhouse had been nothing but a pipedream. And I wouldn't now. I'd be too embarrassed to admit that I couldn't afford to put a proper roof over my own head. The way things were panning out, come next Thursday, Jess and I would be living in my car. Locally, there was no emergency housing, and I was low on the priority list anyway because I had no dependants. There were no hostels or cheap hotels, let alone ones that allowed a dog. A cabin at the caravan park would chew through my meagre savings in the blink of an eye.

'Oh, I haven't decided,' I said, hoping I sounded as if the world was my oyster. 'I will eventually head back to the city, where the boys are.' I hope my nose hadn't grown any longer as I'd added that. I had no desire whatsoever to live in Adelaide again.

He nodded and sipped his tea.

'Do you need a hand with any packing?'

'That's very kind of you, Daisy, but Pam and Leanne, my younger daughter, will come for a week when the house goes on the market. I want them to choose the things they want, and they'll help me deal with the remainder.'

'Might take you more than a week,' I said, remembering how long and tedious it had been packing up and moving out of Mum's old place. And I'd been steadily decluttering since she'd died.

The men had gone by the time Jess and I went home. They'd left the front and back doors wide open, letting out what little warmth there'd been in the house. I forced down some food with a mug of strong coffee and then set about clearing out the kitchen cupboards. Georgia had taken anything she'd wanted, and I put to one side what I'd take. What was left could be returned to the op shop. Or go in the rubbish bin.

Even though activity and layers of clothing kept me warm, it was cold enough for condensation to form on the end of my nose.

I'd intended to share my impending homelessness with Glenys when I'd been out there on Sunday. But after she'd recounted the row with Trevor, I just couldn't. I know she would have wanted to help and would have offered for me stay there until I found some-where suitable—and I might have been tempted to accept. But not now, not knowing how Trev felt, and with Charlie staying out there for who knew how much longer.

Adam had rung the evening before, full of concern and angst. Bec had Covid and he had a sore throat, again. I should keep away from them, at least in the short term. I did my best to allay his fears about the urgency of my situation. It did nothing to allay my own fears.

But what could, and should, one expect of their friends and fam-ily at a time like this? In the past I'd never expected anything, satisfied with my own self-sufficiency. But time was running out and so were my options. I wasn't as young and resourceful as I'd once been, nor as resilient. It was cavalier to say, even to myself, that I'd live in my car when I knew it would be downright disgust-ing, even for a few nights, and especially with winter setting in.

Down on my knees emptying a cupboard, I almost gave in to despair. I could have curled into a ball and let myself die right there and then. If only it were that easy. But then I felt Jess, warm and solid beside me, her cold wet nose pressed against my cheek. I put my arm around her and buried my face into her hair to muffle my sobs.

54

Kate

When I peered in through the front window, I saw Daisy. She sat by the north-facing window in a solitary shaft of sunlight, Jess sprawled at her feet. Her eyes were closed. She appeared diminished; her recent illness and then being turfed out of her home was taking its toll. I rapped on the window. She jumped and her eyes flew open.

She let me in. The old house felt cold and hollow. I shivered.

'By the afternoon it's not too bad in the sun,' she said, lacklustre, and returned to her chair. I pulled up its mate and we sat side by side.

'I see you've been packing.'

She glanced at the partially filled boxes. 'I've made a start. Not a big job, by any means,' she said, and arched an eyebrow. 'Kieran and a mate will collect the fridge and sofa bed next Thursday morning. The woman at the op shop bought the twin tub for her daughter. The real bonus is, I won't have to clean the house or tidy the yard before I move out.'

'Come and stay with me,' I said. 'Today. Now. This place is horrible.'

She didn't answer, or even look my way, and the offer hung in the air between us.

I cleared my throat. 'Jess can sleep in the garage.' On hearing her name, the dog briefly raised her head and looked at me.

The chair complained when Daisy moved. She angled herself around to look at me. 'It's hard, Kate. I feel so ashamed. I've always made my own way, managed somehow, with whatever life chose to dish out. I've never been beholden to anyone. But this?' She swallowed hard, and closed her eyes. 'It's almost more than I can bear,' she whispered.

I held my breath; tears thickened my throat.

She opened her eyes and smiled. 'Please, don't misinterpret what I'm saying, Kate. I appreciate your offer, but I'll stay put for the duration. I feel as if I must. And the rent's already paid. If it turns out that by next Thursday I have nowhere to go, you can rest assured knowing that Jess and I will be on your doorstep well before sundown. And I promise, we won't overstay our welcome.'

I swallowed my tears. 'You're amazing, Daisy. I would have gone down in a screaming heap long before now, dealing with what you are.'

'You've had your fair share to deal with, Kate, and you haven't gone down in a screaming heap.'

'No, but I almost did. If not for you and Rhonda and my GP forcing me to face up to the unpleasant things so I could learn to live again.'

'Don't worry, I've had my moments, my own little pity-party. Several of them, if you must know. The older I get, the lower the lows seem to be, and the harder it is to pick myself up again. But in the end, what choice do I have?'

'Never forget you have friends, Daisy, who're there to help pick you up. Who *want* to help pick you up, because you helped them. You just need to let them. Now, shall I put the kettle on?'

'Yes!' she said with a glimmer of her old spark. 'And I have cake. Apple and cinnamon. Glenys makes sure I'm never without cake.'

★ ★ ★

An hour later the sun had shifted and I was winding up to go when Georgia breezed in, on her way home from a day shift. I hadn't fully made up my mind yet whether I like her or not. At first she'd reminded me of a younger Daisy, but then the few times I'd been in her company since I'd noticed she lacked the kindness and compassion her grandmother had had at roughly the same age. Then I caught sight of the blow-heater tucked under her arm and readjusted my opinion slightly.

'We can do without the heater for a week, Gran,' she said, plugging it in and turning it on. 'Don't worry, I'll pay the electricity bill. Have you organised to have the meter read?'

'They'll do it Friday morning when they cut the power off,' Daisy said. 'And thank you for the heater.'

'It's bloody cold in here. I don't know how you put up with it.'

Daisy didn't comment. There were only two chairs and we were sitting in them. Georgia stood in front of the heater.

'How are you, Mrs Hannaford?' She stooped to peer through the front window. 'I didn't see your car.'

'I'm on foot,' I said.

'I suppose Gran has you out pounding the pavements with her.' She turned to Daisy. 'You won't believe this, Gran, but Jake's back. And he's got a job at Roxby Downs. Lisa said he was devastated over her losing—get this—*his* baby.'

Daisy's mouth turned down at the corners. 'Well I never. What about Kieran's mate? How's he?'

'Gutted.'

Daisy wrinkled her nose. 'I'm sure he'll get over it, the poor love.'

I listened to this exchange with bemusement. Gutted? That's what you did to fish.

'How's work?' Daisy said, and Georgia tilted her hand from side to side.

'Busy. Never lets up. I've requested holidays. I've got a couple of weeks owing. We're going to paint the inside of the house.'

No news to me. Kieran had shared the plans he had for the house when he'd last cleaned my swimming pool. I listened now as Georgia told Daisy about *her* plans for the house. She was headstrong, I could see that, and from what I knew of Kieran, he had a stubborn streak a mile wide. He knew what he wanted. If they lasted, it wouldn't be without fireworks.

Daisy caught my eye. She winked.

After Georgia had gone, without even asking her grandmother how she was, I said, 'Do you think it'll last?'

'Anyone's guess. But there'll never be a dull moment in the meantime.'

I walked home smiling to myself and wondering what it would have been like to have a few more fireworks in my marriage. It'd had its share of dull moments, that's for sure.

★ ★ ★

Tom called me that night. When his name flashed on the screen, my heart stuttered.

'How are you?' he said, when I answered with a tentative hello.

'I'm well.'

We exchanged pleasantries and news of his family, and then he coughed, cleared his throat and said, 'I have a proposition for you, Kate. Hear me out and then tell me what you think. I won't be offended if you say no.'

'All right,' I said, slowly, hoping he and Helena weren't going on holiday and wanting me to look after the children. I wasn't ready for that!

'I'd like to meet Dennis's brother, the farmer, and his family, and yes, I'd like them to meet me. What if I took a few days off and picked you up on the way and we drove to the Eyre Peninsula to visit them?'

I hadn't been expecting that.

'In spring I have a conference in Sydney. My plan is to reach out to the other brother when I'm there.'

'Well, they are your uncles,' I said. 'There are cousins. Lewis and Molly have three children, and grandchildren. Derek never married. Whether there are children …'

'Of course,' he said. 'What do you think? Will you come? Introduce me?'

'Do you need me to introduce you?' After all, he'd had no qualms fronting up on my doorstep when there was more at stake than meeting the relatives.

'No, but I'd like you to, Kate. It would be advantageous to us all if you and I were to show a united front. Don't you think?'

How could I argue with that? It would be a shock for Lewis; perhaps less so for Molly. If Tom and I presented a united front, that is, we both told the same story, there'd be less room for speculation about the events surrounding Tom's conception.

'Yes, I'll come,' I said. 'Because you're right, Dennis doesn't deserve to have his reputation tarnished by unnecessary speculation.'

I could hear the smile in his voice when he said, 'That's wonderful. Thank you, Kate.'

'When were you thinking of making the trip?'

'Not for a few weeks. It'll take me that long to rearrange things and clear my calendar for a few days. It'll be either side of a weekend. I'll chat to Helena and get back to you in the next day or two, how's that?' He sounded excited.

'I don't have any plans that are set in concrete,' I said, finding myself caught up in his excitement. 'I'll look forward to hearing from you.'

After we'd disconnected, I stood stock-still and stared at the phone in my hand. We'd spend hours in the car travelling, days in each other's company. What better way was there to get to know someone? Happiness filled me from the inside out. *I must tell Daisy*, I thought, and scrolled through to her number. Tomorrow morning I'd pop across the street and share the news with Rhonda. She'd be thrilled. She'd told me that each instalment of '*A day in the life of Kate*' was far more enthralling than her favourite soapie!

55

Daisy

Charlie dropped by Friday morning. He had on his work clothes. Jess and I were on the front verandah, barely back from our walk with Kate. I was taking off my muddy sneakers. Walking wise, I was almost up to speed again, post-influenza. Kate had been on cloud nine, bursting with excitement over her forthcoming trip with Tom. It was only a fortnight away. She'd planned what she was taking right down to the last handkerchief. I had memories of this bright, care-free Kate from decades ago. I'd glimpsed her in the lead-up to her wedding and through the first months of marriage, until disappoint-ment, jealousy and bitterness had pushed her into the background.

'Are you coming in?' I said to Charlie.

He followed me in, hat in hand. 'I thought we might go for a drive on Sunday,' he said, fiddling with the brim. 'Up to Appila and out to the springs. Take a picnic lunch, boil the billy.'

He looked ill-at-ease, and with I jolt of comprehension, I realised he was nervous. I wriggled my feet into my slippers. I needed a new pair.

'What is this?' I said, amused by his discomfort. 'Are you asking me out on a date?'

'You can call it that if you like.' His lips twitched as he tried not to smile.

'Did Glenys put you up to it?' I hadn't missed the way she'd watched Charlie and me that Sunday I went to the farm for lunch, her eyes twinkling with starry anticipation. When she wasn't throwing daggers Trev's way.

'She did not,' Charlie said, offended now. 'But when I told her what I had in mind she offered to put the picnic lunch together.'

'I'd have to check my calendar,' I said airily.

He rolled his eyes. 'Go on then, check your calendar.'

I took out my phone, knowing full well I had nothing on.

'We went to Appila Springs for a picnic one other time. Do you remember?'

'How could I ever forget,' he said.

I'm sure it was where Gareth had been conceived. It'd been a cold, clear winter's day. There'd been no-one else around, and we'd sunned ourselves on the rocks afterwards. We'd had bread and cheese for lunch. Fresh oranges. Charlie had made billy tea. We'd been falling in love. I looked at him now; the same man in so many ways, but different in so many more. Of course, we'd both aged. And I'd changed as well, in fundamental ways. Life did that to you.

'Don't overthink it, Daisy,' he said, quietly, his expression solemn. He knew where I'd drifted. 'It is what it is. We can't change any of it, no matter how much we might want to. It's what we do from now on that matters.'

'In my wildest dreams I have never imagined a moment like this,' I said, and folded my arms, hugging myself.

'I have,' he said, his gaze boring into me.

I frowned. Charlie chuckled. 'There you go again, overthinking it all. Don't. We had a heap of fun together when we were young. We enjoyed the same things. It was the best time of my life. Remember how much we used to make each other laugh?'

'Yeah, I do remember,' I said. 'But then life got serious pretty fast, for me anyway. I don't know what you're hoping for, Charlie, but I don't know if I can move past all our baggage. I don't know if I have it in me any more to be that magnanimous.

'My life has been hard, and foolish old woman that I am, I let myself be seduced by an idea that would have made my life easier and more comfortable. Me, of all people, should have known that if something sounds too good to be true, it more than likely is. What I'm saying is, Charlie, my risk-taking days are over.'

'You know Gareth regrets the whole debacle and Tess tore strips off him for leaving you high and dry.'

'I bet she did, but all the regret in the world won't give me back my home. In five days, I'll be homeless. I've very little to fall back on, and I'm not just talking about money or possessions.'

'So what are you going to do?'

'Survive, as best as I can. Kate offered for me to stay with her until I can sort something else out. And so did Adam, but their place is so small and they're all sick at present so even that's not an option for now. And Jay? We both know he barely manages to look out for himself, wherever he might be.'

'What about Gareth? Didn't he offer?' he said, astounded.

'Quite the contrary. He made it very clear that I couldn't live with them, as if I would want to. No-one gets it: I don't *want* to live with anyone. I'd give anything not to be in this predicament.'

After I'd turned on the blow heater I went to the sink and filled the electric kettle. I hadn't had breakfast yet and that could account for my lightheadedness. Charlie stood at the front window, gazing out. He'd dropped his hat onto one of the folding chairs.

'Tea?'

He nodded.

'So what are *you* going to do?' I said, standing beside him while the kettle boiled. Perhaps I'd catch a glimpse of whatever it was that always captured his attention outside the window. Outside any and every window.

'Trev won't need me for much longer, and I'll have to collect Bruno sometime. I've made a lot of contacts over the years, and I won't have any trouble picking up as much work as I need.'

'But aren't you getting a bit old for the sort of work you do? It'd be fairly physical.'

He turned to me and smiled. His eyes twinkled. It was as if the sun came out. How could he still have that effect on me, after everything? I wanted to stamp my foot.

'Nah,' he said. 'I might have slowed down a bit, but there's a lotta life left in these old bones.'

Feeling more frustrated and confused than ever, I went and made the tea and two slices of toast for myself.

We sat in the canvas chairs, hunched over the blow heater. I shared my crusts with Jess.

'This is a bit like camping, but without the campfire,' I said. 'Speaking of which, when do you want to take your camp table?'

'When you don't need it any longer.'

'Wednesday. I can bring it out, if you're not coming in.'

'Fair enough. I'll let you know.' He drained his tea mug, took it to the sink and washed it. Then he clamped his hat onto his head. 'So, are we on for Sunday?'

'Why not,' I said. 'Let's have a real campfire, instead of a pretend one.'

'Done. Be ready at nine.'

'Is Jess included in your invitation?'

'Goes without saying, Daisy. You oughta know that.'

Instead of sitting and brooding after he'd gone, I cleared out the linen press, which took me all of fifteen minutes. No need to wipe over the shelves, but I did it anyway. Then I rugged up and we walked to the library to return books. I splurged on the usual cappuccino on the way home.

★ ★ ★

Sunday dawned bright and clear. Charlie showed up early and we were on the road by nine. When I'd woken up, way before the alarm, I'd made a conscious decision to enjoy the day for what it was: an outing I wouldn't otherwise have been having. The most ambiguous part was with whom I was having said outing. Was Charlie an old friend, a new friend, my estranged husband, my ex-husband ...? I really didn't know.

'I haven't been up this way for years,' I said as the scenery sped past. 'I'd forgotten how beautiful the Southern Flinders Ranges are.'

Untidy vineyards waiting to be pruned had given way to paddocks tinged with green and dotted with sheep. Huge, silvery gums swayed overhead and, lower down, the odd splotch of yellow where a native acacia flowered.

'It's drier than I remember. No moisture in the subsoil,' Charlie said. 'Trev held back for as long as he could to put in a crop. Don't reckon it'll amount to much unless there's a lot more rain.'

'The seasons are changing, much less rain than I remember. Winters were always drizzly and foggy for days on end. Wet washing hanging around all the time. Oh, look, kangaroos ...'

Sun slanted in through the windscreen, warming the cabin. Jess was curled up on the back seat, sleeping. I took in the passing countryside. Charlie appeared relaxed and comfortable behind the wheel. I was enjoying myself.

When we stopped to stretch our legs Charlie bought a *Sunday Mail* and shouted me a coffee. 'Too early for an ice cream,' he said. 'Pity.'

We wandered up and down the town's main street, dead as a doornail on a cold Sunday morning. Then we drove northeast out to the springs. Back in the late seventies, the picnic ground near the springs had been pretty basic. Locals used to picnic and barbecue there on weekends. I was surprised by the amenities we found this time, and the number of caravaners camping on the flat, higher ground. We found a secluded spot down near the springs. Charlie had brought firewood, a barbecue plate and the requisite billy and tea. Glenys had sent sausages and lamb chops, bread and a salad, sultana cake for dessert.

We climbed around the rocks and walked up the gorge as far as we could go. Lunch was perfect. I could see Charlie was in his element, building a fire and cooking out in the open. Jess loved it all. By tacit agreement we didn't mention the past, or the future, instead we took pleasure in the present.

'I smell like a campfire,' I said, when Charlie pulled into the driveway at the house. House? When had I stopped thinking of it as my home? It was almost dark. I was pleasantly weary. 'A wonderful day, thank you, Charlie.' Before I knew what I was doing, I'd stretched across the console and kissed him on the cheek. His skin was warm and he smelled of woodsmoke too. I forced myself back into the seat, gathering my day pack off the floor. Neither of us spoke for what seemed like an age.

Then Charlie said, 'I'll come in Wednesday, collect the camp table. If there's anything else you need done, anything at all, I'll do it then.'

'All right.' Two days before I'd see him again. Instinct told me he was readying to leave, and who knows when I'd see him again after that. Myriad emotions vied for space. I went with resignation. 'I'll see you then, and thanks again for today.'

'It was my pleasure, Daisy,' he said. 'I had a good time, too.'

I didn't know if he sounded sad or regretful, or if he was just tired and keen to get back to Glenys and Trev's. I let Jess out of the back seat and Charlie waited until we were inside the house before he tooted and drove off. The joy of the day kept me warm until bedtime.

56

Kate

Daisy was coming to stay. Tomorrow. I flitted around making the final touches to the guest room. The one I'd chosen for her had never been used before. The bed and the bedlinen were all new and never once slept in since we'd moved into the house. Dennis couldn't understand why we'd needed three guest rooms. I was beginning to see his point. Molly and Lewis had stayed twice, or was it only once? Now the bed in that room was strewn with clothes and the suitcase I'd take on my trip with Tom.

I'd chosen this room for Daisy because it was closest to the door to the garage so she could listen out for Jess. God knows why I was nervous about her staying, but I was. Looking forward to it, but I had been on my own for a while now. Added to that was the anxiety about how long she'd stay; if my idea of outstaying her welcome would be different than hers.

We'd walked together that morning and she'd told me about the Sunday outing with Charlie. Her expression had glowed with the retelling. Something had twisted inside of me. Jealousy. I'd wanted to hate him, but found that I couldn't. Not if he could put a smile on the face of someone who'd become such a dear friend to me. Someone who had not much else to smile about right now.

She'd said she thought he was getting close to leaving.

'How do you know? Did he say so?'

'Not in so many words, but I feel it,' she said, and she'd touched her fingertips to her heart ever so fleetingly. I don't think she even knew that she'd done it.

'Does it bother you? That he's going? He only came for a visit, after all.'

'I don't know how I should feel, Kate,' she'd said, and her confusion was plain to see. 'We've talked about a lot of things from the past. Cleared the air, in a funny sort of a way.' She'd shaken her head and looked off into the distance.

Her next comment had been about the weather.

But I'd thought about that part of our conversation for some time afterwards. How would I feel if I were her? Confused would be the least of it. She was alone and the most vulnerable she'd probably ever been. Charlie was someone familiar from the past; they had a history together. As well as three sons and a handful of grandchildren.

At lunch time I went to the bakery and bought pasties, and took them around to have with Daisy. Yesterday, I'd had my follow-up appointment with the GP, and we'd both been pleasantly surprised: I'd dropped two kilograms and my blood pressure was back in the normal range. My cholesterol had come down a whisker. Early days.

'It's all the walking,' I'd said to him. Most days included a walk, if not with Daisy then by myself.

'And have you cut back on the wine?'

'Yes. Substantially.'

He'd studied me for several seconds. 'You seem happier in yourself, Kate.'

'I am. My life has taken a turn for the better, and I have things to look forward to. I feel well; the best I have for a long time.'

'Nevertheless, I'll see you again in three months,' he'd said, with a supercilious smirk. 'Make sure you haven't fallen off the wagon.'

★ ★ ★

Daisy was loading several plastic tubs with coloured lids into the back of her car when I arrived. Jess was sitting on the verandah, watching. That dog knew something was up. I parked by the kerb.

'Lunch,' I called, and waved the paper bags.

'Is it that time already?'

'What's in the tubs?'

'Gear that I won't need until I find a place to live.' She looked tired and her brightness was forced. I'd never asked her where she was hoping to live, I'd just assumed she'd stay in the vicinity. But then she hadn't found anywhere suitable so far.

'Rents would be cheaper in the country, wouldn't they?'

'You'd think so,' she agreed. 'But that hasn't been my experience to date.' She closed the back of the station wagon with a thud. 'Take this place for example … and I've finally conceded that it is the dump everyone says it is, but have a guess how much rent we were paying each week?'

'No idea,' I said. She told me and the figure made my eyes water. Wow, was I ever out of touch; I hadn't rented since before I was married. The amount she'd quoted would have put a dent in my generous monthly income. How did people on benefits manage? Simple: they didn't, they lived in their cars or couch-surfed with friends and relatives.

'Don't worry, I'll find something,' she said. 'Just let me get through the next few days, give myself time to regroup, and I'll be out of your hair before you know it.'

'That's not what I meant, Daisy. I'd just assumed that you'd stay in the area. But you've never said, and while Georgia's here, all your other grandchildren are in Adelaide.'

'So they are,' she said. She accepted one of the paper bags and opened it. 'Oh, a pasty. Lovely. Meat and three veg. Come on in. Avail yourself of my stunning hospitality while you still can.' She gave a dry, self-deprecating laugh.

When I went inside, the house was spotless. It smelled of Pine O Cleen, old age and emptiness. 'You told me you weren't going to clean the place,' I said.

'What else have I had to do? I'll empty out the fridge in the morning. Kieran's coming at ten to pick it up. And the potted plants on the back verandah.'

'Did the woman's husband pick up the washing machine?'

'Yesterday afternoon. Georgia asked me over for tea tonight. I said no. I'm not very good company at the moment.'

We sat at the camp table and ate the lukewarm pasties out of the paper bags. Daisy provided tomato sauce.

'What time shall I come to your place tomorrow?' she said after she'd folded her empty paper bag and smoothed the tablecloth on the camp table several times.

'It's not a motel, with check-in and check-out times. Come whenever you're ready. I'll be home all day.'

'Okay,' she said, with what could have been a smile or a grimace. Her glance flicked briefly to me, then away. 'Don't think I'm not grateful, Kate, because I am. I just haven't got my head around the enormity of being homeless. It's overwhelming.'

I didn't know what to say, so I didn't say anything. I vowed then and there to make her stay with me as comfortable as I could. While there wasn't anything about my home that I didn't like, it was *my* home and Daisy would be a visitor.

Sensing she wanted to be on her own, I left not long after that. I'd been so looking forward to having her stay, and I still was. However, my earlier enthusiasm had been tempered with the reality of how it might be for her until she found a home: always a visitor.

A familiar 4WD with roof racks was turning into Daisy's street as I turned out of it. Charlie. So he hadn't left town yet. My feelings about that were mixed, which was a surprise in itself. I went home and planned what I'd serve Daisy for dinner the following evening.

57

Daisy

After Kate went I sat motionless and let myself absorb the silence. It was my silence, uncluttered by anybody else's noise or energy. I'd never before appreciated how precious that silence could be. Then Jess barked, a car door slammed and I heard the rumble of Charlie's voice when he spoke to the dog. He'd come for his camp table. I'd be eating my evening meal off my lap.

Charlie knocked and came straight in. I didn't get up. He closed the door behind him. 'Are you all right?' he said. He was dressed in his usual work jeans and flannelette shirt. He dropped his hat onto the table.

'Just sitting and cogitating. Enjoying the peace and quiet. Kate brought pasties for lunch. She's only just left.'

'I thought it was her flash car I passed at the corner.'

He went to the sink and filled the kettle. A reflex action that made me smile.

'A drink of tea?' he said, and turned to face me. 'And what might you be smiling at?'

'You. Not Polly, but Charlie put the kettle on, we'll all have tea.'

'Don't mind the odd brew,' he said, his smile broadening. The kettle hissed and popped as it came to the boil. He made the tea and brought it to the table.

'There's cake in the tin if you want a piece.'

'I've not long eaten,' he said, and sat down. 'Jay rang this morning. He's got a job on a property in the Top End. They grow fruit and vegetables, apparently.'

'Is he up that way now?'

'Yep. Flew up a few days ago.'

This was all news to me.

Charlie took in my disgruntled expression and said, 'I suggested he visit his mother, but I couldn't force him to. He hasn't got a vehicle and he was bunking with a mate. I loaned him the money for the airfare. I know I'll get it back.'

'You've loaned him money before?'

'A few hundred here and there. It's the least I could do.'

I drank my tea and digested that bit of information. It occurred to me that Charlie had been more of a presence in our sons' lives than they'd ever let on to me. 'Jay never did have his feet as firmly planted on the ground as the other two did,' I said.

Charlie grunted in acknowledgement.

'My aim was never to favour one over the other, in anything, but I'll admit that Jay has always been a bit of a puzzle. With Adam and Gareth, what you see is what you get.'

'Jay's a lot like Colin. Peas in a pod if you ask me.'

'Where is your brother these days? Do you keep in touch?'

'Lives in WA, down south, in a community set up by a group of Vietnam vets for other veterans who don't fit in elsewhere. I ring him every so often. He sounds happy enough. He always asks after you.' Charlie's grin was slow and cheeky, and then he nudged my foot with his own. 'I reckon Col was sweet on you. Can't say that I blame him. The old man always thought you were all right.' His grin faded. 'He was another one who said I didn't deserve you.'

'I hardly knew Colin, but he always treated me with respect, and honestly, Charlie, I didn't have a lot of time for your dad. The way you two would get together and wind the boys up when they were little … Sometimes I could have easily killed you both.'

'Yeah. All water under the bridge now, Daisy. Go again?' He held up his empty mug.

'Not for me, thanks. Has Trev given you the afternoon off?'

'There're a couple more jobs he's got for me to do. Reckon I'll finish them by the weekend. His back's pretty good now.' He made himself more tea. 'So you're at Kate's from tomorrow?' he said when he sat down again.

'She's "prepared" one of her "guest rooms" for me. Jess is allowed to sleep in the garage. The backyard isn't that big.'

'*One* of her guest rooms? And I'll bet the dog won't be too pleased about being relegated to the garage. Imagine if Kate steps in one of her—'

'It's very kind of her to offer me a place to stay,' I said, cutting him off, because that had already crossed my mind.

'But you'll hate being there.'

My sigh was long and deep. 'Yes, I will. You should see her house … the yard … the swimming pool. Everything is perfect. I'm almost too scared to touch anything, in case I break it or leave dirty fingermarks. But the main reason I'll hate it is because it's not my home. I don't have a home any more, and I can't see how I'll ever be able to afford one.' The tears came hot and swift and unexpected. I pressed the heels of my hands into my eyes in an attempt to hold them back.

'What of my dignity, Charlie, my privacy? My right to have my own space and my own place in the world? And without other options, I'll have to appear grateful for the largesse of my friends and family, even if I don't want to be, and it will be awful and exhausting!'

His chair creaked as he moved. He cleared his throat. 'Then come with me,' he said.

Not sure I'd heard him right, I slowly took my hands away from my eyes. The longer I looked at him, the clearer he became.

'Why?' I said, on a whisper.

'I think you'd enjoy seeing the outback. You could treat it as a long overdue holiday. Or if you wanted to, you could work a bit. There's no end of seasonal jobs if you're willing and able.'

I felt hot, then cold. I couldn't think. I stood and sat down again. He didn't take his eyes off me.

'Daisy.' He laid a hand on my arm. It steadied me. 'I *want* you to come with me. We were good together, once upon a time. I know it was mainly me that stuffed it all up, and I'm sorry for that, but we're older and wiser and I know if we *both* want it, we could be good together again. I'm tired of being on my own—aren't you?'

Go with him? A holiday? Together? Thoughts tumbled through my mind, way too fast to grab a hold of a single one.

'But what would we tell the kids?'

He threw back his head and laughed. 'Nothing! Let them make of it what they will. It would be our business, not theirs.'

'But where would we go? Where would I sleep? I don't have a tent or a swag. And there's Jess.'

'It'll be nothing five star, I'll grant you that. And one or two dogs in the back of the vehicle makes no difference to me, and it won't matter to Bruno. We can buy you a swag. You travel light.'

'Goodness me,' I said. 'What made you decide to ask me?'

He shrugged. 'I came back, hoping … The boys have kept me in the loop. When Gareth told me about his project, well, it set my alarm bells ringing. Then old Bill died. It was as good a time as any to come and see how things were for you. I had no idea it'd all pan out the way it has.'

'It's a helluva lot to take in, Charlie. I'm where I am because I fell for something that sounded too good to be true, and it was. Will what you're offering be the same? What happens when you do get too old for the life? What then? I could be back to square one, only I'll be even older and less able.'

'I can understand that,' he said. 'I have some savings put aside. Neither of us are extravagant or wasteful. I know we'd manage. I failed you once, Daisy, and I will do everything in my power not to fail you again. You have my word on that.'

I so desperately wanted to believe him. 'Have you told anyone that you were going to ask me to go with you?'

'Nope.'

'Not even Glenys?'

'Not even Glenys. But her being who she is, she's always hoped that one day I wouldn't be on my own any more. And she thinks the world of you.'

I rested my elbows on the table and massaged my temples. 'I'll need time to think about this,' I said.

'Wouldn't expect anything less. But Trev has given in to Glenys, and Bridgette and her husband will be moving in for the duration. I won't ask them to put me up past when I've finished working for Trev. I was thinking the middle of next week … The weekend at the latest.'

'As soon as that!'

'You're already packed up. Shouldn't be too much left to do.'

'What about my mail and things like that?'

'You still get snail mail? Have it redirected to Kate or Georgia. Ask them to send it on to wherever we'll be. They'd do that, wouldn't they?'

There was so much to consider. Charlie stayed and I plied him with questions; anything and everything from where he did his washing to where he had his vehicle serviced. We had an early tea. Leftovers. After we'd eaten, all that remained in the fridge was milk and butter and a few eggs.

After he'd gone and with little else to do, I went to bed with a hot water bottle and a book. When I turned off the light I lay awake, eyes wide in the darkness, imagining how it would be to see Charlies's outback with him as the guide. My heart raced at the thought. Jess snored gently in her bed on the floor beside me.

58

Daisy and Kate

'What do you think?' Kate said.

'It's lovely. I can't remember ever staying in a room so lovely.' Daisy stood on the threshold of Kate's biggest guest room, her suitcase beside her.

'I'm glad you like it.' Kate's chest puffed out with pride. 'There's an electric blanket on the bed. I've put towels in the bathroom. The heating's on, but I turn it off at night. You're welcome to open the window.' Kate was prattling on but she was helpless to stop. 'You must make yourself at home. If you want a cup of tea, anything, just help yourself. There are coat hangers in the wardrobe; sing out if you need more.'

'I'm sure I'll be very comfortable, thank you, and I doubt I'll need more coat hangers. But thanks just the same.'

Kate backed out of the room. 'I'll let you settle in, shall I? Have a lie down if that's what you do in the afternoons.' Her words petered out and she spun on her heel and scurried off.

Daisy studied the bed. It was huge, immaculate. If she lay down on it she'd dent it, mar its pristine smoothness. She glanced at the floor. Would the carpet feel as soft on her backside as it did underfoot? 'Don't be ridiculous,' she muttered, with a mental eye roll. Plenty of time to sleep on the ground in the weeks and months to come. A frisson of excitement and anticipation shot through her. Did that mean she was going to say yes to Charlie's offer? She pushed her battered suitcase out of sight on the other side of the bed. Pointless unpacking too much when she didn't know how long she'd be staying.

Daisy found Kate in the family room, sitting and staring out the window. She startled when Daisy cleared her throat.

'Is everything all right? Shall I make tea?'

'Charlie's leaving in about a week,' Daisy said. 'He's asked me to go with him.' She perched on the edge of the sofa.

Kate had noticed that something had changed in the past twenty-four hours. From the moment Daisy'd stepped through the door, her demeanour had been different. There was a lightness about her that had been missing for some time.

'So he is going to take you away from me again,' Kate said, her voice flat. 'I had a feeling he might.'

Daisy squared her shoulders. 'I haven't decided yet whether I'll go with him. There's a lot to consider.'

'You'll go with him. And if I was in your position, so would I.'

'Would you?'

'Yes! Although it irks me to admit it, Daisy, Blind Freddy could see that the man cares for you. And what an adventure you'll have.'

'But it's not without its risks.'

'Of course it's not, that's what makes it so exciting.'

'But am I too old?'

'For which part? Taking such a trip, or taking it with Charlie?'

'Both, I guess. Sleeping on the ground in a swag might turn out be the least of my worries. Along with neither of us being spring chickens any more, Charlie's record for reliability is far from stellar.'

'Of course you'd have misgivings, you wouldn't be normal if you didn't. And please—' Kate paused and held up her hand in emphasis. 'Please, do not take this the wrong way and think that I don't want you here—quite the contrary—but have you really thought through the alternative?

'I know this house is huge, but it's *my* home. What if in a few weeks you start to resent being here? Not having your own home and the freedom to come and go as you please. Being at the behest of others because it turns out that you can't afford a place of your own. What then?'

Daisy settled into the soft embrace of the sofa. Kate's admission had surprised her. Shocked her, actually. 'I have thought all of those things, but when you say them out loud it makes them all the more real. Makes it so I can't pretend it will be different than that, when I know deep down that it won't. You have so much and I have so little.'

Kate's gaze dropped to her hands resting in her lap; her laugh was laced with irony. 'Material possessions, Daisy, that's what I have. Your life has a richness and a purpose that mine will never have; has never had. I envy you that, and always have.'

'But what of Tom and his family? There's a chance there for you to at least have the experience of grandchildren, if not children.'

'We'll see. I hope that's how it works out in the end. It'll be a steep learning curve for me, and although I'm looking forward to my trip with Tom, I'm not letting myself get too excited about the possibilities, in case it all falls over.'

'Just be your true self, Kate, and they'll like you well enough. If they're smart they'll realise just how much you have to offer, and I don't mean material things.'

Kate pursed her lips. 'So when are you leaving?'

'Charlie wants to go in a week, ten days on the outside. Trev won't need his help for much longer.'

'So what's holding you back?'

Daisy shifted in the seat. 'It all sounds a bit too good to be true, and I swore after Gareth's townhouse project that I'd never fall for that again.'

'But what have you got left to lose, Daisy? As harsh as that might sound, and as much as I can hardly believe I'm saying it to you.'

'It's not harsh and it's true. I don't have a great deal left to lose.'

'But a lot to gain if it does work out. Are you happy when you're with him? You were in the beginning. Nauseatingly so.'

'I think I could be happy with him again. If I can treat the past for what it is: the past. Get around all the baggage. In so many ways, we know each other. We share children and grandchildren, and it would be wonderful if we did it *together*. And I'm beginning to respect the man he's become.'

'A pity it's taken him this long to grow up,' Kate said with her usual acerbity. 'The man's almost seventy.'

Daisy laughed. 'He would agree with you, wholeheartedly.'

'When will you tell him you'll go with him?'

'Tomorrow. Glenys has invited me out to the farm for tea. You too, if you want to come. From this weekend her youngest daughter and her husband will be staying with them until their new house is built. Trev's not exactly over the moon about it. Glenys might need another friend close by.'

'That's kind of her to invite me.'

'She says you're my friend and I'm family so that makes you practically family.'

'Okay,' Kate said, and her eyes widened, much as Daisy's had when Glenys had first said it. 'And Daisy, if it doesn't work with

Charlie, you're welcome to come back here. Stay for as long as you need to.'

'Thank you, Kate, for offering to be my safety net. You know, Dennis would be so proud of you. How you've been with Tom. You could just as easily have had nothing more to do with him after he showed up with the letter from his mother.'

Kate brushed at an imaginary spot on her black woollen slacks. 'It's the least I can do. I was never an easy person. When we moved here we finally started to settle into retirement, and into each other, at last, and he seemed on the verge of contentment. And then he died. It wasn't fair, none of it.' She lifted her chin, sat taller. 'Then Tom presented himself. And like you and Charlie, I feel as if I've been given a second chance. I don't want to muff it.'

'You won't. They'll love you.'

Several seconds ticked by and then Kate slapped her palms against her thighs and stood up. 'Now then, that's enough of the serious stuff. I don't care what the doctor says—this calls for wine. Preferably with bubbles, because we have to celebrate.'

Several minutes later, Daisy and Kate raised their glasses to friends lost and friends found, and to new beginnings.

Epilogue

Daisy and Kate
One year later

Daisy and Charlie had argued about which of them had first come up with the idea of renewing their marriage vows. Charlie said it had been him one night when they'd been stargazing in the saltbush near Uluṟu. Daisy insisted it'd been her when they'd been cruising down the Katherine River. In the end it didn't matter whose idea it was, because it meant they were on their way home to South Australia for a visit, and family and friends would celebrate with them.

Daisy had envisaged a simple affair, nothing more than a family picnic or barbecue. They'd exchange the vows they'd written themselves and then catch up with folk not seen for a year or more. But then Kate got involved and the whole thing quickly blew out into something altogether different.

'You must have what you didn't have all those years ago, Daisy: a proper wedding,' Kate said. They were talking on the phone. Daisy was in Coober Pedy. 'I insist you have it here. My place is the perfect venue.'

'Kate! We're on our way home now. We'll be with you in a couple of days and we can only stay for a fortnight because we have more work in WA. There won't be time to arrange the sort of shindig you're talking about.'

'Leave everything to me,' Kate said, undeterred. 'All you and Charlie need to do is show up, have prepared what you want to say to each other and enjoy yourselves.'

'You don't have to do this, Kate.'

'I know I don't, but it's my way of saying thank you, so please let me. You popping up in my life again saved me from myself. You and that dog.'

Daisy pressed the phone to her other ear. 'What is it I'm meant to say? Oh, I remember ... Thank you, Kate, that is very generous and thoughtful of you.'

Kate chuckled. 'You're learning.'

'And I mean it. But *no* gifts, Kate. I do not want anyone bringing gifts. There's nowhere to put them and that's not what this is about. It's about me and Charlie wanting to recommit to each other, and share that with our family and close friends.'

'All right! I concede, no gifts, but let's do the rest with the style it deserves.'

Daisy laughed. 'You sound happy, Kate.'

'Believe it or not, I am. I've become a Meals on Wheels volunteer. I stayed at Tom and Helena's on the long weekend and looked after the kids while they had a few days away. *And* the twins are coming to stay in the next school holidays. I can't wait. They are terrific kids. I've got so many things planned for us to do. It's been wonderful getting to know them all.'

When they'd disconnected, Daisy recounted the conversation to Charlie. He raised his eyebrows, but made no comment. She could see he was busting to say something, but he kept his mouth shut.

She had to admire his control, and accept that Charlie and Kate would only ever tolerate each other, and only because of her.

★ ★ ★

In true Kate style, the planned celebration could only be described as lavish. No expense had been spared. Charlie said it was completely over the top. Daisy was inclined to agree, and couldn't stop herself imagining what she'd do with the money Kate was spending. But her friend was having the time of her life and Daisy would not begrudge her that.

The only thing Kate didn't have a hand in was the dress Daisy would wear on the day. Almost the moment they'd arrived home, and at Glenys's urging, Daisy chose a dress style and Glenys came up with suitable fabric and made the garment in a matter of days. It was gorgeous.

'We mustn't let Charlie see the dress until the day,' Glenys insisted after the final fitting.

'Why not?' Daisy said, flummoxed by it all.

'Because it's not the done thing,' Glenys replied, and that was an end to it. The dress was whisked away until it was required.

★ ★ ★

The big day arrived. It was July and the days were short and the nights long. Everyone had their fingers crossed that it wouldn't rain. Charlie stayed at the farm the night before; Daisy stayed with Kate. When she woke after seven hours of dreamless sleep, she knew in her heart that what she and Charlie would do that day was the right thing for them. Not to say there hadn't been bumps along the way and wouldn't be more in the future—they'd been apart for over two decades. But what better way to get to know each other all over again than to spend months on the road together. Sleeping under the stars, no-one else within cooee. Relying entirely on each other.

For Daisy, there'd been some serious soul-searching. Reflecting on the time from the comfort of the queen-sized bed in Kate's best guest room, she realised she'd relished every minute of it.

Kate tapped on the door. 'I've made you a cup of tea.'

'I'll get up.'

'No, stay there. This is your day.' She came into the room bearing a tray made up with her finest china.

Daisy elbowed herself into a sitting position, propping herself up with pillows. Kate poured the tea and perched on the edge of the bed.

'So, how do you feel?'

'I feel good. I'm looking forward to the day, and thank you so much for it, Kate. What you've made happen in such a short time has made my head spin.'

'Everyone has pitched in. Tess and Bec have been terrific. And Helena. It was her friend who decorated the cake at such short notice. It's just a shame Jay couldn't be here.'

'We caught up with him when we were in the Top End. He loves his job. Where he lives is a beautiful spot. Seeing him thrive was good for his mother's soul.'

Kate smiled. 'Eighteen months ago I would never have believed any of this was possible. The morning I first watched you walk by with Jess, I could hardly believe my eyes.'

Daisy's cup gave a delicate clink when she replaced it on its saucer. 'I used to feel as if someone was watching us. It was you!'

Kate stood and put her empty cup onto the tray. 'And that day you barged in uninvited; I was dreadfully rude, but you persisted and I'm so grateful you did.' She topped up Daisy's cup from the pot. 'Stay there until you're ready to get up. The hairdresser comes at nine thirty. I'll make toast when you're up.'

Daisy sipped the second cup of tea, gazed out the window and wondered what Charlie was up to. Jess and Bruno were out at the farm with him. Daisy missed all three of them. This was the first night they'd been apart in the past year. She climbed out of bed and pinched herself, to remind herself that this was really happening to her.

★★★

The guests started arriving from eleven thirty. The formal proceedings were at twelve thirty, to be followed by a catered buffet lunch, with the appropriate liquid refreshments.

Gareth had been primed to walk his mother down the aisle, that is, from the garage to the patio, which had been decorated with floral arrangements, gauzy chiffon bows and fairy lights. Daisy wanted to laugh out loud when the "Wedding March" swelled from a speaker near the sliding door.

Her dress was a simple ivory-coloured sheath with a lace bodice and sleeves. She hoped she didn't topple off the matching heels. Kate hadn't missed a thing. There was something old: a bracelet Daisy had given her when they'd first become friends; something new: a pair of diamond stud earrings the kids had all clubbed in together to buy; something borrowed: a diamond and sapphire brooch that had belonged to Glenys's mum; and something blue: the palest blue, softest cotton handkerchief with a lacy border crocheted by Rhonda Hall.

'You look beautiful,' Charlie said when Gareth delivered Daisy to him. He couldn't take his eyes off her. He was standing under an arch covered in flowers and fairy lights, and looked decidedly ill-at-ease in a suit.

'You scrub up all right yourself. I've never seen you in suit and tie before.' Daisy linked her fingers with his and gave his warm hand a squeeze. He returned the pressure and his shoulders softened.

'And you won't ever again, so make the most of it.' He ran his finger around the inside of his shirt collar. 'I feel as if I'm being slowly choked to death.'

In his role as MC, Tom came to stand beside them, handsome and perfectly at ease in his Armani suit and tie. How like his father he was.

'Are you guys good to go?'

Daisy and Charlie nodded.

The music faded away and Tom welcomed everyone and thanked them for coming.

'It is a privilege to share this very special occasion with Daisy and Charlie. Thank you, Kate, for making this happen, and for your kindness and generosity, to us all.

'On Saturday the sixth of November 1976, Daisy Miller married Charles Toogood. My father, Dennis Hannaford, and his wife Kate were the witnesses to that union. After a lifetime of ups and downs, Daisy and Charlie are here today because they wanted to recommit to the vows they made back then. That's all I'll say before I hand over to them.'

A patter of applause from the thirty or so adults and children looking on and Tom moved off to one side.

Daisy stepped forward and said, 'Thanks, Tom, and we're thrilled to have you and your family here to share this celebration with us. We're sorry Dennis isn't here. Thank you, Kate, from the bottom of my heart. You are a dear, dear friend. And to our children and grandchildren: I'll bet you never expected to see this day.'

Laughter and another patter of applause.

She turned and linked hands with Charlie so they were facing each other beneath the arch.

'Charlie Toogood, who would have thought we'd find each other again, but life is full of surprises. I married you forty-six years ago because I was pregnant, and also because I'd fallen in love with you. Over the years that love sure was tried and tested, and I'd accepted that it'd eventually been snuffed out. But I was wrong, there was an ember still there, it just needed more oxygen.

'Here and now I pledge what is left of my life to yours. No matter where life leads us from now on, I know that as long as you are there, that's where I'm meant to be.'

Charlie's eyes glistened and his grip on Daisy's hand tightened. He cleared his throat.

'When I first clapped eyes on Daisy Miller I was serving behind the bar at Dennis and Kate's wedding. Well, I couldn't take my eyes off her then, and I can't now. For me, I reckon it was love at first sight. Everyone said she was too good for me. Back then, they were probably right. But Daisy Miller is the best thing that's ever happened to me, and I will always regret that it took me nearly a lifetime to fully appreciate that.

'Thanks to you, Daisy, we have three terrific sons, two delightful daughters-in-law and six fabulous grandchildren. What more could a man ask for?

'I promise to be there for you, always. That I've made you laugh again makes my heart sing. I love you, and let's keep loving and laughing for as long as we're able.'

Gareth called out, 'Now you can kiss the bride, Dad,' and everyone laughed.

Charlie kissed his bride. There were whoops of delight and more clapping. Jess pushed her way through the crowd and yipped.

Tom stepped up beside them, a glass of bubbles in his hand, 'Please charge your glasses. To Daisy and Charlie!'

Everyone cheered.

Kate hugged Daisy.

'Thank you,' Daisy whispered. 'What a perfect day.'

'My pleasure. And what you both said, well, I teared up. Now I'll go and get lunch happening.' She rushed off towards the kitchen.

The family milled around, offering best wishes and congratulations. Max Purdue, leaning heavily on Pamela's arm, shook Daisy's hand and wished her well.

Ryan high-fived and said, 'Way to go, Gran.' He was nearly as tall as his dad, and filling out nicely. Five more months of school and then he'd work full time on the farm for Trev. They were going to give it a year and see if he was as keen after that.

Georgia hugged her. 'You look awesome, Gran.'

'Where's Kieran?' Daisy said, glancing around. She hadn't caught up with her granddaughter for more than five minutes since she'd been home.

'It's about over, Gran. We've had fun but he has no ambition past renovating his house and cleaning swimming pools. Basically, he's boring.'

'Oh.'

'I'm off to the UK and Europe in a month's time.'

'What about Lisa?'

'She's moving to Roxby Downs to be with Jake. Got a job at the hospital. Do you want a glass of bubbly?' Without waiting for an answer, Georgia rushed off in search of wine.

Gareth and Adam were talking to Charlie. Adam clapped his father on the shoulder. 'Jeez, Dad, nice speech. All this time a poet and we didn't know it. You do have hidden depths. Congratulations. Mum's a keeper. Look after her.'

Charlie slung an arm around his wife's shoulders and pulled her close. 'You have my word on that.'

Kate called out that lunch was being served. Daisy linked her hand with Charlie's. It was warm, the skin rough and callused. She loved the feel of his fingers intertwined with hers. She smiled up at her husband and they set about enjoying what turned out to be one of the best days of her life.

Author note

The inspiration for Daisy and Kate can be attributed to my very own experience. It went something like this: several years ago, a nursing friend unexpectedly contacted me via my website meredithappleyard.com.au after she'd picked up one of my books in a bookshop. We'd become close friends once upon a time when we'd worked together in a small country hospital. Our parting way back when was not at all acrimonious, unlike Daisy and Kate, rather our lives went in separate directions and we just drifted apart.

Imagine my happy surprise when I heard from her again after such a long time. We exchanged emails and then caught up face-to-face. When we met it was as if the intervening years dropped away. It has been wonderful to reconnect with her and our 'new' friendship goes from strength to strength.

This got me thinking about the nature of friendship, how important it is in our lives, how precious it can be and how downright destructive when things go wrong. The outcome of that pondering formed the basis for the story of Daisy and Kate.

As part of my 'research' for writing Daisy and Kate I read, and can recommend, the following books:

True Friendship, by Patti Miller, 2022, UQP

Grandmothers: Essays by 21st Century Grandmothers, edited by Helen Elliott, 2020, The text Publishing Company

The Friendship Cure; the art of friendship and why it matters more than ever, by Kate Leaver, 2018, HarperCollins

Acknowledgements

Another successful team effort!

Thank you to Team HQ: Johanna Baker, Suzanne O'Sullivan, Rochelle Fernandez and marketing manager Jo Monroe. And the delightful cover? Thank you Louisa Maggio. I love it, and so do my friends!

Thanks again to freelance editor Kylie Mason and proofreader Pauline O'Carolan. You'd think by now I'd remember it's 'kerb' and not 'curb'.

A special thanks to Susan Wilson for telling her story and referring me on to the Polycystic Ovary Syndrome Association of Australia for more information.

And once again a huge thank you to the Home Team: My husband Ken, sister Sandra, dear friends Pat and Sue. Where would I be without you?

It would be remiss of me not to mention and thank The Second Saturday Book Club. This diverse group of women meets for several hours every month and I am in awe of the collective experience and wisdom they posses, and willingly share. And of course we laugh, a lot.

And to you dear reader, thank you. I know I've said it before but you are the reason we keep doing this.

talk about it

Let's talk about books.

Join the conversation:

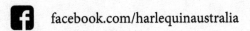 facebook.com/harlequinaustralia

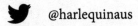 @harlequinaus

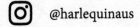 @harlequinaus

harpercollins.com.au/hq

If you love reading and want to know about our
authors and titles, then let's talk about it.